L

CW01456738

A story of The Suburban Dead

By T.A. Sorsby

Get in touch via:
https://tasorsby.wordpress.com/
https://www.facebook.com/TASorsby/
https://twitter.com/T_A_Sorsby

This story is dedicated to everyone who made it happen –
from close friends and family, to beta readers, final
reviewers, and anyone who bought it just to shut me up.
You're an odd assortment of people, but so are the
characters. So that's okay.

T

Also in this series:

Emergency

One

I woke up with the sound of the amplifiers still ringing in my ears, a dull, resonant buzz. It clashed annoyingly with the electric chicken wailing of my alarm clock. I allowed myself a groan.

Chilly early winter air wafted against my arm as I slammed my hand down on top of the clock's little bumper, imagining I was actually hitting a chicken on the head – like in that old cartoon with the caveman family.

I folded myself into a snug cocoon for a minute or so. The air up on the fourteenth floor always had more of a sting to it, but eventually I emerged from the sheets and shivered my way over to the bathroom to make use of the facilities. I brushed my teeth extra hard, trying to get rid of the flat-tongued taste of last night's drinking. It probably wasn't such a great idea to see a Saturday night gig with the missus and her housemates when you have to be up before seven.

Once I made myself up like a passable imitation for a human being, I got dressed for work – seeing as it was a work day and all – Sunday post was never the busiest, but I'm sure the boss would laugh if I showed up nude.

Nobody would accuse me of being up to date with the latest fashions. Dark blue jeans found themselves extracted from the pile of finished ironing, and were pulled on alongside a shirt from the last Some Bad Men tour. Yawning my way through to the rest of my apartment, I turned the kitchen radio on and put my cowboy boots by the radiator to warm up. I did warn you about the fashion.

The radio piped out some middle-of-the-road soft rock while I prepared a healthy breakfast of grilled bacon and scrambled eggs on toast. That's sorta healthy, right? At least it wasn't all fried. When the music stopped, the presenter came on for the news. The station wasn't run by the VBC, but news bulletins for most radio stations across Voison still come from Auntie Veeb.

3

'Live at seven from VBC Tower in Orphen, this is the hourly update,' it began.

I tuned it out while I grilled bacon and put whipped eggs in the microwave to scramble. The morning was too short for scrubbing pans. The news of the day was largely boring; Consuls pushing legislative changes through the Senate, the President making an address about the super-bug in Rojas, and all the worsening rioting out in the East, where their dictators and pseudo-electorates were calling press bans as close to home as Redmond.

I'd been there on holiday, only a couple of years ago. Hard to think that a tourist hotspot only a six hour flight away was being torn apart from within. I always kept an eye on foreign news since one of the guys I went on that holiday with worked a camera for the VBC, and last I'd heard, was out there now. When they were filming on the seafront I could swear he'd picked a spot right where we took a group photo.

After cleaning off my plate and doing the washing up, I unhooked my leather jacket from the hat-stand; a real antique number that looked out of place beside the rest of my modern black and white décor, and draped it over the sofa while I brushed my hair. Long hair on a guy doesn't look great if excessively tousled. Black curls look especially tatty if you don't keep a handle on them.

I fished my mobile from one of the pockets and flipped it open to see I had a message from my special lady friend. She'd been on at me about getting a new phone, but this one still worked. I didn't need to check my email on the move.

'How's it hanging? You and me still painting the town red tomorrow night? Well. Giving it an undercoat…love x'

'Feeling fine, still on for tomorrow milady xx' I replied, before snapping it shut so her picture flashed up on the clock screen. I couldn't help but smile.

Katy's hair was short, platinum blonde, and always worn spiked up. Except for when she was at work, where it was just plain messy. I'd met her on-shift, and with the scruffy hair-do and shapeless blue hospital scrubs, I was just powerless to

4

resist – as she picked broken glass out of my scalp with a pair of tweezers. I'd seen her outside of work a few hours later, and she looked even cuter with a silver stud in her nose. On some people it looked a bit garish; on her it had been known to make my jeans feel small.

I tugged on my jacket and zipped her up, leather creaking. I liked the jacket, in winter especially. It was fur-lined and snug, with a racy red stripe across the chest that stopped it from being mistaken for a biker's jacket rather than a motorcycle jacket. It was also non-uniform for couriers at the post office, but my boss was cool with it, and it wasn't like head office sent people around to check up on us.

There were only three apartments on our floor at castle tower. The whole block had been gutted and renovated a year or so before I moved in, knocking some of the pokier flats into larger, modernised apartments and giving a facelift to the rest.

Not every flat was occupied, and the neighbourhood wasn't exactly gentrified, so the rent was manageable enough for my single-bed place. Even so, it'd have been nice to share it with someone. Katy and I had talked about it plenty, but she'd decided splitting the bills three ways at her current place would help her save for a deposit on a real house.

One of my neighbours in modernised, budget living was just leaving as I was, coming from the two-bed apartment at the end of the hall.

Neville Roberts lived with his daughter Morgan, and worked a lot of shifts for a lot of hours at a major law firm downtown; security guard, not "attorney at law". He was a first rate father, but only around as often as he could be, since he had to work all those hours just to afford the creeping rent and shiny things that teenage daughters seem to need.

I knew Morgan better than her dad. We weren't strangers, but we'd never spent much time together. Most of our conversations went through Morgan, checking in on each other by proxy, but every now and then we'd bump into each other in the corridor.

5

Neville's shifts meant that half the time he was just coming home from work as she was leaving for college, or vice-versa. So when my own shifts at the post office allowed, me and my lovely lass would keep her company, either at Katy's place or mine. It felt wrong to call it babysitting, since Morgan was seventeen-going-on-twentysomething.

Even so, we'd had quite the influence on the kid. She'd fallen into the rock scene, and Katy and Morgan were kinda like best friends, despite there being more than half a decade between them. They even played for the same field hockey team every weekend, but I'm a terrible sportsman by comparison, so when we looked after her we usually played video games or watched movies…But never a rom-com, since Katy has this thing about them where she cries.

Neville was in uniform; pressed navy blue shirt, black slacks, with a heroic utility belt and bronze-effect security service shield. His weapon holster was empty – he didn't like having guns around the house with an inquisitive teen about.

'Morning.' He smiled, giving me the nod as we fell into step along the corridor, sharing a companionable silence as we waited for the elevator. He must have shaved this morning – his cologne was strong, a familiar, old school aftershave. Perfect for a day protecting the legal elite.

'So what's the plan for the day, Mr Kelly?' Neville asked as we stepped through the pinging doors together, riding down from the top floor to the bottom.

'Got work until around five, but I have to swing by Hannah-Smith's to pick something up for later,' I hummed, 'pretty much a boring day. Never anything on TV, is there?' I added, starting to feel uncomfortable with the way Neville was staring at me.

'Hannah-Smith's? Seriously?' he asked, grinning like a cartoon cat, 'Well I never pegged Katy for the type. Erm, that's to say, I didn't think she'd, you know, not that she wouldn't be great, you know.'

'Nice back-pedal there.' I noted.

'I liked it too.' he nodded, the pair of us grinning like co-conspirators when the plot begins to thicken. 'You need a lift in?' he asked.

'If you're going my way, thanks.'

Neville tuned into a different morning station to me, so we got the news again at the half-hour. Apparently some contaminated livestock had been imported, and now our noble homeland of the Voison Republic was looking at exposure to that East Rojas super-bug, some "Human Rabies" thing. A pang of worry shot through me, thinking Katy might be exposed to that at work. At least she worked at County General. She'd told me last time there was a health scare that Mercy Hospital was the infectious disease specialist. County was surgical.

Nobody in the post depot noticed me come in, twenty or so minutes early. Even Gladys, the mail-matriarch, was too absorbed in a TV news report about Centre for Disease Control contingents shipping out across the country in preparation for the "ERHR" crisis. So I filled in my timesheet like I'd started half an hour early. As a trusted Senior Delivery Specialist, I'm on flexi time.

Don't look at me like that! They won't let me take the courier motorcycle home for personal use, leaving me pedestrian and almost perpetually a few minutes late for work. It's a wonder I don't fudge my timesheets more often, the way bus prices keep bumping up – three silver and a shilling for a day pass, now that's worth eyeballing someone over.

Using one of the post office's statutory smoking breaks between parcel deliveries, I slinked away on the bike to pick up my little box from Hannah-Smith's jewellers, and got back before anyone seemed to remember that I don't actually smoke.

As the day went by all I could think about was how much I wanted it to be over so I could get on with tomorrow. Tomorrow was a big thing, and the biggest event of my Sunday was when I almost got a ticket for being illegally parked for a grand total of two minutes.

The owner of the pawnshop across the street from castle tower had stepped out for a while, leaving some kid, maybe his, in charge of the store. One of the duties of Senior Couriers was handling licenced materials, and I always seemed to get stuck with the problem packages.

I'd had to explain to the kid that he needed to provide a licence to accept firearms in the post – National Service papers are enough to buy one yourself when you go straight to the dealer, but I needed to see a store licence, since he'd be selling them on. He wasn't getting it, but I'd been here before, so I told him where the boss kept his paperwork.

It was that close to the end of my shift that if I could take the bike home, I could just flop right onto my sofa, instead of heading back into town and getting a bus. You see my pain now?

Because of some traffic accident blocking the main route out of town, I ended up getting back home about half an hour later than usual; and feeling even better about the timesheet thing, thanks. I reached into the fridge and fetched myself a frosty beer to drink in the shower – multi-tasking I call it, and hung my towel up just before the six o'clock news.

The flatscreen warmed up and flashed to life just in time for me to see the pictures of several people; forced school photo type smiles for the kids, and happy wedding photos for the parents. A woman's voice spoke over them, sympathetic, but neutral;

'…gruesome murder of this Overbridge family will surely touch the hearts of this small community.' the reporter finished, cutting back to the presenters in the studio.

'Thanks Gillian,' the suit said, shuffling papers on the desk. 'Police informed us at a press conference earlier today that they are treating the deaths as gang or possibly cult related, due to the condition of the victims, and tying it in with several similar murders across the county in the last few days, as far south as Orphen and as far north as Kilmister.'

I sighed, and changed the channel, gambling I'd see nothing overseas tonight. It's not that I didn't care about the news, or the murders or the victims. I knew that TV could make problems seem far away and irrelevant, even though Overbridge wasn't more than an hour or so drive from Greenfield on the motorway. I just thought there'd be something less depressing to watch on a Sunday night.

Monday was one of my days of rest; a busy postal day I was lucky enough to rarely be on rota for, since most of my co-workers liked their weekends spent at home. But I'd be meeting Katy later on – which meant an entire day of puppy-sized butterflies in my stomach. She got off work at six, eight hours of eternity away, which gave me a little time to prepare myself for the night ahead. I fired up the games console, colonising distant solar systems, then started watching a movie over a late lunch. There came a knocking from my door as I was putting the dishes away.

I'd been expecting a package today, so had actually gotten dressed. I'm not above spending a day in my bathrobe, but I hate it when people answer the door like that to me, so I put the tiniest bit of effort in today.

'Tiernan Kelly,' the postie said as I opened the door. He'd pronounced it right – *tea-air-nan*. My grandmother had called it a traditional name. People at school had called it stupid. 'Thought it had to be you.'

'Hey Terry.' I greeted, taking the signing pad and stylus from his outstretched hand. As I passed it back, I caught the colour of his face. 'You look awful.'

He was the other Senior Courier at our warehouse, and I was sure that my tendency to get the awkward deliveries was no coincidence. I took the small package from him, handing the signing pad back.

'Something I ate, I think.' He said, 'Sunday Dinner isn't sitting right. You have a good weekend shift?' he asked, the faintest trace of a smirk on his green-tinged face.

'Just the best. Thanks.' I added, when the door was already half-closed. Our working relationship was brisk.

9

Morgan was supposed to be coming over after college, so I tidied up a bit, tackling the laundry pile with the film in the background. She text at about half three to say she was going to hang out with one of her friends, get on with some coursework assignment instead. I finished the laundry, but suddenly running the vacuum around didn't seem like such a big deal until Katy text, asking after Morgan. A pang of guilt urged me into domestic action.

I filled her in as we text back and forth, but her replies were shorter and further between than usual. Something was happening at the hospital, she'd tell me about it later.

After the hours had ticked by, I showered and shaved. Preening completed, I tugged on my best jeans, a silky black shirt and my jacket. I hadn't bought it for work; I could have used a ratty old postal one for that. Katy's 'hog', as she called it, was one of those huge bikes with the ridiculous tasselled handlebars and the engine that rumbled people's teacups like there was an approaching dinosaur. With the vibrations coming off that engine, I didn't feel totally safe with her driving; so I bought a real expensive jacket and matching helmet.

I brushed my hair, dabbed on just enough stinging aftershave to be noticeable but not overpowering, then grabbed the box from Hannah-Smith's and deposited the contents into the package Terry had delivered – a double-thick steel DVD case. It just about fit in one of my roomy jacket pockets.

Just as I was coming out of the flats, Katy was pulling up on her bike; in all its black, tasselled and shining glory. She had one of those open faced helmets, with the aviator goggles and everything.

'A wizard is never late.' Katy said, raising her voice over the rumble of the engine. I could hear her dirty-times smile playing across her lips, and was again glad that I'd come…prepared.

'She arrives precisely when she means to.' I smirked, climbing onto the bike behind her, and unclipping my helmet from her side-saddle. I slipped my hands around her waist in a familiar gesture, and she wriggled herself closer to me.

'Hold tight.' she warned.

'As always.' I said, trying for romantic, but settling for just being heard over the engine.

We rode to our favourite watering hole, a cheapish and relatively cheerful place in the city centre. A great venue for a quiet night's drink. She parked the bike in a little courtyard around the back entrance, hung her helmet on the handlebars, and as we dismounted, turned to face me properly.

She took my helmet off and put it on the other handle before wrapping her arms around the back of my neck. I slipped mine around her waist again, under her jacket. The skin-to-skin contact made her shiver slightly, hopefully not just from the temperature. Our lips met, and parted. We didn't break the kiss for nearly a minute, by which time I was starting to feel more than a little warmed up; despite her lips being cold from the ride. Open faced helmets – the price of being awesome.

The other place that backed onto the courtyard was a biker hangout, so Katy's hog fit right in alongside the other 'choppers'. We were known faces in there, but tonight we fancied a quieter atmosphere. With their bikes outside too, we knew our helmets weren't going anywhere.

Our hands slid together as we walked inside, more of an old style pub than a bar. She picked a table out while I went to the bar and waited for some service. The place wasn't exactly a hive of activity on Mondays, but tonight it was especially dead. Maybe everyone was stuck in the traffic we'd hit on the way in. Must've been a hockey game on or something.

I put the few cents change into the charity box on the bar, and took a sip of ale to steady my nerves a little. Those puppies in my stomach from this morning had grown into big, slathering hounds, and were worrying at my intestines. I blinked at the image, and mused the various meanings of the word 'worry'.

11

'What's up?' she asked, 'You look more smiley than usual.'

'I like the top,' I beamed, recovering nicely, 'it really brings out your everything.'

It wasn't a lie, it just wasn't the answer she was looking for. Her black halter top that was cut so generously, from the male perspective at least, that I could see the bra she was wearing. Lacy, black, and my favourite.

She blushed slightly at the compliment, and adjusted the top in a way that made it seem like she was covering up, but really made little difference.

'So what did you get up to today?' I asked, sitting across from her and taking a glance at the big TV, showing some new music video on mute. I never got why they did that either.

'Dad called.' She said, raising her eyebrows. Tough subject. 'Wanted to know if I'd gotten the birthday present.'

A tablet computer, fancy, new, high end. She'd donated it.

'What'd you tell him?'

'Exactly what he didn't want to hear,' she grinned, 'the truth. He contained himself, but I could tell he wasn't happy at the thought of sick kids playing Tomb of Damocles on his two-hundred-silver tablet.'

'A better plan than smashing it,' I congratulated her. 'How was work today then? Nobody threw up blood on you again, did they?'

'Thankfully not,' Katy snorted, somehow making the noise charming. 'Something weird did happen though.'

'What's weirder than blood vomit?' I grinned, wondering if any other couples talked about this kind of thing on dates.

'You don't hang out in hospitals much, do you?' she asked rhetorically. 'This doctor pronounced a guy DOA, which wasn't hard because he was as white as a sheet from blood loss, then sent him down to the slabs. This is just at the start of my shift, right.' she paused, taking a slurp of her fizzy blackcurrant drink. 'So just as I'm about to clock off there's this call to security, from the morgue. The guy from earlier isn't as

12

dead as everyone thought. Gets off the gurney and bites the assistant coroner.'

'The dead guy?' I asked, raising an eyebrow. She gave me a 'don't interrupt' look, and carried on.

'Yeah, the dead guy. He bites the coroner, security get him restrained and have to put a muzzle on him. We've got him staying in for overnight observation, and the supposed-to-be dead guy in restraints in a private room. Most extreme case of ERHR I've heard of.' she added.

'You think its East Rojas Rabies, or just the normal kind?' I asked, looking over to the TV again. News update.

'Regular rabies takes months to incubate in humans, and it's almost always fatal by the time symptoms show. But from what we've heard of ERHR…the neuro symptoms…don't…hang on…' she added, trailing off, and looking over at the TV screen too. 'Can we get volume on this thing?' she shouted over her shoulder to the bar. The lone barman obliged.

'…related to the murder in Overbridge, possibly conducted by the same gang the police are now looking for. Residents of the smaller communities in Greenfield are advised to keep an eye out and report any strange activity to the police immediately.'

'What's up?' I frowned, looking at her expression and matching it. She didn't reply, so I touched her arm, 'Terra to Katy, you in there?'

'Oh, erm, nothing, just those murders. Been following it on the radio at work. The police better catch these assholes.' she frowned, shaking her head.

'Yeah, I get you.' I smiled. 'But I won't let any cannibal cults eat my girlfriend. Say,' I gasped theatrically, 'I think I should go home with you tonight, just to keep you safe.'

She brightened up immediately, letting out a bubbly laugh and turning her sunshine smile onto me. I put my hand on the table, palm up, and she locked her fingers with mine.

'In other news,' the TV persisted, 'the spread of East Rojas Human Rabies, or the ERHR super-bug, has accelerated.

13

Anyone exhibiting symptoms should call this number for the Greenfield CDC, and avoid travel, spreading the infection to others…'

Two

We'd been holding each other for a few minutes, while the afterglow faded. She really did glow. Her bare skin felt so warm against mine. Her back was pressed up against me, a hand on my thigh while my arms held her close. I felt her breath moving the hairs on my arms, and smiled when I heard her contented sigh. My cue, I kissed the back of her neck, slid my arms away from her and sat up.

'Where're you going, Kelly?' she muttered, turning onto her back, her eyes flicking down to my chest. I'm no bodybuilder, but I keep in decent shape.

'Absolutely nowhere...' I thought, reaching to the side of the bed for my jacket.

Her room was never the tidiest of places and already the book from her nightstand, a refresher handbook from her EMT days, had somehow fallen onto my jacket. I put it back on the stand, pulled the steel DVD case out of my pocket, and then lay back down next to her. I held it up in the air, and with a little laugh, she walked her fingers up my arm and pinched it out of my hand.

'Some Bad Men's new tour album?' she smiled, 'High Heels & Brushed Steel, the greatest hits. So you *were* listening when I told you what I wanted for my birthday.'

'Even if it wasn't out in time for your birthday, I thought our anniversary was a good enough day to give you...something else.' I fought a grin, trying not to give the game away. She softly touched my cheek, sweeping a tendril of black hair behind my ear.

We had been together longer than anyone else we knew, a full two years. Longer by half than any other relationship I'd been in, and long enough for me to remember when our anniversary was without setting a calendar alarm on my phone this year.

15

There was always a lot of fire when we got together, a lot of passion, and you'd think after a couple of years that it'd dim somewhat. Not a chance. We still didn't manage to get fully undressed most of time, even if a few shirt buttons popped or a pair of tights split. Tonight, Katy was still wearing my favourite bra, the lace sculpting her cleavage, offering it out.

'What the hell…?' she said, opening the special edition case. Something small and metal fell from it, and nestled between her breasts; drawing a gasp from her as cold silver touched warm skin.

The ring I'd had made for her at Hannah-Smith's was customised to match the old Northern Voison-pattern tattoo that wrapped around her arm near her shoulder. The design was reminiscent of waves on the sea, but since the ancient North was so fond of stone carving, the waves were angular and rigid, like the sea had frozen. I wouldn't want to get my girl just a plain old diamond now, would I?

'Do you want to get married, Katy?' I asked her, my stomach in knots. I held my breath.

'Oh my Gods…' she whispered, one hand actually going to her mouth. 'Dude,' she snorted, recovering fast, 'you're supposed to propose – then get me into bed!'

I didn't say anything. I just kissed her.

She kissed back, her leg sliding over mine, the DVD case thrown to the floor in all the rolling around we did before we stopped giggling. She sat up, straddling me, and offered me her hand. As gentlemanly and delicately as I could, I slid the silver band onto her index finger, the only finger she didn't already wear a ring on. It fit just perfectly.

'I fucking love you…' she moaned, her lips pressing into mine. I couldn't say anything back, even if I had wanted to.

In the morning I changed into some spare clothes I left at her place, and kissed her at the door to the sound of cooing laughter from her housemates; Laurel and Dani. They were my friends too, after two years courting. It'd been a really great morning, telling them the good news. Katy bit my bottom lip with a growl, grabbing my ass so they could both see.

16

'All mine now!' she laughed.

And that's why I loved my Katy.

I jumped on the bus to town and sat down on one of the many empty seats. Usually the busses from Katy's part of the 'burbs were packed with mid-morning commuters; this morning it was dead, but at least that meant I could take one of the free newspapers, usually gone by the time I started a Tuesday shift.

The front page was split between next month's general election and the ERHR crisis, which looked to be getting worse by the hour. The CDC had drafted all the men they could from the Republic's small standing force, the Territorials, but since most of the Territorial bases were in the South, they'd fallen back on Voison's larger Private Military Companies most everywhere else. Professional soldiers had been an export of the Republic for centuries, but it wasn't often we needed the mercenaries for ourselves.

Greenfield was lucky to have two hospitals. By the looks of it, smaller cities in the 'threatened areas' were directing non-ERHR patients towards Sydow, capital of the midlands and home to one of the major PMCs. They hadn't been hit so badly down there, less contaminated foreign imports, or so the papers guessed.

It was the first time I'd had call to be proud of my home region, from up here in the north – the living was cheaper but I squirmed uncomfortably at the thought of Voison turning to rioting like in the East. From the sounds of it, this super-bug took everyone by surprise. Being a concerned citizen, I put the hotline number into my phone in case anyone needed it. Hopefully not myself, but this looked like it was heading towards a pandemic, so better safe than contagious.

Despite the bus being empty, the roads were a nightmare. I got into work about twenty minutes late this time, undoing yesterday's good work on my time sheet. Even so, I had a spring in my step. I smiled again, looking at the picture of Katy on my phone as I checked my messages. I'd asked if she'd be on-call with this situation going on, but she hadn't gotten back yet.

Suddenly, I was being hugged. Gladys didn't shout when she saw me coming in late. She just walked right up and hugged me, a real rib-cracker, right there in the warehouse.

She'd always been a woman of strong emotions, which I put down to having four kids at home, but she'd never bear-hugged me for being late. Usually I just get a medium-style lecturing about responsibility, and an extra-awkward package delivery.

'Tiernan Kelly! I'm glad to see you're okay,' she said, breaking off the hug and holding me by the shoulders. 'I thought you'd been taken in.'

'Taken in? What do you mean?' I asked, knotting my brow. Nobody uses my first name unless they're Terry or it's *bad*.

'The CDC,' she said, like I was supposed to know what she meant. 'Didn't you know? They're going around looking for anyone showing signs of the virus, men with guns...'

'Yeah, I read about it on the way in. The Territorials are coordinating with the CDC and the mercenaries to secure quarantines around the relief centres. I think we've got Sydow Securities in Greenfield, them or Northern Territories. Think my Gran was in one of them during the War.'

'They're going around, taking the infected away, it's horrible...but better than spreading this thing? I don't know...' She carried on, looking off to one side before snapping her attention back to me. 'You haven't been bitten have you? Scratched?'

'Only in the company of my woman...' I mused.

'Be serious!' Gladys chided, slapping my shoulder. 'They're saying that's how you get it. And drinking contaminated water. And food from Rojas. And it's in the air. But if that were true we'd all have it, wouldn't we? Come on, there's this repeated warning on the TV – you should come see it.'

'They think it's going to hit us as bad as it did in the East?' I asked, as we walked through the warehouse towards the break room, where a few of the other couriers were sat. 'The main strip in Redmond looked like something out of the War, and that used to be a nice place to go for a few cocktails.'

It was a pokey little room with unclaimed packages stacked up along three walls. Usually we'd divide them up around Midwinter if nobody came to claim them, but until then, a large stack served as a TV-stand. National Mail were due to refit our break room three months ago, and while they'd stripped it out they hadn't bothered with the actual redecorating or refurnishing. Although, we still had a coffee machine, set up on a folding table someone had bought from a camping outlet.

'It's still warm.' Gladys said, passing a mug of black gold to me as I checked my phone again. I sipped gratefully, having skipped breakfast. No new messages.

On the TV a male presenter was reading from heavy wad of paper. The bar of text at the bottom scrolled along, telling people that it was a repeated message and flashing up the number for the Greenfield CDC hotline.

'Incubation symptoms include a lack of coherence, pale skin and a rise in temperature. When the virus has incubated do not try to help the infected, call this number immediately and isolate either yourself, or the infected. Busses will stop running at eleven a.m., and all people in Greenfield and the surrounding area are advised to return home immediately and avoid travel.'

'Oh Gods…' Gladys gasped, putting a hand up to her mouth, her eyes widening, 'Terrance, Terrance is in the bathroom, he…he said he wasn't feeling well and he looked so peaky…'

'Ah, shit. That's not good.' I grimaced, taking a big swig of coffee and setting the mug back down. 'I'll go see if he's okay.'

'Don't go near him, weren't you listening?' she panicked, flapping her hand at me, 'You might get it too!'

19

'I won't let him bite me, scratch me, or make me drink dirty water,' I said calmly, putting my palms up in appeasement. 'Let me just go have a word with him, I've got the hotline number, and I'll call it if he's infected. He might have just eaten a bad prawn or something.'

'Oh alright – but I'm coming with you. Some manager I'd be if I didn't supervise this. I'm supposed to be responsible for my boys.' She added, setting her hands into a stern position on her hips.

The bathroom wasn't far from the break room. Workplace efficiency and all that. We walked across the ends of a few aisles, but as soon as we came in sight of the conveniences; bare-brickwork things they'd built just before they took our sofas away, Terry came stumbling out.

'Got to find the stairway…' he mumbled. Or something like that. You know what it's like, when someone mutters in their sleep? That's what it was like. It'd have been funny if he wasn't barely on his feet and the colour of an overcast sky.

'Whoa, Terry man, where are you going?' I asked, stopping so suddenly my boots squeaked on the floor. Gladys stopped beside me.

He muttered something even less coherent, looked at us with the sort of expression you see in movies, where someone gets hit on the back of the head and falls unconscious in the barfight scene. He hit the floor a moment later, knees first, then face, arms limp at his side.

'I got it,' I sniffed, feeling my expression turn sour as I pulled out my phone and found the hotline number. We might not have been on the greatest terms, but I wasn't going to stand there and do nothing. I had to try three or four times until I got through. The lines must've been busy.

'You've reached the Centre for Disease Control, Greenfield hotline speaking, how can I direct your emergency?' the operator lady asked, eerily chipper.

'I'm at the National Mail distribution centre, and I think one of my co-workers has come down with the virus. He's pale, sweating, incoherent and just passed out…'

20

'That sounds like East Rojas, yes. We'll have someone along within ten minutes. In the meantime, do not go near the infected. Isolate them if possible, and if not, isolate the rest of the staff. The CDC official attending will be Doctor Lines.'

'Alright, thanks. Erm, have a nice day.' I added, aiming to match her contagious cheeriness. She hung up.

Me and a couple of the other couriers and packers kept an eye on Terry, keeping well back, while Gladys waited outside. Someone asked if we should get him a pillow, but nobody made a move, even the folks who liked him didn't want to touch him. Right on the ten minute mark, Gladys came back, leading a group of uniforms.

Two wore the white coats of medical staff, and were pulling on masks and gloves as they walked. Bringing up the rear were four men in grey and black urban camouflage decorated with Sydow Security patches. Mercenaries, professional soldiers. They had small but serious looking weapons to hand, boxy, rectangular submachine guns.

Doctor Lines, the older and more bespectacled of the two medics, checked Terry's pulse, his breathing, then nodded solemnly to his colleague.

'We need to get him to Mercy Hospital, quarantine ward.' The doctor reported, sounding tired. This could have been his hundredth callout of the day, and it wasn't even lunchtime. 'Can someone call his family?'

'I have his landline number.' One of my co-workers nodded, taking himself off into the stacks for some privacy.

'Captain Davis, could you bring the gurney and restraints please?' Doctor Lines asked one of the mercenaries before turning to Gladys. 'It'd be wise to close up for the day ma'am, get your staff home safe. Do you all have the hotline number?'

It didn't take us long to lock up and get ready for home. I was about to say goodbye to Gladys and walk for my bus before they stopped running, but she finger-wagged me into silence.

'Nonsense, won't hear a word of it, I'll give you a lift home.'

21

Those who had cars climbed into them, offering lifts to those who used public transport like myself. But it was just me and Gladys in her car, driving in mutual, worried silence.

Every inch of me was screaming that I had to call Katy. She probably already knew what was going on, better than I did. County wasn't where they'd take Greenfield's infected, but still, she'd be on the medical frontlines. She'd still be risking exposure no matter which hospital she worked at. I had visions of her being the one with the blood vomit this time, stumbling out of a bathroom, pale, hair slick with sweat.

Jaw tight, I called her and listened to the dialling tone for a full minute before I gave up. She was probably just busy. Yeah.

'No answer from your Katy?' Gladys frowned. I shook my head.

'She's either not picking up or I can't get through. They'll have her working tonight though. Big emergency like this. Rotten timing…'

'You'll do her no good with worrying. Try her again when you get in, send her a text.' Gladys reassured me, 'She'll be fine, the CDC look like they're handling it.'

'What're you going to do, about this…mess?' I asked, changing the subject.

'Going to pick my kids up, then I think we'll try getting out of town for a few days. We've family in Overbridge we can stay with.'

'Sounds like a good plan.' I nodded, texting Katy. We drove in silence for a few minutes while I composed the message, typing and retyping, not wanting to sound too worried, or overprotective. Just…wanting to know what's happening.

'Tiernan?' she smiled, after I hit send. 'Congratulations.'

It took me a moment to think what she could mean, before I split into a smile of my own. Some women just know these things.

Three

I thanked Gladys for the lift and wished her good luck as she dropped me off on the corner, at the other side of the mini-park between the street and castle tower. Usually I liked walking through the little ring of green space, but all I could think of was getting in and having a long chat with Katy, even if I had to call the A&E desk at County to get through to her. To hell with all those genuine emergency calls.

I met Neville as I reached the car park at the base of the flats. He was just getting out of his old sedan, Morgan getting out of the passenger side. Both of them looked tense; Morgan keeping her eyes on the ground and Neville rolling his shoulder uncomfortably.

Morgan was like a little sister to me, or maybe an adopted daughter, but I'd still say she was good looking. She was slim, on the athletic side rather than skinny side. Katy had once described her as "rather angelic", and was even jealous of her hair, ash brown and almost to her hips. Said it reminded her of when she was in med school. I'd have liked to have met her back then, before the scissors and dye. She'd shown me the old photos.

But Morgan's wholesome looks and cheery demeanour had rubbed shoulders with me and Katy for too long - so she had a tendency to wear floral dresses and pink nail polish, paired with leather trenchcoats and heavy boots – much to her father's amusement. She pulled her school satchel over her shoulder and gave me a wave of greeting.

Neville must have had a day off. I was used to seeing him in uniform, but today he wore comfortable jeans and a windbreaker over a green woolly jumper…with an underarm holster that flashed as he closed his car door. The sight of the gun caught me off balance.

'Heard the news?' Morgan asked as I approached.

23

'Schools out for disease-control.' Neville said, adjusting his jacket to better hide the gun.

'Is that why you're tooled up?' I asked.

'Nah,' he shrugged, showing the gun again accidentally, 'Princess here got all paranoid about the cannibal killers so I said I'd bring my work home with me.'

'Imported plagues and cannibal cults,' she said, almost managing nonchalance, 'what *is* this city coming to?'

The foyer was full of people, so when we opened the doors we had to squeeze our way inside. Most of them had suitcases or backpacks to hand, but there was a feeling in the room that struck a chord with me. Everyone there was afraid of something.

They were all showing it differently. Some of the women looked to have been crying recently, their eyes red or their makeup smudged. Most of the menfolk looked tense, even angry, scratching the back of their heads and pacing back and forth like caged animals. I caught glimpses of conversation. Relatives had been taken into Mercy. A son, a father, a best friend. Nobody was allowed into the hospital unless they were a doctor, a soldier or a patient – no visitors, even for the non-quarantine wards.

A lot of people were talking about leaving the city for a few days, like Gladys, heading into the country, waiting for the danger to pass, like what people did during the bombing back in the War. Suddenly, the landlord's voice cut over the background chatter.

'No, this won't affect your rent like that – I'm leaving too,' he said, 'All payments are suspended until you and me are both back, yes.' The man was sat up on the front desk and he seemed to be fielding questions. Neville stepped up and raised his voice.

'What's going on, Stan?' he asked.

I don't know if the landlord clocked Neville's shoulder holster, or if he was just zoning in on the nearest thing to an authority figure, but he ignored a couple more raised hands, and turned his head to Neville.

24

'Heya, Mr Roberts. A lot of the tenants are going to be moving out of the city while this whole thing settles down. Are you staying?' Stan asked back, a trace of relief in his voice. I got the impression he'd been stuck here for a while.

'Yeah, we are,' Neville said, putting a hand on Morgan's shoulder. She put her hand on top of his, eyes taking in the dishevelled crowd. 'I've already had chickenpox.' he smiled.

Perhaps sensing that the forum was closed, people started shuffling out of the doors behind us, slowly draining the foyer of tenants. I only knew a few faces, and I'd definitely never seen any of them so scared. If they weren't so well dressed, I'd say they looked like refugees. I nodded in greeting at a few of the ones I recognised from the elevator and the co-op, and got the same in return.

'How would you mind looking after the keys for a while? Just until this all blows over?' Stan asked, an optimistic smile on his face. 'I'll freeze your rent for a year.'

'Sounds like fun,' Neville enthused, suddenly beaming at the prospect and accepting a small ring of keys.

'So you're just going to ride it out, huh? Thinking it won't get as bad as in Rojas?' Stan asked.

'That's the hope,' Neville nodded, putting the keys into a jacket pocket. I'm guessing he flashed the gun again. He needed a bigger jacket if he wanted to carry that thing around without being gawked at. Stan knew Neville's gun was licensed; he'd had to fill out paperwork for it when he got the apartment, but even people who had licenses usually didn't just walk around carrying their guns.

'What's that for?' the landlord asked calmly, going behind the desk and grabbing a notepad.

'Just bringing it home for cleaning,' Neville lied, 'but if Human Rabies creeps up on me, I'll pop a cap in its ass.' He said, miming a gun with his fingers.

We chuckled, and the landlord left a note on the desk; his contact info, why the place was so empty, Neville in 1402 has the master keys, that sort of thing. Then he wished us luck and left with a suitcase in hand. The remaining three of us took the

25

elevator up to the penthouse together, and after the third attempt I realised Neville's throat-clearing was prompting me to say something.

'Oh, yeah,' I laughed, getting his subtle hint at last. My mind was elsewhere.

'Am I missing something again?' Morgan sighed, 'Because if this is "man stuff" then you can just let me off here.' She added, inverting the commas in the air.

'Couples stuff, Morgan.' I smiled. 'I've popped the question to Katy.'

Morgan squealed like a kid on Midwinter morning.

'Does this mean she'll be moving in?' she asked, 'Possibly with the addition of tiny feet in cowboy boots?'

'Whoa, whoa, whoa,' Neville said, 'give the man a minute. Congratulations, Kelly.' he added, holding out a manly handshake. I took it with a slightly embarrassed smile, and he clapped me on the shoulder.

'Still saving for a deposit, but we've talked about moving in together…' I shrugged, suddenly in the spotlight.

'Well I think that's a great idea,' Morgan said, folding her arms with a satisfied smile, like it'd been her idea all along.

Katy'd always valued her space, her privacy. There were even locks on a few of the drawers in her room – but that was just because it was an old student house. She'd shared the place since university with Dani, an old friend from back home, and Laurel, who'd simply been looking for new digs. They were thick as thieves now.

On the top floor, I stuck my head out of my place just long enough to hear the Roberts' door close, and Morgan struggle to keep her voice down as she talked to her father about the engagement. I cracked up into a broad grin, but I didn't think Neville would be. Morgan would probably go on about it all day now, even if it would be a distraction from the growing pandemic.

With the warning to stay indoors I guessed I wouldn't be going anywhere for a while. But I still needed to call Katy and make sure she was okay. I punched in County's A&E desk number and chewed my lip for another minute before I hung up. Those pesky hounds started jumping in my stomach again, only this time they had three heads apiece. Nobody was picking up the emergency desk? Again, same result on my landline.

I tried calling friends. I'd come to Greenfield knowing only a couple of people, high school and college friends who'd moved up here for university and never left. Until I met Katy, I didn't have a lot more friends than Jason, the cameraman, Will, a paperwork wrangler, and the host of moderate acquaintances they happened to bring along to the pub or invite to chat in online games.

If you can't get in touch with one person, it's not really a cause for concern. If you can't reach half a dozen names, trying each one on a mobile and a landline – now that's when you can start worrying. I took the back off my mobile, took out the card and blew on it before putting it back in, and trying all the numbers again, just in case I was the problem. I couldn't get a hold of anyone.

Desperately, I knocked on Neville's door and asked to use his phone, just in case mine were both broken. Standing in his kitchen, I stared at my reflection in the black faux-marble worktop as I listened to the busy signals once more. No phone was getting me through to anyone else's.

Maybe it was just the call volume, I thought, trying to reason with myself. So many other people must be trying to get in touch with their friends and family, or the ERHR hotline, the lines and masts must have been jammed up.

I tried my games console, hoping to use one of the chat functions to send out an email or get someone on the other end of a headset, but couldn't connect to the Wireless. Castle tower's network was fine, but it wasn't registering any further signals. If someone on the third floor wanted to play Galaxy Raider with me then we'd be fine, but that didn't do me much good.

My mind started racing again. She was surely working. Everyone with so much as a First Aid badge would be called in

27

to help with something like this. If she went to work and caught the infection, what could I do? Or...no, what if she saw the news report before she left? I crossed my fingers and tried Katy one last time, dialling the girls' house from memory. It connected.

'Kelly? Oh, thank Gods, I was so worried.' Katy sighed.

A lot of people called me Kelly, but for her it was more like a pet name than most people thinking "Tiernan" was weird and old fashioned. In a house full of girls, they'd joked it made them uncomfortable to have a man around the house, so stuck with Kelly. I took it in my stride. Katy's voice sounded stressed, but not like she'd been crying – more like she'd been given some bad news and hadn't quite processed it yet.

'I was too, I called as soon as I got back home,' I told her, 'do you know what's going on at the hospital? Are they sending East Rojas patients to County?' I asked, to confirm my worst fear.

'Yeah,' she said, quietly. 'I don't want you to worry though. Mercy's just getting a little overcrowded, so we're getting some of the overflow. But I shouldn't be treating any ERHR patients, that's the CDC's job. Mainly I'll just be admin, paperwork.' She added, trying to comfort me.

'Can you just...not go in?' I regretted asking it immediately.

'They need me,' she said, firmly. 'This is what I wanted to do when I turned down that job with my parents. Be there for people. Make a difference. I can't bail out on my oaths just because things are getting tough.'

'I know, I'm sorry I said anything, I didn't mean that. I'm just...'

'You're worried you won't be able to return the ring if it's a biohazard.' She sighed. For a second, I thought she was serious. 'I'll be sure to give it a good scrubbing before the cold sweats start.'

'Not funny.' I told her, pacing around my apartment. 'Call me, text me, any chance you get.'

28

She laughed, but it was nervous, fleeting. 'I've got to go, but, just, listen to me for a minute Tiernan,' she stopped, clearing her throat, her voice becoming much quieter and more serious. She used my first name and everything. 'Stay safe, okay? Keep an eye on the news any way you can, stay inside, and please, don't go near the infected. I can't lose you now. I love you. I'll see you later.'

'I love you too…see you later…' I replied.

We hung up.

Four

I slipped into a kinda coma for a minute, imagining Katy getting infected in the line of duty. I know, I know she said it was just paperwork, admin, but it's still a hospital. She could still be asked to help, and help she would. I couldn't bear the thought of her being hurt. I wanted to go down there and grab her, take her back here where it was safe…If she knew I was thinking like such a white knight I'd get such a kicking…

Suddenly I got that feeling that comes after a noise, where you know you've heard something but now it's all quiet. Someone knocked on my door and I jumped, a hot wave of embarrassment making me uncomfortably aware I was still in my jacket.

I walked over to the door and opened it. Before I could even ask her what was wrong, Morgan ducked past me in the doorway, ponytail swinging. My apartment's fairly big, but mostly open plan. Only the bedroom and the bathroom are cut off.

'You've got to see this.' She explained, turning the TV on and picking up the remote.

'Looks like things are getting worse,' Neville said calmly, appearing behind me. 'President just declared a state of emergency, and a few minutes ago the Senate called up all remaining Territorial units to reinforce quarantine areas in the south. The CDC's really worried about Greenfield's infection rate, so they're contracting more mercenaries to block the roads, and there's some kind of riot downtown.'

We all fell quiet, as Morgan searched through the TV guide function for the local news station. It was showing aerial footage of Mercy Hospital, where Something was Happening.

The hospital was just on the edge of the city centre, and the footage was focusing on the main entrance, where several grey military four-by-fours and trucks had parked in a semi-circle on the main road.

As we watched, something was thrown at one of the blockading Humvees and exploded over the roof of the vehicle, covering it in fire and causing some of the men behind the 4x4 to stumble back.

'This shocking footage was taken just a few minutes ago at Mercy Hospital, where victims of the East Rojas virus have been taken by the CDC. According to our on-site reporter, the rioting was sparked by the patients' treatment by PMC soldiers hired to assist in the search for infected citizens. Gillian Allman has more.'

The aerial footage was replaced by a lady reporter, standing some ways down the street from the hospital. I could make out the crowds of people around the CDC blockade, and just about hear the resonating shouts of their protest. She was a fairly safe distance away from the crowd, but she still looked a little worried, beneath the calm, professional, Auntie Veeb training.

'Thanks Matt. I'm outside Mercy Hospital, where a crowd of angry protestors has gathered. I can inform you that only moments ago shots were fired above the heads of the crowd by the soldiers in response to a projectile thrown by the protestors, some of whom have since fled the area.

'According to one bystander who did not wish to appear on camera, concerned family members refused to give up their loved ones to the CDC, which understandably sparked tensions, after leaked footage from Rojas showed unarmed infected civilians being shot by peacekeeping forces.

'As per Parliamentary orders, the soldiers used non-lethal force to separate the infected into a quarantined area set up inside Mercy Hospital. But only a few minutes ago, rioters forced their way inside the hospital and began to harass both the CDC and hospital staff.

'According to a phone call made from inside the hospital by a member of the CDC's medical team; the rioters have barricaded sections of the hospital and are demanding that the soldiers leave. The mercenaries have since declared the entire hospital a quarantine zone.'

The image flicked back to the studio, where the same man was shuffling the same papers. He set one of them aside and I caught a glimpse of black rectangles on the page, the kind that conspiracy theorists love to think about.

'Thanks Gill.' he said, 'We can now tell you that Parliament has authorised the CDC's soldiers to use fully-lethal force to protect the quarantine zone at Mercy Hospital, and have upgraded the state of emergency in Greenfield, Manford and Danecaster Counties to red. Territorial and CDC forces are expected to be establishing checkpoints on the roads within the hour, so travel outside of Greenfield is expected to be restricted to emergency services only.

'Parliament have also issued an official statement, declaring that all citizens infected with East Rojas virus turn themselves in to the CDC immediately, the phone number for which you can find at the bottom of your screen...'

The man flicked his eyes off camera for a moment and, and nodded, his brow furrowed.

'We have breaking news now at Mercy Hospital, coming live from Gillian Allman. Gillian, what's happening out there?' the presenter asked, trying to get the words out quicker.

The image of the woman outside the hospital returned, but now she definitely looked unsettled. Her eyes were a little wide, and she stared at the camera for a moment, mouth hanging slightly open.

'Ah,' she stuttered, casting a look over her shoulder at the hospital. 'Well Matt, we just witnessed an individual inside the hospital struggling to open one of the upper storey windows. The man inside the hospital was then attacked from behind...and... fell through the window, onto the ground...four storeys below. Shots were then fired by the CDC's mercenaries, Sydow Sec, and several more of the protestors outside of the hospital have left the area.'

'Sorry Gill, just to confirm – the CDC fired on the protestors, or the man in the window?' Matt the anchor asked.

32

'I – we aren't sure at this point Matt, though it looks as if more CDC trucks are arriving.' she said, looking somewhere behind the camera.

The camera spun around and refocused on a school-style bus driving towards the hospital. The cameraman kept the lens trained on the bus, painted in the same grey as the Humvees and trucks.

As it drove by, the bus slowed down to let a handsome young soldier in full combat gear, sans-helmet to remain stylish, jump down to the road. He wore the same urban camo I'd seen on the men at the postal warehouse, making him Sydow Securities, I guess. He jogged over to the reporter, and addressed Gill while she was still off camera.

'Ma'am, you can't be filming here,' he said, his tone polite, 'it isn't safe to be near the quarantine zone right now.'

'Sir, sir!' Gillian said, as the camera moved, getting the reporter and the soldier in shot together. 'What is happening inside the hospital?'

'I'm not authorised to comment on any questions addressed by civilians ma'am. A statement has been issued by Parliament, and as you know, it has been announced in local news.'

'But the people surely have a right to know what is going to happen to their families? Does the CDC have the appropriate amount of medicine to deal with a health scare of this size? Do we even have a vaccine or treatment available?' Gill pestered, following the soldier as he moved to catch up with the bus.

Suddenly, the level of volume from the protestors rocketed into something much more aggressive.

'Set them free! Set them free!' you could hear them chanting.

But then a chorus of screams joined with the shouts, and the camera focused in on the bus, just as a spray of blood painted one of the windows red.

The soldier saw it, and turned around. He grabbed Gillian with one hand, and started pulling her back the way

33

he'd come from, away from the bus and the rioters, right into the cameraman who'd been following too closely behind. The picture went all shaky-cam as he tumbled to the ground, the sound crackling as the camera slipped from his grip. We saw nothing but tarmac for a moment.

'Sir, sir! You can't-' she tried to protest, but he cut her off.

The camera didn't pick up what happened next, but the sound of gunfire made the microphone pop again. A moment later, and the cameraman must have regained his footing.

The soldier appeared again, with one of those boxy submachine guns held up to his shoulder. He fired another pair of shots into the side of the bus – *fam-fam*, and then lowered his weapon. The doors of the bus opened, and people began to spill out of each exit, some of them wearing haz-mat suits, trying to shout for order, and some just in plain clothes, running for their lives.

'Gods above!' Neville shouted. I'd pretty much forgotten they were in the room, I'd been looking so intently at the news. 'He's just shooting at people!'

'I don't know.' I said, feeling my blood run cold, 'What was all that blood from? It was fricking spraying…'

'He can't just be shooting the infected like that!' he yelled, 'That's murder!'

'We don't know that's what he's doing,' I said, 'we can't see inside the bus – look at the blood…' I muttered, my stomach in knots just watching it.

'That's murder!' Gillian shouted, standing a few feet behind the soldier, who'd put himself between her and the bus.

'Use of lethal force was authorised.' he said, head tilting down to his shoulder, 'Patient on bus three just turned, had to neutralise the victim but we've lost the bus.'

There was the crackle of his radio, and words that the camera couldn't quite pick up.

'It wasn't my idea to bring them here, blame the CDC official at County, their quarantine's in overflow. Get me a squad here now! Landry out.'

'County was supposed to take the overflow from Mercy…' I thought aloud, 'If there's too many infected in both hospitals...I need to call her again.' My thoughts were spinning, but I was sure I could talk her into staying home, beg her if I needed to.

I patted my pockets for my mobile, couldn't find it, and ran to the landline in the kitchen. I tried dialling the number too quickly, my fingers pressing down two numbers at once. I ground my teeth and carefully redialled, but I got the beeping of a busy line almost immediately.

'Something like this on TV,' Neville said, waving a hand at the screen, 'Line's are going to be buzzing.'

I slammed the phone back into its receiver, but it slipped out, so I had to slam it in again even harder. I found my mobile on the counter and dialled the shortcut for her mobile number. Decent mobile reception shouldn't be hard to come by these days, but as sod's law would have it, I couldn't even get a signal anymore. The "no coverage" icon flashed in the corner of the screen.

On the TV, they'd cut back to the studio, where the anchor was repeating the Parliamentary orders. A scrolling bar at the bottom read 'This message will repeat' – followed by the emergency hotline number.

'I think they've stopped the live broadcast.' Morgan said quietly, 'Guess they don't want people seeing a warzone, don't want people to panic, it kinda got all messed up at the end there, didn't it?' she asked, hugging herself with one arm.

'What do we do now then?' Neville asked, gesturing at the screen like it was going to tell him.

'Stay at home, stay safe, keep an eye on the news…' I said, repeating Katy's warning, and the words that were scrolling along the ticker at the bottom of the TV screen. 'Let's hope this all blows over…I guess that's all we can do. Never thought something like this would happen here…'

I sat down, running my hands through my hair, trying to think clearly. Morgan went straight into my kitchen and put the kettle on. She knew where everything was. Neville sat down next to me, and put a hand to my back in a consolatory fashion.

'What time was she supposed to be in work?' he asked.

'She said she was going in to help with intake, just before you came here. She was leaving in a minute.' I muttered.

'Hey, that's good right? If she's only intake she won't be dealing with the infected beyond the triage stage – or maybe she saw the news? She could still be at home right now, calling in sick or something – but not that kind of sick.' Neville added hurriedly, keeping his voice soft, 'Come on. Try ringing her again in a few minutes, the lines might have cleared.'

'Yeah, yeah,' I nodded, 'Thanks.'

I sat and drank tea with my neighbours while the news played the recorded message. Stay at home, checkpoints established, infected required to turn themselves in, riot at Mercy Hospital. It was about an hour later that they announced that the quarantine around Mercy was now including the entire block, and that they were currently "estimating casualties" at around thirty.

Morgan and Neville left eventually, but I heard them moving about in their apartment until fatigue started to weigh down on me. I turned the volume up on my mobile and the kitchen handset, taking them to bed with me. I tried again before resigning myself to sleep. It'd gotten worse. The landlines weren't just busy, they were completely down.

Five

On Wednesday, me and Neville got together in the late afternoon and started knocking on doors. He'd brought a pencil and a notepad with him, but after we'd got a few floors down we realised he didn't need the register. Most people weren't answering, or weren't present. Out of respect, we didn't barge into their homes. Not yet anyway.

The only remaining tenants were on our floor, and the one below, like a sense of height conferred a sense of safety. The parking lot was empty aside from a massive blue 4x4, a white pickup, and Neville's sedan, everyone was gone. We were alone.

So there was Neville and Morgan, myself, Edgar and Rosie Jameson who lived across the hall from me, and below us only two more people; Damian Grant and Lucile Marchland, 1301 and 1302 respectively. Everyone else had left town, and hells, did that make us feel isolated.

Even though we tenants weren't exactly a tight-knit community, I still knew everyone to a certain extent. I'd helped the Jamesons' son carry furniture up to their apartment, cramming a three-seater sofa into the elevator and somehow getting it out again – a feat I'm sure I wouldn't be able to repeat.

Lucile had only been in town a month or so, working some kind of construction job. She'd thrown herself a flat-warming party, knocking on most doors in the building, with a few people from her job showing up too, but I got the impression she didn't know too many people outside of the job.

I knew Damian as a face about town, setting up sound equipment at small live music venues, working behind the bar, standing out front as security – though he didn't have the bronze shield like Neville. He'd given me a business card once, shouting over the noise of the club in his lilting accent. The card advertised his services as a sound technician, party DJ and roadie – a hell of an odd-jobbing résumé.

Neville scrunched up his list of names and put it in his back pocket while we rode the elevator up from the first floor.

'Not a big turnout for a block of over fifty people.' he said.

'Starting to think you should have skipped town?' I asked.

'I'm not exposing Morgan to ERHR, even if we have to sit up in castle tower with malnutrition.' he replied. 'You've seen the few pictures that got out of Rojas.'

'Yeah.' I nodded, rubbing the bridge of my nose. I shut my eyes a moment, and saw the image of Katy pale and feverish again.

'And down that train of thought madness lies.' Neville said, seeing into my head. 'If the phones clear up she'll call.' he added, patting me on the shoulder uncertainly. Male bonding probably didn't come easily to him, but he'd been trying.

'I just wish we knew more of what was going on. Did the same rioting crap break out at County General or what?' I asked the world. It didn't answer.

I pushed the fourteenth floor button until the doors rattled open onto the penthouse, where Morgan was waiting for us in the hallway.

'Paused something interesting on TV… Come take a look.' she said, leading us into the Roberts' apartment.

It wasn't much different to mine in terms of décor. Comfortable leather sofas, a wooden coffee table, a faux marble surfaced kitchen and a sleek black widescreen you'd have trouble fitting in a smaller elevator.

I'd had the news running since I'd last talked to my fiancée. It was mostly just the same message repeated over and over, with different inflections and slightly different versions, depending on what station you watched. All the channels were dead apart from the news stations, so it was the only thing on anyway.

38

Some made out like the Territorial Army and the CDC's soldiers were letting people through the checkpoints so long as they didn't carry any signs of infection. Another, more reliable station, said that the city had been completely locked down and riots had broken out at some of the motorway checkpoints. Still another station said that police forces and EMTs were touring the city looking for infected, and carrying them off to who-knows where.

I fixed my eyes on the news as Morgan pressed 'play', and watched as the camera panned back to the desk. This was different to all the recorded messages we'd seen earlier. This felt unscripted, and the woman behind the desk was missing the usual cake of TV makeup. Her hands were clasped on the desk in front of her, but her nail polish was chipped and her hands were covered in black smears, like engine grease or something.

'As you can see, we've taken our own advice now, and are staying indoors. The rioting seems to have quietened down, but there are still infected walking around out there. If you make too much noise they try to get in, but if you stay quiet for a while they'll go away.' Gill spoke, the lady reporter from yesterday. She looked around the room for a second, and then turned back to camera. Her shoulders shook as she took a deep breath, before carrying on.

'There'll be no more news after this report. It isn't safe to go outside anymore, but we'll repeat this message for as long as we can. The infected have gone mad, attacking whoever they see with their bare hands...and teeth. They're everywhere you go now, the city isn't safe...' She swallowed, glancing around the room again. 'Those cannibal murders from the start of the week...they have to be related. I don't want to panic anyone,' she said, her voice going a little quieter, 'but I don't think they're really human anymore, like they're something from a movie. Mad, I know. Please, just stay away from them, stay home, or get to somewhere safe and hide. There's no getting out. Last thing we heard was the checkpoints were overrun, or the CDC was holding them with force, shooting

39

anyone who got close. Quarantine is broken, and that means the Territorial or more security forces should come soon to contain the infected.'

She took a break, and sipped from a glass of water. The camera panned around the news office, showing the usual behind-the-scenes broadcasting equipment, news desks and a handful of spectators dressed in camo fatigues; all with military-grade firepower strapped over their shoulders – Sydow Security.

I could see the weather guy from Sunday broadcasts carrying a woman with the help of a soldier with a red cross on her helmet. They set her down on a pile of cushions that looked like they'd been taken off a sofa, and the weather guy started to unpack macabre looking medical tools from the mercenary's pack.

'Just…hold out and wait, don't take any unnecessary risks...' Gill said, the image thundering her words home. 'The power grid will probably fail soon, and when that happens most of the food in the city will start to rot, so ration it with whoever you're with. Wait for the Territorials, the mercenaries, wait for help...and if any infected come knocking…just stay quiet. Stay safe.' she added, looking down. A moment later, the screen flashed to the no-signal card, but after a few seconds, it was replaced by Gill again – and the footage began to play from the start.

'Stay safe…fuck…' Morgan whispered.

'Language.' Neville muttered, unaware he was saying it as he placed a hand on his daughter's shoulder.

'I'll see if anyone didn't get that broadcast.' I spoke, feeling my voice come out a little hoarse.

I walked out into the corridor, just as Edgar did the same. Neville joined us, with Morgan trailing behind. Rosie looked over Edgar's shoulder in the doorway, her straight iron grey hair brushing over his shoulder.

'We need to start working together,' I said. 'We've been holed up with our heads in the sand, and it's about time we started treating this like the disaster it is.' I sighed. 'But I think we need to see what's out there before we go into survival mode, maybe bring our families and friends back here. It's safer than the average twin house if someone's trying to break in.'

'The woman on the news said to stay inside, keep safe.' Neville reminded me.

'I know that...but my fiancée is out there somewhere.' I said, grinding my teeth, my mind flitting back to the injured woman on the cushions, 'I need to make sure she's okay.'

'And I agree with you.' Neville shot back, holding up his hands, 'I was just saying, for the record, so we all know what we're getting in to.'

'Then it's noted. If anyone wants to come with me, I'm heading out in a minute.'

'We'll take my car.' Neville said, throwing me his support, and wheels, I guess. 'Won't be gone long.' He said to Morgan.

'Hope not...' she gave him a weak smile.

'We'll stay.' Rosie said, holding Edgar's shoulder. 'Leave it to you young ones to play at scouts. Right, Ed?'

'Hmm? Okay.' he said, slowly. 'I'd liked to have gone, but if you need to light out of somewhere quick, I'm not going to be good on my leg. I got shot you know, in the knee...' he added with an eye roll. I got the impression his wife reminded him of it more than just walking did. Edgar would have come with me if it wasn't for the hand on his shoulder.

'Yeah, I remember.' I smirked, seeing his eyes.

'Were you going to invite us?' a deeply accented voice asked.

I hadn't heard the elevator rattle open, but Lucile and Damian were just stepping out of it.

'I coming witch you.' Damian raised his voice to carry down the corridor. He was a physically imposing man with dreadlocks brushing the tops of his shoulders; tall, broad, muscular and friendly as they come.

'I'll sit this one out,' Lucile tutted, 'I'm gonna, you know, listen to the nice woman on the TV.' she added as she folded

41

her arms and raised an eyebrow at Damian, looking him up and further up. Petite, blonde and short-haired, she contrasted him in almost every way, save her own muscle. Labourer's biceps flexed with her folded arms, on show with her tank top.

I'm not usually the type to pay attention to the gender stereotype, but it looked as if the menfolk were manning up, while the womenfolk were staying at home.

'Then we leave now.' I said, nobody left to ask.

We dressed warm, grabbing coats and jumpers. Five minutes later, Neville, Damian and myself left castle tower, Neville locking up behind us with Stan's keys.

'Where to first?' he asked, bleeping his sedan open.

'Shotgun.' I called.

'How old are you mon?' Damian snorted, shaking his head. I think it helped diffuse the tension a little.

'Katy's place first. You remember where it is, right?' I asked Neville, getting into the front passenger seat. He'd picked Morgan up from there more than once.

'Yeah, I remember,' he nodded. 'What about after? If we're going to make a drive for everyone's family then we'll need a bigger car.'

'I like to check on me sister, an de little ones. She text me de other day saying she were heading out, I need to be sure they made it,' Damian said, 'you feel?'

'I feel. Where does your sis live?' I asked.

'Terrace housing, over an Greenside.' he answered, his accent turning 'Greenside' into something exotic, rather than a slightly rundown estate. 'If she there, she'll lend her car.'

'We'll go there first then. Katy's is further away, and nobody in her house has a car, just one oversized bike. We'll need more seats if we're bringing more people.'

'Thanks man.' he sighed, his shoulders sagging with relief.

The sun was setting as we left, a light breeze taking with it the last warmth of the day. Even with my jacket, I was cold. Inside Neville's car we were out of the wind, but still needed the heater.

42

Neville got us moving but kept to a slow, wary driving pace. We could see smoke rising from several different fires somewhere in the city, the black clouds standing out clearly against the orange of the sunset. On a long, straight stretch of road on a slight rise overlooking the city centre, we came to the clearest view.

In the waning light, we could make out the blinking lights of a helicopter circling over the city, and with the radio turned off, we could hear the sirens of emergency service vehicles, but there was no sign of anyone as we drove through our neck of the woods.

We must have only been driving for ten minutes when we came to a roadblock. It wasn't military, not a checkpoint. It was a crash, with one of the cars still pouring steam from under the bonnet. One car straddled across both lanes, the other two had somehow crashed into it, making it a sandwich of sharp metal.

Neville rolled his sedan to a stop maybe ten yards back and unbuckled, while I did the same. It was the sort of thing that makes you want to get out and have a look. As we straightened up, a foul smell caught our attention. We glanced at each other over the roof, making sure we were both smelling it.

You don't forget that smell. The rotten, clinging scent of death. Scrub all you want, trim your nose hairs, and put on some of Neville's powerful aftershave, but that smell's only going away once you've gotten used to it. Someone had died in that crash. Died bad.

I moved closer. The nearest car had both its doors on one side open, and I could see dark brown stains – blood – on the seats. It looked like there were two people in the back, one unconscious man, and a woman trying to rouse him. Or so I thought.

'Hey, you okay?' I asked.

I wish I hadn't. The woman's head snapped towards me, her hair covered in blood and grime, obscuring her face. She kept rheumy eyes on me while she crawled backwards out of

43

the car…when she stood up, that's when I could see her properly.

From her chin to the top of her nose was a mask of fresh blood and bared teeth. But her teeth weren't showing because of some animalistic gesture…her top lip was torn away, just gone.

She staggered towards me and reached out with both arms, taking in a ragged wheezing breath and letting out a low moan. The moan carried everything dark; pain, hunger, sadness, and it struck a chord right at the base of my spine that froze my feet for a second. I stared into her eyes, white and glassy, and felt my throat tighten.

'Kelly!' Neville urged, watching the woman step towards me. 'Get away, she's infected!'

'Shit!' I swore, thawing my feet, running back to the car.

She followed, staggering towards me so quickly she almost fell over. Before I could get the car door open, she lunged forwards, falling, and just managed to get a grip with one hand around my ankle. She used the grip to pull herself forwards, groaning and wheezing a little more excitedly. It made the hairs on the back of my neck stand on end. I tried to shake her off, but she had me by the sock.

Damian's shoe came down on the woman's wrist, and I heard the bone snap. He got a hand under my arm and pulled me away from the woman, whose grip was nothing now her wrist had been broken. But she clawed forwards an inch using her other hand, pulling so hard that two of her nails peeled free of her fingers. She didn't even wince.

'What de hell is this shit?' Damian cursed, the pair of us taking a few quick steps backward. 'She a zombie!'

'There's no such thing as zombies.' Neville murmured, looking right at the damn thing while his face turned pale.

'Come to this side of the damn car and tell me that!' I yelled back, watching the rest of the woman's nails tear free as she clawed another inch towards us.

'In the movies they shoot them in their blackest evil hearts.' Neville said distantly, half quoting from some film. He looked to have frozen up too, his face puzzled.

But Damian was on the ball; he grunted with effort and threw open the rear passenger door, hitting the woman in the face with another crack of broken bone. She rolled over, thick blood oozing from her nose, which was so twisted over to one side that she looked like an abstract painting.

'Get in de back!' he shouted, scrambling over the seats to make some room for me.

I followed him in. 'Neville, get us out of here!' I yelled, closing the door just before she could slip her hand inside.

'You're serious?' Neville asked, still outside of the car. 'A zombie? She's just sick…'

'You were looking right at it!' Damian cried, his voice running high pitched with fear.

A deeper, more masculine moan joined that of the woman's. Neville spun around, and saw something in the mess of tangled metal that made him turn green when he faced back towards the car. He looked about ready to vomit right there on the street.

'Yeah, we should go back home.' he said quickly, slamming the car door and ignoring his seatbelt as he put us into reverse. Tyres squealed as he flicked the car around. Damian and I used each other for support, ourselves un-belted, tossed around in the back.

I turned to look out of the rear window as we sped away, watching as two more figures emerged around the side of the crash and the half-faced woman pushed herself back up to her feet. They started lurching after the car with jerking steps, limping after us a little faster than walking pace. We were safe.

'This can't be happening, no way.' I panted, short for breath, noticing my voice squeak a little higher. I swallowed hard and tried to breathe steadily. 'This can't be happening…'

As Neville tore up the streets heading back home, it was like our eyes had been opened. They were everywhere, with their glassy eyes and bloody clothes, staggering in our wake, letting out that awful moan.

Six

We came to a gentle stop back in the parking lot, the engine making little ticking sounds as it cooled. Neville just sat still, one hand on the handbrake and one on the wheel. Damian was holding his head between his hands and staring at the carpet mat, dreads hanging down.

'That just happened.' I tried, hearing my voice come out a little quieter than it should have. I repeated myself, louder, searching for confirmation.

'I broke de woman's arm,' Damian muttered, massaging his temples, 'she didn't feel a thing.'

'I know, I saw…saw her nails tear out. She didn't slow down, just kept coming forwards…' I spoke, seeing it happen all over again in my head.

Neville opened the drivers' side door and started taking in those deep, steady breaths that you take when you're trying not to be sick. I needed air too.

We took a few minutes to pull ourselves together, the terror-induced adrenaline ebbing away, making me feel a little drained, a little weak at the knees. I leaned against the side of the car. Neville's hands shook as he took out the keys to unlock the foyer, but he clenched his fists, steadying himself.

The elevator ride back up was just as tense and jittery, the usual rattling of the lift not helping matters. I slumped, propped up in a corner, Neville damn near chewed his own bottom lip off and Damian just leaned his head against the cold metal doors, misting them up with his breath.

'Zombies man,' he said, a dark laugh in his voice, 'real old Island lore. They like de story what you tell little ones when they misbehaving, try to get them to eat they greens and not play out after dark. Can't be real. Can't.'

'You slammed a car door in one's face, D,' Neville said, looking down at his shoes, 'sounded pretty real from where I was standing.'

47

'You should be proud. Knocking seven shades out of the bogeyman like that.' I offered up.

'I need a brew about now,' he chuckled, forcing a humourless smile and removing his head from the doors.

They shook open onto the top floor, me and Neville following Damian out into the corridor. I could see the big man's shoulders shaking when he breathed. The Jamesons' door was open, but before we'd gotten to it, Edgar appeared. He'd been keeping an ear out for us.

'Well that wasn't slow.' The old man said, raising an eyebrow, 'What's gone on?'

'I need to use your bathroom please.' Damian politely said, Edgar letting him slip by in the doorway.

'Could you get the kettle on?' Neville asked, following in Damian's wake. Edgar looked at me, holding the bag, so to speak.

'We've got big news.' I nodded gravely, just as the sound of Damian's first round of retching came from the bathroom.

About ten minutes later, we had everyone together for a sit-down in the Jamesons' comfortable living room. The old couple were sharing sofa space with Lucile while Damian paced the room, still a little rough around the edges. Morgan was in the kitchen making everyone's tea, while me and Neville sat on the arms of Edgar's big chair, both of us too polite to take the actual seat.

'You remember what that reporter said in the last broadcast? About how ERHR and the cannibal murders are related?' I asked, struggling to think of a way to break the subject of zombies to someone. 'I think she was right. Out there, we saw…there was a woman…'

'Didn't feel pain.' Neville chimed in. 'White as a sheet.'

'She was bent over this guy, her face was…covered in blood…'

'Broke her arm. Can still feel it snap. She wouldn't stop.' Damian muttered, scratching the back of his neck.

'Ah,' Morgan said from the kitchen, 'you think that the East Rojas Human Rabies virus is in actual fact, the cause of

48

the cannibal murders of last week? That somehow the virus is turning people into violent cannibals who attack their victims with their hands and teeth? That these people are in fact…zombies?' she added with a dramatic pause.

I looked at the back of her head, ponytail bobbing about the kitchen. I couldn't tell if she was joking, or just repeating some conspiracy theory she'd read on the Wireless.

'Way to steal my thunder.' I grimaced, looking at the reaction on everyone's face. 'Yeah. That is exactly what I'm getting at, yeah.'

'Zombies?' Rosie scoffed, 'What's this rubbish?'

'East Rojas virus,' Damian said softly, his voice hoarse from throwing up, 'you been seen them pictures? All de infected, grey faces, cuts, nothing behind de eyes. That's what we just seen out there, everywhere.'

'But they get a fever, that's it, isn't it?' Rosie asked, 'Everything I've read about it says that the infected get a fever and a few sores. I haven't seen anything like zombies on the news when they reported from abroad.'

'Well you wouldn't get many people staying around to record stuff like that…people, eating other people.' I tried, 'But they showed us crowds, people with horrible injuries, civic unrest, but not much new in the last few days. I thought it was just because they'd contained it. But if Parliament knew it was coming here, maybe they didn't want to panic people by showing the full extent. If they even knew about it at all. Pretty much every state in the East has imposed a press ban in the last couple weeks.' By the time I'd finished talking, just voicing aloud my own thoughts, I realised people had started listening. It left a deep silence when I shut my mouth.

'Maybe?' Morgan replied, a blanket response as she started to ferry mugs of tea over.

I shrugged. 'Doesn't matter. But what we just saw out there, no question. The cannibal murders, ERHR, it's the same thing. That makes the situation a little more dangerous than just some contagious fever. Out there…that woman, she was after us. She meant to kill us. She wouldn't stop.'

'Zombies aren't real though, they're movie monsters, superstitious myths from backwater cultures…ah, no offence, Mr Grant.' Rosie added, not looking Damian in the eye. He didn't look like he was listening, but would probably have politely ignored her anyway.

He was currently engaged in a staring contest with his tea. There were no end of goblins and other nasties in the mythology of the midlands – wonder how I'd feel if I smashed a living, snarling monster right in the face?

'There was a woman sat in the back of this car. It'd been in a crash,' I told them, 'I thought she was trying to wake the guy. But when she got out of the car, I could see…she'd been…' I faltered, looking for the right word. 'She'd been eating him. Hell, there's no way she should have even been walking around. Half her godsdamn face was missing…' I added, gesturing at my own.

I looked down at the carpet, the vintage floral pattern making me feel even more nauseous. 'She was missing her top lip, not even bleeding from it. She tried to grab me, fell down, and started crawling forwards,' I kept talking, trying to get the words out as quick as possible, so I didn't have to think about it too much. 'She tore out her nails on the tarmac. Damian broke her wrist, and that didn't even slow her down. So come on Missus Jameson, what do you know that can make a person do that?'

'Drugs, or, maybe she wasn't right after the crash? I'm sure there's a perfectly reasonable -' she began, but Edgar cut her off.

'Roe, just hold it? Let the man talk.'

I nodded thanks to Edgar. 'Like I said, this makes things more serious than we thought. This means that it's a lot more dangerous out there than just rioting and quarantines or some disease…if you don't want to call them zombies, then fine, infected, afflicted, whatever. But that's what we saw – a walking corpse. The living dead.'

I know I promised Katy that I'd sit tight, but knowing what kind of danger she could be in? I couldn't bear it. What if she was already like one of those things? What if work got her killed? I had to at least try and find her, bring her somewhere safe. Or safer. Or whatever. I had to know she was okay.

'I'm going back out to look for my fiancée.' I said slowly.

'But you just said it was dangerous!' Lucile exclaimed, pointing a finger, 'And now you want to go back out there, knowing what's waiting? And seriously, if I couldn't smell Damian's breath from here, I'd think ya'll were yanking our chains.' She added.

'Thanks girl,' Damian chuckled, sniffing in another deep breath, 'but we not trying to joke here.'

'Which is why we have to find our families, soon. If they're anything like in the movies, zombies won't know how to use elevators, and from what we saw out there, they'd have trouble with stairs. We're the safest place in the city right now.' I added, feeling a welcome burst of resolve setting in, a purpose. I stood up.

'It's dark now, and we don't know what these things are capable of. Without being able to see them coming…I'll listen to her advice, stay safe. Until tomorrow. Then, I'm going to bring my fiancée back here. I won't ask anyone to come with me, but if you want me to see if I can find your families too, I'll do it. Might need your ride though, if you're cool with it?' I asked Damian.

'I coming witch you.' he nodded, 'Not going to be asking anyone to do something I not willing to do myself.'

'I'm in,' Neville said, raising his hand, 'I have a weapon and know how to use it. Been…a long time since I shot at anyone, but I think I still remember how.'

'Uh,' Lucile hummed, tentatively raising her hand too, 'I don't really know many people in the city, certainly not any I'd be willing to risk my life for. My brothers are all down in Sydow. But if you're serious about this, you might need an extra pair of hands.'

'We'll just hold the fort, shall we, Ed?' Rosie said, putting a hand on Edgar's leg.

'Oh, sure. The knee, you know?' Edgar said, giving me the eye again. I gave him a wink back.

'I've got friends I want to get, the Masons?' Morgan asked.

'I know them too,' Neville agreed, 'family friends. Eldest daughter though, Anita, she's in the police, must be nearly thirty now. Moved out years ago, so it should just be Paul, Marianna and Becky. She might not be there when we call…' Neville added, looking meaningfully at his daughter. The police must have lost more than a few silver shields to this virus.

'Even if we can just get Becky and her parents, it's better than nothing. We can leave a note for Anita, in case she comes looking for them.' Morgan said, siding with optimism.

'We? You're not coming.' Neville said immediately.

'Why not?' I asked. He turned to look at me.

'Because I didn't realise we were insane.' Neville replied, 'You've seen what those things are like, is that really something a child should see?'

'I'm seventeen, Dad,' Morgan said, teenage steel seeping into her voice, 'and I highly doubt anyone knows more about zombies than I do. You even thought about how to kill these things?'

'We're running a rescue mission, not waging a war.' Neville said, trying to fold his arms, nearly spilling tea on the armchair.

'But we might have need to,' I butted in, 'Morgan's seen more horror movies than anyone. She can remind us not to go off alone to investigate strange noises, or say things like "it can't get worse than this."' I added, flashing a smile. It felt good to be smiling, but the image of that half-faced woman slapped me in the mouth, taking that grin away. I looked at him more seriously now.

'I know I said it was safer here. But I can't bear the thought of leaving anyone behind – what if looters come in here? Or we're completely wrong and the infected can just swarm up the stairs? You want her to be…alone?' I asked, meeting his eyes.

'She's seventeen.' Neville said, defiant. 'And Edgar and Rosie would be here.'

'Doubt we'd be much use against men looking to rob.' Edgar grunted, a wrinkle of frustration above his bushy, silver brow. 'I was sixteen when I signed up, back in the War, and a lot of those PMC boys and Territorials won't be much older than her.'

'Yes! I'm nearly national service age, dad,' Morgan appealed to her father, 'we talked about this…'

'Going off for a year or two after college isn't the same as risking yourself to this…infection.'

'I'm old enough to make my own choices…I'll stay in the car. If I'm a burden or I freak out or whatever, then I'll stay home next time, make the tea and keep an eye out. But I just need to see, for myself.'

Neville sighed, thinking about it, but that pretty much settled it. Morgan was coming with us. We spent most of the rest of the night talking, wondering about the infection, how it works, and who we hoped was still out there.

It'd been a tough decision. Not to go off straight away, to drive to Katy's place or the Hospital. I had to remind myself that County General would probably be the second-most dangerous place in the city, right after Mercy.

I thought through the logic of it, a dozen times – if she was there and got out, she'd have come here, or gone home. If she went home, then she wasn't alone – and would probably think I was fucking stupid for going out after dark to fetch her with literal monsters on the streets. But no matter how many times I rationalised it, I knew I was still playing the part of the coward.

The Jamesons had offered to cook, which was a welcome distraction from what was rapidly becoming a brood-a-thon. They had us squeezing around their kitchen island, with a couple of us on trays on the sofa. It was a tense supper.

53

Damian, with assistance from Morgan, had been telling us some of the folklore or movie myths about, you know…those things. Now the aftermath was over, it felt hard to say the word again, like I'd imagined it all. Every time I dared to wish that, I saw fingernails ripping out on the road and cringed into my pasta.

We went back to our apartments pretty late. The Jamesons didn't have much to say to the rest of us though, just offered their home cooking. I reckoned they were taking it the worst. They'd lived through the World War, the most life-changing event the world had ever seen, and now they were being threatened with another unthinkable global disaster. I stared up at the ceiling in bed, and tried to remember what life was like before I went utterly mad.

Just the other day I'd been running people's birthday presents and book orders all over town. I'd been going out for drinks. I'd proposed to the love of my life. I rolled over, shut my eyes and I could smell her shampoo still lingering on my pillow from the last time she stopped over.

I found myself growing tense as I breathed in her scent. That part of me kept asking, why put it off until tomorrow? Wake Neville up, get his car keys, and drive to her now. A more sensible, part of me was in charge though. We shouldn't be out there after nightfall. If I went out there, alone in the dark, I couldn't see them coming, couldn't run, I wouldn't stand a chance. No, it had to be tomorrow, in the daylight, with everyone else. Ugh. Coward.

Rolling over, I tried to get to sleep. All of a sudden, it felt like the walls were closing in on me. I stood up, pulled on a robe and paced through my living room, into the kitchen to make myself a hot chocolate. I was probably beyond the aid of milky drinks at this point, but it was worth a try.

As the kettle boiled, I heard raised voices from across the hallway. Edgar and Rosie were still awake, and getting into it pretty bad. It'd have been rude of me to listen in, so I took my drink back into the bedroom, turned on the bedside lamp and tried to read.

It didn't help me fall asleep, but at least having the lamp on, sitting in the pool of light with my bedroom door closed, that made me feel a little better. My eyes flicked to the darker corners of the room every now and then, but I knew that was just paranoia. I must have fallen asleep at some point; because I had the worst night's rest I can remember.

Seven

You know that feeling you get when somebody wakes you up? You know somebody just shouted your name, or some loud noise just broke you out of sleep, and there's that uncomfortable sensation around your ears that says you're listening too hard? That's how I woke up on Thursday. I lay still in bed, straining my ears to listen for burglars or maybe Katy; coming to surprise me before work. She'd done that before, right after I gave her keys.

It took me a full thirty seconds to remember what'd been happening. In a flash, I saw the reporter at the hospital, that soldier firing into the bus, that dead woman's bared teeth and Damian slamming the car door into her nose.

I swung into action, the cobwebs of sleep suddenly blowing away, and reached under my bed. It's not common for burglars to pick the top floor of tower blocks, but even so, I still had a home-defence kit under the bed. I just never imagined using it. Especially against what Damian had called "de forces of de evil dead".

I groped around in the shadows of my darkened bedroom to find my nicked old baseball bat, rough at the end and fraying on the grip, then straightened up and eyed my bedroom door. Slowly, I tip-toed over and put my ear against it, straining to hear breathing, walking, anything that'd give me a clue as to whether there was a zombie or a person out there. My hand was pecked by pins and needles as I gripped the doorknob. Probably slept on it, but at least I wasn't shaking as I flung the door wide. This time, I was ready.

The apartment was empty.

Even so, I took a careful step forward, leaning this way and that just in case something popped out of a tiny blind spot. Deep breath, and sigh.

'Idiot.' I muttered, tapping my head with the bat.

I set it down against the bathroom door, and fumbled around for the light switch. I clicked it a few times, as if I was trying to pump the electricity to the bulb, but it looked like the power had gone out.

The light in the bedroom was the same, but I could open the curtains in there. Katy had peppered my bathroom with candles to add ambience to our showers, so I found my way around the bathroom in a haze of lavender mood-lighting and made sure the water was still running before I used the toilet.

No power meant no TV, no radio, no phones. No way of keeping in touch with the world from all the way up here. The thought of it stopped me still for a minute, before that sensible part of me reminded the other part that it wasn't like I'd been able to get a hold of anyone anyway. No use crying over spilt milk. Speaking of which.

For breakfast I ate all the yogurts in my fridge, and toyed with the idea of putting all my food out on the balcony under a blanket or something. A memory swam to the front of my mind – a storm, a few years ago, back when I still lived in Dent with my parents. Mother said if you left the door closed on the fridge, it'd keep the stuff good for a day. I'd already opened the door, but maybe I was quick enough, and the stuff in the freezer would be fine for a couple of days at least.

I puffed half a dozen empty pop bottles that I'd meant to take down to recycling back into their original two-litre shapes, and filled them up from the tap. We still had water but there was no telling how long for. So it put them back in the cupboard with the rest of my drinks, then put my boots on and went to rouse everyone else with the bad news.

I listened to Edgar and Rosie's door before I knocked. Yeah, I know I'd said it was rude to listen to their argument last night, but this was the morning. I was making sure they were okay. No sounds came from inside, but since the power was dead I guess there wouldn't be a radio or a TV on anymore. I'd grown used to their constant humming over the last couple of days. Well, the last twenty-something years of my life, actually.

57

Hells, without electricity we couldn't even cook, since Stan installed electric ovens and hobs rather than gas when he did the refurb. But what about the heating? Since it wasn't freezing cold I figured that must still run off a pilot light or something. Lucile would probably know more about that than me – I wasn't sure exactly what she did in construction though.

I knocked three times on the Jamesons' door. Blood thumped through my ears as I strained to hear the slightest of sounds from inside the apartment. After about twenty seconds of silence, I tried again, pounding harder on it this time. I heard a rapid scrabbling sound, like a cat on a tiled floor.

'Kelly?' a voice called out, somewhere behind me.

If anyone tells you I jumped out of my boots and hit the ceiling like a cartoon character, they're a liar.

'Morgan,' I coughed, as my heart dislodged itself from my windpipe, 'morning.'

'I suppose I was sneaking a bit,' she admitted, silently closing the door to her apartment behind her, 'If there were any of them up here, I didn't want them hearing me.'

'I think we'd know if they were up here.' I assured her, despite nearly giving myself a heart attack not twenty minutes ago.

'Better safer than sorrier. I tried Ed and Roe's door earlier, but I figured they must have been sleeping in.' she said, crossing the hallway to lean beside the doorway. She looked like she was sucking a lemon. And wearing one, judging by her pyjama top.

'Someone's cheerful this morning.' I said, taking in her offensively bright shirt, floral shorts and wolfman slippers.

'I slept well, the zombocalypse agrees with me.' she shrugged. 'Worried about them though.' she added, tilting her head at the door. She fished Stan's keys out of a pocket, and dangled them off her finger.

I took them and looked at the Jamesons' door. 'Power's been out for a few hours, I'd hardly call it the apocalypse.'

'Riots, quarantines, soldiers, zombies,' she said, ticking each thing off on her fingers. 'What would you call it?'

58

'You only had to count it on one hand, so we're still good.' I tried to keep a strong face up. I didn't feel it, but if I faked it enough, maybe it'd come.

'That's what I'm calling it anyway.' She nodded, 'Now stop procrastinating and get that door open...'

I listened at the door again for a few seconds, while I found the key labelled 'Apts' – figuring it must work for all of them. Morgan was crossing and uncrossing her arms, eyeing the door with concern. I unlocked it, and slowly pushed it open.

The whole place smelled like boiled sweets, tea and rich food – the kind of old people smell that never gets mentioned in stand-up comedy. But underneath the household aroma was something else, something a little stale and musty.

I followed my nose to the kitchen, Morgan politely wiping her feet before she stepped in behind me. She clicked the door closed, and as the lock snapped back into place, there was that scrambling noise in the kitchen again. I got around the side of the breakfast bar just in time to see a small brown shape dive beneath the skirting board.

'Looks like we have rats now.' I said over my shoulder.

'Was it cute?' Morgan asked, tilting her head around the side of the island, arms still crossed over her chest, like she was afraid to disturb anything.

'Not terribly.' I replied, leaving the kitchen, heading for the bedroom door. I didn't have a problem with rats, but I wondered why it was here. This was the top floor; we didn't even get many spiders...I almost put my hand on the doorknob, but then drew it back.

I had a sneaking suspicion, a dark thought that crept up and started twisting up my guts. Rosie had seemed frightened last night. She didn't want to wait for the Territorials or some "brute" mercenary to come bail her out. And she was talking about how she and Ed were getting on in years.

As we stayed up talking, she had become quieter and quieter. Edgar wasn't the type to do something...drastic. But as you can probably guess, Edgar would do whatever she said.

'Same wavelength, huh?' Morgan asked, stepping up beside me. 'I'd have come in earlier, but I didn't want to be alone.'

Morgan put her hand on the doorknob, twisted, and let the door swing open. There was no ominous creak. The thick carpet didn't even make the door stick. Nothing dramatic happened to prepare us for what was inside. There was something peaceful about it, but at the same time, it was so utterly wrong that I stared for ages before I could process it.

The Jamesons were dead.

'Oh no…Oh Gods…' Morgan breathed.

Rosie lay up in bed, propped on a few pillows, with the blanket drawn up to her waist. She'd aged gracefully, however in death her face had sunken, become gaunt. I'd always remember the look on her face. Her expression was like that of sleep, but the way her skin hung, her eyes, darkened…no, there was no way you could mistake her for sleeping.

Her hand lay to the side, underneath Edgar's, who sat in a comfortable wing-backed chair beside the bed. In his free hand he still held a finger of amber liquid in a short crystal tumbler, resting on the arm of the chair.

His head had tilted over to one side, in the shadow you could almost see Granddad taking his afternoon nap after the Sunday roast. He looked better in death than his wife, but him, in that chair, with the glass of whisky…I turned away.

Morgan was already in the living room, her back to me, hands up to her face and head bowed. I walked over to her, feeling like my feet were dragging lead weights behind them, and wrapped my arms around her.

She wriggled to face me and put her head on my shoulder, sliding her arms around my neck. I felt her shaking with the tears she tried not to shed. I held her there until I felt them trail down my arm, then finally let the first of mine run down my cheek, wetting her hair. We stood there for a few minutes, each pretending the other wasn't crying.

'Shouldn't we call an ambulance?' Morgan mumbled into my arm, 'No…stupid…' she sniffed, coughing out a bitter laugh at herself, 'What…what happened?'

I put a hand to the back of her head and smoothed her hair down. 'Wait here,' I said, 'I'll go see…see what I can see.' I tried, looking for the right words.

We pulled away from each other, Morgan sitting down hard on the sofa and drawing a cushion up to her chest. I turned back to face the bedroom and stepped through the doorway, half-closing it behind me. I didn't want to be alone with the bodies, but I didn't think Morgan needed to see them either.

I put my hand over my mouth as my stomach turned again. After yesterday it was becoming familiar. There wasn't anything outwardly gory about them, the Jamesons. But there was a fundamental wrongness about seeing two friends, clearly dead, posed like they've just gone for a nap.

I tried to put the feelings to the back of my mind, and walked over to where Edgar was sitting. I took the tumbler out of his hand, and poured it onto the carpet. That's what old soldiers do when they toast dead comrades, isn't it? "Spill some for me?" I could almost hear him say it, with Rosie chiding me afterwards for messing up the carpet. My imagination is cruel.

The whisky smelled strong, even after a while in the open, but it was just one smell in a mixture of the others. Katy once told me it takes a couple of days for a body to start to smell, depending on the climate or, ugh, carrion. It didn't smell like dead bodies in here, but there was a…toilet-like odour. One of the reasons I had no problem spilling whisky to hide the smell. I cracked the window open wide, and secured the curtains so they wouldn't hang outside.

A bottle of pills lay open on the nightstand, a few of them spilling out onto the carpet. I picked up the bottle and read the back. It was blood pressure medicine, I think. Meant to lower the heart rate, reduce stress levels. Edgar must have still woke up some mornings thinking he was back in the War, in the POW camp with his leg all shot up.

I fixed the cap back on the bottle and walked into their bathroom to return it to the medicine cabinet. I caught sight of their toothbrushes on the sink, one pink and one blue, still both wet from last night. Fuck.

More tears started welling up, along with something else, down in my gut. I put the bottle back in the medicine cabinet and slammed the door closed. The magnetic lock didn't settle, so I slammed it again, and again, until it did.

If I'd have gone out last night, would they have still done it? Was my indecision, my fear, a factor in their decision? If I'd have showed them that there was still hope out there, hope their kids and grandkids might still be alive, would they have still taken those pills?

I sat myself down on the edge of their bathtub and dropped my face into my hands. I don't know how long I sat there, the pit of my stomach twisting into knots. After a while, Morgan came in, holding a glass of water out to me. I don't know why, but I felt better after I passed the empty glass back.

'Why?' I asked her, shaking my head and looking at the lino floor.

'I used to always drink water when I was sad, I thought it gave me more tears to cry.' she smiled weakly, sitting down next to me on the tub.

I spluttered out a few short bursts of air, too bitter to be called a laugh. 'I meant…why did they do it?'

'I knew what you meant, I was just trying to cheerify you with a childhood memory.' she smiled again, looking at me, taking a shaky breath. Tears still streaked her face, her eyes were red and puffy. Some women could make crying look endearing or dignified, like a classy movie actress. Morgan looked just awful. 'Kinda stupid, huh?'

It started as another bitter laugh, but before I knew it, I was chuckling, great big bursts of laughter running up from my gut, where I'd felt such pain a moment earlier. Morgan joined me, laughing youthfully, infectious, like she's just watched the cat do something cute. If you can't laugh about the bad shit in life, you'll go mad. That's the lesson here.

'No laws against it, and no hospitals to go do it in safely right now. I guess Rosie just couldn't handle the thought of it,' she finally said, cutting my laughter dead, 'I don't know.'

'It was selfish,' I said quietly, that sudden humour gone now, 'Selfish of them.'

'In some ways. But in some ways, it was self-less,' she corrected me. 'If this really is the apocalypse – and I'm not really saying it is, hells it's only been a couple of days – but if this is the end of the world, then they just made things easier for us. They were old, they wouldn't be good on the stairs with Edgar's knee and they were two more mouths to feed if this doesn't just "blow over".'

'That's a little cold.' I muttered, still finding myself nodding, 'But they were old. Knee. Yeah.' I said, teeth clenched, eyes still welling up. Maybe she had given me more tears.

'Come on,' Morgan said, standing up and offering me a hand, 'there's something you should see in the kitchen. I thought I heard the rat come back but I found this.'

'Found what?' I asked, taking her hand, following her back into the kitchen. I was glad to be out of that room.

Morgan went behind the breakfast counter and slid a sleek wooden presentation case over to me. Inside was a revolver, set into the felt lining of the box. A plaque in the lid read the date of manufacture, and Edgar's name was engraved before the words, 'For honourable service'.

It was and old breech-loader, and heavier than it looked with that short barrel. But there were three newer looking speedloaders in the box too. I put it back inside and closed the lid with a smile. Sly old dog. At least we would have something to remember him by.

I looked back towards the bedroom, and saw Edgar in my mind again, cruel imagination working overtime. He smiled and nodded, sat up in his chair with his drink. I burst into another short laugh, failing to blink back the tears again.

'They knew what they were doing.' I sniffed. 'Taking the burden off us. Giving us something to defend ourselves with.'

'Wish they hadn't though.' Morgan said, folding her arms.

Yeah. Me too.

Now, that feeling, that knot in the pit of my stomach. I didn't shy away from it. I embraced it, unravelled the tangles and laid it flat. That knot would have been rope enough to hang myself by, but I wouldn't let it come to that. Not for anyone.

If this was what happens when people lost hope, then I'd never let it happen again. I looked at Morgan, eyes flicking to the bedroom door, and decided I wasn't going to be a burden either. But unlike Ed and Rosie, I wasn't going to just check out. I was going to do something…I wasn't going to sit on my hands, never again.

Eight

I knocked on Neville's door and waited for him to answer, trying to shake the image of Edgar Jameson, glass in hand, out of my head.

'Wondered where you'd…' he said, as he was opening the door, hair mussed up, wearing lounging-about clothes. 'Ah, Kelly, nevermind. Morgan with you?' he added, craning his neck to see around me.

'She's in the Jamesons' place.' I said, rushing into my next words to get them out of the way with. 'Listen, Neville, I've got some bad news.'

'She's ticked Rosie off with an innocuous comment?' Neville asked, eyebrows climbing.

'Not quite. Edgar and Rosie are dead.'

Neville inhaled deeply, and breathed out a long sigh.

'Wee-ll…' he winced, 'I guess I'll have to ground her.'

'I-uh-what?' I faltered.

'Joking,' he sighed again, leaning against his door now. He looked down at his slippers intently. 'What happened to them? Will they…turn? Is that how it works?'

'It looks like they overdosed on Ed's heart medication. I think you have to be bitten or scratched or something to turn into one.' I added, glancing over my shoulder – just in case.

'Movies aren't documentaries,' Neville shrugged, 'but I don't want to take their hearts out, if that is the way you do it. Give me five minutes to get some clothes on, there should be some shovels in Stan's flat.'

I was glad he was on the same wavelength as me – and taking it better than I was. Damian had said something last night, about the old Island myths of zombies. They rose from the grave, so you had to pin them back to their coffins with a wooden stake, through the heart. I guess that was where the whole thing about staking vampires came from. But this was

65

real life, not old stories. We meant to bury them, but beyond that I'd be uncomfortable doing anything else.

Since Edgar and Rosie didn't have graves yet, that also posed a problem if these were the kind of zombies from the folklore. Can't pin them to their grave if they haven't got one. But if they were the zombies from the movies of today, then they wouldn't rise up unless they'd become infected. Yeah, in short, we had no clue what we were doing at this point.

Given how the zombies we were dealing with have spread as a pandemic, I'd say we were going with the movie-monster theory; but even if we weren't, I knew that none of us could leave them to rot in that apartment.

'We're probably safe to bury them. I don't want to, erm, mutilate?' I half-asked, 'No, not messing up anyone's body. Not unless we need to.'

'I'm right with you there,' Neville said, 'don't set off without me, we should be on the buddy system at all times.'

'Sure, I'll be in, uh,' I struggled, hooking a thumb towards the Jamesons' old place, 'yeah, see you in a few.'

I returned to find Morgan sat on one of the kitchen stools, staring at the revolver in the presentation case. Not like she was contemplating using it or anything, she just had a sour look about her.

'Didn't want to worry us.' she said. 'When men commit suicide, they tend to do it big or noisy, like a gun or jumping into traffic. Statistically, it's women who take overdoses, or cut themselves. Guess we know whose idea this was.' She added, her voice turning bitter. I'd seen her muster up teenage hatred for some of the kids in her college, but I'd never heard her this angry.

'She was never my favourite either.' I agreed, putting a hand on Morgan's back and sliding onto the stool next to her. She snorted, and made a whip-crack motion with her hand. 'But at least Edgar left us this. If it's still bad out there, we'll need more firepower than just your dad's handgun.'

'Heh,' Morgan coughed, a lump still in her throat, 'maybe it was Ed's idea not to use the gun, save us the bullets. Zombie movies first came about post-war. A bit of Islander myth plus the creeping threat of new regimes rising out of dead ones. They're all metaphors really.'

I pulled her in for another hug, and wondered if we'd live to see the all clear. It was a fleeting thought, but still…two of us were down, with five to go. The world had only ended a couple of days back. Neville came in to find Morgan resting her head on my shoulder. I gave her one last squeeze, before we pulled apart.

He whistled through his teeth, and looked down at the presentation case. 'Old gun. Edgar's, from the War?'

'Yeah. Left it surreptitiously on the counter.' Morgan supplied, 'Do you think it still works?'

'Revolver like that? Built to last.' he said. 'Do you know how to shoot, Kelly?' he asked me.

'Face your opponent on a dusty street, eye them up dramatically, and when the clock strikes noon you hold it at your waist and pull the trigger as fast as possible.'

He smirked, and picked up the case, reading the little info card. 'It's a Tetley Mark Four,' – I could pretty much hear him pronouncing the four as 'IV' – 'uses thirty-eight rounds. After the War it became the staple police sidearm until only a few years ago. I had one, back then, modernised version. But like I said, these things were made to last. Built to withstand the trenches.' He repeated, examining the gun closely.

'Didn't realise you were a gun nut.' I said, impressed by his knowledge. Of course, knowing nothing about guns besides what I'd seen in films or games, that wouldn't take much.

'I don't like having them around the house,' he said, glancing at Morgan, 'But I used to read magazines. Still have a few back issues on the coffee table, gave them a thumbing last night. If the Territorials or the CDC's mercs can't put this thing down, if life doesn't return to normal…might be useful to know your guns. Do you know how to use those speedloaders?' he asked.

67

'Seen them before, yeah, but I've never fired a gun. Much less an antique.' I shrugged.

'Thought you'd done your NS?' he raised an eyebrow.

'I'm on my last year to defer, got to sign up in six months or so. Katy…she's one of the reasons I put it off, and with it looming, it's one of the reasons I proposed.'

'Makes sense to me,' he nodded, passing me the gun. I hesitated, hand halfway out to it. 'Would feel much better if you'd been trained, but you just put the bullets in the chambers, twist the knob on the loader, and then put it in your pocket so you can use it again later.'

'I'm not too comfortable with a weapon myself,' I told him, taking the offered weapon, 'it won't leave my pocket unless its needed.'

'Good plan,' Morgan said, 'Plus, ten silver says the deadites will be attracted to the sound.'

'That's why we'll be taking Damian's tank instead of your dad's car,' I replied, picking up the gun, 'We should be able to outrun any of them, or just ram into them if it gets too hairy. Do these things have safeties?' I asked Neville, carefully examining the old pistol.

'No, you'll have to cock the hammer,' – Morgan stifled a snigger – 'when you fire, so it's a good gun for you to learn with, forces you to pace your shots. I'd take you and Morgan on the range, but I don't think we can afford the ammo.'

'No prob. Thanks Neville. Could you do me a favour?' I added.

'What do you need?'

'Wrap Ed and Rosie up in some bed sheets or something. I'll fill Damian and Lucile in on what's happened; maybe they can help us with the burial.'

'I'll help, but fair warning,' Morgan scrunched her face, 'the sheets are soiled.'

Neville nodded, understanding. If the bodies were wrapped up they wouldn't just be easier to carry and easier to look at, but it'd be harder for them to move if they had the inclination to. Neville either didn't mind being around dead folk and urine, or he didn't want to break the bad news to the guys downstairs. So I went to take care of that, while Morgan helped Neville with the task of handling the deceased. I didn't envy them.

I could still see Edgar when I blinked, even hear him talking at the back of my head, little whisps of memories from helping him move furniture, or eating with them last night.

Last thing I heard before leaving the Jamesons' place was Neville, complaining about the stairs. Of course. No power, no elevator. I guess his light-hearted look at the situation would probably help. I leaned against the stairway door, silently agreeing with him. Fourteen floors up…I hope you've got sympathy for how many times we'd have to do that hike.

The stairs were a boring, typical tower block affair. Plain concrete, red safety rail; but with windows all the way down, overlooking the city. It was pretty much the same view as ever, except for everything having gone to hell.

Streamers of smoke were still rising from a dozen places, most of them looking like the city centre, or out in the industrial districts. Some were new, but some of those blazes had been going for a while now. The smoke was rolling across the city, probably giving everything a nice coating of apocalyptic grime like every B-movie horror ever made. Why are there always random sheets of paper littering the streets in those things anyway?

I could make out just one vehicle moving along the roads, too far away to see what it was, just a moving spec in the distance. The city looked like it was in its death throes, but with so few signs of life out there, I hoped that meant a lot of people made it out, or were holding up like us, staying behind barricaded doors, rationing their food.

My mood was dipping as I crossed the length of the corridor to Damian's place. I knocked politely. Another flash of memory struck me; standing outside the Jamesons', knocking on their door, finding them dead. I really, really hoped Damian would answer. Just before I knocked again, the door opened.

69

Damian stood there, bright eyed and bushy haired – if dreadlocks had another state of being, I didn't know it. Sockless, shirtless, wearing old jeans, a pleasant smile and dual-wielding a cup of tea and a rollup; I've never seen a man looking more relaxed, before or since. Just the sight of him took the edge of my own anxiety. I realised I'd been balling my fists, ready to fight, and slowly unclenched them at my sides.

I eyed his tea for a second, wondering how he got it. He must have noticed.

'Hey man,' he said, 'have a camp stove, to boil de water. Fancy a brew? I got loads more gas for it.'

'No thanks. Got some news that might ruin your morning though.' I said, rubbing the back of my neck.

'What's going an?' he asked, taking a distracting sip of tea. Hot food and drink. I was used to eggs, toast or bacon for breakfast. Having only had yoghurt and already fought off the urge to vomit, my body was giving me displeased signals. Hope he was right about having plenty of camping gas.

'Edgar…Rosie. They overdosed last night, heart medication. Couldn't have been accidental.' I said, rushing my words again, like I couldn't face them. 'They killed themselves.' I added, fighting back against that fear.

'Aww…' he tried, his bottom lip tensing up. He shook his head, looking at the doorframe like it'd made a foul smell. When he spoke again, his teeth were almost clenched. 'Why man?'

'Way I see it…they didn't want to be a burden. Or at least Rosie didn't, and she talked Ed around to it.'

'I can see why they'd think that. Old, none too spry witch Ed's knee, but…I can't believe it, you know? Shouldn't have…' he trailed off, shaking his head. 'What we going to do with de bodies? Are they…moving?'

'No, or, not yet at least. Neville's getting them ready now. We'll carry them downstairs and bury them in the park.'

'What if they come back?' he asked, pursing his lips.

'We'll deal with that if it happens. These are our neighbours, friends…I can't just…not them. Not unless we need to.'

'Right man.' Damian nodded, 'Respect for de dead, so long as they stay that way.' He put his rollup in his mouth, and I bumped the offered fist. His expression was tense, brow furrowed, eyebrows together. Pretty much a mirror of my own. I guess we were bonding.

'I'll go tell Lucile.' I said, 'See you in a little while.'

'Nah man,' Damian said, 'don't worry, I'll take care of that.'

I saw movement behind him in the dim apartment, a form under a blanket on his sofa, a glimpse of blonde hair. Naturally I jumped to a conclusion.

'Heh,' I said, managing to turn it into a cough in case she was listening, 'well thanks Damian. See you in a few.'

'Yeah man,' he smiled, 'we…I be up in a bit. If you can carry one down, we'll get de other.'

I left Damian and Lucile to their devices. I guess people have different ways to deal with the bad. Neville and me had tried to laugh off Edgar and Rosie's deaths. Damian and Lucile had comforted each other about the state of the epidemic. "If tomorrow was your last day" must be a hell of a pick-up line when it can actually be true.

As Neville had accurately predicted, the stairs were a bitch. Fourteen floors and its hard not to count the steps. Seven down, then a landing, seven more down and that's one floor done; all the while trying not to bump Rosie's body against the rail or the walls. It was easier with her wrapped up – in clean sheets too, so the smell wasn't so unpleasant. I could almost imagine I was carrying a rolled up carpet or something. Almost.

'So how'd D take it?' Neville asked.

'He looked like the king of cool before I told him. Seemed more angry than upset, think I took it the same way. He was just standing there with tea and a smoke. Got to see if we can talk him into sharing that camping stove. We'll need a brew-up after this.'

'Or something stronger. What label was on that whisky?'

'A good one. I'm not averse to drinking before noon right now.' I agreed.

We tried to make small talk, tried to forget what it was we were carrying, but it was no good. We switched a couple times when we had to have a rest, taking it in turns to go backwards. Eventually Neville put his back to the door at the bottom of the stairwell and pushed the bar to open it into the foyer.

We had to set her down over a few chairs while we went to look around Stan's ground floor apartment, poking about while we got our breath back, massaging some life back into sore arms.

His was kind of like everyone else's place, but a bit bigger, and clearly for a bachelor. I hadn't seen such an impressive collage of centrefolds on a living room wall since Jason and Will's first student house, when I was first visiting up from Dent. I checked my phone, just in case they, or anyone else, had got through to me.

No missed calls, no texts, no signal. Jason would be somewhere in sunny, plague-torn Redmond with the VBC, while Will had an apartment in a tower block too, over on the other side of the city. I'd been there a couple times, but wasn't a hundred percent sure how to get there. Because of work, my sense of direction about town is usually second to none, but that area wasn't on my rounds often, so I usually cheated with a sat-nav when I had to go there.

Was it worth trying to save him too? Or was that too much? Too far? Too risky? Both Katy and the reporter had told us to stay put. I could ignore their warnings for Katy's sake, and stand by my neighbours as they went for their loved ones, but that was it. With any luck, Will would be able to take care of himself – his apartment building was just like ours, so it wasn't like I'd be brining him anywhere safer. Just dragging everyone across town for no reason.

'In here.' Neville said, reminding me of the task at hand.

He'd found a door off Stan's kitchen that led to a sort of walk-in closet for DIY enthusiasts. Hammers, wrenches, boxes of nails, drills, locks, a rather tall folding ladder – all kinds of landlordly stuff was neatly arranged on the shelves, with a pair of shovels and an electric lawnmower shoved into a corner. I guess he didn't do much gardening. I grabbed the shovels while Neville rifled through Stan's kitchen cupboards.

'Forgot the shopping this week?' I asked.

'Stan's got to have a first aid kit somewhere, we might need it. Not for Rosie, mind. Think she's a bit beyond plasters and icy-hot.'

He found it, a green tin case only a little bigger than a lunchbox. I doubted anything in there would do much good for a zombie bite, but it might not just be zombies we'd find out there. Living rioters could be driving about, taking advantage of the lack of law and order, or maybe one of us would just trip up and cut ourselves on broken glass. Better prepared.

He left it on the reception desk while we carried Rosie outside. I returned for the shovels while he found a good spot; a nice place under the shade of a big old tree – oak maybe? I'm no woodsman. It looked like it'd be a nice patch to sit down on in summer, maybe have a picnic. I think they'd have liked that.

The green-space that formed the miniature park around the apartments was nothing major. A place to walk a lazy dog, somewhere for local kids to have a sneaky cider after dark, that kind of thing. The walkers always picked up their pet's droppings and the kids put their bottles in the bins, so it wasn't the worst place to bury somebody.

There was a tiny artificial pond not too far from where we'd chosen to dig, ringed with pebbles and small stones. I grabbed a handful so we'd have something to mark the graves with.

It was pretty nice outside, sunny but not too bright, breezy, a definite chill in the wind, but not enough for scarves, gloves and bobble hats. Probably one of the last good days

73

before winter set in properly. It would have been a pretty nice day, if not for the dead friends.

Nine

I never thought of it before, digging a grave. You have to sort of get a general idea of where you're going, how big it's going to be, how deep. I'd like to have just gotten on with it, but we had to talk to eyeball the measurements.

Once the macabre mathematics was out of the way with, we broke ground. I didn't count the time it took, I tried not to think about it. I just…I just let time go by. With our arms sore from carrying her down stairs we weren't going to dig deep, just enough. After a while, Damian and Lucile came to us, carrying Edgar's wrapped up body, Morgan trailing behind them.

Sweating, we leaned our shovels against the tree, and lowered Rosie into the grave, while Damian and Lucile eased Edgar down next to her. The grave was only a foot or so deep, and just wide enough to get them both in side by side.

Neither of them tried to get up again, but nobody looked comfortable by the graveside. Morgan was staring at the two wrapped bodies, not really seeing them. She was seeing the nice old couple from next door.

I looked at her for a few seconds, and tried to fix that look on her face into my mind, turn it into a weapon against my fear, a reminder that I had to be strong – that *we* had to be strong. I wouldn't let her lose hope, not like the Jamesons did.

'Anyone want to say a few words?' I asked, dragging my eyes back into the grave.

There was silence.

'I didn't know them too well.' I said, reluctantly. 'But I knew them long enough to tell they were good people. Right now we don't have any idea what the world's like outside of this city, and we've only got one woman's word for what it's like inside it.

'Edgar and Rosie didn't know what life was going to be like anymore. Neither do I. Can't make any promises that

75

we're going to be able to bring our friends, our families, back here to safety. But I can promise that I'm going to try. I'm not just going to give up, I don't care how bad it is our there. I wonder how many people did the same as them? Took their own lives, gave up. I'll always remember them…

'But I wish they hadn't done it.' I sighed, taking up my shovel again. Neville picked his up too. 'Let's just hope that we find our people before they go the same way. Or worse.'

I'm not one of life's great orators, but it'd have to do.

The others watched while we shovelled the earth back over the bodies. Morgan was letting the tears roll freely down her cheeks, but she wasn't making a sound aside from the occasional sniff. I tried to put her to the back of my mind, otherwise I'd start up again too.

Damian had one hand on Morgan's shoulder, the other arm around Lucile's, where she was resting her head on his hand. Her eyes were wet, but the tears weren't streaming. She didn't know them as well as Morgan did, but it's always going to be sad to see someone go, especially people who you'd seen alive and well just last night.

We patted the earth down over Rosie and Edgar, and I prayed that if they did turn into zombies, that it would be enough to keep them down there. My eyes were swimming when I looked up from the grave.

'Right,' I said, steadying myself, 'Right. We said we're heading out today. If you've changed your mind, don't feel ashamed. I think this is a shitty idea too.'

They chuckled, but not a one of them said they'd stay behind. I felt my spirits lift, I think. My back straightened, and it became easier to breathe, easier to lift my head up. It made the tear I'd been holding back roll down my cheek. I swiped at it, and muttered something about getting a move on.

I returned to the Jamesons' place and picked up the revolver, loading it as instructed while I mooched around my kitchen. Six shots, with two reloads, a total of eighteen rounds. I subtracted that from the likely zombie-population of

Greenfield; and came to the conclusion that staying quiet and moving quick were better options.

There were five of us, small enough to move around without drawing much attention, and even if we did, Damian's truck was a proper countryman's all-terrain-vehicle. If it came to a zombie vs. ATV situation I knew which one would come out smashed up.

But if it did come to fighting, Morgan was probably right. Sound would attract zombies, I was sure of it. I shouted to that zombie in the backseat of the wreck, and only after did it come towards me. So with that knowledge, I needed a quiet weapon, and my slugger was still leaning by the bathroom door. That would do nicely.

I looked at it for a moment, and remembered the last time I'd used it properly. I'd been going to play a game of baseball in the park. Couriers against the office staff. But I saw a guy I thought I recognised when I was in the parking lot. I made my excuses from Gladys, who'd given me a lift, and walked over to say hello, thinking he must be one of Jason's friends, or someone from back in Dent.

The guy was in his car, one of those tiny little boxes, all sleek and modern but with only two seats and a crumple zone that consisted of the driver's face. That was when I recognised him, and promptly made a U-turn, ducking behind a panel van. That bastard.

You remember I told you how I met Katy? How she was picking broken glass out of my head? That was from earlier in the night. Greenfield throws a little mini-festival now and then, plenty of live music and beer tents around the parks. Some drunk at one of the tent stages thought it'd be hilarious to throw a bottle at the band. Only he was a terrible shot.

Well *this* guy, was *the* guy. I'd asked the pretty nurse, half in jest, if she fancied seeing the Some Bad Men tribute act playing one of the evening slots – turns out she was a big fan, and agreed to meet me after work. I didn't expect her to show, but she did. We started talking, and hit it off. But as we were at the bar, that guy showed up, and came onto her like the most stereotypical drunken asshole you can imagine.

When she refused his advances at the nightclub bar, probably as he was so far gone by this point that he could barely talk, he called her every foul name under the sun. I wasn't having any of that – so I promptly strode up to him, balled my fist to punch, and was grabbed on the shoulder from behind.

Katy turned me around for our first kiss – hours after meeting her. She probably did it just to save me from getting kicked out and missing the band, not just because we were getting friendly. Would have still been satisfying to hit him, but the band struck the opening chords to "Midnight Ride" a moment later, so I was happy.

Eight months later however, and there were no bouncers around to kick me out of Cemetery Park. No security cameras in the car park either, a massive security oversight I was suddenly glad of. I waited for him to get out of his car and disappear into the crowds. Then I strolled up to his tiny foreign car, and put its driver's side window in with my bat.

It felt so damn cathartic that I swung the bat down on his windshield too. Shame it was safety glass, but it still made a hell of a crack right across his driver's side. After that, I looked around for any witnesses, then ran like hell towards the baseball game.

True enough, I was thinking about my freshly scarred scalp when I did it. Katy can defend her own virtue well enough, but she was still my girl, and to hell if some drunk was going to call her a whore, even if he'd done it technically before we were an item. You can say I'm an old romantic, but there is such a thing as "love at first sight". It's what made me smash that guy's car up, and it's what made me risk my ass against a city full of zombies.

Coming back to myself, I picked the bat up and rested it on my shoulder, but had to settle for putting the revolver in my pocket with the handle sticking out. I wouldn't be taking out any zombie hearts with a baseball bat, but it'd surely knock them over, and the last one we came face to face with wasn't too steady on her feet.

I played baseball at high school, so it followed that I'd own a bat of my own. Shame the same logic didn't follow on to fencing, which I'd picked up in my senior year at college after watching too many fantasy movies. Hours of swordsmanship lessons, and nothing to show for it. I certainly wasn't spending my money on a "battle-ready" replica from one of those movies, something that'd snap or chip after a couple of knocks. I wanted the real thing, but they're as pricy as firearms and nearly as tightly regulated.

I looked at the empty space by my door, where my sword-cane, my cavalry sabre or my Nordic longsword would lean against, and lamented the passing of historical trades – there were no blacksmiths in the Greenfield listings who worked anything other than lawn furniture and light fittings.

If only Edgar had been an officer, he'd have left me a rapier or something with the pistol. That'd go for the heart, and we'd need more than just a gun and a baseball bat out there, even if we planned on being quick and quiet, the best laid plans always go tits up.

If I hadn't deferred my national service, gotten it out of the way with like my parents said, then I might have been able to come up with a better plan than just "we go out there and find them", but that's what I had and it'd have to do.

After a few more minutes procrastinating, walking in circles around my flat, I put my jacket and my boots on, and took to the stairs. Everyone would be meeting at Damian's ride when they were ready.

'Got to be a backup generator, girl. De stairs will be murder if we using them all de time.' I heard Damian saying as I reached the last of the stairs.

'Specs for residential blocks like this have their lectrics wired down into the basement,' Lucile said, 'makes it easier for sparks to diagnose and fix anything that gets borked up.'

'Sparks?' Damian asked.

79

'Electricians. Come on, that ain't just industry slang, is it?' she asked.

'Whatever it is, sounds good.' I said, running out of breath as I reached the foyer. Even heading down that many stairs was difficult going. 'Worth checking on that now?'

'I might need time with it, if we don't want the whole block to light up like a Solstice tree.' She snorted, 'Just guessing, but I think that might attract the infected, or looters if not. If I did it in the day, less chance they'd notice, but I'm not staying back here on my own while ya'll ride out.'

'What you have to do?' Damian asked.

'Unhook and de-fuse all the electrical connections to the basement, cept the one that powers the elevator. I don't know how long it'd take for me to do, I'm a foreman, and as these northern boys say; "those who can't do, sling their hook in." But if they were any decent sparks who wired it, they'll have left a diagram I can use. If not…looks like we're walking.'

'A job for tomorrow then.' I nodded.

'Whoa, I didn't say I'd do it.' Lucile said, folding her arms, 'I ain't got the right tools in my apartment.'

'There's all kinds of stuff in Stan's place.' I suggested.

'Girl, if you don't do it, I won't be sharing de camping stove with you again.' Damian smirked, folding his arms.

'I was only joshing, dumbass. I ain't giving up coffee for a small chance of electrocution…' she drawled.

We sat down in the foyer, waiting for Neville and Morgan to arrive. It looked like Damian and Lucile had had similar thoughts about bringing weapons along this time, but we didn't mention them. They were just security blankets at this point, I think. Nobody intended to use them.

Damian was twirling a cricket bat between his knees, while Lucile and I shared a similar taste in sporting goods. Her bat was aluminium though, and looked fresh out of the packaging – probably never used to commit an act of criminal damage, much less the intended sport.

If I were the sort of person who reads too much into things, I'd say Lucile didn't really have a friend in the world.

Between throwing a housewarming party for herself, being the only woman in a male-orientated profession – a management figure no less – and not wanting to add anyone to the rescue list, I reckon we were all she had in Greenfield.

No wonder she didn't want to be left here alone. She was probably feeling homesick for Sydow right now. I knew that's where her family lived, but her accent was more of a southern drawl, so I figured they were from further south, originally.

I'd armoured up with my jacket, and again, Lucile seemed to have had a similar idea, wearing a stylishly cut leather coat of her own. Damian had gone with a tan brown trenchcoat that made him look like a Noir detective. All he needed was a fedora and a cigar.

Neville and Morgan were only a few minutes behind me; Neville staving off the winter with a fur-lined denim jacket with jeans only a few shades off the same colour. Now let he who has never gone denim-on-denim cast the first stone. I could see the straps of his shoulder holster cutting across his jumper.

Morgan was dressed like how I figured her mood to be. Gone were the pinks and yellows of earlier. She wore a black shirt, with black jeans, black combat boots and the black leather motorcycle jacket Katy had got her for her birthday. A whole lot of black.

'No weapon?' I asked her, as we walked towards the 4x4.

'Terms of the deal were that I stay in the car this time, but thanks to you, and Edgar, I'm coming. Wouldn't want you guys going after my friends unless I was taking the risk too.'

'You talked yourself onto this mission, not us. You can always turn back. Nobody'll think less of you. Like I said outside, even I think this is a stupid idea and it's my idea.'

'You're in it for love. Me too. Wouldn't miss this for the world.' She smiled up at me.

I tousled her hair and gave her a pat on the back, lowering my voice, 'You're the only backup I need, kiddo.'

Damian's ride was a monster. You know those huge luxury 4x4s that movie stars drive in, killing the planet by inches? Well that was based off a military vehicle of similar size, but with the TVs in the backseat replaced with machine guns. This was the granddaddy ATV that inspired that one. If it wasn't painted sky-blue, it'd get locked up just for looking so mean. Its front bumper – and it was a bumper, fitted for shoving unruly cattle along – came nearly up to my chest. Morgan actually had to give the shorter Lucile a push up.

'Bloody hell, isn't there a law against having monsters like this on the road?' Morgan asked as she belted up. She glanced over her shoulder, into the trunk. You could have probably fit a double mattress in there. 'Why'd you need all this space?'

'Was me Uncle Rob's, he seen how I was struggling carrying speakers an that around to me jobs. He was getting a new one for his farm anyways.' Damian replied.

'What's all this stuff in the back?' I asked.

A half-open duffle bag was nestled between the wheel-arch and the back seats, and I could just make out some vaguely tool-shaped things inside it.

'Stuff me Uncle Rob left in it. Said he didn't want them back. Crowbars, chains for de snow, little shovel, you know, farm stuff.'

'Crowbars, plural?' I asked, belting in.

'I dunno man, I never worked a farm. Maybe you got to pry open sheep when they birthing?'

He turned the key, and the 4x4 hummed into life. As did the radio…

Ten

'…listening to GCR, and that was the hourly update. Next up, we've got some more music for you, to help you keep up that War Time Spirit.' The radio DJ said, before the opening notes of a classic song from the War drifted out of the speakers.

'No fucking way.' Morgan gasped.

'Language.' Neville said, deadpan, staring at the radio in the dashboard like it was about to explode.

'Someone's got a working genny.' Lucile leaned forward.

'Someone's still alive out there. The woman on the TV made out like it was all over.' I gawped. 'And they've got a working broadcast tower…'

'They can use to talk to de TA, de CDC,' Damian said, finishing my train of thought, 'maybe they already have?'

'What station did he say?' Neville asked.

'GCR.' Damian said, starting to smile, 'I hate de daytime tunes but I sure we can get there quick enough.'

'Whoa, wait.' I said, putting my hands up to get everyone's attention, 'Just wait a minute. I've delivered to GCR before. There isn't any rush to get there.'

'Why's that?' Damian asked. He still hadn't driven out of the parking lot.

'It's got a big-time security fence, and clearly a generator too. Place is more like a fort than a radio station. Our people don't have that kind of protection. We save our people, then we drive to the station. GCR can wait.' I added. I noticed everyone was turned towards me, even Neville was craning his neck around from the seat in front.

'They could know a way out of the city,' Neville pointed out, 'maybe they know something we don't.'

'Then we stay tuned, see what news they share with us. But even if they do have a way out, even if the CDC have come up with something, then we're still going to need to bring our people to safety. We can't just abandon them. We go later.'

Nobody said anything, but a silence fell that wasn't entirely comfortable. I think they knew I was right. But it was a tough call. Hearing that radio come to life with something other than a repeated broadcast, that was exciting. It got the blood pumping – gave us a glimmer of hope.

There was just no reason to race to the station right now. We had more important things to take care of – like our friends and families.

'Long live de king.' Damian slowly said, 'Alright man, I was going to me Lydia first anyway. Radio can wait until we all together.'

'Damian's sister first,' I nodded, 'it's closest. Then the Masons for Neville and Morgan. You said they weren't far from Greenside, right?'

'Right.' Morgan nodded.

'And then Katy's.' I said, 'With any luck we'll be able to pick up another car at the Masons', or make room in that warehouse you call a trunk.' I added. Damian smirked.

We drove out of the parking lot, through the mini-park, and out past the crash from earlier – the, ugh, zombies, long since moved on. Even in my head I had to force myself to say the word. After that, we were in dead streets. There were a lot more crashes than just the one we'd seen earlier.

With panic on the streets, people must have been taking all kinds of risks to try and get out of the city, and that meant dodging around the traffic caused by all the other people who had the same idea. Some roads were blocked off entirely.

All it takes is one idiot running a red light and then an entire intersection gets blocked off. Couple that with a few zombies, a few people trapped in their cars, and multiply it by half the crossroads in the city…the road network was screwed.

A lot of cars were just abandoned; doors and trunks hanging open where people grabbed their stuff and bolted. But as we mounted the pavement to go around an old white van, I saw into the driver's side. Red-faced and bloodied, trapped by

84

its seatbelt, one of them turned to snarl at us as we drove by. A lot of cars had bloodied windshields and doors hiding whatever happened in there from view.

Like running the reds, it only takes one person trying to transport an infected, and you've got a big old mess when they turn. I remembered that soldier on TV, firing into the blood-smeared bus. Suddenly it didn't seem so cruel, didn't seem like he'd just murdered someone. He'd put down a turned infected. A zombie.

We'd only been driving for about ten minutes before Damian had to make his second three-point turn, avoiding another in-car abattoir where the pavement was too narrow to go around it.

By the time we came to the third one, he was so tired of it that he just used the cattle bumper, and nudged aside the burned out wreck of an unidentifiable car. It'd somehow caught fire, and if the street around it was anything to go by, exploded. A few other cars nearby had their windows blown out, and the street was littered with glass that crunched under the tires.

Metal screeched as our bumper came up against the wreck and its bare wheels ground against the tarmac. The noise hurt my ears worse than nails on a chalkboard, so I tried to look out of the window to distract myself.

The nearest zombie was just across the road, and already moving straight towards us. No wonder, with a noise like that to grab its attention. It dragged its feet, shoulders slouched, mouth hanging open, making that, hollow, dead sound, like a ghostly yawn.

As it got closer, I realised it couldn't close its mouth if it wanted to. Sinew and muscle lay bare on one side of its jaw, with the bone jutting through the skin. If it felt pain like any human would, it'd be dead by now.

Seeing that made the reality set in a little more, made me feel like an idiot for bringing people out here, not listening to my Katy's advice, or that Gillian woman, on TV. But that was the coward talking. The guy who had to sleep with the light on once the walls closed in. I shut that voice out.

Damian cleared the obstruction before the zombie could get any closer. Lucile was giving Damian directions, as she took a different route to pretty much the same place; a construction project right across the road from Damian's sister's house. But that zombie wasn't the last we'd see on our way.

We drove down streets where packs of them were knelt on the pavement, bent double over bodies, so many of them that thankfully we couldn't see what they were doing. When they heard us coming, they'd look up from the thing beneath them, and start pushing themselves to their feet. That's when you saw the body. Fresh kills must have been more tempting than carrion.

Another sadistic flash from my imagination showed the Jamesons' graveside, teeming with zombies clawing at the earth. I put it to the back of my mind as best I could.

Once or twice we'd also drive by somewhere we thought people had been recently – smashed windows at the front of little independent shops, looted shelves within. At one point I was sure I'd seen curtains twitching in an upstairs window as we swerved through another blocked up road, but nobody waved hello. Better to stay quiet, especially with a big, scary truck rolling by to drag the dead away with it.

We finally got to a stretch of clear road, a dual-carriageway roundabout just outside of the centre, where I felt I could breathe easy again. I heard Lucile let out a sigh of relief, and Neville cracked his window open a little.

We must have been driving for close to an hour before we took the roundabout, but as we were halfway around, the old wartime music was cut off and a cheery little jingle played. 'G-C-R, Radio Two!'

All attention was firmly aimed at the radio.

'Good afternoon listeners, I'm your host, Carl Sachs – coming to you live from GCR, rain, shine, or apocalyptic pandemic. Here's our hourly update.'

'How can he sound so cheerful?' Lucile asked. 'It's like this ain't even phased him.'

'Show must go on?' I shrugged.

'News from the field indicates a high population of the infected, or "zombies", around the city centre. If you are heading out of your homes today, the advice is not to head downtown, for fear of cannibal dismemberment.

'For those of you listeners who don't already know, the Territorial Army has increased the threat level of the situation to "Code Red", which did include changing the bulb. Sadly, this means that the Territorial will not, and I repeat, *not* be riding in to save the day, as the vast majority of TA forces have been called back to protect Orphen, our administrative capitol, at all costs.'

'No, oh no no…' I heard Neville saying in the front seat. It was like his worst fears had come true.

'However…GCR has been in contact with the CDC, which is now under new management. Rather than trying to contain the virus, which has reportedly spread to most major population centres in the country, the new CDC along with the Private Military Companies still in operation, are setting up refugee centres in the uninfected areas for anyone able to escape the old quarantine zones.

'Now, I know power's out across the board, so chances are there's only a few of you who can still hear me. But if you can make it to GCR, fifty-four Shoreham Street, we'll be able to keep you safe until a CDC contingent arrives to evacuate us.

'But for now my dear listeners, stay safe. Here are some more classics for you, to help you remember that It's Not All Bad News.'

Nobody said a thing. There was just the sound of the engine and the wartime music as we rolled steadily on to Greenside.

'My Gods,' Neville said, 'major population centres? Every city like this? Did he mean just us, or the rest of the Republic? The Commonwealth? Globally?'

87

'What did he mean about the CDC? New management?' Lucile asked, at the same time. 'This doesn't make any sense, why would they stop trying to contain the infection?'

'Quiet.' I said, a little louder than I meant to. Everyone turned to look at me again, even Damian risked a glance over his shoulder. 'Please.' I added, remembering my manners.

'The TA is protecting Parliament and the capitol. They're not going to "put down" the infection like the woman on TV said. It must be so widespread they've given up. If the CDC isn't trying to contain the infection either, that means the quarantine is now so thoroughly fucked that it's like trying to plug the holes in a colander with your fingers. Instead of herding the infected into one area, they're herding the non-infected.

'That's our best bet now, for survival. Not just us, but as a country, I suppose. But I'm still saying we leave off GCR for now. I still want my fiancée back before anything else. Compared to that, the radio station is still not a priority. For me, at least.' I added.

I looked over at Lucile, who didn't look pleased. 'I get it. You've all got people to look for. I understand, making them safe before we look into this. But we will, right? We'll go there, get evacuated?'

'If they have a line on getting out of the city, of course. I just won't leave without her.' I nodded.

Maybe Katy was already at the GCR building, or maybe she was at home, without power, without a radio tuned to just the right station. I'd be exploring that option before I locked myself in a broadcast booth and waited for the cavalry.

Looking back on it, it's like all we were doing was running around in circles, waiting for some white knight to come charging in. All we were doing was trying to find more damsels to add to our number. I guess, I'm trying to say…I totally had no idea what I was doing. And people were listening to me. And doing what I said. Maybe things would have worked out differently if Neville was in charge.

Damian pulled into an estate area that seemed to be undergoing reconstruction. The terraced housing was slowly being demolished and replaced with larger builds, semi-detached duplexes and a couple of mini-mansions. This old working-class neighbourhood was being gentrified.

The road was narrow, maybe enough for two cars to pass by each other, but with the 4x4; Damian had to veer wildly over to either side to avoid parked vehicles. But at least these were parked and not just abandoned.

Wish I could say the same for the homes though. Nearly every door was open, or else had the ground-floor windows smashed. Hopefully people got out before the infected spread to here.

Damian rolled us to a gentle stop outside one of the few remaining rows of terraces, skirting the edge of the planned estate that Lucile said she was working on.

The corrugated metal boundary across the street separated the old from the new, and it didn't surprise me to see flyers pinned to the lampposts, encouraging the residents to stand up for their homes and spit in the eye of the planning authorities.

'Guess I'll never see that finished, huh?' Lucile said, looking at the construction site, then guiltily at the back of Damian's head. Guess the development had come up in conversation.

'Right, I be back, one minute.' Damian said, not listening, unbuckling and sliding out of the car. Neville didn't ask if he needed backup, he just followed him out, pulling his gun from his holster as they moved closer.

Damian fished a set of keys out of his trenchcoat and unlocked the front door. It wasn't smashed. That was a good sign at least.

I unbelted, knelt between the two front seats, and started fiddling around with radio buttons to try to find another active station. After about twenty pushes of the scanning buttons, Morgan cleared her throat and politely tapped me on the shoulder.

'We've got company.' she whispered. I turned to see her looking out of the rear windscreen, 'It's of the zombified kind and its heading straight for us.'

Eleven

We grabbed our bats and swung our doors open. I was first out, followed by Lucile. I was tall enough to slide down onto the road, but Lucile sort of jumped.

'Wait here.' I told Morgan.

'Heh, no problem…' she said with a nervous laugh.

We shut our doors and walked a few paces, giving us room to swing and squaring off against the oncoming zombie like we were in a spaghetti western.

The cowboy at the other end of the street was wearing jogger's sweatpants and the remains of an expensive running vest. And he was sprinting. *Sprinting*. Not like a regular person would sprint either. His arms were waving all over the place and he wasn't quite running for us in a straight line, like he couldn't keep his balance. It'd have been funny, if he wasn't almost certainly trying to kill us. This guy was clearly infected.

'Zombie.' I forced myself to think, trying to focus on the conclusions we'd drawn from our first encounter. It didn't want to talk, it couldn't feel pain, and it was not human.

'Undead fitness freaks?' Lucile snorted.

'Maybe it makes a difference, what you did when you were alive?' I shuddered, setting my shoulders in place for a swing.

'How're we gonna to do this?' Lucile asked, doing the same. She was swinging from right to left – so she wouldn't hit me in the back.

'Break its legs,' I said, something I've never said before. 'If it's hearts we need to destroy then we've got the wrong tool for the job.'

'But legs we like, gotcha.'

'Be ready.' I said, taking a step forwards.

The zombie was seconds away, and if my heart wasn't racing a moment ago, it sure as hell was now. I felt the prickling heat from terror-fuelled adrenaline running up my back, and everything was brought into sharper focus. I tried not to see the way the zombie's skin hung loose on its face, or how dark blood was slowly oozing out of a gaping wound on its shoulder, the vest was torn away, or how what might have been bone was pressing sharply against the material on the other side, but every gory detail was vying for my attention.

I tried instead to imagine its head as an oversized novelty baseball, which I was about to whack right out of Cemetery Park. My bat connected with the side of its skull, the force of the blow sending ripples of shock up my arm, buzzing my fingers numb.

I was…surprised, by the results. Having no sense of balance, a blow straight to the head sent it over to the right, tumbling down on to the road and using the rest of its forward momentum to roll onto its back.

A dark smear stained the end of my bat, and I looked down to check that there wasn't any on my clothes. That's when I noticed the blood, the zombie's blood. It was thick, congealed, almost black. Lifeless. They don't have a functioning circulatory system – their hearts don't pump. So what'd be the point of destroying a defunct system, you know, scientifically? The lore wasn't holding up.

I didn't know if Lucile had thought the same, or if she was just pumped up for the fight. She brought the bat down on the closest target for her swing – the zombie's head. I've never seen a baseball bat employed as a golf club before, but damn. It made a sound that I really, truly, cannot describe.

She whacked the top of its head, all the force of the blow going into the body, down through the skull and onto the spine. It must have been like diving head first onto concrete. Dark grey fluid started to seep out of wide cracks in the skull.

I had to look away but the smell reached my nostrils; something more rancid than death itself – it'd only been a couple of days, no way should this guy have smelled so ripe already. With no escaping the smell, I forced myself to look down on it again, and readied myself to bring the bat down on its legs, just in case.

92

But after a few seconds, I lowered my swing. It wasn't moving. Lucile was on the same page as me now, for sure. The blood. It wasn't bleeding living, red, oxygenated blood. It was just seeping brown, necrotic gore.

'Folklore be damned,' Lucile said, giving the thing a prod with the end of her bat, 'ain't the heart we need to kill. The head. Got to get them in the head.'

'Their hearts aren't pumping any blood. How do they move? Breathe? I know they breathe, I've heard them doing it, right before they moan.' I said, shaking my head and looking down at the thing. For once I was more confused than horrified. I didn't even want to throw up, despite the smell, and all the…fluids.

'Could really use a smoke right now.' Lucile said, shaking her hair, 'I've got the shakes, look at my hand…'

I knew how she felt.

'Come on people,' Neville shouted to us, leading the way back out of Damian's sister's house, 'let's just get the hell out of here.'

'No one there man,' Damian said, following him out, with blood on the end of his cricket bat. 'Some dead guy was eating de housecat, real fucking sick.' he spat.

'What about your sister?' I asked, as we climbed back into the 4x4. Lucile needed Morgan to give her a hand up again.

'Gone. Lydia, de kids, everything gone,' he said, turning the ignition, 'clothes, food, suitcases. They packed up, but I don't know where they'd go. Uncle Rob's maybe. Car's gone. But no note, no nothing.' He added, slamming a hand down on the steering wheel. 'Less just get de fuck out of here.'

'You want me to drive?' Neville asked quietly.

'Nah I…I be fine, it's all good. Maybe they with de CDC or some shit, I dunno.' he cringed, shaking his head. I could see his jaw was tense, and he was avoiding looking at Neville. 'Who been messing with me radio?' he asked, carrying on the drive down the street.

Morgan produced baby wipes from her pocket, for Lucile and me, so we could set about cleaning the blackened blood off our bats. Apologetically, Neville passed Damian's cricket bat to her, so she could do it for him. I gave up when I realised the blood had soaked into all the frays and notches on mine. Lucile had more luck with her smooth-finish aluminium.

Damian eventually found a way out of the estate that didn't involve driving over the top of other vehicles, so we were back on the main roads after only mild cursing, with Morgan giving him directions towards the Mason place.

Even after most of the folks in the car had just been toe-to-toe with a zombie, there wasn't as much tension in the air as I thought there'd be. I was tearing myself up inside, my guts writhing around like snakes trying to find a way out, thinking about the city, the county, the whole Republic. But everyone else looked…calm. Well, calmer than I felt at least.

I glanced across at Morgan, who was just looking out of the front window with her lips pursed; more concerned than afraid. When she spoke, her voice didn't shake or come out weak, just steady, maybe thicker, with a side of worry.

Lucile looked like she'd gotten past panic and was just…going with it. If I ignored the blood that'd streaked into Damian's cricket bat, I could pretend we were just going down to the park for the afternoon.

Is this how quick the rest of the country would be adjusting? There was no power, no TV, the government was hiding behind a nation's worth of soldiers, and packs of walking corpses were roaming the streets. We'd accepted that in just a couple of days. We had to. It was that or go mad.

I think people just accept the reality they've been given, try to muddle through and do their best. Either that or they take the easy way out. Rosie, Edgar…I felt my muscles tense with the urge to hit something. The way things were going, I wouldn't have to wait long.

I looked out of the window again as we passed a pickup truck loaded up with suitcases, its cab's windows smashed in. A few yards down the pavement, a woman's body was pinned down beneath four of them; clothes reddened and torn. People were still alive out there, trying to escape…and largely failing, from what we were seeing. Maybe this rescue mission business was a worse idea than I thought.

Neville tuned us back into GCR as we got onto the city centre roads. Not being a huge residential area meant that not many people had driven through the centre when they were trying to evacuate. Still, some roads were blocked off here and there, grey military trucks, 4x4s and armoured personnel carriers pulled across into makeshift checkpoints, or wrecks like the ones we'd seen earlier, so a twenty minute drive to the Masons' house took closer to forty.

By the time we cleared the city and were back in the suburbs, my knees had started to lock up, that feeling of wanting to hit something not going away, all that nervous energy settling in my joints. I suppose it was better than being scared again, like when I'd seen my first one at that car crash.

Damian pulled up a rise and into a fancy 'cul-de-sac'. You couldn't just say it was a dead-end, because the people here had paid to live on a 'cul-de-sac'. Suburbanites.

The lawns were immaculately trimmed, a couple of them neatly ringed off from the neighbour's lawn by a pigmy hedge you'd barely have to raise your foot to step over.

All the houses were two storeys and built up slight inclines, so that the lawns sloped gently down to the sidewalk. Paths laid down in pretty coloured masonry tiles led down to the recycling bins and trash cans. The whole thing was so middle class and picturesque it'd make Katy sneer just out of anarchistic principal. Places like this reminded her of her family.

Morgan kept Damian driving onwards, about halfway down the left-hand side of the cul-de-sac, where he parked up and set the handbrake.

'Their car's not here.' Neville observed.

'Might be caught up in traffic, ya'll seen the roads.' Lucile drawled. 'Could be they abandoned ship and ran home.'

'Something else not right, seen?' Damian muttered.

95

'No zombies.' Neville nodded, sitting forward in his seat for a better view of the road, 'This is residential, not even that far from Mercy. Shouldn't exactly be crawling with them but...its quiet-'

'Don't say it-' I tried, before he could finish.

'-too quiet.' Lucile grimaced, finishing for him. It's not often you get a setup like that.

I looked out of the window, already accustomed to seeing zombies emerging from alleyways and looking up from dead bodies, getting to their feet to after us and letting out that godsawful moan. There was none of that here. The place was just as she'd said, it was too quiet.

Morgan unbuckled her seatbelt, but Neville piped up from the front, 'Where do you think you're going?'

'To see if Becky's family are still alive?' Morgan replied, her voice taking on the first chords of an argument.

'I thought the agreement was that you wait in the car?' her father reminded her.

She sent a quick look my way, but I didn't say anything. If the vibe we were getting from this place was right, I didn't want Morgan far from our ride. But I couldn't just tell her that. I'd be agreeing with her father, and thus, not being a good mate.

'Young Roberts, Marchland, Grant,' I said, stiffening my voice, 'stick with the vehicle. Roberts Senior, you're with me on the door.'

'Aye captain.' Morgan nodded with a sarcastic salute. She folded her arms and glanced at me, disappointed but there was the shadow of a smirk there. I felt a little rush of embarrassment as Lucile turned to raise an eyebrow at me, but I met it with one of my own. Her lips twitched up, shaking her head.

Everyone dismounted, except Morgan. She swung her legs over the side of the backseats and watched Neville and me head up the path to what must have been the Masons' place. Lucile and Damian walked to the front bumper and kept an eye out.

'Nice move back there, very diplomatic.' Neville muttered when we were out of earshot, 'You find it easy to talk to kids?'

'Wasn't too long since I was her age,' I replied, 'she just doesn't want to feel useless. She's a doer, you need to let her do more.' I tried not to sound critical.

'Given our circumstances, do you think that's a good idea?' he said, his voice growing harsher.

'Who knows how long this could last?' I replied, pretending not to notice. 'We could be eating ice cream at the movies this time next week, or we could be poking through an abandoned supermarket looking for the last tin of beans. I don't know which way the world is swinging and I'd rather know she's ready for the worst.'

'But you're not her father.' Neville said, a definite edge to his words this time.

Gulp. I liked Neville, but I was starting to get the impression he wasn't overly impressed with me sticking up for the Independent Morgan Front so much.

'I know, Neville.' I said, 'But you're not the only one who cares about her. You remember how we both froze up at the crash?'

He nodded, listening.

'Maybe if that wasn't the first zombie we'd seen, we'd have been more like Damian. Prepared. Doing something about it. She's seen what the city's like now, what zombies are like, maybe she won't freeze up if she comes face to face with one.'

'I really don't want that to happen.' Neville said, looking intently across the street.

'Me nether. But given our circumstances…' I shrugged, echoing him. He smiled, and held a hand up in surrender.

'We'll see.'

I knocked on the door, making it a little musical, so it wouldn't be mistaken for a zombie trying to beat the door down. I blinked for a moment, and I was standing outside the

Jamesons' door again. I wondered, if in the end, things would have turned out differently if they had been with us.

But a sound, or something else, snapped me right back out of it. Have you ever heard a dog whistle? You don't hear the sound so much as you feel it, like a tinny buzz. This was more booming, resounding, but it still struck something inside my ear, inside my head. Something wasn't right.

Twelve

I had to take a step back to keep my balance. My vision blurred, growing fuzzy at the edges.

'What the hell was that?' Neville asked, sounding like he was standing further away than just a few feet, like I was hearing him from the other side of a thick window.

I looked back over at the 4x4, my vision coming back to me. The others must have heard it too. Morgan was getting ready to close her door, while Lucile and Damian were readying their bats.

The not-noise boomed out again, my eyes blurring and balance wavering for just a moment this time, like I'd gotten used to it.

'We should go inside, check the place out.' Neville said, keeping his voice low. I got the sense he'd rather have been indoors right now and I seconded that strongly.

'Let me look first, then you can shoot the lock or whatever.' I said, not wanting to exit one lot of weirdness and walk into another.

'I actually have a spare key, but hey…' he mumbled.

I knelt down in front of the door, glad that the house owners hadn't bought a mailbox, but had the conventional letter flap instead. I could see stairs to the right, and the open door to their living room on my left, with the red-linoleum kitchen straight down the middle of the hall.

I was scanning the corners when the family pooch padded out of the living room. It was probably a small child's cuddly toy once, but now it had grown up it could probably fight off a band of burglars single-pawed. It turned towards me, and dropped into a pouncing stance, jaw hanging open. That's when I noticed what was wrong in this picture.

The kitchen floor wasn't red – it was blood. More of it speckled the hall's cream carpet with red footprints, human and canine, leading upstairs. The dog's muzzle was coated in it, and its legs were stained almost up to the knees.

Its eyes were strangely glassy, white, reflecting the light like when you see footage of people through nightvision cameras, like those stupid "ghost hunters" on haunted-house TV shows.

It opened its mouth and saliva dangled from its teeth. Instead of a bark, it let out the sub-audible boom we'd not-heard a minute ago. I jumped to my feet and let the letterbox snap closed, just as the dog threw its full weight against the door, silently roaring.

'What's going on?' Neville asked, pulling his gun out, aiming it at the door uncertainly, setting his feet apart in a marksman's stance. He opened his jaw wide, as if trying to pop his ears.

'The dog's infected.' I said, pulling my own gun out clumsily and resting my bat against my shoulder. Swinging it at the letterbox wouldn't do me much good.

'What?' Neville said sharply, 'You've got to be kidding me.'

'Take a look for yourself, go ahead!' I answered, voice rising with the panic. I knew it wasn't getting through that door, but something about the bark was unsettling me, more than the quietened streets had already.

Neville bent down and opened the flap of the letterbox with the barrel of his pistol. Immediately, the dog was pawing away at it, trying to bite through the letterbox. The door shook as the dog barrelled into it again.

'It could just be rabid?' He tried.

'We thought East Rojas was human rabies.' I reminded him, 'Did you see its eyes?'

'No, let me have another look…' he snarked, putting his gun up against the flap again.

I saw movement, half a dozen silent shapes bounding over the hedges, coming straight for us across the gardens on Neville's side. More dogs. I shouted out to him, but I could barely hear the sound of my own voice above the growing buzzing in my ears. He turned to me, frowning, forgetting the letterbox. I jabbed a finger over his shoulder. He spun around and raised his gun in a practiced motion.

At least the sound wasn't upsetting our balance anymore; otherwise Neville would never have made the shot with a handgun at that distance. He put the first dog down two gardens away, and took his time with the next shot, taking out a sheepdog as it leapt the next hedge. Two shots, two hits. I never knew my neighbour could do that.

Even though I was stood right next to him, his shots sounded about as loud as someone slamming their hand on the table, barely getting through the buzz from the weird, silent-barking from the oncoming pack.

I looked over to my right and saw Lucile and Damian running up the path towards us, to get our backs. Morgan was leaning over the front seats, doors closed and face whitening. I wondered if she'd watched us take down that zombie earlier.

When I looked back, the dogs were much closer. I dropped my bat, fumbled the hammer back and aimed my gun inexpertly at the leading dog. The trigger wasn't as stiff as I expected – Edgar must have kept the antique pristine. One moment I was pulling it, the next, the hammer fell. *Bam.* The dog dropped to its side and lay panting. I felt a surge of pride, and resisted the urge to punch the air.

I wasn't quite prepared for the recoil. It made my hand feel strange, like holding on to your phone when it vibrates, but a hundred times stronger. I didn't have time to make a second shot, but Neville had already fired twice more, a quick double-tap, *bam-bam*.

The last dog reached us at the door. It pounced through the air, towards Neville, and I only had that split second to act. I jumped forward, putting myself between the shining-eyed retriever and my neighbour, punching my gun upwards, hitting it under the jaw. I pulled the trigger. The hammer clicked down into an empty chamber. Of course, I forgot to cock it.

The force of my punch and its own momentum sent the dog flying into the side of the house, where it bounced off the white wall and landed in the flowerbeds. My fingers didn't feel sore from the blow, the trigger-guard and barrel had protected my hand like a knuckle duster.

I cocked the hammer back and aimed down at the dog, already stumbling to its feet. This time, without the disorientating barking of the pack, the shot was loud. Like someone slamming a metal pipe on an empty trash can.

'Shit…' Neville gasped, taking a step backwards and thumping a hand on his chest, as if to dislodge his heart from his mouth, 'Thought it had me there.'

'No problem….' I panted, out of breath even though I'd only moved a couple of feet. I swallowed down my pulse and looked around the street for any more surprises.

I'd shot at something, and I'd hit it too. I'd stood between Neville and that dog, and I didn't even think about it. On the one hand, I was proud of myself, feeling a kind of heroic rush – we'd been attacked and we'd come through, defeated our assailants. But on the other hand, we'd still been attacked. Twice now, things had come at us and tried to kill us. That shit just doesn't happen to people in the real world. It was fucking dangerous out here.

'I think I see what you meant now, the dogs *are* infected. Their eyes, and that bark…' he trailed off, looking at Damian and Lucile for confirmation.

'I saw, I heard, yeah.' Damian nodded, looking down at the retriever's body. 'Me ears still ringing.'

Lucile walked over to the dog that I'd shot first, and lifted her bat up. I turned away, but I heard the wet crunch as it broke the dog's skull open.

'I don't think we need to do that, Lucile.' I said, still not looking, 'Neville's dogs dropped just as easy as they would have if they weren't infected.'

'Can't be too careful?' Lucile shrugged, sounding a little reluctant to stop. I think she'd found an outlet.

'Permission to make more loud noises?' Neville asked, pointing his gun at the door, which shook again. There was still one dog left.

'Granted. But we need to be out of here as soon as we can, if Morgan's theory about noise bringing more trouble holds.' I nodded.

Neville put a bullet through the door, just above the letterbox. I wanted to hear a little whine as the dog keeled over, to know it'd been hit, but all I heard was the sudden quiet of the door no longer rattling against its hinges. That'd have to do.

With it dead I could finally breathe easy, and was suddenly hit by a wave of exhaustion. My knees weakened, and I turned their sudden jelly-like state into an excuse to pick my baseball bat up. I used it like a cane to get back on my feet.

'Can we go inside?' Morgan asked, tentatively leaning out of the rear window.

'We've come this far.' Neville nodded, looking back to his daughter.

He fished a keyring out of his jacket and looked for the right one while the rest of us stood scanning the surrounding gardens, growing more and more paranoid. That was a lot of dogs for one little estate. Someone was either a real animal lover, or infected dogs formed themselves into packs. No telling how many more could be out there in suburbia – or what happened to the cats.

And who heard of rabid animals sticking in packs? Maybe if this was the same infection; it'd have different effects on the brains and bodies of any creature it'd take hold in? The zombies from earlier –most we'd seen had been slow, ponderously limping towards us, but the last one we'd seen had come for us at a dead sprint. No pun intended.

Maybe that doesn't sound weird to you, but realising there were potentially hundreds of surprises waiting for us was a little concerning to say the least. At least there were no zombies here. Either the dogs scared them away, or, as I found more likely, they were smart enough to go where the dead weren't.

Neville opened the door a crack, setting both hands back on his gun before nudging it further with his foot. The door stopped about half way, coming up against the limp dog. He stepped around the door, gun flicking between the living room and the kitchen. Morgan was set to follow him in, but I put a hand on her shoulder.

'Let him see.' I muttered, so he couldn't hear.

'Clear.' Neville announced a few seconds later.

I let her go in after him, and politely waited outside with Damian and Lucile.

'What do ya'll think?' Lucile asked, concerned. 'They okay?'

I dipped my head, and looked back towards the door. 'There was blood all over the carpet, kitchen floor. Dog was covered in it too.'

Damian sniffed loudly, and turned to look around the cul-de-sac again.

'How about you, man?' I asked.

'Longest time Lydia an I been without talking since our Ma died. But I be right.' he nodded, not turning around, his voice a little deeper.

A gunshot rang out from inside, muffled by the walls. People started yelling, Morgan, her father, and someone else.

I was already through the door before I knew what I was doing, bat under my arm and revolver in hand, thumbing the hammer back. I followed Neville's yelling upstairs, where he was pinned to the side of the wall beside the first door on the left. Light was shining into the dim corridor through a bullet-hole in the door.

'Cease fire, cease fire!' he shouted.

'Who are you? Looters?' a woman's voice was yelling back, from inside the room. Holy shit, someone did survive.

'It's Neville, Morgan's father!' he shouted back, 'I already said that!'

'Who else? There's more than one gun out there - I heard more than one gun!'

'I'm a friend of Morgan's too,' I said, bringing the volume down, 'my name's Kelly.'

'You've…you've got a funny voice for a girl, Kelly.' The woman replied, uncertainly.

'I work out.' I shrugged, looking at Neville's bemused expression and matching it.

I heard the woman in the room let out something halfway between a laugh and a cry. She was hurting. An uncomfortable half a minute passed before the woman in the room called out again, her voice strained, 'Got no choice anyway…I need some help in here.'

Neville looked at me, hooking a thumb at himself and then the door. I shook my head, and tapped my own chest. I felt stupid for doing it, but I then patted myself on the back. I think he understood.

'I'm coming in.' I warned.

I entered the room while Neville waited outside, covering the door. It was the room of a teenage girl. The name 'Rebecca' was written on a license plate hanging off the door, a few feet above the bullet hole, several dints, and a set of peeling claw marks. Morgan was just coming up the stairs, Neville put a hand out to signal her to stop. She didn't need to see what was inside, no matter how prepared I wanted her to be.

Becky, I assume, was laid out on her bed. The sheets were soaked through with blood, and her face was a deathly pale-brown, tan skin turning to grey. A set of human teeth marks showed red and raw on her neck.

A neat hole sat right in the middle of her forehead.

I dragged my eyes from that strangely demure little wound. Across from her was a living woman, tall, brunette, somewhere near thirty with pale brown skin, Rojas descent maybe, and if circumstances were different I'd say she was pretty.

105

She sat in a chair across from the door, turned away from a vanity table-come-desk. Her left hand held a tea-towel to her shoulder, while her right held a gun; firmly pointed at me.

Thirteen

She caught me looking at the gun, and rolled her eyes.

'I haven't asked you to drop yours, so don't worry about mine, okay?' she said slowly. I nodded. 'I would appreciate it, if you could put it away though.'

I did as she asked, setting my bat down against the bed first, carefully putting my gun in my jacket pocket and slowly lowering my hands again.

She wore black trousers and a dirty vest-top that was stained with so many different things that I didn't want to hazard a guess at them. A belt hung with different pouches and holsters was lying on the desk beside her...along with a silver police shield.

'Who're you?' I asked her.

'Anita Mason.' She replied, passing up the opportunity to drop rank and flicking the gun around the side of the bed, 'Come give me a hand, Mr Kelly.'

I tried not to look at the body on the bed as I walked around it. I kept my eyes on Anita, bleeding quite badly down her right arm, but still managing to keep the gun pointed at me without so much as a waver.

'Can I trust you?' she asked.

'Given how much you're bleeding, I don't think you have the luxury of choice.' I said, kneeling down to examine her wounds.

'You're little Morgan's babysitter, right? Answer the Godsdamn question.' She demanded.

'Yeah. You can trust me. Morgan's here too.' I promised, meeting her eyes for a long second. Bloody babysitter.

She sagged down in the chair a few inches, and I realised she wasn't all that tall, just confident, commanding. That ran out when her pain threshold did.

'Hurts like hell,' she said through her teeth, 'there's a FAK in my tac-belt. First, I need you to find the antiseptic and spray it on my arm when I tell you to.'

'Were you bitten?' I asked, trying not to think about what it meant if she said yes.

'By a dog, not an infected.' She replied, 'Don't think you turn if you get bit by the dogs.'

'What if you do?' I asked.

'You know when I said not to worry about my gun? I take that back.' She added in a whisper, looking down at me. Her eyes were red from crying, but she was still keeping strong. I couldn't *not* help her.

I searched through the pouches on her belt until I found it, a pull-out mini first aid kit.

'If I turn out to be wrong, you can shoot me yourself, Kelly. Now, open that pack of bandages. You're going to have to go under my armpit with them, the bite's all around my right shoulder. Get the tape and the spray ready because this is going to *bleed* when I let go.'

I did as she asked, and used the little scissors to cut off a few strips of the medical tape, and hung them off the arm of the chair.

'Just like wrapping solstice presents.' she grimaced, 'Hurry up, I'm dying here.' She added, glancing to her sister, on the bed. She looked back down at her knees, her face grim.

I nodded when I was set, and she removed the towel she'd been pressing against the bite, long soaked through with blood. Underneath, the dog had sunk its teeth into her shoulder pretty deep, and likely cut some important bit of plumbing that bled like crazy. I'm a delivery boy, not a doctor, but a couple of those punctures looked pretty serious.

She must have killed the dog or pried its teeth off, because the wound was neat, not like she'd ripped herself away from it. I tried to focus on what she said about wrapping solstice presents, rather than on the blood pumping freely out of the three or four biggest punctures.

108

I quickly sprayed the antiseptic over her shoulder, amid a wave of shivers and pained hisses. Then I stood so I could get around the back too, where she hadn't been able to keep as much pressure on. Blood had stained the cushions of the chair beneath her back.

She was looking noticeably paler as I started wrapping her shoulder up in the bandages, working around her bra strap, but she didn't cry out, just hissed through her gritted teeth. I taped the bandage in place across her back and the top of her arm, and took a step back to see if I'd left anything.

'Congratulations,' she said, leaning over to one side in the chair, her gun slipping from her hands, thumping softly on the carpet, 'you probably just saved my life…' she trailing off. I barely caught her before she hit the floor.

'Somebody, I need help in here!' I shouted towards the door.

I heard heavy footsteps bounding up the stairs, Damian clearing the side of the door a moment later, cricket bat in hand. He took one look at me holding the unconscious woman, and dropped it.

Damian was stronger, so he took her shoulders while I got her legs. We carefully moved her out of the bedroom, the room where her sister's body lay, and negotiated her down the stairs without hitting her on anything.

Neville and Morgan were knelt on the lawn, hugging. I couldn't see her face from here, but what with the Jamesons this morning and Becky now…she'd be worse than broken up, words wouldn't do what she was feeling any justice.

I felt my ears ring again, and got another dose of blurred vision. Lucile pointed towards the end of the road, where more dogs were slipping out of an alleyway and sniffing the air. We got the wounded officer into the back seat, Lucile and Morgan climbing into the warehouse-sized boot and grabbing onto straps to give Anita and myself a little room.

Anita Mason, Rebecca Mason's big-sister, woke as we mounted the pavement, turning to speed away from the cul-de-sac. The new dogs were haring right after us, their barks not carrying the same bite anymore, either because we were in the car, or we'd become desensitised to it.

Morgan hadn't looked into Becky's room, but Neville had told her that she was dead, that there was nothing they could do for her. Apparently the parents – Paul and Marianna – were dead in the kitchen. Which Morgan had seen. She didn't say a word, all the way back to the flats. She just looked out of the rear window with this blank stare.

I wished we could have stayed behind to bury them, like we had the Jamesons. Leaving the three bodies there left a sour taste in my mouth, but if we fought the dogs we risked more injuries. Maybe more deaths.

Anita looked up at me, blinking her eyes open. Laid across the backseats, her head was in my lap.

'Whe…' she tried, her throat closing up on her.

'You're in Damian's ride. We're heading back to our safehouse.' I told her, keeping my voice as soft as I could.

'Wha…' she tried again.

'You held on until I'd finished patching you up, but then you passed out. You're still bleeding, but the bandages haven't soaked through yet. I think you might need a few stitches. Hopefully we have some in our own medical kit.'

She cleared her throat. 'Do you always talk so much?' she said weakly.

'Only when I'm rescuing folk.' I said seriously. 'I picked your stuff up. Badge, gun, belt.'

'Let her rest, Kelly.' Lucile said from behind me, 'She still might not pull through. And she still might be infected.'

'An optimist huh?' Anita smirked, creasing up lines of blood on the side of her face. She fell silent for the rest of the ride, and passed back into sleep, rather than unconsciousness. She must have been exhausted. I still kept a close eye on her, and had my gun out beside my leg, just in case.

Despite the safety of the upper floors, it wasn't practical to carry her all the way back upstairs when we got home. Damian helped me again, carrying her through to Stan's apartment and setting her on the sofa, where she muttered

110

something about his interesting collage before drifting off again.

'Neville,' Lucile said, walking to Stan's kitchen, 'get me the medical kit and a cigarette lighter.'

'You going to stitch her up?' Damian asked.

'No, I'm going to roll her a smoke.' She sniped. 'Of course I am. Don't think any of ya'll got the stones for it.' She added, washing her hands in the sink. We still had hot water, but there was no telling how long the city's pump stations would last before shutting down.

'Kelly, I want you to hold her head, don't need her thrashing around if she gets lucid again.' Lucile continued, nudging a coffee table closer to the sofa with her knee. 'And just in case she is infected, don't let any of the blood get in your mouth or eyes.'

'Why would I do that anyway?' I asked, my hands already streaked with Anita's drying blood. I'd tried not to touch anything on the way here, though I'd need to wipe my gun down at least.

Lucile used some kitchen scissors to snip away what was left of Anita's vest…sleeve? Would you call that bit at the top a 'sleeve'? Anyway, she cut that away while I slid her bra strap off her shoulder, out of the way. No sense in ruining it.

'Perv.' Lucile joked, pulling on a pair of blue latex gloves from Stan's first aid kit, with the snap usually associated with airport security. I ignored her.

Neville and Morgan were nowhere to be seen while Lucile worked, peeling back the bandages I'd put in place and identifying the worst of the wounds, the ones that meant she'd be dead before they healed on their own.

She cleaned her hands off again with antiseptic wipes, and had us do the same too, but it was more of a formality, with my hands already caked. I should have washed up too.

Then she used a cigarette lighter from my jacket pocket – I don't smoke, but Katy does – to sterilise the hooked needle. I tried not to look while she pulled it through Anita's skin. Luckily, Anita was too far into sleep to do more than whimper.

111

Lucile was right, I didn't have the stones. Needles just went right through me… so to speak.

Anita was still out as the three of us re-bandaged her with the more complete equipment from Stan's kit. We used soaking pads, gauze, and then put the bandages over them, taping them in place more thoroughly. I put pillows under her head and tried to make her as comfortable as I could.

'So. What if she's infected?' Lucile asked, taking the first turn at the sink. She probably used more hand soap than water.

Maybe Lucile was an optimist after all. Warning us that Anita might be infected with the virus, then getting her hands dirty in an attempt to save her life? Not the actions of a worst-case-scenario thinker.

'Then we deal with that when it happens.' I replied.

'I ain't saying we kill her now,' Lucile said defensively, 'If I thought she was going to die I wouldn't have wasted my time there, I'd have started on the elevator. I'm just thinking, you know, in case shit.' She added in her drawl. I adjusted "optimist" to "realist".

'We seen about that when de time comes.' Damian intoned, his voice deep with concern, 'For now, we wait an see if she even pull through.'

'I seen worse on site. Once saw a chainsaw belt snap clean off and into the side of a man's neck. Of course, he actually got to see an emergency room. But I reckon she'll be okay.' Lucile tried for reassuring.

'Where you learn to do that?' Damian asked her.

'My Nat-Service,' she shrugged, 'I had some trauma training before I went engineering. Got kicked out after a while. I'm so-so with the blood, but show me the soft and squishy bits and I'll show you my lunch. Either of you two served yet? You handled that gun alright.' She added, nodding towards me.

'No, I was due to soon, before this.' I waved a vague gesture.

112

'That's why you popped de question to your girl, right?' Damian chuckled. 'I not been yet either. Glad about it now. Gods know what de TA are having to deal with.'

We washed up and left Lucile in there to watch her. Neville and Morgan were sitting in the foyer. I caught the image of myself as a doctor, walking out of an important surgery and meeting the family. I shook my head and pinned it on the increasing deficit of sanity in my life.

Morgan was sat next to Neville, his arm around her shoulder. Neither of them were crying at the moment, but from their eyes, I could tell they had been. Now they were just sat there, staring quietly into space.

'She's alive.' I said, 'Lucile says she'll probably make it, and she's the closest thing we have to a doctor. She does good work.'

'Maybe they'll have a doctor at GCR,' Neville suggested, 'you said yourself, we should go there eventually. Why not now?'

'I said that it wasn't a priority…' I corrected him, looking down at the carpet, 'I guess it might be after all, if there's a life on the line. What time is it?'

'It's passed five o'clock.' Neville replied, checking his watch. 'Sunset should be around six.' He added, looking at the sky, already beginning to darken.

'Shit.' I muttered, sitting down next to Morgan. Damian was pacing the foyer behind us. 'Alright. Alright, if Anita wakes up by half-past, I'm saying she's fine, and I'm going for Katy…but if she doesn't wake up…GCR.'

'We have three cars,' Neville reminded me, 'mine, Damian's, and I'm guessing that's Lucile's pickup outside.'

'Hadn't thought about that. Do we really want to split up?' I asked, biting my lip.

'Let's just see what happens first.'

I was torn between selfishly pursuing Katy, chasing down my chance to save her, and the life of another woman. But I tried to reason it away. I tried to think that Anita was potentially infected and maybe there was nothing we could do

113

to save her. But I still made the selfish choice. And I'm not proud to say I'd probably make it again.

Minutes ticked by like hours. After a few weeks, Morgan rested her head on Neville's shoulder and started to cry again. He pulled her in closer and tried not to follow suit, just kept his eyes on the darkening sky.

'Twenty past.' He muttered.

He had a box of nine-millimetre rounds on the floor in front of him, but comforting Morgan, he was no longer able to reload his and Anita's guns, which'd been set out on the little table. They were different models, but used the same bullets, I guessed. I reloaded them for him, both guns, all four magazines, trying to familiarise myself with the weapons. Anita's had been all but empty. Wonder what she'd been through.

Just shy of ten bullets rattled around the box when I set it down. Even if Anita didn't pull through, at least we'd have an extra gun. I tried the maths again, Greenfield minus bullets equals zombies. The result wasn't much better.

But we'd set out to save people – those were always going to be shots well fired, in my opinion. Still…with no cavalry coming to Greenfield, us and those bullets, we were on our own. So we really needed another steady pair of hands.

Fourteen

Lucile came out of the apartment.

'She seems to have lost a fair amount of blood, but a little time, a lot of painkillers and some rest, and she should be back on her feet. She's awake.' She added with a nod.

I was up like a shot, so quick I nearly took Morgan with me, who'd been holding my hand after I'd done with the guns. She made a noise of amused protest and wiped the last tear from her eye.

Lucile sat back down on the sofa, nursing Anita's head on the pillows beside her lap and making her drink water through a straw. We filed in. I took the armchair while everyone else got on the second sofa. Anita didn't look any worse, but she didn't look any better either. Pale, blood-stained, she looked half-dead – which is way better than undead by anyone's reckoning.

'I really need a shower.' She grunted, her voice rough.

'We've still got hot water,' I smiled, 'Lucile. Could you help her with that?'

'Sure. You want me to take a crack at the genny too? For the elevator?' she asked.

'If you've got the time, please.'

'Sure thing boss.' She hummed.

I hoped she felt valued, rather than bossed about. Like her skillset was needed. I sure wished my skillset was in demand right about now, but delivering packages didn't seem applicable to the current situation; unless you counted delivering Anita to Stan's apartment. You'd probably need to sign for something like that.

'You feeling okay?' I asked Anita.

'A hell of a lot better than I was a couple of hours ago, because of you guys.' She nodded, 'Thanks for getting me out of there. I…couldn't be in that room any longer, and, too cut

115

up to run far.' She said, turning her head away. "Cut up". She wasn't just talking about the bite there.

I looked over to Morgan, staring intently at the carpet. They'd both lost Becky, a sister and a best friend.

The darkened apartment, and the darkening mood, reminded me that the sun was setting – it'd be more dangerous out there after dark, where we couldn't see what was coming. I certainly wasn't leaving Katy out there another night.

I looked to Neville, then Damian. They seemed to be waiting for me to speak.

'Come on then,' I sighed, putting on a brave face even as I looked out at the sky, 'one more job for today.'

'You a busy man, Kelly?' Anita asked.

'I've got to go save my fiancée.'

Lucile chimed in. 'This Katy, she must be some special lady for you to want to risk your ass like this. How long did you say you'd been engaged?'

'Three days.' I grimaced, 'I haven't even seen her since she put the ring on.'

'I'm not sure if you're a romantic, or a remedial.' Lucile laughed, 'But good luck out there. Come back in one piece.' She added, glancing toward Damian. They shared a look.

The menfolk were walking out into the foyer, when Morgan caught up with us.

'I want to come too.' She sniffed, eyes still puffy.

'Morgan…' her father said, despondent.

'Katy's my friend, I want to help.' She said, her voice shaking.

She was looking for something to take her mind off of losing more people she cared about. I got that, I understood that. But this wasn't just something therapeutic, something cathartic, like digging a grave or drinking your way through a Kilmister wake. Night would fall while we were out, and while I wanted her ready to face those things out there, seeing them at night might do her more harm than good.

I walked past Neville, and brought Morgan in for a hug.

116

'Stay here with Anita, kiddo.' I mumbled into her ear, 'Talk to her. She just lost her sister and she'll want to talk to someone about that. You two can help each other through this. You've been so brave today, but you ought to sit this out...'

'I don't want to just sit here and be useless.' She said, 'I need to be doing something.'

'Then make sure Anita's okay. Help her get cleaned up, keep her company while Lucile has a go at that generator.'

She squeezed me uncomfortably tight, gave a great sniff, and let me go.

'You going to be okay?' I asked.

'If today doesn't leave me traumatised into professional therapy, yeah, I'll be good.' She shot back, smiling weakly. 'You bring her home, yeah?'

'Damn right I will.' I said, bumping fists with her.

I was a little glad to leave Morgan and Anita alone. Maybe that's somewhat uncaring on my part, but I don't mean it that way. I wasn't trying to get her out of the way because I didn't care, just the opposite. You know me by now. But aside from keeping her out of the night, I didn't want to see her in pain.

Grief doesn't sit well with me. Like Morgan, I needed something to do while my mind processed it. I'd had a friend die when I was a teenager. Car crash. Closed casket. Never got to say goodbye. Being around other people's grief, that didn't help me, I needed to process it solo.

Digging the grave, or the aforementioned wake, that's not to everyone's tastes. But maybe helping Anita get cleaned up would be more her speed – and if she helped Lucile save us all from a trip on the stairs, I could live with myself.

'This is dangerous,' Neville said as we left the building, and Morgan's earshot. 'We should wait until the morning.'

He'd left Anita's loaded gun behind in Stan's flat, just in case something happened while someone was in the shower. I didn't feel comfortable with treating Anita like a timebomb, but I couldn't see any other options short of just euthanizing her now, and I certainly felt that was a last resort. Maybe we

117

could have tied her down, but if she wasn't infected, she'd probably hold it against us later.

'You can always turn back.' I suggested, still heading for the 4x4.

'Nah, I'm good,' he said, nonchalantly rubbernecking around the parking lot, hand on his gun.

I called shotgun again, and we mounted up in silence, headlights off so we wouldn't attract so much attention. The clock was getting closer to six as we were pulling onto the road, the world cast into shades of darkening grey, blue and brown. No streetlights flickered to life, so as we drove our eyes just adjusted to the lengthening shadows.

I gave Damian directions, trying to stay away from roads we already knew were blocked, but we still came to a couple of dead ends, having to mount the curb or simply shove a car out of the way. I'd thought Damian would be worried about damaging his 4x4, but the cattle bumper on the front seemed tough enough to take on a herd of bison.

After a while, Damian had to give up peering out of the window, and turn his lights on. Now we were a noisy, brightly lit target for the zombies. It was probably just my imagination, but I hadn't seen that many zeds on the road before we were lit up. Now, it was different.

Dark shapes moved on the streets outside, every one of them a zombie in my mind. I know that most of them would just have been wrecked cars, newsstands or mailboxes but the thought that they were out there, watching us, set my teeth on edge. I chewed my tongue and continued to eat the silence.

Damian drove carefully; never going above fifteen or twenty miles an hour, plenty of stopping distance if he saw another roadblock. He could see about forty yards in front of him thanks to his halogens, but it wasn't enough as we came face-to-face with another row of smashed up cars, and carefully negotiated the pavement around them. Something else bumped into the side of the 4x4 and groaned into the night. I wiped sweaty palms on my jeans.

Damian was silent in concentration, while Neville was visibly trying to gather his fraying nerves. I looked behind me to see him checking his gun again, resting the bat Lucile had gave him between his legs. Then I looked back out of the window and wondered why I was quiet.

Butterflies in my stomach reminded me of Katy, and the thrill of driving to meet her was strangely not dulled by the obvious danger. I'd love to ride to her rescue. Despite how she'd scoff at the whole white-knight notion, I'd still get a kick out of it. Replace the horse with Damian's ride and I was all set, though I doubt getting a lift off your friend would be considered very chivalric.

I was getting excited, despite the zombies, despite the darkness, despite the icy doubt that was still creeping into the back of my mind. 'What if she isn't here?' it whispered. 'What if you're going to get them killed, for nothing?'

We were driving for ages, well past sunset, before Neville leaned forwards from the back, and pointed up at the skyline. 'Do you see that?' he asked over my shoulder.

The moon cast just enough light to let me make out a plume of smoke rising into the sky, not too far away. That wasn't unusual. I'd seen smoke out in the city from the top of castle tower, but this looked like it was on our way to Katy's. As Damian pulled us even closer, I began to realise it wasn't just on the way. It was there. We turned the last corner a moment later, driving up a short hill of terraced houses before the road flattened out again.

Someone had built a bonfire in the middle of the street, using smashed up household furniture. Chairs, tables, wardrobes, and dozens of misshapen, fire-warped things I couldn't even guess what they used to be. They'd probably doused the whole thing in gasoline and lit it up. But Who? Katy? As a kind of emergency signal perhaps?

Damian parked us a safe distance back from it. I looked out of the window and cautiously opened my door before dropping down to the street, gun in one hand and bat in the other. There weren't any zombies here, and I wasn't getting the same vibe I got at the Mason house, so I was guessing there were no dogs either. But I knew something wasn't right, and I hadn't picked up on it yet.

The fire was big enough to light up the fronts of three or four houses on either side of the street. This whole area used to be student housing I think, before I'd moved to the city. It'd been invested in by former tenants and renovated into the classy kind of place that 'young professionals' lived in, but where it was still socially acceptable to share houses with your old university mates.

No candlelight flickered in any of the windows, the only light here was coming from the bonfire. My heart began to speed up when I realised that I'd be a pretty neat looking target; standing in front of the only light for miles around. Zombie, dog, anything. My neck began to itch, and the hairs on the back of my arms stood on end.

I turned full circle, looking for whatever was setting my teeth on edge. It felt like…someone was watching me. Corny, I know, but those primal instincts are there for a reason.

'Hello?' I asked the night.

The fire crackled, something within it popping, sounding for all the world like a spitting slice of bacon.

'Get back in.' Neville said, just loud enough for me to hear, 'I don't like this.'

'I know, it doesn't feel right…' I muttered, still looking around for the source of my discomfort.

'Get in man!' Damain repeated, clearly spooked, 'That's not just wood on de fire!'

I finally twigged, something filtering through my senses. The smell of burning meat. I spun around to the bonfire, and met eyes with the empty sockets of a charred human corpse.

Gunfire split the silence, something a lot bigger than my dinky revolver. It cracked into the road next to my foot, kicking up chips of tarmac.

Instinct took a hold of me, fight-or-flight, and before I knew it I was cowering on the other side of the 4x4. It's called

120

"taking cover" if you do it in a manly fashion, but I think I might have let out an un-manly noise while I did it.

'I'm alive, I'm alive!' I started shouting, that little voice in the back of my head wondering if that meant they'd stop shooting, or just shoot some more.

'You're tooled up too,' a familiar female voice called out. 'Lose the piece mate, and nobody get out of the bloody truck.'

Fifteen

'Laurel?' I shouted back.

There was a lengthy silence.

'Who're you?' she asked, her tone confused.

'It's Tiernan Kelly you idiot!' I yelled, getting back to my feet. There was another pause, punctuated by the sound of something on the fire doing the unthinkable bacon noise again.

'Oh,' Laurel called out, quieter this time. 'I suppose you'd better come in then.'

'Too right!' I shouted back, splitting into a grin.

I saw a flicker of movement in the front-bedroom window of their house - Katy, Laurel and Danni's house. I ran around the 4x4 and towards the door; the other two shrugging to each other and following. Damian locked the doors with a click of his keys.

I waited in the front garden, a little rockery that we used to sit out on in summer, reading our books to each other and cracking open cold bottles. I ran my fingers through my hair, trying to look presentable.

Laurel opened the front door, at first a crack, then fully when she saw my face. She stood as a vague silhouette against the dim glow of candlelight from the kitchen, a tall, willowy woman with ash blonde hair that she usually straightened to halfway down her back. In the last few days, she'd trimmed it to a more severe cut.

It hung wet, freshly washed, grazing the shoulders of a comfy looking dressing gown, under which she wore some roomy jeans and a grey blouse. A scoped hunting rifle was slung on a strap across her back, and she carried a carpenter's hammer through one of her belt loops. Leaning up against the wall beside the door was a pile of smashed up furniture, rough and ready planks for a barricade.

'I was setting myself up for a last stand,' She said, catching where I'd been looking, 'really, really glad to see a friendly face.' she stressed, putting an arm around me on the doorstep and bringing me in for a hug. I reciprocated. As she moved, the sleeve of her dressing gown rode up and I saw a streak of blood staining the cuff of her blouse. I put it out of my mind, and focused on the important.

'It's good to see you too.' I said, squeezing her tight for a moment. 'Everyone okay? How's Katy?' I asked as we filed into the hallway. She closed the door behind us, sliding the lock and the chain in place. I stood on tip-toe, trying to look into the kitchen, to see if my fiancée was in there.

'You must be the world's only surviving brain donor, coming out here after dark.' Laurel said, looking me up and down, her eyes lingering on the gun, 'Zeds will've heard the shots, but I guess you already know that.'

'Not just zombies out there.' I said, lips pursed, leaning to one side to look up the stairs, hoping to see my girl. 'What's with the artillery, by the way?' I asked.

'Bloke up the road was a hunter,' she sighed, looking more serious, 'but he's dead now.'

'What happened?' Damian asked.

'We made a play for safety in numbers, about ten, twelve of us. Fella had a gun and the experience to use it,' she said, eyes flicking to Neville's shoulder holster, 'but before we figured what you had to do to stop the bastards, the sitting room window was smashed in and the front door was off its hinges. Me and Danni, we ran upstairs, jumped out the window.' She swallowed hard, 'Left everyone down there. Ain't proud.' she added, jaw tight.

'But in all the panic, one of them…before we…' Laurel sniffed hard and put a hand up to her forehead. When she spoke again, she had a lump in her throat. 'They caught her and…they bit Danni and –' she stopped talking, shut her eyes and shook her head slowly.

A bucket of ice water fell into my gut.

'What about Katy? Is she hurt too?' I demanded, my voice rising.

123

'Katy?' Laurel said, putting a hand on my shoulder, pushing me backwards. I'd stepped into her personal space. 'Katy left before this all started, she's not here.'

'What the fuck do you mean?' I shouted, taking a step back, and forcing myself to tone it down. 'Sorry, sorry. What do you mean? Where is she?'

'Gone,' Laurel said, as Neville put a hand down on my shoulder. Damian did the same for the other one, and squeezed hard. 'Not dead, just gone. She packed a bag and turned into work after her call with you, even after seeing all that "stay in your homes" bull on the news.'

'Did she say anything else?' Neville asked, beating me to it.

My throat was closed and I wasn't sure what was welling up faster, my eyes or my anger. My vision was blurring, and that urge to hit something grew even greater, forcing me to clench and unclench my fists. I paced into the kitchen and turned the tap on, splashing the water on my face until I could take full breaths again.

The kitchen was all decorated in pastel shades. Blue cupboards, yellow curtains, green worktops, relaxing colours that were totally failing me. I remembered helping Katy paint it. But she wasn't here now.

'She wanted us to go with her, said we might be safer at the hospital, that there were soldiers and police there. Talk of forting County up or something. But we couldn't, didn't want to go, we listened to the news. We thought she'd be back again, when she saw how the roads were. But her bike must have gotten through.'

Her bike. Why didn't I notice her bike wasn't outside?

'Her parents,' I stammered, 'her parents live in Linkoln, she must have gone to them - can't have really gone to the hospital...'

'You know she'd have sooner chewed a wasp mate – I thought she'd made it to your place.' Laurel said, stepping up behind me at the sink.

'Maybe she's still at the hospital?'

124

'Maybe Kell, maybe they managed to hold out in County…' Laurel said, like she was trying to appease me. But then her voice changed, almost to a whisper. 'They bit Danni.'

'You already said they…they…' I said, mouth hanging open, 'Oh my Gods. They bit Danni. She's infected?'

'She was bitten,' Laurel repeated, 'That doesn't mean she's infected, does it?'

'I think so.' I turned to see her, my face probably as sour as her's.

'I'm gonna to need more than "I think so", Kell!' Laurel yelled, her voice fracturing.

'What happened to the hunter?' I asked.

'Perry…' Laurel said, taking a step back from me, realising she was in my personal space now. 'He was mobbed by them in the living room. When I went back to his place, there was a pool of blood…'

'And?' I asked, casting a glance back to Neville and Damian, wisely waiting out in the hall, both trying to blend with the wallpaper.

'And his body was gone.' she murmured, a tear forming in the corner of one eye. She bit her lip and stared at the kitchen cupboards.

'Were there drag marks, or footprints?' I asked.

'F-footprints…' Laurel said, lowering her head.

'He got mobbed by a dozen zombies, infected, murdered, and I'm guessing a few hours later, you put a bullet through his head and threw him on the bonfire.' I said, losing patience. 'Fucking hell, Danni's infected and you're keeping her upstairs?'

Laurel nodded, and turned away from me. That put her looking at Damian. She looked back to me again.

'Why does that mean she'll turn, huh?' Laurel growled, pushing me back against the fridge. I could see tears rolling down her cheeks, glinting back the candlelight in the kitchen.

I stepped forward again, put my arms around Laurel, and drew her close to me before she broke down completely. She knew what infection meant, she just didn't want to admit

125

she didn't have the power to do anything about it. Laurel and Danni were like family, and Laurel knew that she would have to watch her sister die…or even help her along, like Anita and Becky Mason. Those planks in the hallway, they weren't for barricading the front door. She'd have done that already. They were for whatever room Danni was laid up in.

Laurel balled her hands into fists, scrunching my jacket up in her grip. She shuddered violently for a moment, as the tears finally burst out. We stayed that way for a while, Damian and Neville never coming into the kitchen.

'I'll go and see what I can see,' I said eventually, mirroring what I'd said at the Jamesons. It had only been that morning, though now the sun has set it seemed like a week had passed; after their deaths, fighting those freaky dogs and Anita's impromptu-surgery, everything was moving so fast.

I gently pushed Laurel away from me, and rested my hands on her shoulders. 'Pack up all the supplies you can, we'll be leaving soon.'

'You think your flat is safer than here?' she asked, her voice shaking, her face ruined with tears.

'Lots of stairs, you know they're not good with stairs. Plus, we don't have a big bonfire outside advertising our dramatic last stand,' I smiled, 'Go on, pack up your stuff.'

'Already done,' she sniffed, tilting her head to the living room, 'Packed up to move to Perry's, I'm all set, and…and without Danni…I'll be ready.'

I left her crying in the kitchen, Damian sweeping in after me with a nod, and joined Neville in the corridor.

'Infection probably passes through bites.' Neville said.

'I know,' I said, scratching my chin, thinking.

'That means she's infected. She'll turn into one of them soon.' he continued.

'I know that too,' I grunted, shaking my head.

'What're you going to do about it?' Neville asked, folding his arms.

I knew what I'd want done to me if I was infected. The thought of becoming one of those mindless bastards was enough to make me understand Rosie's choice – and she hadn't even seen them. I saw myself, empty eyed, wandering the streets, looking for the living to eat. Then I saw in the distance; a woman in biker leathers with short blonde hair and a cute piercing. I pinched the bridge of my nose and closed my eyes tightly.

'What are you going to do?' Neville repeated.

'The humane thing.' I said, putting conviction in my voice even if I didn't feel it in my bones.

I walked up the stairs. I knew I was in the right house, all the boards creaked in the right places and the banister wobbled enough to let me know it needed fixing. But I felt like I was in a different world as I took the first steps onto the landing, and saw the candlelight coming out from underneath Danni's door. It was a back bedroom, not visible from the road, or I'd have seen the lights earlier. I wondered if any zombies were making their way across the back gardens, drawn to the light peeking around the curtains.

I pushed the door open until it knocked against the wall, but it took me a few more seconds to work up the nerve to step through it.

Danni, Katy and Laurel could have passed for sisters. I hadn't really thought about it until now. All three of them were blondes of one flavour or another. Laurel's ashen hair was a dirtier shade, Katy's was almost bleach blonde from the dye, and Danni's was usually the colour of cornfields in summer. It wasn't that colour now. It was heavy with sweat, clinging to her cheeks and her neck as if she was in the grip of a terrible fever.

Her eyes slowly turned to watch me enter the room, but there wasn't much left of Danni looking out from behind them. She wasn't a zombie yet, but if I needed anything to convince me she was infected, it was the look in her eyes. She knew she was dead, it was just a matter of time…and circumstance.

Bloodied bandages made from bedsheets were wrapped around her forearm and held in place with cell-o-tape, and

127

several more cuts and scratches were exposed on her arms, probably from jumping out of that upstairs window.

'Danni…' I said softly.

She didn't say anything, but she nodded her head weakly, almost so little that you wouldn't notice.

'Danni, I know you've been bitten.'

Another nod.

'Do you want us to leave you here, or do you want me to…' I started the sentence strong, but I couldn't finish it. The words caught in my throat, and I swallowed hard to clear them.

For all I knew, Danni wasn't seeing me, I could have been just some feverish illusion. A guy she knew, offering to take the pain all away. Danni just nodded. It wasn't subtle this time. She gave it her all, which wasn't much.

I pulled Edgar's wartime sidearm out of my pocket, thumbed the hammer and aimed it at Danni's head, from not ten feet away. I meant to pull the trigger as soon as I saw the sights were lined up, but my finger wouldn't stick to the plan.

Euthanasia had been legal for decades, people with fatal illnesses or untreatable chronic pains had been able to go through a process of dying on their own terms since I was born. I'd grown up with the concept of putting somebody out of their misery. But my finger remained unresponsive.

My guts were in on it too, alive; writhing and struggling as I tried to come to terms with ending the life of my friend. Pulling a trigger is different to pressing the plunger on a needle. But she was infected, and this wasn't just a matter of whether or not I wanted to pull that trigger. She wanted to die. I'd want the same, but my finger wasn't listening to reason. I started to sweat, and my breath quickened.

Then thunder clapped in the room, with a burst of light like the flash of a photograph. The picture of Danielle's brain matter splattering an old foreign movie poster was imprinted in my mind, forever.

Sixteen

I turned and stumbled, pushing Neville and his smoking gun out of the doorway, and just about made it to the bathroom before my insides finally had their say.

Vomit burned up my throat and splattered down into the bowl of the toilet, as my vision swam with streamers of purple and orange, along with the image of bone fragments and gore streaking that black and white poster.

I reeled back from the toilet and fell onto my ass, propping myself up with one hand and covering my mouth with the other. I tried to get my breathing under control, I always found that helped stop more coming up.

Neville offered me a hand up and I took it, almost falling into him as the strength of his pull heaved me a little too far. I fought my stomach back in line before I threw up on his shoes, though at that point, I felt like I should have.

'The fuck?' I growled at him.

'You couldn't do it, it needed to be done,' he replied, his voice low but even, 'you said it yourself. It was the humane thing. There wasn't much left of her anymore.'

I knew what he said made sense. It was what I'd been telling myself only a few moments earlier, but Gods above. If you'd have been there, maybe you'd feel the same. It was cold. And it wasn't like Neville – not the Neville I knew.

'I didn't know her,' Neville said, 'So it was easier for me. Thought I'd save you the trouble.' His choice of words was poor.

'I wanted the trouble, you shit!' I snarled, something red flaring inside me, forcing me to shove Neville back, 'She was a friend – you were a stranger to her!'

'Exactly. You think she'd want that eating away at you?' Neville asked, keeping his voice quiet, despite mine. 'It's done now. Let's get out of here. Let's get back home and you can grill me about it all you damn well please, Kelly.'

He turned away and took to the stairs before I'd thought of a decent reply. I wanted to punch him, but I knew he was right, and I was only venting my own frustration, my inability to act. I wanted to go home and thump the pillows until I fell asleep. I settled for kicking the top of the banister, finally breaking one of the props out of its creaky moorings.

Ugh. Suddenly I was more embarrassed than angry. Having a tantrum, breaking something. Now wasn't the time for that. I walked down the corridor - avoiding Danni's room, the door mercifully closed. I opened the door to Katy's and managed not to slam it closed behind me like an angry teen.

It was dark in her room, but I found her long-tipped lighter and knew where all the candles were. She was big on mood lighting. Big aromatherapy candles, tea-lights in little lanterns and stained-glass cups. When the room was flickering, I set the lighter down and let out a breath I didn't realise I'd been holding.

It must have been a big old bag she'd packed. Patches clear from dust stood out on her dressing table, where I knew a ring-bound photobook and her tiny makeup case had sat. I looked along her shelves, noticing a couple gaps in her reading library. I couldn't find the Some Bad Men album I'd used as a ring box either.

That…cheered me up a little. She'd really taken a lot of things with her, but it wasn't all clothes and shoes. Keepsakes, mementos, the really important stuff, they were all missing. I hoped she was out there right now, listening to that CD. I sat down on the edge of the bed. Wherever she was, she loved me. I knew that.

I tried to lay the information out in front of me, give it all a good going over. She'd taken so much stuff, it wasn't like she was leaving the house expecting to return later. She knew she'd be gone a while. Not talking to her parents, that cut them out as an option. So she'd either packed her bags for a long stay at the hospital – Laurel did say they were "forting up", or she'd intended to come to me.

130

Why the fuck had she taken off, asked Laurel and Danni to go with her, and not given me the same option? Maybe I was feeling a little shorter-tempered than usual, because I wanted to start smashing shit up again. I looked over to the corner, where she kept her and Morgan's hockey sticks - handy clubs at this point. Only Morgan's stood there, Katy's gone, as if she knew she might need a weapon…or just wanted a big handle for her duffel bag.

I didn't go caveman, didn't smash anything else, but the urge was still there. I knew that when it was gone, all I'd be left with were tears. That grief I'd been working so hard to avoid. Edgar, Rosie, dead. Damian's sister, his nephews and nieces, gone. The Mason family, killed by their fucking dog.

'Where is she?' I asked myself, my voice swallowed by the dancing shadows.

I opened drawers and cupboards, looking for some clue, some note, anything. All I found were more empty spaces where things used to be. Appropriate, I guess. Even her private drawers, the ones with the tiny locks on, were unlocked now. I felt bad for searching them, and save for the, ahem, toy drawer, even they were emptied, whatever secrets she kept were gone.

Maybe it was the aromatherapy, the smell of lavender and vanilla, but I didn't feel like slamming the drawers. I left everything, whatever was left, as I found it. Finally I picked up Morgan's stick and left Katy's room, closing the door behind me carefully. At the bottom of the stairs, everyone was waiting for me. They looked up and stopped talking as I came into view.

Laurel had a camping backpack on her shoulders, and her rifle in her hands. Neville was holding two stacked cardboard boxes of what looked like tinned food and bottled drink. Damian had another one under his arm, and carried his and Neville's bats in the other hand.

'What's all this about dogs?' Laurel asked. I could see her face was still blotchy from crying. She was changing the subject, offering an olive branch to all involved.

131

I wasn't sure I could take it and wipe my conscience clean of Danielle's death. But I only had to hold it together until nobody could see me fall apart. There'd be time to dwell on it later.

A bitter, cynical part of me remembered a thought I'd had earlier. About it being tougher to deal with death when it was a friend, someone your own age, as opposed to an aging war vet and his long-suffering wife.

'They had ghost eyes, like from haunted house TV shows, you seen?' Damian nodded, trying to smile. Although even he couldn't manage it for long, not tonight. 'They bark, made everything weird.'

'You said they didn't make a sound.' Laurel said, pulling off that long sniff you do after a really long cry.

'Something subsonic.' I nodded, heading for the front door, taking the branch and not thinking about *Le Movie Poster*, or Becky Mason, who looked to have gone out the same way.

We left that house with the candles still burning, and I half-hoped that the whole place would burn down. If the world ever got back to normal, I wouldn't want Katy going back there anyway. She saw the bad side of people every day at work, but she didn't need to see what happened to Danni.

Walking down the path, past the little front rockery and out into the street, I remembered leaving the Masons in their house, no burial, no cremation. Laurel didn't say anything about moving Danni, or putting her on the fire in the street. Guess she didn't want her burning with the zombies, as if that'd taint her remains.

I took the bats off of Damian when we got to the 4x4, so he could get his hands in order with the keys. We loaded the boxes into the backseats, Neville and Laurel climbing up in there after them.

I belted up, rested my bat between my legs, and opened the window enough for the wind to batter my face when we started moving. I still felt like I was going to be sick, and Damian was looking at me like he was worried I was going to do it in his front seat.

132

He drove just as carefully back home, but I wasn't watching the scenery this time. My mind was elsewhere. I swung backwards and forwards in thought, half asleep. It'd been a busy day.

If Katy was still alive, where could she be? Obviously County Hospital was a top candidate, but perhaps she'd have gotten out of there when the trouble started - but if that were true, why hadn't she made it to my place?

What if she wasn't alive? Was she even now walking the streets looking for…food? Or if she was still breathing, then what was she doing? Was she with this new CDC, or the Territorials, helping people? I prayed that wherever she was, whoever she was with, that she was okay. I had images, visions running around in my head.

Katy, on her massive hog, shotgun stuck down into the slot at her feet, a meaty soundtrack playing in her earphones. She rode by a zombie, and casually blew its head away as she went, riding towards a military encampment on the horizon.

I saw her kneeling over a wounded soldier, administering emergency first aid to a gunshot, some friendly fire incident. The guy was bleeding out, but she was keeping him stabilised with her hoodie, bunching it up and pressing it against his chest, like in the movies.

But then I saw the soldier reach up and grab her by the hair, pulling her down to his mouth, and it wasn't to hear his last words. She tried to get away from the zed, but he was too strong.

'Behave!' Damian shouted, grabbing my arm, shaking.

I opened my eyes, and blinked them back into focus. I was still sat in the front passenger seat. Damian was looking at me, lips tight, brow furrowed.

'Sorry…' I muttered, voice tight.

'You started twitching, muttering.' he said, letting go of my wrists, 'Shouted but you didn't wake up.'

I coughed, leaning forward in my seat, the taste of vomit lying heavy on my tongue. I dry-wretched, the air rubbing at the back of my throat like sandpaper.

133

'Not in de car, man.' Damian moaned, reaching across and opening my door.

Apparently I didn't have anything left to throw up, and my stomach lining was being stubborn. I coughed again and sat up, muttering something about needing a drink.

A bottle of water appeared over the headrest, and I took it, spitting some out of the door and draining half of it in one. It cut off the worst of the puke taste, but I knew that wouldn't go any time soon. I'd probably wake up in the morning with it.

'Must have nodded off.' I said, passing the water back over the headrest.

'Erm, best hold onto that Kell.' Laurel said, not unkindly.

Everyone dismounted, but I sat for a while longer. I put my head against the dashboard. The cool plastic felt soothing. Damian and Neville were carrying Laurel's supply boxes into the foyer, but Laurel stayed behind.

She stood in the open door at my side of the 4x4, and offered me a hand down. I took it, and she pulled me closer, squeezing her arms around my shoulders and holding me reassuringly tight. The night was turning cold outside of the climate-controlled vehicle, and it was nice to have a warm, living person to hold onto.

'Thank you.' she said quietly, her head on my shoulder. 'I was all ready to…call it, back there. Seeing you, other people…maybe it's not as bad as it could be.'

'All I did was drive by…' I said, rubbing my hands on her shoulders.

'It was enough.' she nodded, breaking the hug. 'So, you sure you've got room for me? We going to have to bunk together?' she chuckled, gesturing at the fourteen storeys of living space.

'Going to assess the situation inside.' I replied, waving a hand at the glass doors, 'We've got wounded. Possibly infected.'

'Like Danni.' Laurel said, looking over her shoulder, at the doors. 'If this Anita woman, if she's like Danni…will you?'

I just nodded. It'd be me this time, not Neville.

We grabbed our gear; tins, rifle and bats, and found Neville, Damian and Morgan waiting for us in the foyer. Morgan was sat in candlelight, boiling a pan of water over a camping stove – probably the one from Damian's apartment – and had a bunch of cups set out on a squat magazine table, along with milk and sugar. My Gods, she's an angel.

I knew that coming back home without Katy was going to draw some questions from her, but I was too tired, too drained, and I didn't have the answers myself. Where was she? Why didn't she come to me? Or did she come to me, and something happened on the way? I gave Morgan a smile, feeling my lips turn up but my expression was still probably grim.

'Builder's, two sugars.' I said, making my way to Stan's apartment, keeping my head down.

'But what-?' Morgan tried.

'Later.' I snapped, feeling the word come out too harsh, too fast. 'Please.' I added to soften, 'Just a minute, okay?'

I opened the door to Stan's apartment and walked inside, shutting the door behind me. I wanted to lock it, my hand hovering over the catch, but they might hear the latch click. Like Katy's room and the foyer, candles were the only light source, giving just enough to see by.

The flat smelled like antiseptic, and I could hear the shower running. Good, nobody to see me losing it. I drank the rest of the bottled water Laurel had given me, and slid my cowboy boots off on the doormat. I checked my gun was still in my trousers before I crossed into the kitchen and filled the bottle back up, splashing more water on my face as I went. Hot tears mixed in with the cold water. By the time I'd stopped running the tap, I couldn't hear the shower anymore. I'd probably spoiled the water pressure.

Stan's sofa was comfortable, and in the darkened apartment I couldn't see the flecks and splotches of blood that must have been at the other end; where Lucile had employed her rudimentary medical training. I hoped it'd be enough.

135

The sound of the bedroom door opening pulled my eyes away, Anita jumped backwards, her towel slipping. I looked down before I saw more than the bin-bag taped over her bandages – but that took my eyes past her well-toned legs.

'Sorry, sorry,' I said, waving one hand and putting the other over my eyes, 'my bad. Shouldn't just sit around in the dark.'

'You saved my life, Kelly.' Anita replied. 'If you wanted a peep show, all you had to do was ask.' she added, but there was no smile in the line, reflexive banter but her heart wasn't in it.

'Funny. You got clothes?' I asked, still keeping my eyes politely shut.

'Ones that aren't ruined? No. My house is out on the way to Overbridge, I'd usually take the motorway to get here, so I'm not asking for a ride. Lucile said she knew a woman who might be a similar size and brought some stuff down from her apartment.'

'Theft and looting, that not against the law?' I asked, scratching my head theatrically.

'A little B&E to retain my modesty, I think I can live with that,' she shrugged. 'Not like there's anyone left to call it in to.'

'No police, at all?' I asked.

'Haven't been able to raise anybody on my radio, but that could mean anything. I'm not going to write everyone off yet – just don't have a means of getting in touch if there are.'

'I should leave you to it, you and your modesty, I just wanted to see if you were alright.' I said.

'I can't see to be sure, but I bet you're blushing. Stop being such a kid. Come on, I'll need you to help me get dressed.'

'I'm a married man. Almost.' I protested, smiling weakly.

This might sound a little strange, and don't ask me why, but after everything that'd happened tonight, being in the vicinity of a semi-nude woman was making me feel a lot better. I sat up and followed Anita into the bedroom, where yet more candles awaited.

136

Seventeen

Despite the flattering lighting and her almost-nudity, there wasn't as much sexual tension as you might expect. Her family was dead, and she was wounded - or possibly worse.

'Turn around while I put some knickers on.' She said.

As she asked, I turned around and stared at the wall. Her shadow dropped the towel – and while there was no funny business going on in here, that was a lot nicer to look at than the other thing's I'd been imagining when I closed my eyes.

I kept my gaze averted but offered a supportive shoulder as Anita Mason gingerly stepped into her stolen underwear, making a small sound of discomfort when she pulled them up. She picked up the tracksuit bottoms from the bed and stepped into those too, before peeling back the tape on the bin-bag over her bandages, and throwing that down on the bed.

'Could you clasp me in?' She asked.

I helped her get her arms through the straps of a white bra, noticing the way her back muscles moved under her skin. Her arms were toned too, and probably carried more muscle than mine.

'Thank Gods she didn't get you a frontsie.' I joked.

'Guy like you mustn't be used to this.' she said, finding a hint of a smile from somewhere.

'Huh?' I managed, my voice a little deeper than I would have liked.

'More used to taking them off, right?' she chuckled. 'Drop the strap on the wound side, I don't need it digging in.'

'Well what guy makes a habit of helping his girl get dressed? Usually it's the undressing you do for each other.' I answered, helping her wriggle in to a loose long-sleeved top.

'Your fiancée then…' Anita said, 'the one you went for earlier, instead of the radio station.'

'How'd you know about that?'

'Lucile told me. She also got little Morgan to help me shower so she could work on the generator, but I didn't need her help past getting my bandages covered.' She replied. 'So you didn't find her then?'

'No. Found two of our friends.'

'You don't sound too happy about that.' She said, turning to face me as she adjusted the shirt. Lucile might have found someone of a similar size, but Anita was a little taller than them and had the build of an athlete, the shirt barely meeting the top of her bottoms. With the chill in the air, she used it as an under-shirt and pulled on a longer blouse over the top. It was a mismatched outfit, but comfort is worth more than style when you've got a shoulder wound.

'One of them was infected. Neville…euthanised her. Wasn't pretty.' I sniffed, wrinkling my nose. 'The other one, Laurel, she's alive. She's back here with us now.'

'What happened to your fiancée?' Anita asked, gently broaching the subject.

'Chance she went back to work. She's a nurse at County General. Or maybe she's with the TA, or the CDC's soldiers. We heard they were under new leadership.' I shrugged.

'County, you said? I hope not.' Anita said, giving my shoulder a squeeze before removing her hand.

'Why not?'

'I was at County. With some of the CDC, soldiers and doctors. We were going to fortify the place, but the infected got out of control, way too fast. We tried to evacuate the healthy, but…I'll tell you later. I'll tell everyone at once.' She sighed, her face twisting, shoulders tensing up as she folded her arms.

I gave her a hug. It seemed to be the thing to do. Or maybe I was just being a little touchy-feely after seeing her shadow in the buff. She hugged back, and let out a deep breath, her head resting against my chest – she was taller than Lucile, but shorter than Laurel and Morgan.

'You smell like vomit. You should get a shower while the water's still hot.' She suggested. Like I said – no sexual tension.

'Come on, blow the candles out. We'll go join the others.' I said, giving her a pat on her uninjured shoulder.

We picked up the medical kit and Anita's clothes, then left Stan's apartment. I got my shoes on and dropped the latch behind us, since it was only polite. Though after all that had happened, if Stan ever came home the least of his problems would be burglars.

There was a dim rumbling sound, growing louder. Suddenly the elevator doors rattled open, and florescent lighting spilled out into the foyer, almost too bright to look at after coming out of the candlelight in Stan's place. Lucile stood between the doors, her silhouette slightly misshapen because of the tool belt around her waist.

'Generator's running on near-empty, make it quick.' She said, clapping her hands, 'Let's move, people.'

'Angel of mercy,' Damian said, starting to pack away the tea and coffee making facilities, 'my feet are killing me.'

Neville pressed a mug of tea into my hand as we piled into the elevator, the seven of us having to breathe in a little.

'I'm calling a meeting,' I said, 'take your time, have a shower, fill every seal-able container you can with water, then come to Edgar and Rosie's place. We got lucky today. We need to make sure we're prepared tomorrow.'

Lucile and Damian got off on the thirteenth floor. On the fourteenth, Neville and Morgan went back home to get showered and changed, while I let Anita and Lucile into my place.

Anita settled down onto the sofa while I found some candles under the sink and lit them around the room for her. Then I went to light Katy's bathroom ones. I was just putting a covered tea-light in the soap tray when I turned around to find Laurel in the doorway, arms folded, watching me.

'You do this for all the girls?' she asked.

'Only the ones I rescue from suicidal last stands.' I replied, trying not to think about Danni or Becky again.

I moved for the doorway, but she barely budged an inch, forcing me to edge past her to get out. She smirked at me and asked, 'Could you hand me a spare towel?'

'I'll even get one for your hair. Liking the new cut, by the way.' I added, moving into the bedroom, where I kept the spare towels and linens and such.

As I came out of the bedroom, I looked over into the living room. Anita's was still on the sofa, her eyes were closed and her head rolled back onto the cushions as I watched. A rush of fear went right through me, a cold flush rising, and I looked around for where I'd put my bat. But then I saw her chest rising up and down. She'd only nodded off.

Not to wake her, I quietly nudged the bathroom door open, steam already misting up the mirror over the sink. I threw the towel onto the closed lid of the toilet and shut the door. They weren't prudes in that house, Laurel herself had walked in on me in the shower one morning and stayed to brush her teeth, but I had stuff to be getting on with that'd need a different sink.

Laurel took about twenty minutes. She found me in the kitchen, scrubbing the blood out of my baseball bat's many dinks and nicks. Anita was still sleeping, but she was dead to the world, so to speak.

'All yours.' She said, draping the hair towel over her shoulders, letting it air dry rather than wrapping it.

'You use up all the hot water again?' I asked. It was a long-standing tradition that she shower last at the ladies' house.

'Tried. Your boiler just doesn't know when to quit. Hey,' she added, putting a hand on my chest as we passed by the sofa and sleeping Anita. 'I'm sorry I don't know more.'

'That's not your fault, we're all in the dark here.' I shook my head.

'Maybe. But I should have gone with her. We should have stuck together, had a better chance. If she's…if she's gone…' Laurel trailed off, her voice cracking.

141

'We're not crossing that bridge.' I told her, placing my hand over hers. 'We're here now, and if we made it then there's no reason to think she hasn't.'

'Right, right…' Laurel nodded, her eyes welling up. 'She's tough. She'll be okay, yeah.'

'I'm going to get cleaned up. Be back soon.' I added, meeting her eyes. 'We stick together from here out, you and me. We'll find her.'

I locked myself in the bathroom and ran a sink of cold water while I stripped out of my clothes. I felt the patches of dried blood on my shirt, and figured there'd be some on my jeans too, so I made sure my pockets were empty before I dumped them both into the sink. Yes, it was a deep sink, one of those big bowl-type ones that sits above the stand. I've filled it with ice and used it as a beer bucket before.

Katy once told me that the best thing for getting blood out of your clothes was spitting on the stain, and then sucking. I'd actually used that for tiny cuts and such and it wasn't bad, but it seemed a fair assumption that the blood in these clothes should go nowhere near the mouth. So I went with the old fashioned cold water method.

The air was still thick and steamy from Laurel's shower, making it a little too humid for comfort, but by the time I'd gotten under the water I didn't care. There was too much blood on my hands, literally speaking.

Laurel must have had a lot of Danni's blood on her, she wasn't just trying to drain the boiler. I took as long as she did, maybe longer, scrubbing the red lines out of all the creases and wrinkles in my hands with a nail-brush. It hurt, but it let me know I was clean again. I rested my head against the shower wall and let the water pound the muscles in my back for a while. I didn't know when I'd next have a hot shower, so enjoyed the moment for a while longer, until Morgan politely knocked on the bathroom door.

'Lucile's making dinner. Everyone's going to be in Edgar and Rosie's place, like you said.' She called. 'You okay in there?'

142

'I'm okay, Morgan.' I said, my voice a little rough.

'Heh, yeah, me too.' She replied.

I sighed and turned off the water, but didn't get out of the shower for another minute, just dripped off and breathed in the steam. Eventually though, I had to face everyone. I felt like I could just curl up and sleep for a week, but at the same time, I could still feel the anger I'd felt earlier. The confusion about why Katy hadn't come to see me. Was she alive? Dead? I was no better off than I was this morning – worse even, for having come so close, from having exhausted all good options.

I towelled off and changed into some pyjama bottoms and an old grey shirt, then wrung my wet clothes out in the shower, putting them on the radiator while the heating was still on. Water would probably still pool under the radiator, so I put my already damp towel down on the floor underneath. It was something at least.

I crossed the hallway and opened the door to the Jamesons' apartment. Everyone was sat in a big circle on the floor, backs against sofas and chairs or just sat cross legged around the camping stove, where a chunky soup was steaming away. If you included the kitchen stools there were enough seats for everyone, I guess they just felt this was more…social, somehow.

Neville was passing Edgar's bottle of whisky around, not one to let something like that go to waste. I sat down between Laurel and Anita, and the bottle made its way to me.

I tipped it back and drank to Edgar's memory, wondering what he'd say if he were here now. Would he risk going out again, knowing what's out there? Or would he tell us to stay put, horde the food and wait for this to blow over?

What would Katy do? How would she want me to play this? I know if I were in her position, I wouldn't want people risking themselves to come looking for me. But I couldn't stand the thought of her out there alone. I drank again, and passed the bottle on to Laurel.

Lucile dished out the soup with a big ladle, while Morgan handed a loaf of sliced bread around, the use-by-date

143

just coming up. It probably wasn't such a good idea to be drinking on nothing but soup and bread, but when the bottle came around again, I took another long pull.

Anita had a thousand-yard stare fixed while she was eating, spaced out, looking at the little fire under the cooking pot, burning away from the nozzle on the gas bottle. Only after everyone had finished eating did I see her blink. The last of the booze ended up in front of her, and she finished it off in one long swig. Her voice was still burning with it when she started to speak. She'd seen me looking, started talking with just me listening, but after a few seconds, everyone quietened down, and was leaning in.

'So…the entire Moss Way Precinct was detailed to help the CDC at County General. Even before the rioting at Mercy, there was an overflow of infected patients. Not all of them were really infected. Some of them just had similar symptoms – fever, confusion, shortness of breath.' She added, taking in a long breath as if to confirm she was uninfected. She looked up, noticed everyone watching, then kept her eyes on the stove as she carried on.

'Three busses of suspected infected were taken to Mercy so that County could stay open to the public, outside of the quarantine. We were trying to contain the infected in just one hospital. But even with police and soldiers, the CDC couldn't get all of the infected out. A few families heard that if their people went to Mercy, they weren't coming out again. They took their relatives up into a ward and locked themselves in, hiding. We finally had to follow the screaming to find them.' She said, a tear starting to well up in her eye.

'When we did…they weren't human anymore.' She said, her voice grating, a lump in her throat. 'The families that'd taken their infected up there were all dead. There were about twenty…z-zombies, give or take. By the time we'd opened fire, we were too late.

'A lot of people ran, even some of the mercenaries. When you empty a magazine into something you expect it to go down. Zombies don't. You're trained to shoot for the centre

144

mass, that's what kills people – but by the time we figured out it was headshots, they were pushing us further back from the wards and we were running out of ammo. They're not all slow…some of them ran. Gods…I swear some of them could climb up the fucking walls…The doctors were trying to get the patients out while we screened them in front…' she started wiping the tears away with the sleeve of her borrowed shirt.

'We didn't have many guys left as we got out to the parking lot. Four ambulances got out, I think? Six or seven patients or staff on each, two or three cops or mercs, really crammed in there. One of them got separated in the traffic, one of them crashed. I was on one of the others. Got separated on the roads. We made it almost to the Greenfield-Danecaster motorway checkpoint, but things weren't much better there.' She swallowed hard, tears freely rolling down her face now.

'Four lane traffic jam, hundreds of cars back. We got out on foot, had to fight our way through panicking civilians, belted-up zeds in the cars or ones busting out of them. One of the patients got dragged through a window and two zeds ripped his throat out. Sergeant Mosley went down after that. Friendly fucking fire, some scared, angry civilian. Weren't even halfway there…' she sniffed, her mouth twitching up at one side.

'And when we got to the checkpoint?' she said, shaking her head, Starting to laugh. 'Everyone was dead! Doctors, soldiers, police…and zombies everywhere.'

I felt I knew what was coming, but I needed her to say it.

'And do you want to know what was on the other side of that checkpoint?' she asked, looking up at us all. The room was silent, my throat was tight.

'Another four lane jam. Far back as the eye could see.'

145

Eighteen

Hundreds of cars lined up to get out of Greenfield, and hundreds more lined up to get in. That was just one of half a dozen motorway routes they would have screened. Anyone who tried to evacuate would have been stuck in hell's own rush hour – no wonder we hadn't seen anyone on the roads. Add into that the non-motorway routes, dual carriageways and the village roads…no wonder quarantine broke under its own weight.

That night I dreamt of the other cities, wondered if it had all played out the same way there, or if the CDC had fought harder, if people had been less stupid - the rioting at Mercy certainly wouldn't have helped the CDC's men keep the zombies contained. Was there a place left untouched by this disease? Was it spreading globally now?

I dreamt of a city, nothing left but empty buildings and streets full of deserted cars. I saw a walled-in motorway road, packed from lane to lane with smashed up cars and zombies, clawing at either side of the checkpoints, each side wanting to be on the other.

I woke up suddenly, sitting bolt upright. I thought I'd heard a motorcycle engine rumble by, but then I realised the noise was coming from the bathroom. The flush. I looked beside me and saw short-cut blonde hair. My heart caught in my mouth for a moment as it tussled about, a pretty face turning to look up at me.

Laurel blinked her eyes at me and smirked.

'Last night was wonderful.' she mumbled, sleep-flirting.

'Morning?' I replied, my rapier wit taking a lunge.

Anita was sleeping in the Jamesons' bed, unconcerned by the recent occupants but more worried that she was going to turn into a zombie in her sleep and kill anyone she shared a room with. We'd also turned the mattress and changed the sheets – it didn't smell so bad anymore.

She didn't cheer up much after sharing her story, and I was worried enough about her that I took her equipment belt away when I went to bed, just in case she decided to do something drastic, like the previous occupants. But who was in my bathroom?

Since they'd woken me up with the flush, I figured it wasn't a zombie, so instead of grabbing Edgar's or Anita's gun off my nightstand, I pulled a shirt off the floor. I can't sleep unless I fill a certain quota of nudity. I get too warm, even in winter. Nod in agreement, tell me I'm not the only one.

Usually I just go with the boxers, but I wore pyjama bottoms to stay decent for Laurel, who talked me out of sleeping on the sofa. I think that unlike Anita, she didn't want to be left alone, and truthfully, neither did I.

'Last night was wonderful.' She repeated, sitting up next to me, losing the sultry edge. 'I've never ate campsite-style in someone's sitting room before. It was an experience. One I'm sure to re-live in the coming days, but hey – fun.' She added with a tilt of her head.

'Someone's in the bathroom.' I said, my brain still slightly fuzzy from sleep.

I swung my legs out of bed and was just opening my bedroom door when the bathroom one opened. Morgan stepped out, wearing a big pink dressing gown that made her look like an effeminate yeti.

'Morning, stud.' She said flatly. 'Don't hang around much, do you?'

I narrowed my eyes at her and closed the bedroom door behind me. I gave her a tight hug, but she didn't hug back.

'I'm sorry I couldn't talk in front of everyone else.' I said quietly, following her lead out into the living room.

'You could have taken me off to one side.' She said, suddenly turning around. It was like she'd hit me, I had to take a step back. 'I want to know what happened to her.'

'So do I…' I hesitated, feeling my throat tighten by saying it out loud. 'Laurel doesn't know either. Her bike wasn't at the house, she'd packed up some of her things, clothes, photos…' I

147

was going to carry on talking; about how she might be at the hospital or might be with the CDC, but my voice just gave up on me.

I flumped down on the sofa, and within seconds Morgan was nestling under my arm, her's going across my shoulders. We sat there and hugged in silence. It was a little like finding Edgar and Rosie yesterday. Same time - nearly the same place. Both of us pretending the other wasn't crying, because we're tougher than that.

We didn't sit there for long. I heard Laurel getting out of bed in the other room and wiped my tears away with my free hand. I went to the bathroom to make use of the facilities and make sure my clothes and towel hadn't made a mess from last night, but it looked like Morgan had already sorted that out. They were almost dry, still hung up over the big radiator but a lot neater than I could manage. I tried the hot tap and washed my face, but the water wasn't getting any hotter by the time I was done. The boiler had finally cut out. No gas, no heating.

Laurel used the bathroom after me, while I put some new clothes on. Even though there were twelve entirely empty floors underneath us, we never even suggested she make herself comfortable in one of the spare apartments. Like a human herding instinct, we all stuck together.

'So what brought you here?' I asked Morgan, raising my voice to carry from my bedroom.

'Couldn't sleep. Been camped out on your sofa for the last hour or three.' Morgan replied.

'You bring a book?' I asked, trading the pyjama bottoms for some old jeans that'd long since frayed at the knees.

'You know it.' She said, probably getting back to it.

I opened my wardrobe, a sea of t-shirts for every occasion – except perhaps, the zombie-apocalypse. I went with the same Some Bad Men shirt I'd worn the night I'd proposed to Katy. Maybe it'd impart its luck to me again. I stuck my gun into my pocket and picked up Anita's belt, jealously eyeing its holster as the nose of the revolver dug into my leg.

148

'My dad had an idea for keeping the perishables from, you know, perishing?' Morgan said, turning over a page. 'We've got a coolbox for those barbecues in the park that I've heard so much about. Dad thinks if we all put our ice in there, we can keep stuff from our freezers good for another day or two.'

'Worth a try. I haven't opened my freezer yet so it should still be cold.' I shrugged, an idea striking me. Morgan was a doer, she needed to be doing. 'Would you mind doing that for us today?'

'Doing what?' Morgan frowned, putting her book down again. She hates being talked to while she's reading, but somehow manages to talk herself.

'Get the ice from everyone's freezer and pack it up with what food you think is worth saving.' I said, leaning against the kitchen island, 'Even if it only keeps meat from spoiling for another day, it's worth it if we don't have to use up our entire tinned food ration.'

'Sounds like an important job,' she said, kneeling up on the sofa, 'what's the catch?'

Inspiration struck once more. 'You have to get Anita to help you do it. It'll take her mind off things, and it's not so strenuous as to pop her stitches. If we're gone long enough, it might be worth going through the whole tower, apartment by apartment.'

'For ice?' Morgan asked, raising her eyebrows.

'For everything. A lot of food's going to go bad, no matter how much ice we can scrounge. Everyone's going to have at least a few tins in their cupboards. Soup, beans, tuna.'

'The prospect of surviving the next week, let alone months, on tuna alone does not entice me into decisive action.' She said, smiling. 'But sure, sounds like fun. Hey, do I get a gun? Could be zombies in any of those apartments.'

'You get Anita, and she'll have a gun.' I shrugged.

'No fair. You took it off her last night.' She replied, folding her arms and giving me a glare, but holding back a smirk.

'I was worried about her last night. Things always look better in the morning. Now come on, and get dressed. I want everyone next door in half an hour. If they're up. We need breakfast and I need to give everyone their jobs.'

'You know, back in the truck when we elected you El Presidente, I don't think we were being serious.'

'Too late now, somebody has to do it.' I said, clapping my hands together. 'You've awakened my long-dormant sense of organisation and forward planning.'

'Gods have mercy on our souls.' Morgan sighed, rolling her eyes and returning to her book.

My newfound sense of purpose lasted only until I got out into the hallway. Someone did need to lead these people, but why the hell should it be me? That little voice in the back of my head spoke up again. No National Service award, no practical qualifications besides my driving licences. I wasn't even a team leader at work. What makes me think I'm the man for the job?

'Because the only real authority figure around here kinda has PTSD and Neville's still asleep. So why not you?' I muttered to the corridor. I'd already decided to do my best by these people, my friends, to make sure they didn't lose hope like the Jamesons did. It wasn't a million miles from that decision to the one to lead.

I opened the door to the Jamesons' old apartment, what I was starting to think of as our group's little headquarters. I wasn't prepared to find Anita out of bed. She was standing at the kitchen sink, scrubbing out the cooking pot Lucile had used for the soup. It'd soaked overnight, but with the only water now running cold, it couldn't have been a pleasant task.

'Good morning!' she said over her shoulder, positively beaming. I was a little taken aback.

'You're up early.' I keenly observed.

'Wanted to make myself useful,' she said, scrubbing away in a pair of marigolds. Marigolds? Who actually wore those? 'I wanted to thank you for bringing me in. But I also planned on slapping you for taking my gun away, so would

150

you kindly come over here? I don't want to drip dirty water all on the carpet.'

'I think I'll pass, thanks.' I hummed. 'You're feeling better?'

'Thinking about it. What happened.' she spoke, staring deep into the dirty water in the sink, like it had shown her the answers. 'What happened was terrible. The hospital. Getting home. Mum, Dad, Rebecca...then that thing that used to be our dog? But it wasn't the worst part. What you're going through now – not knowing if who you love is alive or dead, that's the worst part. It was better, when I got home. Even after everything that happened there, it was still better than not knowing.'

'I'm sorry about what happened Anita. If we'd have gotten there sooner...'

'No, don't think like that.' She sniffed, 'I keep having to tell myself - you can't change the past. Got no reason to live there.'

I set her belt down on the kitchen island and picked up the tea-towel. We worked through the domestics, she washed, I dried, and then we both had fun trying to find where everything went back.

Not long after that, Damian and Lucile walked in, bearing gifts of processed meats and bread. It felt eerily like a self-catering holiday, only with even more of that sense that everything's about to go wrong.

Neville, Morgan and Laurel weren't far behind them, with more stuff from mine and Neville's fridges that was running out of date. Pretty much the only thing to do with all this random crap was make sandwiches, so that's what happened.

Between Morgan, Laurel and Anita, they set up a little production line, while the rest of us sat at the kitchen island and watched. Once a sandwich was made, it was double-wrapped in film, then put into a plastic box saved from someone's previous takeaway. We'd be well stocked for sandwiches, and while it never tasted exactly right, I knew you could eat them a few days later, if you kept them wrapped and cool enough. Up here, keeping them cool was just a matter of putting them on the balcony.

'What're our options?' Lucile asked, the only woman not making sandwiches in the kitchen. Morgan and Anita were there because they needed to feel useful. I think Laurel was there so she could pick at the food.

'Only one stick out to my mind.' Damian replied, 'GCR.'

'Radio station's on the agenda. There's things to do around here as well though.' I pointed out. 'Lucile, is there anything more you can do with the generator? Just divert power up to the top two floors? Or get the heating back?'

It wasn't uncomfortably cold yet, must have been a warm day out, but even with triple glazing it was going to get colder sooner rather than later.

'I was thinking on that last night, took me ages to doze off.' Lucile said, rolling a stiff shoulder. 'The fuse box ain't as new as I expected, should be able to do some tampering without setting off surge protection or the like. But the heating's a different thing, not a chance on that.' She added with a nod. 'We'd still need diesel for the lectrics but it's a definite maybe.'

'Shopping-slash-to-do-list then.' I said, sitting up on my stool. 'You do what you can for the generator. Since its daylight I guess it doesn't matter if the whole building lights up, no zombies are going to notice?'

'What if I wanted to go to GCR?' she folded her arms.

'Could you still find time for the generator?' I suggested, as her spanner landed firmly in my works. 'It is pretty important, Lucile.'

'Lu's kidding. She hate that station.' Damian grinned.

I gave her a sideways look, and she gave me a wry smirk, just messing with me.

'You've got that covered then. We need the top two floors and the elevator powered, if you can. If we're going to use the lights, make sure to draw the curtains or black out the windows, but mainly, we need power for fridges and freezers

152

would help us make the food last. While you're on that, Neville, Damian, Laurel and me are going to check out GCR, see what the situation is there.'

'Why me?' Laurel asked, slapping some cured meat onto the chopping board, trimming the fat. Watching her butter the bread with cheese spread reminded my stomach that it lost a meal yesterday.

'Because you have a gun. And you drive a small tank.' I added, before Damian could protest his lack of firearm. 'And while we're there, Morgan and Anita are going to be sorting our food supply, right Morgan?'

'Aye aye, captain.' She said with enthusiasm, but no salute, as she was handling a knife at the time. 'We'll leave the freezers up here closed, if Lucile's able the get the power back then we'll add what we find to them.'

'If you guys come across anything else useful while you're searching, bring it too if you can. Doubt anyone would have left a gun or their first aid kits behind, but you never know. Good tools, impromptu weapons, use your judgement.'

I don't know if I should have been, but I was surprised to see everyone just going along with what I'd said. They probably wouldn't have assigned tasks any differently themselves, but they say a good leader never gives an order they don't know will be followed – and I'd stand by that. All my worst bosses had been micro-managers, and all my best had kept their hands off. People knew their stuff, they just needed someone to co-ordinate from time to time, someone to get the ball rolling. If I was going to lead, I'd take a leaf out of their book.

Nineteen

The look of the sky showed half a chance of rain, so Neville and Damian went to change into something more suitable before we set off. Neville appeared in an old puffed-up winter jacket, and Damian wore the same noir-detective coat he had before. Laurel had decided it'd be a great idea if she borrowed one of my old leather jackets. She was a tall girl but didn't have my shoulders. It buried her.

Damian had his cricket bat, I still had my old wooden whacking-stick and Laurel had her carpenter's hammer slipped through one of her belt-loops. With the rifle and a pair of handguns between us, I felt like we were a little under armed for what was out there. Which Neville had picked up on.

'If we're going to be riding the highway to the danger zone every day, shouldn't we keep an eye out for more firepower?' he asked as we emerged into the foyer.

'Perry said that there were a few places out of town, but only one hunting store in the city, place where he got this,' Laurel said, tilting her head back at her rifle, 'but I figure it'll have been stripped clean by now, it's stock'll be in demand.'

'Deerstalkers and lumberjack-jackets?' Neville asked.

'Hunting rifles and revolvers.' Laurel replied, clearly not familiar with Neville's brand of humour. 'Scoped and unscoped.'

'You get pistols with scopes an them?' Damian asked, bleeping his ride's doors unlocked.

'Fun, but in the same way as a desert eagle.' Neville said, pulling himself up into the back. 'Too big and bulky to be called a sidearm, and that's kinda the point of pistols generally. I guess some hunters would use them though, if they want to give the deer a chance. Like bow-hunting.' He added with a shrug.

'You read that in one of your old magazines too?' I asked.

154

'Nope.' He left it at that.

'Pawnshop across the road has guns.' I replied. Left it at that.

Damian paused with his keys in the ignition, and flicked his gaze between Neville and myself.

'You didn't think to tell us this sooner?' Neville said.

'Only just remembered. The guy wasn't happy he had to show a valid licence for a box labelled as firearms. I told him your Service papers are enough to buy it from a dealer, and even then you've got to apply for a licence at the same time. He wouldn't have it, but hey, that's not just policy. It's the law.'

'We've been out there twice already,' Neville said, 'and there was a shop full of guns. Just up the road?'

'You thought he just dealt in wristwatches and potentially-stolen jewellery?' I grinned, looking over the headrest. Neville looked a little pissed off and Laurel was smiling faintly. 'Sorry, only just thought about it. Besides, remember what we said about guns being loud and possibly attracting zombies?'

'Still would have been good to have them.' Neville said, as Damian started to drive us out of the mini-park. Yeah, I felt a little bad. But I had other things on my mind, alright?

He drove us up onto the main road and parked at the curbside, where we all dismounted. The pawnshop was one of a little rectangle of shops built around a fountain that hadn't pumped in years, and was now more of an arboretum for weeds.

At the far end of the little concrete plaza was a run-down old arcade, on the left was the co-op I usually bought all my food from, and on the right was the pawnshop, squeezed in between a barber's and a pub that'd been boarded up for the last few months – seemed rough, I'd never been in.

With the shutters down on all the windows and no people around, the place felt a little too empty, foreboding. All it needed was tumbleweed to complete the ghost town look. Just as I was thinking it, an empty crisp packet drifted up in a sudden gust of wind. The sound of Damian's coat flapping echoed around the plaza. We spread out.

'That crowbar in your trunk should get through those shutters.' Laurel told us, waving a hand at the closed up co-op, which would solve any food issues we had, not that we had any right now. Still, we were lucky to find it intact.

'But won't get through this...' Damian said, giving the pawnshop door a solid kick.

'Security door.' Neville hummed, something in his area of expertise, 'Wooden cover, over steel. They're real tough. Can't drill the lock, can't crowbar them out.'

'What about going in through the top floor?' I suggested, looking up at the building. A lot of these old shops had flats above them that the owners used as storage, if they didn't live there. There were security bars over the window, but no shutter.

'Should be able to find the right size drill bits in Stan's place.' Neville said, rubbing his hands, a man set to do some work.

'Great, we should get on it this afternoon.' I said, turning back to the 4x4.

'What? Why not now?' Neville asked, a trace of laughter in his voice, 'It'd take us an hour at most.'

'Because GCR's a more important concern right now.' I said, turning around again.

'You sure changed your tune from last night.' He shot back.

'That's different. That was about rounding up survivors, not looting small businesses.' I frowned, seeing the way this was going. I know what you're thinking – we'd have been better off with more guns. Obviously we would, you know I was already thinking it. But hear me out.

'We can barely protect ourselves, what's to say we can save other people? There's four of us here and only three guns.' Neville said, his voice growing a little louder. Damian and Lucile just stood at the side-lines, no wallpaper to blend with out here.

156

'We have the 4x4, we don't need to get into any fighting. We're just going to GCR to see what the situation with the CDC is. We probably don't need more guns for that.'

'Probably? And what if the situation's bad? What if we break down on the way there?' he said, gesticulating at me.

'Then we have guns already, and other, quieter, weapons – staying off their radar is better than getting into a firefight with them. We're not defenceless and we shouldn't be at GCR long. Plus, we'd need to come back to loot the co-op anyway,' I said, forcing my voice quieter and giving a little nod to Laurel, 'so we'll get the guns. Just not now.'

'I don't see why we can't –' Neville started to say, but he was cut off. Something pounded on the pawnshop security door.

'Shit, someone alive in there?' Damian asked the door.

My vision blurred for a moment as my ears popped. Neville put his hand up to the side of his head in discomfort, and Damian began to back away from the door. Even though it was reinforced, he still wasn't taking any chances.

'Ghost dog.' He said, 'Trapped inside.'

'Well there's one reason, I guess.' Neville sighed, giving me a half-apologetic look. 'I'm in no hurry to cross paths with one of these things again, but…you *sure* you don't want to do this now? Wouldn't it be better to have them and not need them, than the other way around?'

'What kind of impression would we give to the guys at GCR if we introduced ourselves armed to the teeth?' I asked, giving him a similarly apologetic smile. 'We might get asked to hand over our weapons anyway, then we might not get them back afterwards and we'll be down whatever we find in there too – if we have too many guns, they could also just open fire on sight if they're twitchy.'

'Damn. Let's get it done with then,' Neville sighed, shaking his head, 'feeling like this is going to be a long bloody day.'

'Idle hands and that.' Damian said, cutting me off before I could say something I'd regret.

By now we pretty much knew the blocked roads and the ones we could just about squeeze through, so it didn't take us long to get onto the city centre's main roadways. But as we got closer to the centre, taking one of the major thoroughfares, we started to notice the zombies more.

There'd still been a few of them, trailing in our big blue wake as we drove by the wrecks and side-streets, but as we got onto the main roads a hell of a lot of them were trying to cross, heading out of the centre and into the suburbs.

'They're migrating.' Laurel snorted as we had to swerve around a group of half a dozen, just crossing the dual carriageway.

'They going where de food is.' Damian said, his tone a lot less casual. 'Centre must be a dead zone. Nobody left they can find. So they moving out into more residential streets.'

'Shit.' Neville muttered, 'Won't be long until they get as far out as castle tower. You swear we're going back for those guns?'

I didn't answer him. I looked out of the window as we drove by another zombie, a runner, coming full speed for my door. We turned a corner and it was gone. It was easy to feel safer inside Damian's rolling fortress, in daytime especially, but I didn't kid myself, we were still riding into the danger zone, as he'd said.

GCR, Shoreham Street, was over on the other side of the city, out through the centre and out through the suburbs again. Pretty much as far as you could get from our tower and still be in city limits. The centre's roads gave way to suburban streets and eventually to a secluded woodland road with sloping hills either side. There were houses within a hundred yards on either side, but the long driveways and tall old pines gave the place privacy.

Out past there and we were getting closer to GCR. I'd delivered to there before, so I knew what to expect of the area. It was upper class, all white stone cladding and black slate roofs, with immaculate green gardens and maybe a kid riding a tricycle down the perfectly pristine pavement.

158

It wasn't like that anymore. The first thing I saw as we left the woods was an upturned car smouldering away on one of the lawns, a dead woman lying on the grass a few feet away with a trail of gore leading back to the car. Looking at the tyre tracks in the road and the massive gouge in the lawn, she'd swerved to avoid hitting something, and the car had just rolled over.

Damian slowed down as we cruised along the street. Somehow, a burglar alarm was still going off in the distance, which would explain why there were no zombies around here. They were definitely attracted to sound. Laurel pointed out of the window at a group of a dozen zeds, their backs all turned to us, staggering in the direction of the noise.

Suddenly there came a crunch. We'd driven over some broken glass. It took them a slow second, but all of them turned towards us, staggering, unbalanced, their eyes empty, white and unfocused. After the first one let out that cold, hollow moan, the rest of them joined in. They were coming towards us.

'How far away are we?' Laurel asked, her voice going high.

'That's the broadcast mast, up there,' I told her, pointing out of the front windscreen, 'get us to it, now!'

Damian floored it, and I jerked back into my seat. The tyres screeched and the engine let out a brief roar as Damian worked up a gear. He cleared the length of the street and took the first left, trying to put some houses between us and the zombies, to break the line of sight, but all he ended up doing was driving us into another loose crowd of them, heading for the alarm. Fifteen, maybe as many as twenty.

As the 4x4 thundered by them, still picking up pace, narrowly avoiding parked cars on either side, they turned and started to shuffle after us, a few of them breaking from the herd and clumsily sprinting. One of the runners got a hand to the bumper, but we were going too fast for it to hang on.

Damian had to slow down as GCR came into sight, but there were zombies coming out of the woodwork everywhere.

159

One staggered through the remains of a front door, another rose up with a mouth full of bloodied teeth from a body draped over a garden fence. I looked out of the back window and saw the sprinting zombies come around the corner, still chasing.

'The gates, drive up to the gates!' I yelled, taking out my pistol and checking the chamber. Four shots, I'd never reloaded, the speedloaders were still in my jacket pocket and I didn't think I had time now. I should have been more like Neville, checking my gun every two minutes. Stupid.

GCR was a two-storey building, L-shaped, built around its car park and surrounded by a thick steel wire fence about ten feet high. If it wasn't painted green then the locals would have had something to say about it being an eyesore. The gates were electronically locked; no way we could open them from the outside unless we had the right code. But there was an intercom.

'Stay inside, get ready to drive but don't fucking leave me here!' I yelled, jumping from the safety of the 4x4 as we pulled up in front of the gates.

I pressed the white doorbell button on the intercom, and a little hum from inside the box told me it was working. I looked around the side of the 4x4, trying to gauge how far away the closest zombie was. It was way closer than I expected, maybe fifty yards, and heading straight for me. They were just smart enough to know I was exposed.

Suddenly, like a whip-crack on steroids, a noise split the sound of the growing zombie moans. The running zed's head exploded. Dark pieces splattered down in a red mist as the zombie fell over backwards, hitting the pavement not with a thump, but more of a squelch. I heard the steady *click-clack* of a bolt being drawn back, as Laurel prepped her rifle for another shot.

'I've seen flattened snails with more speed! Get a move on!' she yelled.

I pressed the bell button again, tried keeping it pressed, tried pressing it as many times as I could, but nobody was

160

answering. I took a step back, and aimed my pistol at it. Maybe it didn't only work in the movies.

Laurel fired her rifle again, another miniature crack of thunder, and yelled 'Runners are nearly here! What's taking so long?'

'This better work…' I muttered through gritted teeth, hearing the moans of the zombies growing louder.

I did not want to hear an "I told you so" from Neville.

Twenty

'Hello?' a voice crackled over the intercom. I lowered my gun.

'Hello! Yes! Can you hear me?' I yelled at the box, not seeing any obvious hold-to-talk button.

'Hear you? I can see you!' an excited male voice replied. I recognised it as the radio DJ. 'Come in, quick!'

The gates began to open, two sections coming apart in the middle, going at a fair speed but a lot slower than we needed. I ran through them, signalling over my back for Damian to follow. He narrowly squeezed through the gates without losing any paintwork but forcing a wing mirror back on its hinge. Immediately they started to close behind us.

Two of the runners made it through as the 4x4 drove past me, heading for the empty parking spaces - didn't look like the DJ drove to work. The runners let out something halfway between a moan and a scream, and steamed straight for me. My bat was in the 4x4 and there wasn't anywhere for me to turn and run to, so I planted my feet, took a deep breath, and raised my gun.

My shot took one in the neck. It was moving around so much and it was so fucking close that I didn't have time to line up the headshot. Still, it went down onto its back and I didn't have time to make sure it was dead. The second zombie was already on me.

It grabbed onto my arm with both hands and yanked me forwards, pulling me into him. I was more than happy to oblige; pushing off with my back foot and ramming it shoulder-first, as hard as I could.

Dead fingers couldn't find purchase on the leather of my jacket, its grip slipped, and I sent it flying to the ground, screaming and growling and already thrashing its way back onto its feet. I aimed my gun and fired. I'd forgotten to thumb the hammer back again.

As it clacked down into an empty chamber, I made a mental note to learn how to use a gun properly, let alone shoot it accurately. So I cocked the hammer with the heel of my palm, the cylinder revolving, and jammed the gun against its forehead before firing. Like a puppet with its strings cut, it crumpled to the ground.

A wave of heat came over me now the danger had passed, leaving my fingers tingling and my jacket feeling uncomfortably hot. I looked over at the 4x4 to see everyone else just getting out, looking over at me.

'Thanks for all your help there,' I said, taking a deep breath and glancing down at the two bodies. I'd planned on following that somewhat passive-aggressive statement up, but I got distracted.

The first one I'd shot was jerking around, twitching wildly, clenching and unclenching its fists and kicking its legs randomly. I leaned over it and saw I'd shot it right in the middle of the neck, probably lodged the bullet in the spine. I thumbed the hammer and finished it off. I'm not sadistic, but in hindsight I should have saved the ammo.

'I was trying to line a shot up, but you insisted in going toe-to-toe.' Neville frowned, unsure whether to be approving, or chide me for not running away.

'Nice work.' Laurel congratulated.

'Lucky is what I was.' I said, feeling my breath still coming quick after the adrenaline burst.

The glass front doors opened up, and a squat balding man in a lurid yellow floral shirt stood in the doorway, beaming from ear to ear. He didn't sound as smooth as he did on the radio.

'That was fantastic!' Carl Sachs, GCR Radio DJ grinned, 'The shots will have them crawling all over here, but…fantastic!'

'He should have seen us yesterday with the dogs…' Neville muttered under his breath.

'People, real, live people,' Sachs mused, walking closer to inspect us all, 'and with guns! You *must* be with the CDC? We

163

weren't expecting you for days – but hey, I'm not complaining.'

'We're not with de CDC,' Damian said, lifting his bat up onto his shoulder, definitely not a mercenary's weapon, 'seen, we thought you were in contact with them?'

As much as it was nice to see another person, if Carl Sachs wasn't in contact with the world beyond, this trip had been pretty pointless and I'd almost got eaten for nothing. So I was put off the man from the get-go.

'We were…' Carl said, 'Hopefully will be again. Look, why don't you come inside, have a drink or two?'

'We came because we thought you had contact with an evacuation group,' Neville said, 'not because we thought you were throwing a kegger.'

'I'll tell you everything, if you come inside.' Sachs said, looking at the fence, his face turning paler.

Zombies were starting to come up against the fence, putting their fingers in through the stiff wires or beating against them with their fists. The moaning was growing louder as more of them came into view around the houses. Now there were only about half a dozen, but if the moans were bringing in more of them, we could get stuck in here in no time.

'We're going to get trapped in here,' Laurel said, reading my mind and still holding her rifle ready, 'that fence looks tough but it won't keep a hundred of them out.'

'They've come before,' Sachs said, 'if you go inside and turn off the lights they go away when something else comes along.'

'What came along last time?' I asked.

'Someone started that burglar alarm. If we're lucky they'll go back to it if we-'

'If we go inside.' Neville said, giving me a longer look this time. I understood it.

This guy was way too keen on getting us to go in there with him, or so it seemed. That or he was just really scared of that fence coming down. Either way, we were keeping our

164

weapons to hand. This was our only lead on CDC evacuation, so we had to risk it.

I broke open the top of my pistol and shook out the last bullet into my hand, and then put the speedloader in just how Neville had told me. I clicked the weapon closed but didn't put the gun away, just left it out at my side and slipped the spare bullet into my pocket with the other speedloaders.

'We'll go inside then,' I said, 'looks like it's about to rain anyway.'

'Great! The girls are going to be so happy to know someone else is out there.' Sachs enthused.

We followed Sachs into the building, and when his back was turned I saw Neville quietly slip his pistol back out of its holster and hold it at his lower back. Laurel and Damian weren't giving any clues that they knew what me and Neville were doing, but I knew they weren't stupid.

Something was twigging my instincts again about Carl Sachs. Not in the same was as at Katy's house, or with the dogs, but something else. Sachs wasn't being forthcoming with any information, not outside anyway, and he seemed to want to get us in here rather badly.

'So how many are in your group?' Neville asked, as we walked through the darkened reception area, to a set of stairs behind the desk. Offices went off in both directions on the ground floor, the places I'd delivered to before.

'Eight. No there were eight. Six, in total.' Sachs corrected, 'Conrad and Pieter are out at the moment, so it's just me and the girls back here, holding up.'

'You got a lot of firepower?' Neville pressed, digging for information, probably trying to tell if Sachs was playing it straight with him by using his super-security-guard senses.

'Mary has her old shotgun, but the boys took their guns with them when they left. It's the fence that keeps the dead out.' Sachs said, sounding downright relieved now we were inside.

He led us up to the second floor, where we emerged into another dimly lit corridor, thanks to the skylights. To the left

165

were the toilets and a maintenance room, but we went right, past recording booths and private offices where frosted glass turned everything beyond into a blurry black shape. Neville eyed them warily.

Windows overlooked the car park and the gathering zeds at the gate, but I didn't stop to stare. We turned the corner in the L-shape, where there were more offices and closed doors further along the corridor, but we stopped at a door marked 'Meeting Room' in black etching, where candlelight flickered against the translucent glass.

Carl opened the door and I tried to take in as much information as I could, just in case something nefarious was about to happen. There were two women in the room, one with a double-barrelled shotgun on the table not far from her, and the other with no obvious weapons. The table was littered with tinned food, camping utensils and cooking equipment, except for between the two women, where a patch had been cleared for a card game.

'One missing.' Neville muttered to me as Carl walked ahead into the room, out of earshot.

Neville was right. If there were six of them all together, two away, and three in this room, there was still someone else here; waiting in the dark rooms, behind frosted glass. Waiting to catch us off guard…That, or they were in the bathroom.

'Everyone, this is Beth, one of our interns at GCR,' Sachs said, gesturing gracefully at the blonde woman of the pair.

She was dressed in a pencil skirt and smart white shirt with a suit jacket and fake-tan; standard office attire. Kinda strange at a time like this. She even had her hair and makeup done, but I guess some people are just like that, especially young girls with something to prove. She flashed us a look that was pretty hard to read. Somewhere between suspicion and relief.

'And this is Mary, who came to us just yesterday.' Sachs continued, gesturing at the other woman who was dressed as a polar opposite to Beth; worn dungarees and a red chequered shirt, with her straw-brown hair pulled back into a bun. She

166

was probably in her early fifties, with a tan from hours working in the sun, not sitting in a salon. She gave us a nod and put her cards down.

'Beth, Mary, this is…' Sachs said, opening the floor for us.

'Captain Kelly.' I said, stepping forward first, 'This is my team. Neville Roberts, Damian Grant and Laurel Daniels.'

Maybe if I gave the impression we meant business, whatever trouble Sachs had planned wouldn't go down, if he did have any planned at all. We could have just been paranoid.

'You're with the CDC?' Beth asked, sounding a little hopeful.

'No, ma'am.' Neville said, giving her a nod and not just taking my lead, but running a marathon with it. 'We're working with local law enforcement,' he said with a professional tone, 'here to see if the claims Mr Sachs made on the radio are true. Have you really been in contact with the CDC? Have you arranged evacuation?' – Local law enforcement he said. The Police? With my hair? They must have thought I was undercover in a garage band.

'Police? Wow.' Sachs said, genuinely without a trace of sarcasm, taking a seat at the head of the long table, 'Come in, sit down, help yourself to a refreshment – there must be something in this pile from the top shelf. Or can you not drink on duty?'

'We're on a tight schedule. Maybe next time, Mr Sachs.' I said, noticing how none of them answered Neville. 'We need to ascertain when the CDC is coming to evacuate your group.'

'Sit down, please, I'll tell you the story.' Sachs said, motioning to the seats, 'It won't take long.'

I gave everyone the nod, and we took up seats down the side of the table, across from the women, with me sat at the head, next to Sachs and closest to the door. I rested my gun on my knee, aimed roughly at his crotch, and I guessed Neville was next to me, aiming his gun at Mary, the one with the shotgun beside her.

'After the state of emergency was declared,' Sachs began, 'I stockpiled supplies up here, in the studio. It's safer than my

167

house and I have the broadcast tower here, still powered by the emergency generator. I figured I could do some good, keep everyone's spirits up until this all blew over.

'But after a while,' he swallowed, looking down at the table, 'I realised that this wasn't just a virus...I let someone in through the fence, hiding a bite. After they died, we put the body in one of the offices until we knew what to do,' he said, looking at Beth whose eyes were darting from us newcomers, to the door. Hmm.

'He came back... about an hour later, started banging on the door, wailing. Conrad had to put him down...carry the body outside of the fence.' He said, clearing his throat, 'But after that, the CDC contacted us through the relay, a unit commander for their task force. He said that they were evacuating the cities, setting up refugee centres, so we were to get as many people to come here as we could...

'But as you can see, there aren't many of us. Maybe some tried to get here and couldn't make it, or maybe just not that many people can hear the radio anymore. How did you hear it?' he added, excitedly.

'Our ATV.' Damian said, 'Precinct doesn't have any power.'

'Fantastic.' Sachs beamed, 'Perhaps more people have taken to their cars and heard about us.'

'Mr Sachs,' Neville interrupted, 'when we were outside you made it sound as if the CDC were no longer in contact with you. When is the last time you spoke to them?'

'Last night,' he replied, 'we're supposed to check in three times a day, seven in the morning, one in the afternoon, and ten at night. Since the War, all radio stations are required to maintain two-way towers for emergencies. Ours was outdated, we were waiting on replacement parts.'

'What do you need to get the receiver working again?' I asked, 'Maybe we have it.'

'They, Conrad and Pieter,' he stressed, 'are already out there, searching that hardware place near the new supermarket, they think they can bodge something together.

168

Kind of you to offer though, but I think what we really need now are numbers for safety.'

'When do you expect to have your communications back up?' Neville asked, ignoring his last comment.

'By check-in tonight.' He smiled, looking relieved.

'That's promising.' Neville said sternly, 'Let's hope you can get your receiver back.'

'You said there had been eight of you.' I pressed, 'You lose more to infection?'

'Eight. Yes, I mean, no,' Sachs faltered, nothing like as confident as his radio persona, 'one couple went out to get supplies, they live nearby and thought they could be back before long. We haven't seen them since…assumed the worst had happened.'

There was a moment of silence, as Sachs looked down at the table. Neville's expression was completely neutral, but I knew he'd be taking it all in.

'So Mr Sachs. Carl. I feel as though I need to ask,' Laurel said, breaking the silence and planting her finger down with a look at Sachs. 'Where's your sixth man?'

Twenty One

'Sixth man?' Sachs asked, smiling nervously, 'Did I say there were six of us? Oh I'm sorry, I meant five. There were six. That man Conrad had to kill, you see.'

Alarm bells started ringing in my head, and I thumbed the hammer back on my pistol. Neville had been adjusting his position in his chair, and stopped halfway through the motion, holding his breath.

'Shit, that de time?' Damian said, looking down at his wrist, where he wore nearly a dozen bangles but no watch, 'We got to be reporting into de lieutenant.'

'Right.' I said, standing up to my feet so quickly the chair wobbled precariously behind me. 'Mason will be pissed.'

'Leaving a-already?' Beth stuttered, leaning forward in her chair, her eyes flicking to the doorway again. Why weren't her eyes going to the shotgun?

'They'll be back.' Mary said, reaching across and putting a hand over Beth's, which seemed to calm her a little.

'Okay, alright, I understand, officers.' Sachs said, saying the word 'officers' a little louder than normal, like he was making allowances for the hard of hearing.

Sachs led us out of the building, I took a position walking next to him, while Neville brought up the rear, guns still out and at our sides – we didn't care if Sachs saw. Those alarms of mine didn't stop ringing until we were out of the building, and Carl was seeing us off.

While we were inside, the rain had started up at a steady pace, but it hadn't deterred the zombies one bit. Thirty or more were clustered around the fence on the side of the houses, but the mob was growing slowly, pressing up against the gate.

'Mind if I talk to you a moment, Mr Sachs?' Neville asked, keeping up his professional airs. He took Sachs off to one side, while the three of us waited by the 4x4.

'Somethin ain't right in there,' Damian said, before I could. 'Not just talking about keeping de numbers straight.'

'Eight guys. Six. Five…' Laurel nodded at him. 'Couldn't wait to get us in, lapped up the police cover, and with you two here, we ain't exactly convincing.'

'Must be desperate.' The big man said, his eyes flicking over to the fence, and the blocked gate. 'Speaking of desperate…'

Laurel seemed to know what to do. She trotted over to the gate, whistling like you might at a dog, and running the tip of her rifle over the fence with a metallic clicking sound. The zeds pressed themselves against the mesh fence with renewed interest, feverish moans taking on an edge of…anticipation.

'Gods, what's she doing?' Damian asked, glancing back and forth between us.

Clattering her rifle along the fence, she led the zombies away from the gate and around to the left side, splitting our undead audience between the left and right sides – but leaving the gate cleared.

'I know they not getting through any time soon,' Damian said to her, 'but what de hell was that?'

'They're thick as anything,' she said, defensive, 'give them bait and they'll go for it every time. About the smartest I've seen them get is knowing the difference between a door and a wall, but they can't seem to tell the gate from the rest of the fence.'

'So you're the zed whisperer?' I asked just as Neville and Carl Sachs started heading back our way.

'Come back soon, alright?' Sachs said, his voice wavering slightly. 'We'll be checking in tonight.'

'We've got to leave if you want us to come back.' Laurel said, not even trying to sound polite.

'Yes, of course. Safe travels!' Sachs said, closing the door to the building, and scurrying off behind the reception desk.

We climbed up into our ride. In the back, Neville kept his gun out, and despite the rain, Laurel wound her window most of the way down, leaning out to look at GCR.

171

'We even thinking of coming back here?' Damian asked, as he turned us around to face the gate.

'Something really isn't kosher in there.' Laurel said, eyes fixed on the windows of the building, 'He was giddy when we showed up, but kept his mouth shut until he had us inside. What did you two talk about?' Laurel added, glancing at Neville.

'I subtly asked him if there was a reason he felt he couldn't tell me anything. You know, the, "blink twice if you're being coerced" technique.' He replied.

'Result?' she asked, resting her rifle on the open window, pointed vaguely back towards the radio station.

'Inconclusive. His face screwed up, but he didn't say anything more about it. Or blink twice. I don't think we should come back here. The sixth man's in there, and he wasn't just shy. The way that girl's eyes were all over, way she couldn't sit still. Something was going on.'

'What your guess?' Damian asked, flicking his eyes up to the rear-view. The gates hasn't opened yet, and I could feel the tension rising.

'Could be they're there against their will.' Neville shrugged, 'Just a gut feeling, it's not like we've got hard evidence. Sachs couldn't remember how many were in his group, so either he's so badly frazzled he genuinely doesn't remember, or he's just using his best guess as to how many people are keeping him there.'

'They're our only link to evacuation.' I sighed, relieved as the gates began to open. 'I don't like it, but we'll have to go back. Tomorrow. When we have more guns.' I added, with a look over the seat to Neville.

'You admitting you were wrong about not needing guns for a simple recon job?' he asked.

'It got complicated.' I bit my tongue.

We'd gotten out of there unscathed and as far as I was concerned, that was a success. But I didn't like the thought of going back there unprepared. If what Neville said was true, there could be a handful of bad sorts hanging around that

172

place putting the pressure on DJ Sachs. In a city of Greenfield's size there were bound to be all kinds of crooks, and they'd want to get evacuated as much as anyone else.

Laurel wound her window up before Damian drove through the gates, only then did I realise she didn't have it aimed out for zombies. He gave the engine some gas and we clipped the first zed that tried to come through, sending it spinning onto the pavement.

It seemed they knew the difference between gate and fence when it started to open up, but the all-terrain battering ram ploughed on down the road, the zeds turning to follow us, coming away from the fence. Guess we were the new distraction.

I set my gun back into safety and manoeuvred it into my pocket as we took the same roads back the way we'd came. They were desolate this time, not a single zombie on them. Damian sped us back into the woods before settling to a safer speed.

'Pawnshop then?' he asked.

'Yeah. Let's get some guns.' I said, with a little smile.

Ownership of firearms wasn't exactly uncommon in Voison, but you couldn't find a gun store in every town. First, to own a gun you have to have completed your National Service, one or two years spent in the Republic's standing armed forces, the Territorials. Some people went career with it, but most people looking to stay in the military joined a private military company, better pay and training but higher risk – and if you believed their detractors, less scruples.

Your service papers let you apply for a firearms licence, but that's still not the end of it. After that you've got a written and practical competency test – repeated every five years - a thirty day administration period and once you've purchased a firearm you need to keep your address current on the census so an inspector can complete an annual safety check to make sure you're storing them correctly. Every six months, if you've got kids under sixteen at your address. Most people didn't bother.

173

We listened to GCR on the way back to the flats. A few songs played before Carl Sachs' voice came over the airwaves.

'Welcome back to the program,' he said, 'we hope you're all having a safe and infection-free day out there in sunny Greenfield. These next ones go out to a group of deputies who stopped by the station earlier today. Safe trails my friends, I hope you come back real soon.'

More zeds were making their way out of the centre and into the suburbs. We saw a few of them gathered around the base of a tree as we drove by central park, probably trying to get their hands on a cat or a squirrel that'd taken refuge there. I guess that explained how the dogs could get infected, just need enough zeds to corner them.

The clock on the dashboard spun on, getting on around one o'clock by the time we arrived back at the flats to pick up the stuff we needed for the B&E on the pawnshop. The rain was just about easing off too, but it was definitely getting colder as the day went on.

Damian and Laurel waited with the vehicle while me and Neville grabbed the stuff from Stan's place. I carried the folding ladder while Neville took the biggest power drill and a box of assorted attachments for un-screwing the bolts on the window bars.

As I was coming out with the ladder, Neville holding the door for me, I noticed Laurel and Damian standing outside, waving up at the apartments. Looking up as we came out with our tools, I could make out Morgan and Anita just a few storeys up, craning over the balcony.

'How's it going?' Neville asked.

'Plenty of food and water left behind,' Anita supplied, 'slim pickings on the medicine, unless you've all got killer headaches. Zero on weapons too – standard stuff, kitchen knives and screwdrivers, but nothing we don't have already.'

'More coolboxes and ice though,' Morgan added, 'so if our tinkerer can't fix the electrics, we'll at least have a couple days more chill-power.'

174

'You guys got to there from the top floor already?' I asked, surprised.

'Negative, we're going bottom to top, taking it careful.' Anita shouted back, 'Met one of the locals, but he didn't give me much trouble. Were your neighbours always so handsy?'

'Stay safe, okay?' Neville called up.

'You too Dad.' Morgan answered. The two of them disappeared from view.

A brief pang of guilt went through me, realising I'd asked Morgan and Anita to expose themselves to danger like that. I hadn't expected anybody from castle tower to be infected, much less lock themselves at home with it and pose us a danger.

I looked at Neville, one hand on his hip, the other on his chin. He wouldn't have wanted Morgan facing danger without being there, but in my defence, I arranged her an armed, professional escort. Still. I'd have felt better being there too. I hoped they wouldn't come across any more of our former neighbours.

'You good?' I asked him, expecting another argument.

'She's in good hands.' He nodded, and I took that as us being okay.

We got in. The ladder didn't quite fit, so Damian drove with the boot open while Neville leaned over the backseat, holding onto it. Laurel and I kept our eyes out of the windows, on opposite sides, but there wasn't a lot of shuffling foot traffic out here yet.

We pulled up at the curb again; two wheels up on the grass verge that separated the road form the plaza. Just as we were getting out, Laurel slid her rifle off her shoulder, frowning.

'Hey.' She called out, softly, so only we could hear. 'Everyone, off the road, up here.' She bent double as she went, and we all followed suit.

We didn't know what she'd heard, but there was an urgency in her voice that made us listen. Neville and I dragged the ladder out and ran with it, bent as Laurel had been, for all

175

the good it'd do us, carrying ten feet of ladder. Damian closed the boot and hurried after us.

Laurel got behind the broken fountain and knelt down, keeping her head low. We laid the ladder down flat, vertical to the road, so it couldn't be seen behind the fountain. We all crouched down, peering through the long weeds and spiky grass that'd grown up through the tiles. Someone must have tried turning it into a flower patch at some point, but that was a lost cause even before this started.

'Wha-?' Neville tried, but Laurel slapped him on the shoulder.

I heard it then, the sound of a throaty engine, definitely coming closer. The echo around the plaza made it hard to tell where it was coming from, but we didn't have to wait long to see. A shiny black SUV drove into sight, heading out of the city. Sat in the pickup-bed were four guys with sizable guns, two of them in camo-gear with matching tactical vests, two more in similar gear, but done up in black.

The SUV slowed down as it passed the plaza, the armed men taking a look at Damian's 4x4, scanning the shop fronts. One of them aimed their rifle in the plaza, something too big to be civilian-legal. I closed my eyes, as if he'd feel one less set of eyes on him.

Half-opening one a moment later, he was lowering the rifle. He couldn't see us for the weeds - and I'd signed a petition to get the fountain cleaned up a few weeks ago.

'See anything?' I heard a male voice ask.

'Nothing. Truck looks abandoned.' Another man replied.

'Looks in good nick, ATV, probably just needs a fill-up. We'll come back for it later.' The first voice said, before the engine growled a little louder, and the SUV pulled away, engine rumbling.

'No one's taking my ride.' Damian muttered as we all got back to our feet.

'Who were those guys?' Laurel asked.

'Fatigues, tactical vests...' Neville muttered, 'and some serious looking guns. Territorials maybe? Not all of them would have fallen in to protect Parliament. Or maybe some of the PMC guys.'

'Soldiers riding around in an SUV?' Damian asked, 'Stealing my ride?'

'Sound engineers robbing pawnshops for guns?' Neville replied smartly.

'Desperate times.' I nodded, 'If they are TA, we should still be out of here before they come back. We haven't heard anything about the TA besides that order to pull back to Orphen, and the Sydow Security guys we saw on the news all had their own trucks.'

'Lot of acronyms flying around these days,' Laurel said, mostly to herself, 'the country's FUBAR so the TA's CO makes sure Orphen's OK, meanwhile the CDC have PMCs setting up DMZs...'

'And here I am, stuck in the middle with you...' Neville smirked. She caught it, and gave an amused huff.

We got back to our feet, a little shiver running through me as the fear faded. I tried to brush it off, and clapped Damian on the back.

'Nobody's taking your truck. We'll get gone before they've got a chance to come back.' I said.

'You sure?' Damian asked, 'Going to take a while to get everything out of there.' He gestured at the co-op, its shutters drawn down.

'Between Morgan and the fuzz it sounds like we'll be all set for supplies, why bother?' Laurel asked.

'Perishables - if we don't eat them, they'll go to waste.' I suggested.

'Keeps us out of our tins for as long as possible.' Neville added. Good. We were back to agreeing with each other.

If this evacuation thing with the radio station was a bust, we were looking at a long-haul stay at castle tower. In that case, having a stocked grocery store right across the street was a miracle, and we'd need to strip everything from it we could - every crunchy granola bar, every bottle of overpriced mineral water. Enough food to last one person a month was only going

177

to be enough to get three people through ten days – and we numbered seven.

'Better safe, you know.' Damian said to Laurel, raising his eyebrows. 'If it don't pan out at de radio station, could be needing more gas for de stove, or we going to need to get a fire going to cook.'

'Thinking we take a trip out to a camping store?' Neville asked him, as I picked the ladder up from behind the fountain.

'I think it's a plan, for just-in-case.' He gave a sideways nod.

'If we have to go full-on survivor mode…' Laurel mused, trailing off, 'lot of places we could go. Stuff to get. Things we can do. Fortify the ground floor for starters, like we should've done at Perry's place.'

'Not a bad idea. We'll add it to the list.' I said.

We set the ladder up under the pawn shop's upper-storey window, Neville footing me while I climbed. Being a step-ladder rather than one with rungs, I was able to use the topmost step to look through the drillbits, picking out and arranging the likely looking ones.

It still took me a couple of tries to find the right size drillbit to go around the heavy-duty bolts, and even when I did find it, the paintwork over the bars had so many layers that the drill groaned for a second before it actually started to unscrew them.

I started on the centre bar, and by the time I'd unscrewed two of the damn things, dropping them down to the side of the ladder, my arms were getting pretty tired of holding the massive drill, having to reach up to get the bolts at the top. But I soldiered on until four of the bars were out, just enough for me to squeeze through. I'd saved the last bar to smash the window out with.

Taking a firm grip on one of the remaining bars with my left hand, I raised the bar over my head with my right, bringing it down with as much force as I could.

There's a peculiar thing that runs through your mind, or at least some people's minds, when they're about to

178

deliberately break something. It's a moment's hesitation, dating back to childhood. Once you've broken this, you won't be able to fix it. It's going to be loud. And you might get in trouble.

Bung.

As it turned out, the window was made of sterner stuff than I'd thought. I almost lost my balance, hugging up against the bars as the ladder wobbled slightly before Neville stopped it. Just a second later, my ears popped as the dog we'd not-heard earlier threw itself against the window. My heart skipped a beat as I flinched back, almost letting go of the bars before I realised if I couldn't smash the window with a metal bar, a dog wasn't going to bite through it.

I couldn't see it through the drawn curtains, but a beige coloured lump banged up against the glass again, my hearing fading in and out of white noise as it silently snarled and howled at me.

'Window's like, toughened glass or something.' I said down to Neville, 'We got anything heavier than this?'

'Could shoot it out?' he suggested.

Laurel took the hammer out of her belt-loop, and offered it up to me. 'Save the gunshots for a last resort.'

I threw the metal bar away, where it clattered to the cracked concrete, and accepted the hammer from Laurel. It had a bit more heft to it than the bar did. I noticed Damian concealing the bars and bolts in the overgrown fountain, hiding the evidence in case those guys in the SUV came back and saw something amiss.

Again, I pushed through the urge to hesitate, swinging the blunt head hard against the glass. A tiny spiderweb of cracks spread out about for a foot on the window.

'Give it beans, you big girl!' Laurel encouraged, almost laughing.

I chuckled, swinging the hammer again, three more times. With the last swing it cracked through the window, expanding the crackling web across the whole pane. When I pulled the hammer back out, it took a big sliver of the glass

179

with it, and the rest of the window began to collapse, falling like sharp snow onto the pavement in front of the shop. I looked down to see Neville still bracing the ladder with his feet, but he'd thought ahead, and already put his hood up to avoid the falling glass.

The rapid rustle and crack of moving fabric snapped my attention back to the window, where the outline of a gaping maw, complete with teeth, was straining up against the curtains. Canine spittle marked the cheap fabric. Thrashing it's head this way and that, snapping its jaws shut, it was actually managing to tear through the thin material, reducing it to sodden rags as it tried to get at its next meal.

Twenty Two

Reflex took over, and I lashed out with the hammer, cracking the dog right on the nose. There'd have been a howl or a whimper if it were a normal dog, but all I heard was a thump as it fell to the floor on the other side of the window.

I hooked the hammer around one of the bars and took out my gun, cocking the hammer back and taking a deep breath before using my other hand to lift up the curtain.

The room beyond was sparse, but clearly lived in. Bland green wallpaper, inoffensive worn red carpeting, the bed was unmade and clothes were spilling out of a wardrobe that had probably been put together out of a flat-pack. A desk with a home-computer sat across from the bed, the only thing that stopped the bedroom from looking like a cheap hotel room.

That and the shining-eyed Rottweiler struggling to get to its feet. Blood dripped from its muzzle where it was missing a tooth. I aimed, fired, and watched the dog collapse to the carpet, a pool of blood rapidly spreading from the hole in its chest, giving the faded carpet back its colour. The smell of gunsmoke tickled my nostrils, but underneath it was the unmistakable scent of the dog's, you know, business, which it must have been doing somewhere in the room.

'Is it dead?' Laurel asked.

'Yeah.' I said, taking the hammer and passing it back down to her. 'How loud was the shot?'

'Muffled,' Neville replied, 'still loud, but probably enough time, distance and drapes between those guys in the SUV and us.'

'Still,' Laurel hummed, 'I'm going to head over to the corner, keep an eye out.'

'I'll open the door from the inside, give me two minutes.'

I used the barrel of my gun to clear the glass from the top and bottom of the window, before stowing it away and grabbing a hold of the bars on either side of the gap. I started

181

climbing through the window, caught my leg on the sill, and fell forward onto the bed.

'Smooth.' I said, getting to my feet and brushing off the dog hair.

Revolver back out, I stepped out of the pungent bedroom onto a landing with two other doors and a set of stairs leading down to the right. The door to the left was open, looking into a tiny bathroom with an absolutely foul looking shower, hadn't been cleaned in years. The door to the right was closed, but there were no doggy-claw marks on the door, so I didn't think anyone would be hiding out in there.

Carefully, I turned the handle and pushed the door open, taking a step back and aiming my gun. Nothing moved in the room beyond, a living room with a tiny kitchenette shoved in the back corner. I walked inside, weapon still ready, aiming it around the room like an enthusiastic rookie on a police TV show. The pawnshop owner, or maybe that kid he'd had minding the store, they could be around here somewhere.

Two mismatched sofas faced a mammoth widescreen – one sofa ancient, in orange and brown stripes, the other modern, all leather. Next to the TV were three games consoles, two of them just different models of the same, and just like everything else in the room – from the odd bookshelves to the mismatched weightlifting bars – they had little white tags on them, marking them for resale.

'Looks like he lives with whatever his customers sell him.' I thought to myself, looking closer at the books and seeing an entire shelf devoted to the same tacky bestseller from a few years back. The white tags did not read for a lot of shillings.

I gave the place a quick once-over for weapons, pulling out the drawers of a mahogany desk and lifting up the shutter on an antique bureau, not finding anything bigger than a letter opener. Nothing in the kitchen either – like Anita had said, it was all knives and screwdrivers, nothing major. Unless he'd already sold them on, I figured the guns would all be downstairs.

182

So I left the living-kitchen-come-storeroom and took to the stairs. There was door at the bottom, meant to separate the residential from the commercial, but it was left open. I emerged into the shop proper, a fairly large room with waist-high display cases along the walls, various stands and shelves arranged in the middle, and a glass-topped counter to the right of the stairs.

I didn't register any of the items on display, was just checking for danger first. That's when I saw a cupboard just behind the counter, built under the stairs. There were scratches on the door. Claw marks from the ghost dog. Someone might have been alive in that cupboard.

Can you imagine it? Trapped in a cupboard under the stairs, sitting for hours or days in the dark, with no toilet, no food and no water? As I got closer, I caught it, the smell coming out of the cupboard was foul, and so I figured I'd help the poor guy out. Least I could do after I'd smashed his bedroom window in.

Amateur hour, top to bottom.

'Hey!' I called out, opening the cupboard door, 'It's safe now, the-shit!'

A rancid figure lurched out of the dark, baring broken bloodied teeth in an animal gesture of hunger. The store owner. I tried to block its reaching hands with mine, pushing them out of the way and trying to shove it back into the cupboard.

But I failed, shoved it back into the side of the doorframe, dropping my gun in the process. It lurched forwards again, mouth hanging open, grabbing onto my shoulders and pushing me back into the counter. A shock of fear shot through my mind and I saw myself being pinned down to the counter while the zombie ripped my throat out. It pushed me further over the counter, bending my back and leaning in to bite.

Terrified adrenaline kicked in once more. I shoved the zombie's shoulders with all my strength, throwing it to the side, but it gripped so tightly onto my jacket that I had to roll with it. I ended up on top, pinning it to the counter now, our

183

positions reversed. I grabbed the front of its shirt and tried to slam its head against the glass.

It was too strong. They aren't limited by muscle pains or human endurance. It's like they use the full muscle power of their body, all the time. It started to pull me closer, while I struggled to push away, keeping my hands pressing down on its collar bone, away from its mouth.

'Fuck you!' I yelled, suddenly reversing tactics, pulling the thing up instead of pushing against it.

That gave it what it wanted and then some, letting its own strength carry it past me and into the side-on position of the open cupboard door, where the impact of the blow shook its grip loose of my jacket.

I didn't want to get tied down into another hand-to-hand with it. I knew I'd gotten lucky again. So I vaulted over the display, catching a glimpse of what was inside it: the guns.

But they were there, unloaded, behind glass and locks, and I was standing there like a dick while the zombie staggered around the side. Seeing so many of them out on the roads you kinda think they're slow movers, but when you're stuck with one in an enclosed space, your biggest advantage, your speed, doesn't mean a whole lot.

I ran further into the shop, hearing my heartbeat pounding in my ears, and cast a look at the door. There were way too many locks and chains on that damn thing for me to get them all undone. Not before the zombie got to me. So I had to find something in the shop to club it to death with.

I felt like that bald guy in that pulp action movie, he's in the pawnshop, picks up the baseball bat, then the chainsaw and then the… other thing. It was like my prayers had been answered. I looked at one of the display cases at the right side of the room, just in the corner by the window displays.

A fucking collection of swords.

I knew that I couldn't break the glass upstairs without a hammer, but this probably wasn't security glazing and I was not thinking clearly. If I was, I'd have never thought I could get away with it.

184

But I ran over to the display case and ploughed my elbow down into it as hard as I could, shattering the glass in one blow and probably inviting a hell of a bruise in the process, but at the time, I couldn't feel anything but the pounding of blood in my ears. I cast a look over my shoulder and saw the zombie coming for me, knocking over a display stand half-full of sunglasses and reaching out with both arms, that empty moan coming from its cracked lips.

I grasped the handle of the closest weapon, short-bladed, heavy, and pulled it over the hooks that kept it on display. I didn't count on it also being secured to the case with plastic cable – it let me get the sword two or three feet out of its moorings before snapping to full extension. Well, shit.

I dropped it, ducked under the zed's arms and ran back into the shop, towards the counter. If it had to lurch around it again, I'd have time to pick up my gun and fire. But it was really hauling ass after me. I made it to the counter, glanced back as I swung my leg over, and saw it pulling itself along, grabbing the shelves and pumping its legs, every step nearly falling down. I was glad the pawn shop owner wasn't one of the fitness freaks we'd seen, but the bastard worked out, if those pawned weights upstairs were any indication.

I got on my hands and knees and looked around for my gun, but I couldn't see it anywhere. It'd probably gotten kicked into the cupboard in the fight, and there was so much junk in there I didn't want to get trapped looking for it. I looked at the back of the counter, and saw nothing but locks between me and the guns inside – which were still going to be unloaded anyway. Damn, damn, damn...

The zombie reached over the counter and grabbed me by the curls, dead hands getting a grip on my nice clean hair. Pain and fear froze me for a moment as the zombie pulled, hauling itself onto the counter and pulling me closer. Fuck!

I grabbed its wrists, my hands making contact with the cold, clammy skin of the dead. I gagged and choked as I tried to stop its hands from pulling – not shoving it away like I should have, because that'd have hurt like hell. It pulled itself

185

over the counter and fell on top of me, letting out another moan, right by my fucking ear.

I tried to push it away, but all I succeeded in doing was putting my arm in its mouth – covered by the tough leather there was no way it was getting through, but it was only a matter of time until something happened. It'd just wrestle me until the adrenaline faded, or it'd pull its mouth free and go for the exposed skin on my wrist.

'Holy shit. This is it. I am going to die.'

My brain failed me. I couldn't think.

I'd forgotten I had friends.

The claw-side of a hammer cracked into the back of the zombie's head, and its grip on my hair slacked as someone hauled the zombie off me, using the lodged hammer as a handle.

I looked up at the ceiling for a moment while my heart thudded in my throat, my vision narrowing on a patch of ceiling. Laurel's face filled the tunnel, and I felt myself cough out a laugh, while tears welled up in my eyes. I felt cold, hot, sick, tired, buzzed, all at the same time. I could barely breathe past the pace of my pulse and all I could think of was how close that zombie's mouth had been to my ear, the smell of its decayed breath as it moaned.

Laurel knelt down and pulled me into her lap, wrapping her arms around me and smoothing my hair down. She put her chin on my shoulder and started whispering.

'It's okay, you're okay now, everything's fine, it's dead, you're alive, you're fine…' she kept saying, over and over until I had the energy to reach up and touch her hand.

'I'm good.' I said, my voice coming out rough. 'I'm good.' I said again, giving her hand a squeeze.

'Are you…did it…?' she tried, her voice wavering.

'No, it didn't bite me.' I coughed, putting more force into my voice. 'Nearly. Nearly got me there, but…' I cleared my throat, and used the counter to pull myself up to my feet. 'You saved me. You saved my life.' I mumbled, feeling a hot tear

186

streak for my chin. It tickled, and I wiped it away with an irritated grunt. 'Really thought I'd had it there.'

'Just need good friends at your back.' Laurel smiled weakly. I saw her eyes were shining, wet, just on the verge of tears herself.

I clasped my arms around her shoulders, and she slid her's around my waist, locking her fingers and pulling me closer. Neville came down the stairs a moment later, and almost tripped over the body of the zombie.

'Whoa, can't just leave this stuff lying around,' he tutted, 'could hurt someone.' He added, putting his foot on the zombie's head to brace it while he pulled the hammer out with a wet crunch and a sneer of disgust.

He saw us both hugging, me holding onto Laurel like she was the last piece of dry land in the ocean.

'What happened?' he asked, his voice growing serious.

'Shit.' Laurel said, breaking the hug and turning around, 'Shit happened. We should never have let him go in alone.' She shot, before striding off to unlock the front door.

Neville looked me up and down, searching for a bite mark, most likely. 'Are you okay?'

'Peachy.' I replied, running a hand through my hair. I could still feel its clammy hands on me. 'How did you know to come in?'

'Screaming, breaking glass, zombie moans.' Neville said, not even trying to act casual, like usual. 'What's the matter? You too busy to yell for help?' he said quietly, his voice taking on a definite edge.

I sighed, and sat down on the counter, holding my head.

'Wasn't thinking straight.' I muttered, 'Almost forgot you guys were outside until I heard Laurel running down the stairs.'

'Buddy system, I told you yesterday.' Neville said, his tone plainly accusing me now, quite rightly, of being an idiot. 'Nobody's going anywhere alone from now on, okay? Always pairs or more.'

187

'Alright man,' I said, holding up a hand in surrender, 'it's my fault. Just…don't go on about it. Didn't we come here to do something?' I asked.

'Yeah,' he sighed, shaking his head and looking down for a second, 'yeah. We'd better hurry up. No telling when those guys will be back for Damian's ride.'

'Not gonna happen.' Damian said, appearing in the doorway. 'You good?'

'I'm fine, quit asking.' I said, taking a deep breath, trying to live up to those words.

I found my gun in the cupboard under the stairs, while Neville searched the body for the keys to the cabinets and display cases. Laurel and Damian were supposed to be browsing the selection, but Laurel's eyes were on me more than the shelves.

Most of the pawnshop's stock was the kind of stuff you'd expect. Old boomboxes, game consoles, a few bits of signed sporting memorabilia, TVs, DVD players, even one or two home-computer towers.

But hell yes, there were a few things there we could use. Having been getting by with baseball bats and a pair of pistols, we finally had a chance to add a little extra firepower to our group. But to my absolute horror, the sword wasn't real.

It looked like a nice sword too. Not showy, not fancy, not like an action-hero's oversized crotch-extension, just a functional straight-up sword. As it turned out, it was a "battle-ready" replica – they all were. Heavy pieces of steel that'd nick their edges in one or two hits, if the blade didn't slide out of its fixings first. I'd have liked a sword. It'd have made me feel better, especially after nearly dying.

Nevertheless. We did find a few things we could use. Once we had the key to the display cases, Neville grabbed a few plastic bags and started shopping. There wasn't too much, this wasn't a gun-store, but there were enough new toys to make nearly getting eaten worthwhile.

188

Twenty Three

'M1943.' Neville said, bagging up an old magazine-loading handgun I'd seen countless times in movies or games. 'Solid gun. Plenty of soldiers use an updated version, chambered for the same ammo, so we've got half a chance of finding more. Spare magazine, and a holster too.'

'Who's getting that one?' Laurel asked.

'We'll divvy them up when we get back to the flats,' I said, 'I don't want to be around when those guys in the SUV come back.'

The next pistol in the bag was a lot smaller than the M19, shorter barrel, shorter grip, like it was intended for a smaller hand or concealed carry. The M19 looked its age with all that faded brushed steel, but so did this, with modern plastics and carbon fibre. It too had a spare magazine and a belt-clipping holster. With all of the holsters flying around, I was starting to feel a little jealous.

'Seg 357. Some police prefer these to the nine-mills that Anita and I have,' Neville said, 'more shots in a magazine, lighter, more modern. But I'm of the school of thought that people are going to make less trouble around a bigger gun, so I'm not sold.'

The third pistol was a revolver, the bigger, more badassed cousin to Edgar's old Tetley. If people were willing to misbehave around smaller guns, then this was a real peacemaker. Polished steel and a dark wooden handle matched rather nicely with the shoulder-rigging holster it came with.

'Problem with this Cobra, no speedloader here.' Neville said, dropping the ammo box into the bag and throwing it to me. 'Box feels a little light too, but we'll do a proper count when we get back. I don't want to be here too long either.'

That was it for handguns, but while Neville was doing his shopping, Damian was at the other end of the store doing his. He had a long shotgun strapped over one shoulder and a sheathed blade as long as my forearm in his hand.

'Me Uncle Robb has one of these on de farm.' He said, tilting his head back to the shotgun, 'You mind if I keep this one?'

'You ever fired a shotgun before?' Neville asked.

'He took me hunting once,' Damian smiled, 'didn't get anything, so we shot bottles instead.' He smiled, a happy memory. A man his size probably wouldn't have much of a problem handling the recoil from a shotgun.

'What's that?' I asked, pointing at the sheath in his hand.

'From the War, I think. Matches your gun.' He said, passing it to me. It was bloody heavy; and the sheath was all metal, more of a case with straps and buckles.

'And it's not even my birthday.' I said, pulling out the bayonet and grinning at Damian, 'I'll almost-die more often if you get me more stuff like this.'

Most people, people who don't watch a lot of history documentaries, think bayonets were just for the end of guns. Before they started manufacturing specialised trench-knives, the bayonet filled that function, with a lot of them never seeing use under a rifle barrel. I fastened the sheath to my belt; where it carried a reassuring weight. I'd never get caught without protection again.

'Saw you were upset at de state of de swords.' Damian said, 'Now unless we got anything else, we got to be going. Lucile's going to need de diesel, and if we going to be doing much more driving, my ride could do with a top up.'

We still had the co-op to loot for food, but if our SUV friends would be making another appearance, that could wait until tonight, or tomorrow – we risked losing the food I guess, but we had to, they had too much firepower to argue over it. Neville grabbed the guns, Damian wedged his shotgun by the driver's seat and we piled into his ride once more.

'Any ideas where we could find some gas then?' Laurel asked, 'I'm betting silvers to sandwiches every gas station in

190

the city will be tapped – and do pumps even work without power?'

'If we could steal an oil tanker we'd have all the gas we'd ever need.' Neville hummed, as Damian got the engine running.

'Are you actually suggesting that?' Laurel snorted. 'Where would we find one? A truck stop? I don't know if you heard last night, but the motorways are a little bit fucked.'

'Children.' Damian said, flicking his eyes to the rear-view mirror as he pulled away from the curb.

'Head to the garage, Smith Casey's,' I said, 'we'll get a hand-pump. Plenty of cars and vans blocking up the roads, and even if someone's already thought to tap them, I'm betting they're not all dry. Except for those soldiers we haven't had to share the road with anyone.'

'Sounds like a plan.' Neville said, unfazed by Laurel's teasing. 'You know where Smith Casey's is?' he asked Damian.

The big man nodded, and drove off past the flats, into suburbia again, and on towards Hillside. Most of the houses out near us weren't modern by any standards. Pebble-dash exteriors for the most part – a neighbourhood where the windows might get smashed but the lawn will always be trimmed.

Smith Casey's wasn't far. Maybe fifteen minutes on clear roads; which, since this road wasn't on a main route, we had. It took a steep climb uphill at the side of a park, the kind of place fun-fares set up in the summer months, and when the road got level again we were there; quick as a flash. No messing about with roadblocks, taking detours or anything…Yeah, I should have probably realised that meant something else was going to go wrong.

Smith Casey's was a squat little place with a big gas station-style shelter out front that was a little taller than the building itself. But instead of there being actual gasoline pumps, there were supply cupboards and coiled hoses for valeting cars. At the back left of the forecourt was a rolling metal door way bigger than you'd find on anyone's house garage, with an ordinary, person-sized door cut into it. I knew that the pokey office was through another door on the right side of the building, behind a truck that was up on blocks.

Damian leaned over the steering wheel to peer through the windscreen. As we pulled onto the forecourt, I saw it too – a man, walking across the concrete with a bit of a bustle in his step. More people, live people. My heart raced faster as I wound my window down to call out to him.

However, as the rumble of our engine caught his attention, he spun around to face us. There was a mass of chewed flesh and missing pieces, where his throat should be. I thought I even saw the grizzly tube of his windpipe, but it was too much, I had to look away from this one. I felt my breath stick in my throat as I fought to wind the window back up.

'Damn, he almost looked alive.' Damian muttered, hand going to his shotgun, even though he hadn't loaded it yet, the shells still in his pocket.

The zombie's jaw dropped open as it raised its head to the sky, letting rip this primal, animal scream that bounced around the sheltered forecourt. That wasn't the kind of moan we'd been hearing earlier, this was something else. I pulled out my pistol, broke the top open and checked the chambers. Five shots loaded.

'Wasn't limping as much as the others, not running at us either, but it is definitely not alive – not human.'

It started to stride towards us, a little faster than walking pace, but not breaking out into the sprint that we'd seen some of them do. Its eyes were fixed on us.

Damian urged us forwards again and turned off to the left, like he was manoeuvring for a naval broadside. With the volume it put into that scream, I wasn't going to risk attracting more of them by firing off rounds here; but the zombie still needed taking care of.

I opened the door at the same as Neville, the sound of it echoing around the forecourt, along with the thuds of us dropping to the concrete. I pulled my bat out of the front seat and reached over to get Damian's too. I tossed it over to Neville, who gave me a quick nod – "you first."

I didn't feel the same adrenaline I'd felt the first time I'd squared off against a zombie, back in Greenside with Lucile. Maybe because I'd seen a lot more of them now, gotten used to the idea that the dead were up and walking. I guess people can adapt to just about anything.

The zombie hissed at us, *hissed* - like a freaking snake, and took three blindingly quick steps forwards, moving faster than I was anticipating. I stepped forwards to meet it with the bat raised to my shoulder, and turned into the swing like a pro.

I hit it out of the park.

My bat crunched into the side of the zombie's head, sending tremors of force up my arms. It spun to the ground, its hiss abruptly cut short. Neville looked down at it with the cricket bat raised above his head for the coup de grace, but the zed didn't move again. He lowered the bat.

'We're getting good at this.' He commented, working a crick out of his neck. Damian brought the 4x4 around, parking it in the centre of the shelter.

'They still moving out of de centre,' he said, bleeping his ride locked after they had gotten out, 'going where de food is. We're in the DMZ now.'

'Demilitarized zone?' Laurel asked.

'Deadmen zone.' Neville supplied, his voice taking on a dark humour.

Nobody said anything. We looked down at the body of the screamer, and I wondered what other twists in the virus we'd end up seeing. It was the uncertainty, back then. It was scarier than the zombies themselves; not knowing if we were going to get mobbed by stray dogs, charged by runners from side alleys, screamed at, moaned at or wailed at. Neville had been right earlier. We had needed these guns from the get-go.

'Come on then.' I said after the lengthy pause. 'Let's get what we came here for and get the hell out before the rest of them show up.'

193

Everyone kept a few paces behind me while I walked to see if the garage door was unlocked. Damian was spinning his cricket bat between his hands; Neville had his nine-mill out, trained at the ground, while Laurel was resting her rifle against her shoulder, all casual like.

Sticking my bat under my arm, I tried the round handle on the small door, and was relieved when it actually opened. I let out a grunt of frustration when the chain-lock stopped it from opening more than a few inches. I thought I heard something move around inside, a scuffing, scuttling sound, but I guessed it was just the rattling of the chain lock. If there's one major lesson I'll take away from the early days, it's always to trust your first guess.

'Come on, let's try the other door.' Neville said, leading us back to the other end of the building.

There weren't many windows to Smith Casey's on the garage side, but the offices had some nasty old shutter-shaded windows. I'd been inside before, so I knew they had skylights in the garage, but it still always seemed such a dingy, dusty place, even with the lights on.

I'd done a little stint as an apprentice in a place like Smith Casey's, back in Dent, just after I'd left high school, and while I was still doing a few days of college. I didn't have grades enough to stick around for much higher education after I'd be done there, so I'd gone with the best of both worlds - edge my bets with study and some practical job experience. Plus, earned some pub money.

That being more than ten years back, what I'd forgotten about automotive engineering could probably have filled a book or two. Change a tyre, swap doors and bumpers, replace windows and windshields, I could probably still manage that without too much swearing - but don't come see me if you need your suspension replacing. I never finished the apprenticeship but some basic vehicular knowledge helped me get my gig at National Mail.

The office door was made from ancient, greening wood, and Neville broke it open with just one stern kick, leading the

194

way into the room beyond gun first, sweeping the corners and checking the lines, or whatever gun-people do. Laurel snorted and glanced over her shoulder at me, rolling her eyes. I flashed her a smile and a shrug.

'Boys will be boys…' she chuckled, while Neville went out of earshot. I looked behind us, the back of my neck starting to itch.

The office was a tiny room, a little sliver cut from the side of the building. Just after the door was an old leather sofa on the right, and an equally antique front desk a little further in. Passed that were a couple of other desks stacked high with paperwork, except for one that had a computer setup. It kinda reminded me of the offices in the back of the post office warehouse, and it even had that "burned coffee and stale pastry" smell.

For a moment I wondered about Gladys, my boss. Did she get her kids out of the city? Or did she get caught up in that whole checkpoint mess? I shook my head. Nothing I could do about it, either way. But I hoped she got out okay.

I looked at the side of the front door as I brought up the rear, admiring Neville's professional handiwork with the breaking and entering. That's when I saw that it hadn't even been locked. That raised an eyebrow.

'Hey.' I muttered, keeping my voice as low as I could but still trying to reach Neville, who was almost at the other end of the room, at the door to the workshop area. 'Hey.' I repeated, a little louder. 'Door was unlocked. We might not be alone.'

'I kicked the door in. Too late to be quiet.' He said, still dropping his voice a little. 'Come over here, cover me.'

I squeezed between Laurel, Damian and the desks and stood at one side of the grease-smudged door that led into the garage, while Neville took up the other side. The door had the same yellowing shutter-shades as the front windows, so he put his fingers between them and sneaked a peek through into the room beyond.

All I could see was gloom, much like in the office. The rain may have stopped but the sky wasn't exactly bright so the skylights weren't doing much, and without power all the switches would be useless.

'We need to start carrying torches.' Laurel said to herself, checking her rifle, 'Maybe I can tape one onto here…'

We took a minute, nobody wanting to make the first move, just letting our eyes adjust as we stared through the shades into the inky dark. There was something almost religious about the shafts of soft light coming down into the blackness.

'Alright,' Neville said, 'I can't see anything moving. I'm going in. Watch my back.'

'Roger. Or you know, whatever.' I nodded, leaning my bat against the wall so I could take a two-handed grip on my gun.

Neville opened the door and stepped through it, raising his gun. That's when the screaming started.

Twenty Four

My ears gave a painful protest to the noise, almost enough for me to think the place was full of ghost dogs, but when the light started pouring in from the other end of the garage, I realised that the door was rolling up. It jerked and jolted, moving up only a few inches at a time while we watched.

'You won't take me!' a man's voice shrieked; hysterical.

'After him!' Neville shouted, as the man ducked under the partially-hoisted garage door. It must have been a security thing – someone runs, you chase them.

We sprinted across the room, but Neville caught his foot on something in the dark, and slammed shoulder-first into the side of the hydraulic car lifter, which had only been a vague shape a moment earlier. He grunted in pain, but waved his arm, signalling for me to keep running.

I did, kicking a toolbox and sending the contents scattering into the light as I neared the door. I ducked under, all agile and flexible, barely breaking my stride, but skidded to a dead stop as I emerged squinting into the light again.

'Fuck!' I spat, backing up and bending down again.

The man, a completely dishevelled looking guy in a shirt and tie, was being held by four or five zombies, as they grabbed and pulled at his clothes, shirt buttons ripping, and the sleeves of his business jacket tearing from the shoulders.

He screamed, yelled, but there was nothing I could do. His hair was slick with sweat already, and his face had taken on a similar sickly pale to Danielle's. He was infected already – 'You won't take me.' he panted. Delirious, he thought they were still rounding up the infected. I hoped for his sake that meant he wouldn't feel what surely came next.

With our 4x4 and our guns, he must have thought we were CDC, bolted because he thought we'd come to cart him away. Gods only know what he thought of the cricket bat.

197

I ducked under the rolling door and back into the gloom, almost hitting Neville as I swung my head back up.

'What're you doing?' he yelled, 'He's getting away!'

The man in the tie screamed; the hairs on the back of my neck pricking up while my spine filled with ice water. He screamed high, absolute terror, and then suddenly he was cut off.

'Oh fuck...' Neville slowly swore, stepping away from the door. 'How many?'

I squatted down to get a look – I'd only seen a few of them clutching him, but there were a lot more than that on the forecourt, and they were all heading for the group that'd snagged the infected accountant.

Damian and Laurel jogged over to us from the office, looking worried.

'We heard a scream, what happened?' Laurel asked.

'Zombies outside, a dozen, maybe more.' I said, keeping my voice low, getting away from the light cast from the rolling door. 'I think they saw me, we can't get to the truck.'

'What do we do?' Neville asked me. I felt the subtle press of eyes on me, and gave a look to Damian.

'I don't want to leave it here, but if we get trapped...'

'We can't leave without it.' Damian said, 'if we can't get away from them quick enough, they follow us right back to de Tower anyway.'

'So we fight?' Laurel asked, checking her gun yet again and patting her belt to make sure her hammer was still there.

'I'm not seeing another option.' I told her, 'But we do this smart. Hold up in the front office, you and me up front, you two at the rear. Really wishing we'd sorted out those new guns about now...'

'Alright, this time it's my bad.' Neville accepted, putting his palms up.

Laurel swung into action, leading the way into the office with Neville and Damian bringing up the rear, as ordered. Neville shut the door behind him, and helped Damian shove

198

one of the desks in front of it, a pot of pencils falling over and knocking hidden shavings onto the desk.

'The door opens the other way!' Neville panicked, laughing nervously.

'Still better than nothing!' Damian shot back, casting a look to the front door – which Neville had kicked in earlier.

'Real good job there with the front door, rentacop!' Laurel snapped over her shoulder.

'What do you want to hear? I'm sorry?' Neville yelled.

'It'd be a bloody start!' she replied.

The door had gotten stuck against a wrinkle in the carpet, and a quick tug wasn't enough to loosen it, so Laurel helped me shove the leather sofa across the doorway. Like Damian said, it was still something. He strode across the room and handed me my bat over the reception desk. I set it down against the sofa.

'You really think this is the time?' I shouted over the both of them. I'd planned on going out there to draw the zombies towards us, but with all this yelling I'd bet they were already on their way.

'If that drongo didn't smash the door in we wouldn't be shouting, would we?' she snarled, turning her anger on me for a second. She sniffed hard, rolled her shoulders and gave me an apologetic look.

'You done?' I asked.

'I'm done.' Laurel nodded.

'Me too.' Neville chimed.

Laurel was about to throw some choice words at the man, but before she had a chance, one of the runners was in the doorway. The sofa was high-backed, but it used the sides of the door to hoist itself high enough to get a foot on the sofa. Whatever insult Laurel was about to hurl transformed into a fierce grunt, as she struck the thing on the nose with the butt of her rifle.

There was the crack of a breaking nose, and the thing dropped off the back of the sofa – just in time for another zombie to line up in the doorway, its face smeared with fresh

199

blood, it's teeth bared; still flecked with meat and gore from that poor man. This one wasn't as fast as the last; she was a slow one, a shambler. It gave me time to pick up my bat and turn the upward momentum into a clumsy swing.

Outside, I could hear them moaning, getting closer, more excited. I'd like to say that's what distracted me, caused me to rush my swing. I hadn't held the bat properly; just catching it on the chin, without enough force to break anything. My grip slipped and it clattered to the floor. I didn't have time to search for it, because the next one was already reaching over the sofa, and more were starting to pile up behind it. The sofa slid an inch across the carpet as the press of zombies shoved forwards, hands reaching out to us.

I dropped to the floor, as low as I could, and braced my shoulder against the leather, boot on the carpet, trying to stay away from those reaching hands, not wanting to get myself into that situation again, but not wanting to lose this barricade either. If I could hold it, Laurel could shoot.

At the back of the office, I heard the window on the door smash, and Neville fire a pair of shots from his nine-mill – while Laurel opened fire above me, the sharp crack of thunder punctuated by the click-clack of the bolt being drawn back. She fired again and again, each round punctuated by the resetting of her bolt. After my ears were well and truly ringing, she lent the rifle up against the wall.

'Mag's empty, mind if I borrow this?' she said, calmly taking the revolver from my unresisting hand.

With just as much calm, she fired again into the mob in the doorway, guaranteed a headshot since she was only stood three feet away. Unlike me, she remembered to thumb the hammer back after her shot, and fired again.

'Three shots left!' I warned her as the body of a zombie slumped over the sofa, a dead hand flopping against the leather only a few inches from my face. I cringed, and felt the sofa slip another inch - getting pushed back with it.

'Thought this was a six-shooter?' she asked, once again, coolly taking aim and putting another bullet through another brain. Compared to the tinned thunder of her rifle, Edgar's revolver sounded dinky.

'Didn't reload after the pawnshop!' I shouted over the sound of another shot.

'The menfolk around here are really pissing me off with their lackadaisical attitude to godsdamn firearm discipline!' she yelled, sparing me time for a disparaging look.

She emptied the gun, and with the last shot I was able to shove the sofa back against the doorway. I risked a glance up, and didn't see a zed left standing. At the other end of the office, I heard Neville crack off another shot, the sound of it echoing around the workshop, followed by the little tinkle of the empty casing hitting the ground somewhere.

Laurel gave me a hand up to my feet, and was about to hand me the revolver back when the first zombie jumped up into the doorway again, the runner. It growled and pulled itself over the sofa, using it as a launching pad for an aerial tackle, right into the side of Laurel.

It's a cliché, I know. But I had forever to watch it sail through the air, face contorted with hate, rage; showing blood-stained teeth and empty, cold eyes. It'd been a woman when it was alive. Dressed in worn jeans and a woollen jumper; comfortable clothes. She probably never expected something was going to rip her throat out. Probably never expected she'd get up and walk again after it did.

The zed collided into Laurel, bearing her down to the carpet where she struck her head, narrowly avoiding hitting the front desk. It reared its head back, strangely snakelike. I didn't have a gun, I didn't have my bat. All I had was a boot and a bayonet.

I kicked the zombie in the head as it lunged down to her neck, the force of the boot rolling it off her and into a clear patch of carpet. Before it had a chance to snatch at her again, I jumped on top of it, sitting on its chest with my knees pinning its arms, and reached to my belt for the bayonet.

I'll always remember how it felt. Driving that knife through bone. Sort of like if you stabbed an Equinox egg.

There's resistance, then a crunch as the blade snaps through the chocolate, and then you crunch through the other side too. It was like that. Only the egg is full of blood and it thrashes about while you do it. It took a few seconds for it to stop twitching. My stomach rolled, but I gritted my teeth and twisted the knife free.

I crawled over to Laurel, pulling her into my lap to check her neck for bites and see if she was still breathing. Her eyes were open and unfocused, but I could see her chest rising and falling – there was no blood on her. I breathed a sigh of relief, and held the side of her face with my free hand, keeping the bayonet ready in my right. I heard Neville fire off another shot.

How many more of them could there be?

'Think we're square.' Laurel said, gasping for breath, blinking her eyes hard.

'We got to stop saving each other like this,' I said, helping her up to her feet, 'people are going to start to talk.'

'Let em.' She coughed, rubbing the side of her neck, where there were flecks of brownish red, 'Thanks Kell.'

Nothing more was coming through our doorway, but there was an annoying tickling sensation on my hand. I looked down, and saw the blackened, congealed dead blood on my bayonet sliding down onto my fingers. I looked about for something to wipe it on, feeling my face twist in disgust; but Laurel was already pulling a pack of moistened tissues out of her pocket.

I wiped the gore off my fingers and did my best with the bayonet, though it was just as pitted and scarred as my baseball bat, the blood working its way into all the grooves and nicks on the blade. Would probably need to sacrifice a toothbrush for cleaning duties. At least the handle was smooth. I slotted it back into its metal sheath, and tried to remember to clean that out too when we got back.

Laurel retrieved my gun from the floor and handed it to me, pulling the bolt back on her rifle and ejecting a small magazine. She reached into her pocket for a handful of long rifle rounds, and started pressing them into the mag.

202

'Where did you learn to shoot like that? I asked, looking her up and down. 'You can't have missed a shot.'

'I did my two years out in Redmond, border patrol while all that bomb scare crap was going off.' She shrugged. 'Never saw any combat, but my unit was in a hot zone, so they said. We ran drills and shot targets just about every day. What about you? Katy said you'd not been for NS yet but there you are with a gun, and not terrible with it.'

'I never fired a gun before yesterday,' I told her, 'this was my neighbour's. The one whose house we were all eating soup in last night.'

'Wondered what happened to whoever lived there…'

'Thought you knew, Morgan was telling Anita last night. They took the quick way out, with some pills. Edgar, he left me this.'

Checking the doorway again, I reached into my jacket for the speedloader, slotting the bullets in place, twisting the knob and flicking my wrist to snap the cylinder closed again, like I'd seen on TV.

'I don't think I'm particularly good with it, but you on the other hand…don't think I've seen you miss a shot. Training make you that good or were you born on a farm or something?'

'Wasn't raised in a barn, that's for sure…' she grunted, eying up the broken door.

'Coast look clear.' Damian said, 'I don't want to be here any longer, seen?'

'What about the pump?' Neville asked.

I holstered my revolver. Or just, you know, put it in my pocket. It was starting to wear a nice groove in the side of my leg.

'I'll have the quickest of quick looks back here,' I said, making my way to the workshop door, 'if you can get out front and keep watch. Yell if I need to run to you. And don't leave me.'

'Going nowhere, man.' Damian grinned, fist bumping me with a shaky hand.

203

The floor of the shop was littered with bodies, half a dozen maybe more, dark shapes in the half-light. I drew my bayonet, kept it to hand while I went from shelf to shelf, looking for what we needed.

I knew you could get ones that were pretty small, about the size of a pint pot with a hose and either end and a crank in the middle, but SC's wasn't the kind of place to carry something like that, something for home use.

A proper autoshop had something like…*that*. I found it, knocked to the floor in the struggle. I carefully picked it up, keeping an eye on the zombie it'd fallen beside. This pump was made for tapping full-sized oil drums. You know old wells in little village squares? The big cylinder, the lever-pump, the spout? It was like that, only in a four foot cylinder and instead of all the underground workings, there was a flexible rubber hose on either end to suck up and spit out the gas.

I returned to the office, to see everyone peering out of the windows, Damian actually leaning out of the doorway.

'All those shots brought more of them,' Neville said over his shoulder, 'can't afford to get entrenched here while every zombie in Hillside throws itself at us.'

'Preaching, choir.' I shot back by way of reply, 'I've got the goods, let's get a move on.'

Damian shoved a pair of corpses that'd slumped on top of the sofa back onto the ground and climbed over, offering a hand to Laurel as she went after him. I went next, and she handed me my bat once I'd done climbing, leaving no useful weapon behind. Neville brought up the rear again.

The forecourt was empty, save for one freshly mobbed accountant, but the streets around us were another story. We'd killed more than a dozen between us, but there were more still coming, all shambling across the road, their moans drifting towards us like an eerie wind.

Damian ran ahead, unlocking the doors and jumping up into the front passenger seat to slide across to the driver's side. Neville held the door open for Laurel as she did the same in the back. I tossed the gas pump into the footwell ahead of me, and Damian had us reversing before I'd even closed my door.

The back end slammed into one of the zombies as he frantically spun the wheel, turning us back onto the road, going hand-over-hand just like the instructors tell you not to. The engine groaned a brief protest as he fumbled a gear change, getting us on our way with a squeal from the tyres.

Scores of them had come out as far from the centre as Hillside. If that trend kept up, we'd be knee-deep in zeds by tomorrow morning. But on the upside? If the zeds were leaving the centre, that meant it was becoming safer.

I needed to go to County General, my last, best hope of finding Katy. With everything Anita had said about what happened there, I had thought it would be suicide. But if the zeds weren't in the centre anymore, a little trip to County might not be as risky as I'd thought. I might still find her.

Twenty Five

We turned into the parking lot outside the apartments, sans diesel, but with the pump, and with the guns. Two out of three ain't bad. Nobody made any moves to get out. A brief wave of heat washed me from head to toe as the image of that pawnshop owner flashed before my eyes, emerging from that cupboard, laying its hands on me. I shut my eyes tight, and then I saw the zombie diving towards Laurel, bearing her to the ground. What if we'd both been bitten? Urgh. I shook my head.

'Pretty good work back there.' I nodded, letting out a breath I didn't realise I'd been holding. 'Held them off like nobody's business.'

'Uh huh.' Laurel said, deliberately not looking at Neville.

'I'm sorry about the door,' he said, picking up on it, 'I guessed it'd be locked and I just kicked it. I'm sorry.'

'Just check first next time, okay? Common sense.' She muttered, opening her door and sliding out.

I jumped out after her, and put a hand on her shoulder as she was coming around the other side.

'We've all got to blow off some steam,' I said, keeping my voice down, 'and I know it's well deserved, but could you lay off him a little?'

'Why'd he have to kick the door?' she asked, not trying to keep her's down. 'Work of a second to check it wasn't locked and he goes all cops on camera?'

'Like I said, we all need to blow off some steam.' I shrugged.

'Stupid is all I'm saying. And the blowback nearly got me killed!' she added, yelling, standing on tip-toe with her fists clenched at her sides. This shit wasn't good for anyone.

'Come on,' I sighed, putting my arm around her and walking her to the foyer, 'let's get some lunch. I've got a few beers in my fridge, you'll feel better.'

When we got into the foyer we saw that Lucile had stuck a post-it note to the elevator doors:

'Diverted power to 14th and elevator. Couldn't do 13th. Tested it, works, ran out of gas.' It read.

Still without power, it looked like we were back to square one with the stairs. I didn't feel much like going out there to pump some diesel right now – I'd rather face the stairs than another zed. We left it in the boot for later.

Me and Laurel took the stairs ahead of the other two, diplomatically separating them so they could cool off. When we breathlessly made it back to the top floor, we saw a welcome mat outside the Jamesons' door. Morgan's combat boots sat beside it, with Lucile and Anita's trainers lined up next to them. Looked kind of weird, boots just out in the hallway. We shrugged to each other and slipped out of our shoes before going inside.

Four family-sized coolboxes were lined up on the kitchen island, in patriotic red, white and blue - only with two white ones in the middle. I had a quick peek inside them while Laurel went to use the bathroom. The red box was full of meat – steaks, sausages and chicken breasts in plastic wrap, with ice piled around, looked like they'd been taken from people's freezers.

The first white box held a similar story in potato products, packets of peas and mixed vegetable servings – the rest of the sandwiches the girls had made earlier were the next box on, still in air-tight plastic lunchboxes, ready to keep for longer. But the blue box had what I was looking for. Our scavenger team were heroes.

I pulled a few of the chilled bottles out for everyone else and made sure the lid was closed properly, just as I'd done with the others, to keep the cool air inside. Edgar kept his bottle opener in the "useless items" drawer next to the sink, being more of a whisky man than a beer drinker.

On the kitchen sides were row upon row of tinned food, seemed like I wasn't the only person who enjoyed beans on toast. Strawberries, pineapple, pear, suspended in fructose syrup. Tinned tomatoes, carrots, sweetcorn…and every flavour of soup under the sun. In some places, the stacks were four or five tins high.

With the tins were pots and jars as well - pickled onions, gherkins, pasta and curry sauces, those noodles and quick-meal dishes where you just add boiling water and get a passable imitation of food if you wait two minutes and keep stirring.

Of course, there were some things in there I didn't like the look of. Like the mushy peas and tinned spaghetti loops. Really don't like the texture of tinned pasta. Beggars can't be choosers, but this beggar had a party-sized coolbox full of meat to get through first. Might only last a few days, but they'd be a good few days.

I noticed one of the cupboard doors hanging open, and found out that some attempt had also been made to load bags of rice and dry pasta into the kitchen cabinets. While I was over there, I saw yet more meat in the sink, wrapped up and defrosting in separate bowls - no cross contamination. A prod revealed they were coming along nicely.

Yet more of the cupboards had been filled with fresh produce, potatoes, peppers, onions, carrots, broccoli and cauliflower. Some of it looked close to the point I'd throw out, so I wondered how much they'd had to leave behind.

I heard voices coming from the corridor, and turned around to greet the guys, wiping my finger off on my jeans.

'Shoes off and you can have a beer.' I hastily commanded as the door opened. Neville and Damian did as they were told, so I handed them their drinks as they came in, to keep them sweet.

'Don't you usually take your shoes off when you're inside?' Neville asked.

'Yeah, but I guess our shoes would probably block the doorway.' I said, nodding to the Jamesons' shoe rack, which still held their shoes. Nobody wanted to throw them out, I guess.

208

Neville went straight into the living room and started unpacking the bags of guns, arranging the boxes and clips neatly, as if for display. Damian just leaned his shotgun against the arm of the sofa, took the box of shells out of his pocket and started loading them in.

'Wish we'd had de sense to do this earlier...' he said to Neville. 'Why have them, and not load them?'

'You didn't load your shotgun either, D.'

'I was driving. Should'a given it to you.'

'Point well made. I think we could all do with putting some more thought into our actions.' He said, looking over to me apologetically. I'm not sure what the scorecard of our fuckups would read right now, but I'm guessing we were square again.

'Yeah, yeah...' I agreed, swigging beer. It was good stuff, import, from across the Cold Sea. One of those names with a lot of zeds in – the letter zed, not our new shorthand for the walking dead.

'Where is everyone?' Neville asked.

Before I could answer, the door opened again, Morgan and Anita coming through, carrying a sizeable cardboard box each. Must have been using them to ferry the tins about. They set them down on the floor by the kitchen island, heavy with more tinned beans and soup from the vacant apartments. Both of them had wet hair at the temples, from working up a sweat.

'Hey guys.' Anita said jovially.

'Thought I heard you come back.' Morgan said, looking down at the coolboxes. 'See anything you like?'

'Much obliged.' I smiled, tipping my beer back again.

I could already feel the tension ebbing away. I usually had one or two after work, enough to take the edge off the postal bureaucracy's latest attempts to screw over our warehouse. If I was going to try taking the edge off today's stress, we'd need to go looking for a stomach pump too.

'Open me one of those bad-boys, will ya?' she asked.

Neville opened his mouth to speak, but Damian gave him the eyeball-equivalent of a soft knock in the ribs. 'Oh come on…'

'…was only going to say it's a bit early in the day…' Neville muttered.

'Killjoy,' I chimed, looking at the clock on the Jamesons' kitchen wall, 'it's almost four.'

I passed more beers out to Anita and Morgan, still barely dinting the impressive number that they'd scavenged from the tower. I guess it wasn't high priority stuff to take with you when you're fleeing a deadly virus. More for us.

'How'd the search go then?' I asked Anita.

'Hit a couple trouble apartments, but I went in ahead and cleared. Kiddo was adamant she was okay with the bodies…'

'Didn't get vomitorial at all, not even once.' Morgan butted in. I saw Neville turn to listen in from the other side of the apartment.

'A close thing,' Anita smirked, 'but she was okay. Neville's keys got us into most apartments, but there were chain locks on the ones with the dead in, had to get a hacksaw from your landlord's place. Most of it was easy going though. Open doors, root through cupboards, stack it all up outside the door then come back when we found boxes big enough.'

'Thanks to you guys, looks like we're not going to have much of an issue with food.' I said gratefully.

'Maybe,' she said, sucking her teeth, 'I had a while to think about this today. Seven of us, right? That's twenty one square meals a day, really. We actually haven't finished bringing stuff up yet, but at a guess, and I'm just eyeballing here…'

I let her think for a minute, tilting her head this way and that.

'If we eat at that pace, four months?' she tried.

'That's…still a lot of time. Plus there's plenty more in the co-op.' I grinned at the news. We were good for supplies. She didn't look too happy though.

210

'Four, six, even eight months with rationing and more food, that isn't forever. We'll run out of water before we run out of food too. There's plenty of fluids we've not brought up yet, pop, juice, more alcohol - which is actually going to dehydrate you, so go easy. But actual water, we'll run out of quickly, since we need it for cooking and cleaning.'

Morgan, who had been filing cupboards with the food haul, paused to turn around. 'Good job we're coming into winter. I've seen loads of plastic tubs, buckets and boxes. If we put them out on the top floor balconies, we can collect rainwater, like earlier today – every drizzle helps.'

'What about the roof?' I asked. 'There's a door in the stairwell that can get us on there.

'Too breezy, up this high,' she said, 'empty buckets are going to go rolling off the edge, or if the wind takes a full one then we lose what we've collected. The high sides of the balconies'll stop that, but I suppose we lose some efficiency if the wind's blowing the rain the wrong way, so we'll have to bucket every balcony.'

'Smart plan Morgan,' Anita smiled, warmly, it touching her eyes, 'she's been a pleasure to burgle with.' She added to Neville.

'Thanks guys. Glad someone's day went better than ours.' I yawned, feeling the beer start to unwind me.

'What happened?' Anita asked.

Damian piped up, 'Shit happened.'

'Tell you later. Where's Lucile anyway?' I asked.

'Fetching some disposable barbecues from Damian's kitchen. Wonder how she knew they were there, huh?' Morgan added with a mutter, so only we could hear.

'One of life's great mysteries. So I guess it's BBQ for dinner tonight? Fantastic.'

'Someone say barbecue?' Laurel asked as she re-emerged from the bathroom. 'I'm a master of the grill.'

'The disposable grill? And no shrimp.' Morgan smirked.

211

'It's a coastal tradition, but I think I can work with that.' Laurel spoke, quite solemnly. 'It won't be the same, that's all I'm saying.'

I think it's really important to keep morale up. Any tensions in the group are going to show if things turn dangerous. We'd already seen what that could mean with Edgar and Rosie, and Neville's lack of thought had really ticked off Laurel. But now everyone was back at the safehouse, together, you could feel the strain, the oppressive air of the outside world, just lift.

I sighed and drank again. I had no solid lead on Katy anymore, and just as little idea whether she was still alive as I had yesterday morning. My best hope of finding her was County General, and even if the zeds were moving out of the city, there'd still be a hell of a risk going there. I was glad for Neville's guns now more than ever.

So that afternoon we had a barbecue, cooking out on the balcony. The last of the dated bread, the defrosted meat, and a box full of beers – all you ever need to have a good time, though I suppose some of the group had insisted there be some salad, I didn't let that put me off. It was nice, relaxing, and almost normal for a Friday afternoon. As soon as the first bite of a charred steak sandwich touched my lips, I was in a private heaven.

Then Laurel slapped my ass with a toasting fork and told me to keep an eye on the sausages.

Not to get all preachy at you, but have you ever noticed how much excess our society has? We have so much food that we need to invent ways of preserving and storing it. Having an entire tower block's worth of frozen food slowly thawing in the kitchen, we'd easily eliminated the short term problem, but unless we got some diesel in that generator, we'd only have it for maybe a couple more days until it started to go bad and we were forced to live off the dry stuff and tins. If we did get power back, we'd even have our electric ovens to do real cooking in.

'So this co-op you mentioned? Maybe it's got a backup generator, you know, for the freezers?' Anita suggested, as we all sat around the living room, drinking and digesting after the meal. Plates of leftovers were being passed around and picked over - we'd eaten well, I was stuffed, but nothing was going to go to waste. Anita had suggested a vote and we'd decided two meals a day were going to have to be enough from now on.

'Maybe,' Lucile nodded, 'Bigger supermarkets do for sure, in case of power cuts. Ain't so sure about our little local though. Anyone up for a little night-raid to check it out?'

'May as well. Being out after sunset's not a thrilling prospect, take it from us' I said, looking from Neville to Damian. 'But it's only up the road. Not far on foot, let alone by car.'

'Don't we have enough food already?' Morgan asked, 'We've stripped the Tower clean and you're still hungry?'

'We've got more stuff to bring up still, but we've been up and down those stairs all day.' Anita mumbled, covering her mouth as she'd just taken a bite from a chicken sandwich.

'Really got our cardio in.' Morgan sighed in agreement. 'First dibs on the deserts…'

'If they do have a backup genny, at the co-op though, it'd be small. Maybe even a portable. Could plug it into our fridges.' Neville suggested, 'Then we wouldn't even need to bother with the big generator in the basement.'

'You're telling me this now?' Lucile drawled, 'I just got that thing jury-rigged.'

'We planning on being here long, anyway?' Anita followed after her, 'Those guys at the radio station, dodgy they may be, but they said they have a way out.'

'I'm taking anything they say with a heap of salt.' I shrugged, 'The way he was acting, I'd look up if he told me the sky was blue.'

'Hope for the best, prepare for the worst.' Anita agreed. It was like the ghost of Edgar-past was there with us. 'Trust your gut, that's what I'd tell you. If you were getting bad vibes from those guys, there's a reason.'

213

'And yet despite that…' I sighed.

'Despite that,' Laurel carried on, as resigned as I was, 'we still need to give it a shot. Evacuation, safezone, could be better than waiting here for Gods know how long.'

'Do we try them tonight?' Lucile asked. Maybe it was the drink, filling her with confidence, making her want to leave the safety of the Tower after dark.

'No, I don't want to be out too long after dark. If we're up for it, then we can go grocery shopping, then come back here for some rest.' I told her, noticing everyone else was paying attention too. 'Like Anita said, we hope for the best but prepare for the worst. The shutters are still down at the co-op right now, might not be that way soon. If there's food to stockpile, then we should be doing it.'

We tooled up after that.

Those who had guns set about loading and reloading them while Neville distributed the new finds. Nobody had drunk enough for Anita to worry about friendly fire, and if it was okay with her, then it was okay with me.

He gave the Seg, the smaller, modern gun, to Lucile. I watched as she loaded the magazines and found the safety, like she knew what she was doing. She emptied the rest of the ammo box into her hand, a little pile of small rounds, and put them in her jacket pocket, slung over the back of the sofa.

Neville took the heavy old pistol for himself, carefully loading each magazine, counting the bullets. Maybe he was doing what I did earlier. Subtract bullets from population of Greenfield, equals a whole heap of trouble; and he didn't even have bullets left to reload. But even so, he slid his nine-mill ammo box over to Anita, his pistol on top.

'Take it. Only eight rounds left in the box, but two loaded guns with spare mags should be enough to go to the shops and back.' He smiled.

Anita reached over the living room coffee table and put her hand over Neville's, squeezing. 'Thanks. I'll take good care of it.'

214

I smirked, waited, and watched while everyone else played with their guns, loading spare magazines and shuffling spare ammo around in their coat pockets. When you get down into single figures, there's no point keeping the empty box around.

Neville looked up after he'd finished with his weapon, and caught me staring. I'm not sure if there wasn't anyone he'd rather have given it to, or he just thought I looked bored. But he passed me the oversized revolver, and the little tin bullet-box.

'No speedloader for that one, but the cylinder rotates itself with each shot. It's a stupidly powerful gun to be giving you, but if all that matters are headshots, better the trained shooters have the magazine capacity. You can only miss six times with this.' He added.

I tried not to be offended, and mostly succeeded.

'Never before has the co-op seen so many well-prepared shoppers.' I said instead.

Finally, a gun that didn't dig into my leg. I loaded the unsurprisingly heavy Cobra, one massive .44 bullet at a time, and secured its holster on my belt, puzzling out the shoulder rigging and detaching it. I even gave a few test draws to see how fast I could. Now that I had a gun to hand, I could put the Tetley in my jacket pocket, and give the sore spot on my leg a chance to heal.

The bullet box had quite a few spare rounds in, but without speedloaders they were of limited use if six shots weren't enough. The damn things didn't fit in Edgar's empty ones.

'Erm, not to pick holes or anything…' Morgan said, 'But some people have two guns, and we're all out of guns. I'm going to be left gunless, if this trend continues.'

'That's the idea.' Neville said, braced for the argument.

'Anyone going to back me up here?' she beseeched the senate. This time I was coming down on her Dad's side. I gave her a little shake of my head and an apologetic look.

215

'Until you know how to shoot, I wouldn't feel comfortable with it.' Neville said, putting his hand on her knee and giving her a weak smile. 'It's just safer for now, okay?'

'Fine.' Morgan said, the beginnings of a teenage pout forming. 'Promise you'll teach me later?'

'If he doesn't, I'll shoot him myself.' Anita said slapping a fresh magazine into one of her guns.

Between us, we had six handguns, a rifle, a shotgun and enough blunt instruments to make a very dull orchestra. In some cases, we had more weapons than hands. Quite inventively, Morgan cut the strap off one of her leather satchels and pinned it with many safeties through the empty carry-loops on Damian's shotgun, so he could sling it over his shoulder.

'Remember everyone,' I said as we were pulling our coats and shoes on in the corridor, 'these things are attracted to sound, so only pull your gun out if it's dire. Stick close together, and coordinate your attacks against the zeds if we need to – and let's hope we don't. We're only off down the shops, after all.'

Twenty Six

The sun was just setting as we were getting ready to leave the flats, suited, booted and all that other stuff that means we were feeling badass. We had guns, bats, bayonets and more than a few of us were wearing leather – how very post-apocalyptic of us. All we needed now were spiky hairstyles, a layer of dirt and bad teeth. Then we could be extras in the summer blockbuster.

I didn't really have to get changed, it wasn't like my clothes were bloodstained or anything, but after being in a few tense situations throughout the day, I'd caught myself the whiff of sweat. Figured my clothes could do with an airing out, and my pits could do with some spray. I abandoned the Some Bad Men t-shirt and donned a plain number, with faded black jeans and my dark steel-toed work boots.

Edgar's revolver went into a jacket pocket, fully loaded but with a loose bullet rattling around - it'd run dry soon, but fortunately we were only going to the shop. If I needed seven shots in two hundred yards, we had bigger things to worry about than ammo conservation. I left the empty speed-loaders on the kitchen side.

The bigger revolver, the Cobra, went in its holster on my right hip. I put the tin bullet box into my other jacket pocket. The rounds were big enough that the gun would probably feel a whole lot lighter once it'd been emptied.

'Strong hand draw.' Anita commented, seeing me fiddling with the holster. There was a loop on the back to run your belt through, so you knew it wasn't going to come off unless your belt did.

'I don't know guns. Is that bad?' I asked, looking down at it.

'Only if you're sat down. Better for standing.' She nodded, 'But generally, it's whatever you feel comfortable with.'

217

Anita wore the same hard-wearing black police trousers we'd found her in, but she'd spent some time cleaning all the blood out. Her white shirt was from a slightly better fitting closet this time, her search for supplies turning up some new outfits. If the world suddenly got back to normal tomorrow, there'd be a whole bunch of people wondering where all their stuff went.

She'd put on Neville's old fur-lined denim jacket, which concealed his shoulder holster and pistol. Her own gun was on her utility belt, along with a telescopic baton, a club-like flashlight and her silver shield. There was even a canister of defence spray – be interesting to see what concentrated capsicum did to a zed, but my guess would be not a whole lot.

'Haven't thought about it in a while,' she mused, reaching her right hand up to Neville's shoulder holster - across her body, then moving it down to the gun on her left side - 'Guess I prefer cross. Looks more professional, less cowboy.'

She was right, the heavy revolver at my hip, close to hand, did make me feel a little more wild west than law enforcement, but we weren't heading out to GCR again tonight, so appearance be damned. The bayonet, secured by a firm steel clip, went on my left side. I felt better for having my baseball bat with me as well - it'd keep the zeds another couple feet away from me if we got into another brawl.

At the thought of having to use my bayonet, I turned to look for Laurel, picking her out of the rest of the party. She was knelt down by the coffee table, taping a flashlight under the barrel of her rifle.

'Here,' I said, kneeling down on the other side of the table, holding the rifle up off the glass, 'I'll hold them, you tape them.'

'Thanks,' she sighed, 'I'm doing a shit job.'

She unwound the tape she'd already done, and we started again. Laurel had kept my other leather jacket, and must have brought some clean clothes with her in that backpack – I wasn't the only one who felt like a change. A

218

purple cami top sat underneath a black blouse. A smart/casual look.

'All better, job's a good un,' she grunted, standing to hook the rifle over her shoulder.

Dark blue jeans were tucked into a pair of sensibly heeled boots that didn't look like too much of an inconvenience to run in. Her jeans were faded like mine, but with a hole in the knee patched over in a not-quite identical shade.

'Recent addition?' I asked, pointing at it.

'Yeah, well, function over fashion right now.' She said, reaching down to smooth her hand over it, looking for any loose stitches.

'What's with the heels then?'

'They're only low. You've seen my stilettos before, right?' She said, crossing her arms, doing potentially distracting things to her bust. It was move that reminded me of Katy.

'Please tell me stripper heels weren't on your essentials list when you packed…' I said, giving her an eyebrow raise.

'No comment.' She replied, matching me.

I shook my head, walking back over to the kitchen, where Lucile and Damian were chatting.

Lucile had dressed somewhere between me and Anita – neat black trousers, grey shirt under her leathers, running shoes, with her new gun holstered in her belt - cross-hand, I noticed. She still carried her baseball bat, tip on the kitchen floor.

She tossed her head back at something Damian said, sweeping her hair back from one ear. Laughter touched her eyes and lit up her smile.

'Hey man,' Damian greeted, seeing me coming, 'nearly ready?'

Lucile turned around, putting her bat up on her shoulder. She was chewing gum, making her look like a batter ready for the pitch. It's amazing what a gun can do for your confidence. Either that or the thing between her and Damian was going well. There was something in the way the small blonde carried

219

herself that reminded me of my Katy, a kind of "bring it on" swagger.

Everything was reminding me of her right now…and with the guns…maybe heading up to the hospital for one last look, maybe that wasn't such a dangerous idea anymore? I lost myself for a moment before remembering I'd been asked a question.

'Erm, I'm good to go. Checking you guys are all set?' I made it into a question.

Damian was pretty calm before he had a gun. He swung into action on day one against our first zombie, rattled him though it did, he soon got himself composed. In his detective coat, with that shotgun in his arms, he looked all set to take on the world. He'd also stopped wearing his beanie.

His dreads made him look even taller without it, tied into a wild, scraggly bun. Guess he'd seen what happened to my hair. Under the coat he wore a white vest and a black shirt, half unbuttoned, with well-worn blue jeans that'd frayed around the ankles from hours of walking.

'I good. Leaving me bat behind, think de shotty will do. Heavy, look strong enough to go clubbing with.'

'Big fish, little fish…shotgun butt.' Lucile smiled, doing the hand motions, but punching an elbow forwards for the last one.

Something poked me in the back. I turned around to find Morgan offering out a small flashlight. She had a couple more hanging off her wrist on lanyards. They were about the size of a tube of toothpaste.

'Courtesy of apartment eight-oh-two, or somewhere around there.' She chirped, a spring in her step as she went to offer the other two to Damian and Lucile.

'Everybody have one, girl?' Damian asked her.

'Except the other ladies, and my Dad. They've got their own.'

Morgan had opted in for all-black again, just like after the funeral. A black shirt was buttoned up to a modest level and her black cargo bottoms were fitted more snugly than the usual cut – might have made the pockets smaller but it'd offer less material for a zed to grab onto.

She'd taped a kitchen knife to the flat side of the hooked end of her hockey stick, and carried it carefully, improvised spear-tip down. Motorcycle boots and the group's fourth leather jacket completed the look of the survivor…and made her look older, though maybe that was the subtle make-up I detected about her eyes.

Hmm. Like the girl back at GCR, in the full office attire. Morgan didn't have fake tan, but they'd both kept their make-up on, like there were some things the end of the world didn't change, you clung to them like a life raft. I was suddenly aware of the mobile phone in my pocket, switched off. Guess I was clingy too.

'Ready?' Neville asked, coming over.

His winter jacket hid his new shoulder holster and would do a good job of keeping off the rain that'd just begun to speckle the windows.

We did a couple last minute things before we set off. Since it was raining, we followed Morgan's advice, sticking a few bowls, basins or clean buckets out on the penthouse balconies, Damian and Lucile going downstairs to cover their own balconies.

'We should just use this drizzle as a rinse-out, and probably boil the first few collections. Right?' Anita asked.

'Yeah, half of these buckets will have been full of cleaning chemicals and all sorts of horribleness.' Morgan agreed, 'So definitely. Ick. We could boil what we get this time and use that to scrub out the collectors for next time with standard washing up liquid.'

Anita nodded approval at the plan. Again, I hoped we weren't going to be staying in castle tower forever, but if evacuation didn't go ahead, or it turned out to be some kind of sham, then we'd need all the supplies we could muster. Hell. We might even have to start farming in the park after winter was through.

The drizzle was just getting into its stride as we squeezed into the cars; Morgan and Anita riding with Neville in his sedan, while Lucile rode shotgun – literally holding the shotgun – in Damian's 4x4, me and Laurel taking up the backseats. The rain was light enough for us not to need the wipers before we got to the rundown plaza, but it did put a chill in the air, like the rain was blowing in straight from the north.

We didn't park on the curb this time. Damian revved his mighty engine up the sloped verge and into the plaza, driving around the left side of the fountain and turning a little around it, so we'd be able to load the shopping into the expansive cargo hold, then drive around the fountain and straight out.

Neville wasn't going to risk taking his car up the verge, didn't have the ground clearance for it, so he parked by the curb. We exited our respective vehicles and gathered outside of the co-op's shutters, clinker-built metal sheeting that could roll up into a long cover across the doorway. Lucile opened up the metal box beside the shutters, where there was only a keyhole and a couple of switches. She produced a little case about the size of a cigarette packet, unzipped it and selected a screwdriver.

I scanned the street as she worked, expecting at any moment to see a grey, dead face appear around the corner. I shivered, told myself it was just the cold, the whispering sound of the soft drizzle, and forced myself to take slow, deep breaths. I was getting bad vibes about this, and they'd only get worse as the sun continued to set, orange light fading to black. I put my hand on the Cobra, tracing the little push-stud that went over the handle to secure it.

'I'm stumped,' Lucile eventually hummed, 'we'd need the right key, or someone better at this sort of thing than me. I've fitted one of these before, but I wouldn't know how to break into one. I could fuck it up and lock it down.' She added, 'So I ain't risking it.'

'Anything you can tell us?' Anita asked.

'It's not alarmed. Ain't a concern if we're to try and force it open.' She took a quick glance up the side of the building, 'No main alarm system either. Once we're through the shutter, don't worry about tripping anything.'

Damian opened the boot of his ride, crawled in, and dragged the duffle bag towards the edge. His Uncle Robb's toolkit consisted of all kinds of junk. Snow chains, a shovel with a folding shaft, a pair of crowbars, one four-foot prybar that didn't quite fit into the bag, half a dozen hammers of different sizes and shapes, a heavyweight red car-jack, a power-drill, a set of bolt-cutters, a box of assorted screwdrivers and a weird tube that looked like it should have been a light fitting…

I could see how some of it could see use on a farmstead, general tools and the like, but some of it was a mystery.

'Soft touch, or go hard?' Damian asked, opening the bag so everyone could get a good look inside.

'Softly.' Neville replied. 'No way can we get the shutters out of their runners without something a lot bigger than a lump hammer. We could try ramming it with the front of your tank, it's got the cattle-bar, but for the noise-'

'And damage.' Damian interjected.

'-and damage, it's not worth it.' Neville agreed, holding his hands up defensively.

The precision approach it was. We'd coax it up enough for someone to get underneath, and try to find a way in from there.

I took one of the crowbars and Neville the other. We jammed them off to each side of the shutter, finding just enough give to let them slip under. Anita appeared with the prybar, the crowbars' oversized big brother, and forced it under the gap. On the count of three, we pressed down, Anita bending double, Neville and myself on our knees.

Damian and Lucile got between us and grabbed the shutter to pull it upwards, but only managed to clear our tools by another couple of inches – the shutters were doing their job, forcing us to strain against whatever mechanism held them

223

down. We pushed the prybar forwards, and a little at a time, managed to get it about a foot off the ground.

I looked over my shoulder to see Laurel keeping an eye on the road, watching for approaching zeds, so I didn't worry about getting a nasty surprise while we worked at it.

Morgan slid the car-jack under the gap, set it, and began to work the lever. Something began to creak as the shutter rattled upwards, a high, tense sound followed by a loud metallic snap which shook the shutter. She got it another inch or so, but it was slow going, the creaking sound starting up again, like we were working backwards against some tooth in a cog.

'It won't budge any further.' Morgan said, still trying to press down on the jack lever. Metal groaned again somewhere inside the mechanisms, but we'd gotten almost two feet to wiggle through, we didn't need to break the thing.

'So we're thinking there's a switch to work these remotely then? It'll probably be in the office.' Neville suggested, setting his crowbar back in the bag. He blew into cupped hands afterwards, trying to breathe some life into cold fingers.

'Neville, you and me.' I said, 'Everyone else, keep watch.'

'Right.' he acknowledged, drawing his weapon from its holster, and a heavy flashlight from an inside pocket. The thing must have been a foot long, thick as a beer-can and as reminiscent of a club as Anita's – part of his security guard kit probably. I took Morgan's tiny light from my pocket and put the lanyard around my left wrist.

Neville got down on his belly and shined his light under the shutter. He called out it was clear, and started to crawl under. I rolled my bat through and went in after him. He gave me a hand back onto my feet when my lanky legs had folded themselves inside. It wasn't exactly claustrophobic in here, but if you had a cat, you wouldn't want to swing it.

The co-op's doors were humble, wooden things painted in a pastel shade of blue, with glass panes halfway up, not security glass or toughened, as far as I could tell. I guess putting security glass behind a steel shutter would have been overkill.

The glass might not have been reinforced, but the doors were chained shut; a heavy length of steel was wrapped around the two door handles and padlocked. The doors themselves probably had their own locks too, but at least there was no alarm system.

'Smash the windows out and climb in?' Neville asked, training his light on the chain and padlock. In the space between the shutters and the doors, our voices seemed to both echo and be muted.

'Be difficult to wheel the supplies out. There's bolt cutters in good old Uncle Robb's bag though,' I replied, kneeling down again to talk to the guys outside, 'Can you hand me the…thank you.' I added, the oversized pliers already passing under the gap.

They were pretty heavy-duty, and with them I got through the steel padlock with a barely a grunt of effort. Neville slipped the chain loose, and tossed it into a corner, before taking the cutters and handing them back outside.

'Cordless drill, please?' he asked in exchange.

'Why?' came Morgan's muffled response.

'Store lock.' Anita provided, obviously up to date on the methods of breaking and entering.

The drill was quite small, smaller than Neville's new pistol, and as with any man with a power tool, he gave it a couple of test-whirrs before pressing it against the lock. There was a brief whine from the lock before the drill-bit spun out a ribbon of metal, spiralling through the lock as if it were plasterboard. Neville drew it back out, and cocked his head to the side.

'This is professional quality.' He muttered, suspiciously.

'Maybe Uncle Robb was a locksmith.' I suggested, keeping my voice as quiet as his. I nudged the door slightly with my foot, and watched it open slowly.

'Possibly. But more than one type of professional might have a drill like this.' Neville replied just as quietly, before passing the drill back under the shutter.

'You reckon Damian's uncle is a thief?' I asked, swinging the door open for Neville. We both knew he was going in first. He knew how to use his gun better than I did, and he had the bigger flashlight.

'One crowbar is happenstance, two crowbars is coincidence, a third, oversized crowbar, in a duffel bag with a lock drill and a blacklight...'

'That's what that was? You reckon the folding shovel is for when he takes people out into the sticks and makes them dig their own grave?' I teased, eyes flicking this way and that, trying to keep the tension down.

'It's weird is all I'm saying.' He answered.

The co-op was dark. There were no windows to let the last rays of the day in, and if there was emergency power backing up the freezers and fridges, it wasn't doing the same for the store's lighting. I used my knowledge of the place to build a mental map in my head, tried to visualise where everything was. Neville shopped here too, and I figured he'd be doing the same.

The front doors put us about halfway along the building, but not halfway along the aisles. To our left would be the majority of the food and a door into the storeroom over in the back corner, to our right; a few more aisles and the checkout tills, with the office doors behind them.

Neville scanned the doorway around the entrance with his flashlight, looking for any kind of switch for the shutters. He found a bank of switches, and flicked them all to the toggled-on position. To our surprise, one light did appear. I thought it was another flashlight at first, but it came shining down from the office doorway.

A small box with two directional bulbs sat just above it, one of the lights pointing straight at us, at the entrance, and the other diffusing light over the checkout area. It made the rest of the store look even darker, and my paranoia started to eat away at me. Stood here in the pool of light, we'd be visible to anything lurking around in the store. I wasn't sure if I saw it or just imagined it, something moving around between the aisles, like The Beast in some horror flick. I shivered again, pointed my light towards where I'd seen the movement, and gritted my teeth.

It was just a trolley, sat in the middle of the aisle. It hadn't moved.

'You good?' Neville asked, keeping his voice low. He was looking out into the aisles too, but he didn't look like he'd seen anything. I tried to take comfort in that, nobody had pushed that trolley, I just hadn't expected it to be there. After the pawnshop, I think I'd begun to develop an irrational fear of shopping.

'Thought I saw something. Empty cart.' I added, taking Edgar's revolver out of my jacket pocket. The weight of the Cobra would have been more comforting, but I knew how to handle the Tetley, and now didn't seem a good time to learn a new gun.

'And you told Lucile off for saying it was too quiet.' He chuckled, his voice still low, making it sound deeper, and slightly sinister.

'Hah-ha...' I found myself nervously grinning, 'Maybe we should split up and look for clues, after all, I heard a strange noise over there, I'm only two weeks from retirement and it can't possibly get any worse than this.'

'Haha. Good one...'

'Guys like me are always cast as comic relief.'

'We're just lucky neither of us are the black guy.' Neville joked. 'Coming in here is like asking to get picked off first.'

227

Twenty Seven

We went quick and quiet along the row of checkouts, one eye fixed on the rest of the store as we went, torches flicking this way and that, making sure the coast was well and truly clear. Neville took the lead, the steadier gunhand.

He squeaked through a hip-height plastic door, shining his flashlight along the little shelves of cigarettes, strong spirits and condoms they kept behind the counter. I followed close behind him, catching the door with my knee as it tried to spring back into the closed position.

The noisy door, our waving lights and footsteps, in my head we were being too loud, too conspicuous. I turned to stare into the darkened shop again, feeling the walls close in. My breath came tight around the pulse in my throat. I tried to fight it, fixing my tiny flashlight against the dark and slowly strafing along the checkouts, re-checking the store aisle by aisle.

Neville's hand on my shoulder told me I'd come too far over.

'Gods, I've never seen you this paranoid.' Neville said, still keeping his voice down, 'Are you okay?'

'Just being careful.' I snapped back.

Neville tentatively lowered his hand.

'Sorry,' I tried again, swallowing hard, 'I don't think I'm doing too well with the dark. This happened to me the other night, after we fought the first one, at that car crash.'

'Where Damian broke its wrist?'

I nodded. 'Couldn't sleep. Felt trapped, hard to breathe. Had to turn the light on.'

'Shame we don't have the lights back yet, but after what we've been through, that's just normal.'

I hadn't turned away from the shelves, maybe it was a guy thing but I didn't want to look at him as I admitted I was afraid of the dark.

228

'You been having trouble sleeping?' I asked him.

'Not when I finally doze off, but it takes me a while,' I saw him shrug, looking down at the floor, 'have to check the door three or four times, been putting every lock on it, and then dragging a chair over too. Morgan thinks I'm nuts. I can't sleep until I know she's sleeping either. According to my watch, I'm on about five hours. Give or take.'

'Mostly take?'

'Mostly. So…I need sleeping pills, and you need a bedside lamp.'

'Sleep's important. We need to stay rested. Light's just a trade-off between letting the monsters see you, and not going insane…'

'I'd rather have you sane, personally.' He said, clapping me on the shoulder, 'Someone needs to look out for Morgan if I don't make it. Gibbering wrecks aren't great role models.'

I nodded, and tried to pull my shit together. 'Understood.'

Neville tried the office door and found it unlocked. Opening it just a crack, he shone his torch through, holding it in a reverse-grip and resting his gun-hand on top, just like you see them doing on TV.

'So how'd you get to sleep last night? Burning candles?' he asked, nudging the door all the way open with his foot, and leaning in to scan the room beyond.

'Didn't need them, I had company, sharing the bed with Laurel - nothing happened.' I quickly added, getting onto my knees to look for a shutter control button under the counters.

'I wouldn't have thought it did, don't worry. You're both dealing with the loss of someone close. It's to be expected you'd grow closer. Maybe not that kind of close…but you know.' He struggled.

'Not that kind of close.' I confirmed. 'Just needed the company.'

Anyone with a pulse could tell you Ms Daniels was a pretty girl. Maybe even my type. Confident, strong, same brand of arrogance that Katy sometimes wore, if we're being

229

candid. I'd never seen her with her guard down, except maybe, last night when she'd been crying for Dani, and this morning, when she'd woken up with me.

I pushed that thought aside, and got my eyes back under the counters. There was a button underneath each till, a red one the size of a doorbell; presumably a panic button in case of robbery. At the till closest to the door, behind Neville, was a metal toggle switch with a printed label above it. With the beam of my tiny flashlight, it read "Shutter Lock".

I flicked it, and heard a very loud *thunk* from outside. Guess it didn't need mains power to work. A moment later, the shutter began to rattle upwards, Damian standing beneath it, pushing upwards with about as much effort as a garage door. Lucile was already putting the car jack back in the duffel bag.

'Clear?' Anita asked, coming in much as Neville had, gun and light in her fancy, trained grip, shining it down the aisles.

'Clear.' I confirmed. She lowered her weapon.

Damian, Lucile and Morgan were next in, weapons held in a relaxed position. Laurel came in last, checking over her shoulder. While everyone was piling into the shop, Neville went into the little office space, gun lowered now. I followed him in.

Bare brick walls were softened here and there by inspirational posters; cats hanging onto tree branches, dolphins with captions like "Teamwork – We're better together!", that kind of thing. A few chairs were arranged around a cheap-looking dining table, and there was a small kitchenette in the corner, complete with microwave, kettle and sink - you know the setup, basic staff room.

We went on through another door marked "Manager", a simple office with a basic computer, filing cabinets, shelves stuffed with folders and loose paperwork around the walls, except in the back corner, where a steel cabinet was marked with a yellow power symbol.

'Could be emergency power, emergency lights, something like that.' I suggested.

230

Neville opened her up, while I kept the light aimed on the switches and read-outs.

'Got one for battery lights here…' he muttered.

There came a buzzing hum from the staff room, where the lights pinged and popped into life.

'We've got light!' Lucile called from the store. 'Good work boys.'

'So far, so good.' Neville confirmed, shutting the electrical box.

Out in the aisles, the overhead lights were still warming up, flickering to life. The abandoned trolley sat halfway along one aisle, The Beast that I'd glimpsed with my torch earlier.

'Freezer section's still fully functioning, think we're in luck for more steak dinners.' Anita informed us, coming back to the doors from a row of deep chest freezers.

'These are emergency lights, right?' Neville asked Lucile, who was seeing if anything was salvageable from the fresh bread stand. 'Why weren't they already on?'

'Probably just fire safety lights, not set up to come on just because of a power outage.' She shrugged one shoulder. 'Not up to code, I can tell ya.'

We left the ladies to guard the entrance, Damian, Neville and myself heading to the back of the store, where a blue security door stood. Unlike the doors at the front of the co-op, this one did have wire-mesh security glass in the top, and a keypad at the side. I tried the handle, but it was locked.

'Seen these locks before, we've got them at work – power outage should have knocked it off. Must be on whatever emergency power the freezers are running on.' Neville guessed.

'How do we get in?' I asked, 'More crowbar?'

'I don't think it's as heavy-duty as the pawnshop door. Tools should get us in.' Neville agreed, sucking his teeth.

'How many digits in your work code?' Damian asked Neville.

'Four, why?'

Damian reached between us, and pressed four numbers on the keypad – one, two, three and four. When that didn't work, he tried two, four, six and eight. The door buzzed, and he pushed it open.

'Most clubs and bars I set up in, they have codes that're easy to remember. Pattern in de numbers or just a line of them. If not that, probably written in de staff room notice board.'

'Nice.' I smirked, 'Saves a job.'

The storeroom didn't have emergency lighting, so Damian led the way in with one of Morgan's mini-flashlights held in the same hand he was using to support the shotgun barrel. It was awkward, but it worked.

The back wasn't warehouse sized, but it was more than half the length of the store, the far wall ending where the office was. It held enough over-filled shelving units to make me smile from ear to ear. If worse came to worse, if we were going to be up in castle tower for the foreseeable future, we'd be alright.

'Jackpot.' Neville beamed, lifting the cardboard flap on a box of tinned beans and sausages. 'We're going to stink out the apartment.'

'Here's hoping we can get out of Greenfield before we need all this.' I gestured, walking down one of the shelves and inspecting the contents. 'Let's get it back home. Might take us a few trips, so pile as much as we can in both cars, then dump it in Stan's living room to keep it out of sight before we can haul it up in the lift.'

Morgan wheeled the trolley over to the doorway. It was shorter and shallower than the big supermarket trolleys you get, but it was better than carrying a box at a time. We managed to load four boxes of beans, biscuits, soup and sundries, but there were plenty more where they came from.

Anita was inspecting the frozen section, packing select items into insulated cool-bags that we'd gotten from near the tills, the kind that you put your frozen stuff in when you went shopping, so it wouldn't start to defrost before you got it back home. Together with a few pre-packaged ice cube bags it might buy us a day or two but it was no better than our coolboxes.

Lucile had stayed to watch the entrance, make sure nothing crept up on us while we were celebrating our win – a trip out of the safehouse completely without incident.

Or…so we thought.

As we were making our way back to the doors, we heard the rumble of an engine, the squeak of tyres, and the shouting of voices.

I abandoned the trolley and ran forward, drawing the Cobra as I went. Footsteps squeaked and pounded on the co-op floor behind me, as the others rushed to keep up.

Lucile let out a yelp, but I got to the doors just in time for her to disappear, dragged sideways. I strafed quickly around the corner after her, my gun raised. I felt the rain coming down faster now. People were moving out of the store behind me, raising their guns up. I hoped Morgan had the good sense to stay inside.

Lucile was being held by a man in camouflage gear – top to bottom. I could see one side of a tactical vest, but the other half of his body was blocked by Lucile. She still had her gun, her bat somewhere on the floor, but her hand was shaking. The man held her like a human shield, crouching slightly to compensate for her height, and pressing a gun up against the side of her head.

'Drop it miss, drop it now.' He barked, using his free hand to search inside her jacket, patting her down in a practiced and professional motion. Lucile dropped her gun, but once it hit the ground she kicked it further towards us, away from him - no, *them*, more than one, and every instinct was telling me they were not friendly.

Another man in similar camo getup was in the pawnshop doorway, while two men in all-black military clothes had spaced themselves between the two camo-guys. They were definitely the team from earlier – which meant their SUV, with at least one man in the cab – was down by the street.

233

'Doorway has an assault weapon, the boys in black are packing handguns but they won't clear the holster before I can put them down.' Anita reported from somewhere far to my left, in cover, behind the fountain and easily loud enough for them to hear. A threat.

We were lined up between the co-op's shuttered area and the back of Damian's truck. That didn't give us a whole lot of cover except for the fountain between the two black-clad gunmen in the middle. The man in the pawnshop doorway and the first man had good lines of fire on us if they'd care to use them.

'I have a shot on the dick holding Lucile.' Laurel chimed from the other side of Damian's ride. 'Want me to check he's as brainless as he looks?'

I didn't dare take my eyes off of the man to see where exactly everyone was, but I saw Damian move up next to me out of the corner of my eye, shotgun braced against his shoulder, aiming between the two men in black. Neville would have the other camo-guy marked.

I figured we'd gotten the drop on these guys. They hadn't thought anyone would be here. Even so, everybody was pointing guns at everybody else.

'Put down your weapons, looters.' The hostage-taker ordered, his voice stern, his hair buzzed short to match.

'On whose authority?' I asked, my gun aimed squarely at him, with both hands. He'd backed up but hadn't gone far, so I was reasonably confident I could put a bullet in him, not Lucile, even with my basic marksmanship.

'The Centre for Disease Control.' He replied after a moment's hesitation.

'Show me your providence.' Anita said. 'If you're with Sydow Security, Blackwood or any of Greenfield's assigned private military companies, you'd have ID.'

'Listen here little lady,' the other camo-guy snapped, pointing a finger with one hand, and angling his shoulder-strapped rifle towards her with the other, 'I don't know where you get off telling us our job-'

234

'Detective Inspector Mason.' She replied, neatly dropping rank. I didn't have to look to know she was holding up her badge, it put something in her voice, straightened the spine, made it more commanding.

There's no formal co-operation between law enforcement and the armed services, national or private. Neville's bronze or Anita's silver shield could no more compel these guys to lay down arms than their stern tones were doing for us. But hopefully having the law on our side would mean…something.

'What's that got to do with us?' the man replied, thrusting out his chin and taking a step forwards. Bugger.

'My entire Precinct and a dozen others were pulled off of our details to assist the CDC PMC's in enforcing the quarantine. I know the procedure. You don't. Ergo – whatever you're selling, we are not buying. Your equipment - are you Territorial Army?'

'Not anymore, had enough of that horseshit…' the guy holding Lucile spat, 'We'll do you a deal-' He added, his bluff rendered transparent.

'You're from the TA?' I asked, butting in, trying to steer the conversation.

'From the base near Overbridge.' the man in the doorway answered. Good. If I kept them talking long enough maybe I could diffuse the tension, get everyone to stop waving guns about for a minute.

'Shut up!' Lucile's captor ordered. Nail in the coffin for that plan, I guess.

'You boys got the order to fall back,' Anita pressed, into interrogation mode, 'protect Orphen, Parliament, the capitol. You must have had a good reason to desert?'

The captor glanced back over to the man in the doorway, shooting daggers at him. 'Risk our lives going halfway across the country for some politicians?' he said, voice dark, 'Leave that to the private sector, the PMCs get paid to fight.'

'You soldiers or what?' Anita scoffed.

235

'Voison's been exporting mercenaries for a thousand years,' doorway man snapped, 'if Parliament wanted a standing army they should have paid for one. People do their time and leave, call us weekend soldiers, part timers – and we're expected to lay down our lives? It's the end of the Republic, *officer*. I'm not getting killed over nothing. '

'You guys only sign up for the uniform? Republic Day parades?' Anita kept niggling. I wasn't sure goading them into action would be a good thing, but maybe she knew what she was doing better than I did.

'Are we going to discuss political history - or acquire the supplies we came for?' one of the men in black asked. His voice was different. Educated. Calm. If you'd have put his voice in a lineup you'd cast him as the villain any day.

'Sir.' The captor barked, a verbal salute. 'Like I said looters, we'll cut you a deal.'

'I'm listening.' I muttered, not sure if I should be talking or Anita. She didn't say anything.

'How about we give you back the girl,' he intoned, speaking with a voice of authority, 'and you give up your guns, the food, and the ATV.'

'Are you serious, or do you have some kind of mental condition we need to be aware of?' Laurel asked with a bitter laugh. 'I'm counting five guns to two. We've caught you with your collective pants down – so give us back our friend, or I'll bore you a new windpipe.'

'You think I'm scared of you, bitch?' he replied, forcing his gun into the side of Lucile's head. She twisted in discomfort. 'One wrong move, *one*, and I will end her!'

'Bitch? That's all you got?' Laurel imitated, putting on the same tones and laughing again. She wasn't giving him the pleasure of getting to her.

'Only one way you and your guys are making it out of here in one piece.' I said, putting on my captain face, addressing the one called "Sir", rather than the man holding my friend. 'You give us back our Lucile there, and you lay down your guns. Times are tough, so we're not going to take them. You come back here in two hours and they'll be right there waiting for you. I'll even leave half the stuff in that store if you take this offer real quick. We're fair off for supplies, but my patience, now that's kinda wearing thin.'

'And who are you supposed to be?' Sir sneered back, 'I know full well you're not all police officers.'

'I'm just a delivery boy. That guy over there? Security guard for one of the law firms downtown. The angry looking Islander next to me - sound engineer, works local bars and clubs, that kind of thing. Your man there's squeezing his squeeze so he's got a lot of cause to use that shotgun. Laurel? What's your day job?'

'I'm a hairdresser.' She replied.

'How many zeds you killed?' I asked her.

'Shit, you mean today, or this week?'

'Now I don't give half a fuck who you think you are.' I told him, taking a deliberate step forward, feeling my blood rising - powerful, in control, I'd put on my game face and people were listening, 'You've got ten seconds to make your mind up because there's another way this can end if you don't snap up my offer.'

'The easy way, and the hard way?' Sir enquired.

'Something like that.' I shot back. I told him my patience was wearing thin and I meant it. 'Nobody has to die tonight.'

The adrenaline was pumping now. There was a warm, tight feeling in all my muscles that assured me that if it came down to fight or flight, I was covered either way.

'Hmm…' he hummed, 'it's tempting. But I don't think -'

I caught Lucile's eye, and she held my gaze for just a second. She was ready to make her move. I nodded.

She threw her head forwards, wet hair hanging limp, then snapped back into her captor's nose. I could hear the impact. As he stumbled back, he pulled the trigger, a gunshot shattering the still of the night.

Lucile had already writhed around in his grip, twisting her body and grabbing something off of the side of his jacket I

237

couldn't see. Her hands appeared, raised up, clutching a knife. She drove it down with both hands.

It all happened so fast, nobody moved until Lucile had driven the blade home, lodging into his collarbone. He screamed in pain, fell to his knees and dropped his gun, staring at the knife in his chest with eyes wide.

Laurel was the first to react. She'd probably adjusted her aim the moment Lucile made her move. The crack of her rifle echoed around the plaza, accompanied by the sound of another man's agonised shout. It went quick from there, and I had to sort the details out in my head later.

Sir fell backwards, clutching at his chest with one hand. He'd tried to pull his gun, but dropped it in the fall. He rolled across the pavement and snatched it up, rolling again to lay on his back and aim up. Neville had been waiting for him, he probably wouldn't have fired if he hadn't gone for the gun. But he did. Neville shot twice, finishing the man off, his gun letting out low, rough barks to accompany the thunderclap of the rifle.

Lucile barrelled into me, shoving me around the corner and back into the shuttered area. She moved closest to the shop, breathless despite only moving a few feet. She gave me the wall spot, allowing me to lean out, since I had the gun. Chips of brickwork flew from the walls before I had a chance to lean out, forcing me to cringe away for a moment. My hands were shaking so much I doubt I'd have hit anything anyway.

Damian's shotgun roared, a deafening blast that knocked the second man off of his feet. It must have sent him sprawling, killed instantly, his chest was turned into a mess of reddened gore and scraps of black cloth.

The man with the assault rifle was no slouch though. As I got my wits about me and aimed out to help, he was running sideways, firing from the hip as he went, spraying bullets wildly across the plaza - suppressing fire, or panicked fire, I'm no expert. I heard the thuds of impact striking the wall behind me before I heard the zips of the incoming rounds.

He was yelling blue murder as he fired, short, chattering bursts of full-auto, from the waist. Not a technique to hit much with, but if you put enough rounds out fast enough, you only needed to get lucky once. Even without shooting anyone, it was keeping heads down - at least, for a moment.

Between bursts, Anita's pistol snapped off a quick one-two at the man, who was halfway down the grass verge now, going out of sight. He fired one last time, kicking up a spurt of concrete dust from the dried up fountain, firing on Anita – but it was Laurel I heard cry out in pain.

I turned to look, and saw her crouched by the back of the truck, holding onto it for support with one hand, her rifle fallen to the ground. She pressed the other hand to the side of her head, from eye to ear, where it was stained with blood.

Twenty Eight

I hurried over, forgetting the danger, and went down to my knees beside her, Morgan appearing a moment later - she had stayed inside while the bullets were flying, but seeing me move, she must have assumed it was safe.

'So much shooting, I thought they must have won...' she flustered, 'what can I do?'

More shots cracked off, twitching my head down instinctively, but they didn't seem intended for us. Tyres screeched as the SUV revved away. Damian was in pursuit, firing another blast from his shotgun at the SUV. I couldn't see it, but I heard the back window shatter.

Laurel sucked a breath in through her teeth and let out a groan. 'I'm hit. I think.' She said, speaking with forced calm, though her jaw was tight. 'Fucking, bastard, never been shot before.'

'Let me see,' I coaxed, reaching up to move her hand. She was reluctant. 'You haven't actually been shot' I told her, 'otherwise you'd be dead. That's good, right?'

'So sweet of you...' she said, lips tight. 'Burns, stings, throbs, all at the same time.'

She moved her hand out of the way, uncovering a long line of red from just above her eyebrow, right back under her hair. Torn flesh showed in a broad line, about as wide as a finger, seared brown at the edges like it'd been burned.

Though her hand was reddened with blood, the wound wasn't much of a bleeder, the bullet had whizzed past and grazed by the look of it - I'm no expert. As gently as I could, I moved her hair out of the way.

I cringed, looking away for a moment. I saw Lucile run into Damian, getting him around the waist in a very big hug. He leaned down and kissed her forehead. She turned to look, her face contorted at the sight of our injured Laurel.

'How bad is it?' Laurel asked, keeping her eyes staring straight ahead. 'Don't look away. Tell me.'

'Umm…' Morgan tried, her eyes fixed on the red and brown streak.

'Do we have wounded?' Anita shouted back, over her shoulder. She and Neville were crouched behind the fountain, guns pointed at the only entrance to the little plaza. I didn't expect to see the survivors from that firefight again, but one of the deserters had emptied a magazine at us. If that didn't grab the attention of a few wandering zeds, we'd be lucky. Especially with them moving out of the city.

'What? Come on!' Laurel panicked, breathlessly losing her calm, 'What's wrong?'

'You said you were a hairdresser, right?' Morgan answered, putting a hand over her's. 'Good news is, nobody's going to notice…'

'There's bad news?'

Laurel was missing about half an inch of her right ear, just the tip, just a little off the top, so to speak. No wonder it stung.

'It's not that bad,' I shot in, before Morgan could rip of the proverbial bandage, 'and you'd hardly notice it if you weren't looking…and keep your hair long…'

'Kell. I swear to Gods if you don't tell me what's wrong, they'll never find your body.' She growled, teeth bared, eyes watering.

Morgan came back in, squeezing Laurel's hand. 'A teeny, tiny, barely noticeable part of your ear is missing.'

Laurel closed her eyes, and took in a deep, shuddering breath, her shoulders rising and falling. I saw the edges of her mouth go through various expressions. They tightened, twitched, and eventually settled on turning up at the edges.

'Are you okay?' Morgan asked, her mouth hanging open.

'What?' Laurel said in reply.

'I said are you okay?' she tried again.

'What?' Laurel called, louder again.

241

My face split into a grin, and I let out a snigger, Morgan turning to give me a horrified look, like this was no time to laugh.

'Speak up girl,' Laurel all but shouted, grabbing Morgan by the shoulders and shaking her, 'Into my good ear!'

Morgan shoved her back, gently.

'Not funny…' she said, cracking out into a grin.

'I'm good officer,' Laurel strained, pulling herself to her feet, 'I'm going to need morphine and some reconstructive bloody surgery, but I'll survive.'

'Damian, cover the road, please.' Anita ordered.

I opened the boot and Morgan got Laurel sat down under the shelter of the raised lid. A little bulb flicked on just above, providing enough light to see by. The heavy drizzle was turning to true rain now, light, cold flecks giving way to fat, freezing droplets. In our pool of light and dry, it felt quite private.

'I'm not gonna whinge about it, I'm bloody fine.' She assured us, but her tight expression said otherwise.

'Where'd you become such a good shot, Laurel?' Anita asked, doing the same thing with her hair as I'd done, run her fingers through, then lift it away, rather than push it straight back.

'Spent most of my service shooting targets on the Redmond border. Before that I'd never held a gun outside of an arcade before,' Laurel answered, happy for a distraction I think, 'wasn't particularly good at those though. Wasted a lot of shillings.'

Anita chuckled, smiling, 'A girl after my own heart. I think the local amusement only stayed open because I filled those machines every weekend. You're a natural shot, you know?'

'Some good.' Laurel waved a hand at the side of her head.

'Bullet grazes will hurt like hell, but you're in no danger. I want to clean it out when we get back, then you'll have to keep it covered. Change your bandages every day like mine.'

242

'Maybe we can do each other.' Laurel smirked.

'Buy me dinner first.' She said back.

The adrenaline was fading, leaving behind a nice pile of endorphins to gorge on. We'd made it through another scrape, with only a graze to show for it. Once again, we'd gotten lucky - the guys in the middle, I'm guessing the squad leaders, had barely even drawn their weapons – handguns too, not the rifles we'd seen them with earlier, only one of them still carried an assault weapon.

If they'd been quicker off the mark, we could have been disarmed, stripped of supplies and missing our transport - that or we'd have been compressing bullet wounds and marking out more plots in the park. And even then, we'd be lucky to be doing that.

'What's the plan?' Neville enquired, coming over as I hovered uncertainly around Laurel and Anita. They'd just gotten to chatting, Morgan sat down on the edge of the boot as well. I looked over to see Damian and Lucile covering the plaza now.

'Lot of rounds just went off here.' I said, feeling the bottom of my stomach drop out, 'We need to move, fast. Get that trolley from inside, and load up the boot. I figured those shots would attract zombies, but if there's more arseholes with guns around, they might respond too.'

'Crap.' Neville muttered, heading back into the co-op.

I turned back to the ladies. 'We're getting out of here, as soon as possible. Laurel, you in a fit state to help, or do you want to go for a little lay down?' I ribbed.

'Good enough to kick your arse.' she grimaced, shuffling off the tailgate.

'Neville's grabbing the trolley. Can you guys get back to the storeroom and load up another? If we only get two runs, at least losing an ear will have been worth something.'

Laurel and Anita got to it.

Morgan stayed a moment.

'You like her?' she asked, uncertainly.

243

'Please, Morgan.' I replied, incredulous. We were doing this now?

'She's her non-identical twin. I see you getting all close. If you didn't care about her, you wouldn't take the piss.' She keenly observed.

'Me and her,' I said, bringing Morgan in for a hug, 'we've lost someone close to us, someone special. We're just working it through.'

'I lost her too, she was my friend too…' Morgan sniffed.

'I know, I know.' I told her, smoothing down the back of her hair, 'You, me and Laurel. We've all lost her. Or, maybe not. Hope not. There's still a chance…' I added, feeling my eyes begin to well up. We squeezed each other tighter.

'If we don't find her,' Morgan sighed, pulling away, her eyes reddened and glistening, 'you have my blessing.'

I blinked. 'Your what?'

'If you and her, you know, want to take comfort…' she said, irritated, wiping away a stray tear.

'Why are you and your father convinced I'm after her?' I shook my head. 'Let's just put a pin in this.'

'Please, let's.' she nodded, wiping a tear from her cheek.

I left her standing there and walked into the plaza for some air, letting the rain have at me. I'd forgotten about the bodies, of the men who'd attacked us, the men who we'd killed. Felt weird to phrase it like that, even though it was self-defence. I walked over to the one who had held Lucile hostage, and tried not to think of him as a person.

I found it easier than I thought.

He'd threatened us, would likely have killed us. He deserved what he got. But I wasn't sure that I could have done what Lucile did. Killed a man like that, no matter how much of a threat he was. I'd done in my share of the zombies so far, but a person…that was different. I'd hesitated at pulling the trigger on Dani. Would it be easier or harder, to kill a stranger? Maybe Neville had the right of it.

Kneeling down next to him, I beat my thoughts into line. He was dead now, no need to get philosophical over it. I put

244

my hand around the knife in his chest and tried to pull it out, but Lucile had really lodged it in there. It wasn't worth wrestling with the corpse over.

His vest had a few odds and ends in it that I was sure we could use, though the vest itself was too bloodied up for me to consider taking it as well. A compass, a few road flares, a small set of binoculars, I pocketed them along with his pistol and a couple spare magazines from specially sized pockets in his vest. There were bigger pockets, probably for bigger magazines, but they were empty. Hmm.

I investigated the other bodies as well, the two in black, recovering similar equipment - the compass, more flares, one of them had a first aid kit and the other a tin opener, of which I only took the former. They too had space for large magazines in their jackets, but the pockets were empty.

That's why they only had handguns. No ammo left for the big stuff, or they were running so dry only one guy in the group was assigned it. If that were the case – that'd make him their best shooter, surely? He can't have wanted to hit anybody, or he'd have done it. That, or maybe he just wanted everyone's head down so he could escape.

Neville came back with the trolley, and the freezer-bag of frozen goods. I helped him load them into the boot while Morgan went to fill another bag. After the awkwardness I'd just had with his daughter, I was glad we were working in silence.

The other happy couple had moved to the edge of the rundown plaza, and waited at the corners for signs of trouble, leaning around them half-hidden. At the sound of the ladies coming out with the second trolley, they came over to join us.

'Sorry man,' Damian shook his head at Neville, 'they shot out de tyres on your car, front two.'

'He sprayed and prayed, and only grazed one of us,' Neville sighed, walking to the edge of the plaza. I half followed him, not wanting him to go too far alone. He came back shaking his head, 'Then he assassinated my car.'

'Made sure we couldn't chase after them.' Damian said.

'Ugh.' Neville remarked, scratching the back of his head.

'We'll get it fixed, some day.' I comforted, putting a hand on his shoulder. I felt bad for him, but I needed to get us out of here. 'Someone give me a hand with this?' I gestured up at the shutters.

'Thinking we come back tomorrow?' Anita asked. 'We're becoming repeat offenders.'

'That's my hope. I'm just going to duck inside, turn the lights off. We might need them again, if we have to come back at night.' I added, going in to do just that. Through the staff room, into the office, flick off the lights. I only then realised that put me in pitch black darkness, and hadn't gotten my flashlight ready.

Feeling a little silly, I picked my way back outside with the help of the little light, grabbing a bottle of bubbly from behind the counter on the way.

'What're you celebrating?' Laurel quirked an eyebrow, twinging as she did.

'Our first firefight, and nobody's dead.' I aimed for cheerful.

I didn't feel it inside, but somebody had to keep spirits up.

'We found loads of booze already, remember?' Anita pointed out.

'Waste not, want not. And I want it all.' I beamed, putting it on for the troops. The post combat shakes had started and even pretending to be okay made me feel a little better.

We pushed the two empty trolleys we'd used back through the doors, then with Damian's help, closed the shutters. No longer locked on that switch behind the counter, we'd be able to just pull them right up again if and when we came back.

Without Neville's sedan, half of us were either walking back, or squeezing in. Since we hadn't even half-filled the massive cargo compartment, and it wouldn't be a squeeze for long, Morgan and I jumped into the back, and held onto straps which seemed to be there for no other purpose I could tell.

Damian engaged the headlights and wipers as we pulled out of the plaza, swerving to avoid Neville's crippled sedan, which he locked with a bleep of his keys as we rode by. With the exception of a grumble from Laurel as we bumped back down onto the road, we went in silence, watching the windows for signs of headlights or shambling shapes.

'Leave the supplies in Stan's place for now,' I said, as we were pulling up outside the flats, 'we'll take them up when we have the elevator powered.'

'Was hoping ya'll were going to say that. I ain't hauling this stuff up for the sake of a night, should we be getting evacuated.' Lucile seconded the motion.

I helped carry the boxes through to Stan's, while Anita and Laurel got comfortable in the foyer with a first aid kit. On my first trip in I saw her gently padding the graze and ragged tip of her ear with disinfectant solution and cotton wool pads, drawing gasps of discomfort. On the next run, she was getting Laurel to hold up gauze to her injuries, then was just finishing up with the bandages and tape as we brought the last of the supplies in.

'Will she make it, doctor?' I asked.

Anita gave me a look, but Laurel replied, 'Tis but a scratch.'

'We'll keep it clean, and it'll heal. The missing bit of ear though, that's not going to grow back.' Anita said, chewing her lip.

'Obviously. Will I have a scar, on my face?'

'Highly likely…' she said sympathetically.

'Awesome.' Laurel tried to grin, but it must have twinged an uncomfortable muscle.

Anita patted her on the shoulder and picked up the first aid kit. 'Someone's going to have to help me change my bandage tonight too. Don't think I've popped any stitches, but I could do with a cleanup and change.'

'I'll play mother when we get up top.' Laurel nodded, 'I believe we did promise to do each other.'

'There a law against innuendo?' I probed. 'Are you good to walk, or do you want to stay down here tonight?'

'The bullet grazed my face, not my leg. Don't ask me to win any beauty contests, but I'll make it upstairs.'

'You'll look fine when we clean the rest of the blood off. I'll keep her stable, if she wobbles.' Anita assured me.

'Here's me thinking we were supposed to keep you stable.' Laurel joked.

I thought it'd hit a little too close to home, but Anita actually chuckled and helped her stand. Maybe it helped, to have someone not walk on eggshells around her. I should never have taken her gun away.

We set off upstairs, and for once, it didn't seem like such a chore. Maybe we were all still buzzing from the fight or just feeling good about being well supplied, but there was a definite note in the air. Battered, bruised as we were, bad as I felt, we'd made it home. So much for a simple trip to the shops. Everything was trying to kill us these days.

Twenty Nine

Up on the top floor, we took our shoes off in the doorway to the safehouse and shed our coats onto the hooks. After emptying out the guns and other odds and ends I'd found on the Territorials, I hung up mine and flumped down onto one end of the sofa with Damian and Lucile, Neville occupying the armchair. Anita went over to the kitchen to sit next to Morgan on one of the stools.

'I'm going to get cleaned up, someone grab me a beer?' Laurel asked, going off towards the bathroom.

'That's a sensible idea.' Neville concurred.

The energy I had coming up those stairs was drained the moment I knew I'd gotten back to safety. That was the price of burning so much adrenaline in a day. I was beat. But could still really use that beer.

'Morgan?' I asked, sounding all weak and weary.

'Would you be a dear?' her father continued.

Morgan opened the beer cooler, took out a cold one, and used the bottle opener. She sipped it, and carried on talking to Anita, who was fighting not to smile.

'I get them,' Damian grunted with the effort of standing up. My legs felt like jelly. 'Girl.' He sighed, patting her firmly on the shoulder, 'that is just cruel.'

He returned with beers for all and a spare for when Laurel emerged. I took a long pull but stopped when a dark thought hit me - if civilisation itself has collapsed, how will we make more beer? We'd have to look into bathtub cider or wine kits if we were going to be stuck here forever. Across from me, Neville eyed his bottle. I wasn't sure, but he might have been thinking the same.

'Hell of a day...' he mused, pressing the bottle to his forehead a moment. They were still fridge cold, and after sweating up the stairs, they were heavenly.

249

'Seem everywhere we go, something goes wrong.' Damian tilted his bottle in agreement.

'Should have had guns for the radio station. And the pawnshop was on my own head, should have been on the buddy system.' I admitted.

'We let you go in there alone, could have just followed you straight up the ladder. Should have.' Neville added, his brow furrowed, 'Fault for that lies with all of us, not just you. None of us should go anywhere alone.'

'We got to watch each other hit the head now?' Lucile smirked.

'Just when we out there.' Damian said, putting his arm around here. 'We safe up here.'

'No arguments here. When that zed had me in the shop, I thought I was done for. If it hadn't been for Laurel…' I trailed off, looking down at my beer.

'There was a moment of confusion on our end,' Neville leaned back in his chair, 'and then Laurel was up that ladder in seconds. I was behind her, but wasn't quick enough.'

'You'd have made it in time. Don't worry.' I reassured him. 'How are you two anyway, you and Laurel?'

'I did screw up at the garage,' he said, keeping his voice low 'but she's got anger management issues. Bad combination, high stress situation.'

That was the mature answer, I guess. Doubt I would have gotten the same one from Laurel. Neville was right, she wasn't known for her level-headedness. Wonder if that got her into trouble during her service, or if it'd helped her reign in an even worse temper.

'You've been through a couple scrapes together now, right?' Lucile piped up. 'You'll have that brothers in arms thing going in no time.'

'I'll make it up to her.' He nodded, taking it in. 'How are you guys coping with all the bullets flying around?'

The sound of a stool scraping gently across the floor twigged my attention over to the kitchen, where Anita and Morgan were hugging. Morgan had her face buried in the crook of Anita's neck, being taller. Anita held the girl tight, and brushed down the back of her hair. I could see Morgan's chest heaving with sobs.

'Think you're needed,' I said to her father.

Neville excused himself, going over to be with the pair. I turned away, to give them some privacy.

'Tough break.' Lucile noted, 'Friend, sister. Going to need each other to get through this.'

'We all need each other to get through this.' I croaked, suddenly feeling my throat go tight.

'You and Laurel.' Lucile said, 'Same thing. I didn't really have anyone to lose up here, but back home I've got a family, and no clue how they're doing. So I know how you're feeling.'

'Think this is the most emotional I've ever seen you,' I pointed out, employing the typical male response of glossing over it.

'Then ya'll love this. The other day, I said to him,' she gestured at Damian, 'that I ain't never had anyone to lose, until we lost everyone. Now that's true Kelly. Aside from a few work friends, I didn't know anybody here, but I'd still feel better off knowing - like they do - what happened to their people. But you, me and Damian, we're stuck in limbo…and I'm sure glad as hell that we're all together, in this…' she cut off, waving her beer-holding hand vaguely.

'She saying she like having friends.' Damian translated.

'Ya'll assholes, but here's to assholes who care.' She corrected, raising her bottle in a toast. 'Now I need one of my carefully rationed smokes. What's the apartment policy?'

'Outside, respect for de previous tenants.' Damian replied, standing up again and going over to his coat.

'Back in a few.' Lucile said, flashing me a "let's never speak of this deep talk" look - half warning, half smiling.

The opening and closing of the balcony door let a breeze roll in, taking the last of the body heat we'd generated on the stairs and nudging the temperature in there to something just the wrong side of comfortable. It also made me realise we had

251

no lighting, and it was bloody dark in here. Guess our eyes had adjusted.

Neville, Morgan and Anita were still huddled in the kitchen, talking in low voices, so I tried not to disturb them or overhear anything as I got the lighter from my jacket pocket.

The candles were still set out from last night, so I just went about the room creating mood lighting, drawing the curtains as I went. Most of them were the little tea lights you can buy sacks of fifty for cheap, but the Jamesons had been old fashioned and practical, so had a few big storm candles for power outages and slender candles for settings on dinner tables, despite not really having a dinner table.

Once the room was lit, it was actually starting to feel a little warmer again. Not sure if that's because of the tiny flames or the warm glow just making the room seem a little cosier.

Laurel exited the bathroom, still self-consciously rubbing around her bandage. She sat down in the armchair, so I groaned onto my feet to retrieve the beer Damian had got her and held it out.

'How's it feel?' I asked.

'Like one inch to my left and we wouldn't be having this conversation.' She muttered, casting a curious glance over to the trio in the kitchen.

'Not sure dwelling on that's going to help,' I tried, 'drink your beer, it's medicinal.'

'Not strong enough. Do we have any painkillers?' she said, lips tight. 'I'm no whiner, but if there's a time for them, it's now.'

'I've got some strong stuff in my place, give me a minute…' I rose once more and grabbed a candle, better to find my way around my kitchen with. The little flashlight was still in my jacket, but I didn't want to waste the battery when candles were already lit.

'I could come with you?' she half-asked.

'It's alright, I know where to look. You should probably be resting.'

252

'Again, shot in the face, not the leg.' She pointed at the bandage.

I chuckled and went over to the door, leaving my beer on the coffee table. Again, I tried to keep as far from Neville, Morgan and Anita as possible, but I still overheard a snippet of conversation. It was about Anita's family.

'…should be buried, like the Jamesons, doesn't feel right.' Morgan sniffed, wiping away a tear.

'I don't like leaving them there, Neville.' Anita said, her voice raw. 'Morgan wants to help me. What do you think?'

'Of course I'll help…' he replied, putting an arm around her.

I respected their privacy, kept quiet and slipped out into the pitch black corridor, lit only in a pool of candlelight. I hadn't bothered locking my apartment, didn't see the point at the moment, so I didn't have to mess around with keys.

It felt wrong at the time, leaving those bodies there, but it wasn't like we had a choice. The neighbourhood dogs chased us off. But with Anita stable now, she could do with the closure. Morgan too.

In my head, a gunshot went off, and red splattered all over a black and white poster. I cringed, closed my eyes a moment in the doorway to my apartment.

If they wanted to go back and bury their family, that was fine with me, I'd carry a shovel myself. But there were some bodies that I couldn't bear to see again. If Laurel asked me to go back to that house and see to Dani's remains, I don't think I could. Too much of a reminder, too much thinking about what could have happened to Katy.

Like the apartment across the corridor, mine was dark and taking on a chill. Moving around with just the candle's flickering light to see by made it a little unsettling, but I knew nobody could be up here, so I put that to the back of my mind, along with thoughts of dead friends and how else that firefight could have ended.

The back of my mind was getting pretty full.

I have an odds and ends drawer in my kitchen, with a big plastic box of meds inside. Stuff for headaches, heartburn, cold and flu remedies, that sort of thing. There was also leftover pain medication from when I got glassed in the head. They were the good stuff, one tablet, must be taken with food, no more than three days in a row, that kind of good. I only had half a dozen left, but Laurel's need for pain relief was greater than my need to hoard supplies. I checked the date on them first though, since they were getting on over two years old now. We were still in the clear.

In my personal pool of candlelight, I left my apartment and returned to the Jamesons'. Neville, Anita and Morgan were on the sofa now, with Damian and Lucile sat on the kitchen stools. I handed the strip of pills to Laurel.

'Just one. Should take it with food, but we only ate like an hour ago. Have a biscuit, you'll be alright. No heavy machinery.' I added, feeling everyone's eyes on me.

I retrieved my beer, in no hurry to talk, then sat down on one of the kitchen stools as well. I took a deep breath, and stalled some more. They were obviously waiting for me.

'So…' Neville encouraged, looking around at everybody, sat in their silence.

'Tomorrow then…' I began, 'tomorrow we're busy. Priority should be getting to Greenfield City Radio, seeing if Mr Sachs has been in contact with the CDC again. Or if he ever was,' I said, throwing a look to Neville, 'I don't think any of us thought he was completely on the level.'

'More going on there than met de eye.' Damian assented, tipping back his bottle.

'So it could be we're getting out of here tomorrow, off to some refugee camp.' I frowned, 'Kinda not sure I like that any better than being stuck here for an indefinite period, but it at least warrants checking out.'

'Think we're all in agreement there,' Laurel said, popping a small pill out of the foil, washing it down with some beer. 'Got to scope it out.'

254

'Do we have time for a detour on the way?' Anita asked, her voice still a little sore.

'Yes. We're doing it.' I told her.

'Doing what?' Lucile asked.

'Putting Becky, Paul and Marianna Mason to rest.' Neville supplied, his voice solemn. 'We're going to go back and bury them.'

Lucile nodded, mouth set to a line. 'We'll keep an eye out for the dogs.'

'Kelly, if you think we should go back to…' Neville started, his voice fading at the look I gave him.

'No,' I shook my head, 'I don't want to go back there. But I'll help you guys.' I added, raising my bottle. It was empty, so I reached for a new one. 'So we head to the cul-de-sac. Then we get out to GCR, and see what's in store for us there. Anyone else got things to put on the list?'

'Diesel,' Damian said, ticking off fingers, 'my ride's getting below quarter-tank. De white pickup outside, anyone know whose it is? Find keys for it yesterday?' he added, to Anita and Morgan. People shook their heads. Neville had assumed it was Lucile's, but I guess he was wrong.

'If we can't drive it, we tap it for gas.' He added.

'We still need to bring some things up from the apartments, more boxes of supplies.' Anita said, 'But they'll keep until the evening.'

'If you two don't want to, I'll do it, I don't mind.' I told them.

'Just don't feel like it right now. We'll see how my homecoming goes.' Anita said, her eyes fixed straight forwards.

'There's also the supplies left in the co-op,' I reminded them, 'we haven't stripped it clean. Plenty of fresh fruit and the like, probably do us good with all the meat and bread we've been eating.'

'We should save the seeds? Like, to plant somewhere?' Morgan suggested.

255

'Yeah,' I nodded, 'we'll need them if we can't get out of this city.'

'What do we do tonight, more importantly?' Neville asked.

'Got any board games?' I suggested.

'Haven't I been through enough?' Laurel sighed.

Thirty

Twist. Pop. Fizz. I'm not massively keen on champagne, but according to Neville this was good stuff. The Jamesons' had appropriate glassware in their cabinets for only six of us, so I poured mine into a regular wine glass when it came to filling my own. I don't know if that's against the rules of sparkling wine or anything, but I'd have drunk it out of a tea-stained mug if there weren't glasses, so…

'A toast then,' I said, handing glasses around, 'to our hosts. Edgar and Rosie Jameson, long may they rest unrisen.'

The chorus cheered, glasses clinked, and sips were taken. As the group broke apart, Laurel sat on one of the kitchen stools. There should have been dim music playing, and a party atmosphere rising, but instead there was only the sound of low chatter, glasses on tables and a game board being set up.

'Why do you think they did it?' she asked. 'The old couple, who lived here before.'

'Not sure.' I shrugged, 'Talked about it with Morgan, we found the bodies. I thought it was stupid, waste of life kinda thing. But she…saw it a different way.'

'How's that?'

'Said they probably didn't want to be a burden on us. Didn't want us to have to take care of them. The lift down the hall, their prescriptions, without them they'd be housebound, sick or in a lot of pain.'

'They didn't want anyone having to take care of them.' Laurel nodded, doing that middle-distance stare some people do when having deep talks.

'Euthanasia, I guess. Without waiting around for the paperwork or being on death's door already.' I added, dropping my own version of the thousand-yard and meeting her eyes. 'Do you want to go back for her?' I asked. She knew who I meant.

'No, she didn't want to be buried. Didn't want to be burned either, so I've no clue what she wanted beyond just, not that.' She added, vaguely waving her hand.

'Sailor's funeral?' I frowned.

Laurel just shrugged, sighing. 'We never talked about it directly. She just said she didn't like the idea of being put under the ground, or her ashes being spread. Morbid on the whole subject, and she never told me anything different, even after the fever took. So she's…' she paused, but grit her teeth and pushed through, 'she's going to lay there in that bed.'

I looked over the other side of the room, where Neville was unpacking the bits for the property trading board game, the old version, where they still used paper money. He was smiling, chatting with Anita and the rest. Was he beat up inside, or was he just tougher than me?

'We can go back, put her somewhere else, if that'd be any better.'

Laurel took a sip of champagne. A big one. 'Forget it. I never want to go back to that house. Got some clothes I wouldn't mind going back for, but a wardrobe ain't worth stepping through that door again, for me. Dani's not going to turn, and that's enough.'

'I was kind of hoping it'd just burn down after we left…' I sighed.

'I'm not against the idea of doing a drive-by firebombing.' She smirked, taking another drink. 'Top me up, I'm terrible at this game, and a sore loser. Should I be drinking on these tablets?' she asked, frowning at the glass a moment.

'Don't think so. Fuck it.' I told her, pouring more in.

Anita walked over with her glass in one hand, and the big green first aid kit in the other. 'Before we begin?'

'Well I did promise,' she replied, putting her glass down, 'let's get you to the bedroom.'

'The bubbly must have gone to my head…' Anita said, twitching her eyebrows, taking Laurel's hand. I couldn't help but laugh, they say it's the best medicine.

'We're doing well….' I muttered to myself, watching them go. Drinking, joking, playing games. Maybe Ed and Rosie should have been here, just to see how well we were doing. We'd have swung by the pharmacy to pick up their meds if they'd have asked.

The ladies left the door open to the bedroom, not sure if that was to signify they weren't actually following through on their innuendo. I stood in the doorway, and whipped out my flashlight. No overtones there.

'Need some light?' I asked.

'Mine's bigger.' Anita said back, passing me her much larger torch. It was heavier than I expected, you really could have used it as a club.

Anita sat up on the bed with her legs tucked into her side, Laurel kneeling beside her. I hovered above, holding the light on Anita's shoulder.

'We should probably have had a look sooner,' Anita said while Laurel peeled away the tape, 'but we were busy. Besides, it doesn't feel any worse.'

Laurel removed the bandage, and placed it messy-side-up on the bed. My light did not reveal a kindly sight. The neat punctures were still there, red and tender, but beyond dried blood covering her back, there were streaks of yellow. We peered closer, and could see it in the wounds as well.

'What?' Anita asked. 'What're you staring at?'

Laurel and I shared a look. 'I don't think I appreciate sugar-coating any more than she does.' She cringed.

'Looks infected.' I told her, keeping my voice low, not to be overheard.

'Shit, how bad is it?' she cursed.

'There's yellow gunk.' Laurel hummed, 'And it's all red around the punctures. What do I do?'

'Clean me up, please.' Anita said, hanging her head for a moment, 'It's going to hurt. The wound's infected, not uncommon for dog bites, so I'm guessing infected dogs are no different.'

'You feverish?' I asked.

259

'No, but if I was, there'd be no telling whether it was the zed-fever, or from my body fighting a standard infection. Not to sound too defensive, but…' she let her voice trail, tilted her head, 'I don't want to die. So let me have this one.'

'You've got it.' I reassured her.

'Light, Kell.' Laurel reminded me.

She set about cleaning the wound, first with simple wet-wipes and cotton buds from the bathroom to get rid of most of the blood and pus - ick - then she got a flannel and dabbed antiseptic solution on it. Anita had twitched and hissed while the wound was cleaned, but this was going to be something else, and she knew it.

As delicately as she could, Laurel set about patting the wound down with the wet flannel. Anita scrunched the bedsheet up into a ball beneath one fist, and dug her nails into her leg with the other hand, but that was just the first pass.

'You've got to keep going,' she grunted, 'if it hurts this bad, its doing me good. Probably an idea to dilute some of that in water, and give it another couple runs with another towel or something.'

'You sure?' Laurel asked. 'Beginning to think I might have been a big whiner with my missing ear.'

'Do it. Please.' She added, 'I don't want to take any chances.'

I sat with her while Laurel went to get a cup from the kitchen - a bathroom cup might have had toilet-flush bacteria at the bottom.

'You're going to be fine.' I told her, hand on her other shoulder, 'This is just a normal infection, like you said, this isn't going to make you turn.'

'I hope so.' She said, putting her hand over mine, but staring straight forwards, keeping her voice level. 'Finding you guys was the best thing that happened to me. If I die, I want you to know, I appreciate everything you've done.'

'Whoa, don't go talking like that, you're going to be fine…' I tried, but she cut me off.

'Listen, I forgive you for the gun thing, and yeah, it annoyed me, especially since you're a civilian with no training,' she quickly injected, 'but it was a good idea. And I know…I know your heart's in the right place, Kelly.'

'You're talking like you're dying…'

'Might be.'

'You were the one who wanted the optimistic outlook.'

'Hah, yeah. Okay.' She said, nodding, still keeping her voice calm. 'Just wanted to say thanks, and that while we don't have the bullets to spare, I can still teach you proper shooting stance. It's no trouble.' She added, looking over her shoulder with a smile. Her face was a little pale and sweaty from the pain she'd been through, but she looked…happy. Ish.

Laurel returned with diluted antiseptic and set to work having a proper clean out of Anita's wounds with a fluffy towel and a lot of squirming. Once it was all over, she dried her off, and bandaged her back up.

'What now?' I asked.

'We didn't find any antibiotics in the apartment search, so I'm just going to have to fight it off on my own,' Anita said, 'that, or we make a run to one of the hospitals, or break into a pharmacy. I'm already asking a lot of people to bury my parents. I don't want to ask any more of you.'

'You can, if you want,' Laurel stage-whispered, 'they're good people.'

'We'll see if I get any worse,' Anita smiled at us both, 'thank you. For everything.'

Back in the living room, I sat with the group to play the game, and hoped it wouldn't last as long as some of the runs I'd had at this game - days spent with players loaning out money for property, trading railway stations and hanging in by a thread. Not that I didn't like it, but we did have stuff to do tomorrow…

Not everyone was into the game however. Lucile, Laurel and Anita went to play cards in the kitchen, using a poker set I'd gone to fetch after the ladies declared their disinterest. We'd been going for maybe ten minutes when a smoking

261

break was declared for those who partook. I went onto the balcony with them anyway, since the rain had stopped it seemed a good point to get some fresh, if slightly smoky, air.

'Should have picked some more smokes up at the store.' Lucile observed, leaning over the edge to look down.

'Always tomorrow,' Damian assured her, 'I got plenty left. But we going to be cutting down, yeah?'

'You can, more for me…' Lucile muttered.

'You got any bad habits you'll miss?' Damian asked me, passing his cig on to Laurel, a social smoker at best.

'Don't know if it's a bad habit, but going online I'll miss. Games with friends, pretty much the only way I stayed in touch with some people.' I shrugged, 'Going to have to make new friends.'

'Texting.' Laurel said after me, 'I thought I'd miss it. Always had my phone on me, always talking to somebody. Since the battery died, I'm actually kinda relieved.'

'Probably for the best then. You'd have to swap ears to take a call now anyway.' I teased. She punched my arm. Damian chuckled, but looked out over the balcony when Laurel turned to him. It hurt more than I think she intended, but I tried not to rub it while she was looking.

'Ready to go back in?' Lucile asked, dabbing her end into an ashtray.

'Hold on,' Laurel said, holding up a hand, 'can you hear that?'

'Give it time before you use that one again,' I said.

'No, seriously, listen…' she muttered, leaning over the balcony railing and peering off towards the road. We joined her, and strained our ears. She'd heard the Deserters' SUV coming before any of us had, that first trip across the road. Sharp ears.

Something was coming, something with a big engine. I ran inside, dashing to the kitchen side where I'd left those binoculars earlier.

'Where's the fire?' Neville asked.

'There's a vehicle coming!' I replied, my voice going louder, excited, worried, a little of both.

My body, tired from the day's labours, didn't know how to respond to this. If they'd heard the gunshots, maybe they were just concerned citizens coming to investigate, or maybe they were reinforcements called in by the Deserters - here to search the area for the group that killed their friends.

'I have another pair of binoculars in my kitchen,' Neville declared, leaping out of his chair and heading for the door, towards his apartment.

Morgan ran ahead of me out onto the balcony, but Anita stopped to pick up Laurel's rifle from beside the door. I let her go ahead as well.

The hairdresser gave a nod of thanks as the policewoman handed her the rifle. She put the strap over her head, and went straight to looking down her scope.

'Let us know what you see.' Anita requested.

'I'll give you live commentary.' Laurel promised.

'I'll share.' I said to Damian, giving him a nod before putting the binoculars up to my eyes.

I know nothing about binoculars. I'm just going to put that out there now. I assume you can adjust them for focus, but these seemed alright for looking up the road.

'Truck's coming,' Laurel mumbled, concentrating, 'can just see headlights, too dark for much else.'

'I've got it too, just coming down the main road now.'

'We know, we can see the headlights too.' Lucile said, giving me a pat on the back.

The headlights and the dark silhouette behind them drew closer to our neck of the woods, towards the little plaza. As the angle of approach changed, the lights pointed to the side rather than right at us, so we got a better look at the truck.

It sat high off the road, the ground clearance to go off-road and the tyres to match. The front cab was flat-faced with four doors, a bit like the front of a fire-truck, only the whole thing was dark green or black, hard to tell in the dark. At the rear of the cab was a canvas-framed shelter over a flat bed.

263

'Looks pretty standard for any kind of military vehicle,' Laurel kept up her commentary, 'might be four guys up in the cab, could be twenty riding under the canvas.'

'I don't want twenty more Deserters about here.' Damian grunted, 'Think we should be reloading guns?'

'I don't want to miss anything, it's going to be the only current-events news we get for a long while.' Lucile drawled.

I looked over to her, reminded of that reporter outside Mercy Hospital, when the riot started, and that mercenary hopped off the bus just before everything went bloody and shaky-cam. She was the same reporter who gave the final broadcast. I hoped she was still alive, holed up in the VBC Studio. Maybe if things didn't pan out at GCR, that'd be a place to swing by, since the zombies had moved out of the city now.

The truck came to a stop as the headlights fell on Neville's car. I could see inside the cab from here, sort of. People were moving around inside, getting ready to disembark.

Thirty One

'You say I missed something?' Neville himself asked, stepping out onto the now crowded balcony.

'Big truck,' I grimaced, 'they just saw your car and they've stopped. If they heard the gunshots they must have worked out this is where they came from.'

'My turn?' Morgan asked me.

Begrudgingly, I handed over the binoculars.

'They're getting out of their truck,' Laurel informed us, 'mixed bag of camouflage and black fatigues again. One of them just went around to the back of the truck and another went to your car,' she said, tilting her head to Neville.

'He's found something in the road,' Neville kept the commentary up, 'bent down to pick it up. You fired at their vehicle, D? Could be an empty shell.'

'Couple more guys getting out the back of the truck. Can't tell from here for sure, doesn't look like they're in uniform, but they're armed. Rifles, shotguns, something like.' Laurel said, sucking her teeth.

'How many's that now?' Lucile asked.

'Six, two more just got out of the front, can't tell if any more are in the back or if they've all gotten out.' Neville said, passing his binoculars off to her.

'Borrow your rifle?' I asked Laurel, wanting to see again.

'Bugger that.' She shot back.

'Can I?' Anita tried.

Laurel shrugged out of the strap, and handed it over. She stuck her tongue out at me. 'That's for all the ear-jokes, those past and them still to come.'

'Their guns are up, and they're entering the plaza.' Anita kept us posted, 'They look well drilled for it, even the couple who may not be in uniform.'

'How come you can't tell?' Damian asked.

265

'Not much difference between camo bottoms you can buy in a store and ones you get because you're a squaddie,' Neville said, passing him his own set of binoculars, 'the others have vests, helmets, geared up. Ones without might just be dressed for the occasion.'

'Guess not everyone goes for a leather-based look?' Lucile suggested. 'Either way…we thinking about putting up one of those road flares, or playing possum?'

'I go with the rodent,' Morgan said with a nervous laugh, handing her the binoculars, 'squeak squeak.'

'That…is a lot of guns.' Lucile nodded. 'They're better armed than the guys we just went up against. Could be Deserters too, but if ya'know…if they are the CDC's legit forces, this could be a good time to wave hello.'

I scratched my chin. She might have been right. It'd certainly save us the trouble of having to deal with Sachs again if she was. But if she wasn't - we'd be advertising our position to another group of Deserters who might take umbrage with us killing their scouting party, looting their bodies, and sending up the mayday signal with their own fireworks.

'They've seen the Deserters' bodies on the ground,' Anita told us, 'they look spooked, checking the plaza for lines of fire - taking cover. You guys didn't lock the pawnshop up?'

'No?' I frowned.

'Two just went in, think they must have seen the broken glass…one of them's in the upstairs window now.'

'Wish we'd have thought of posting a lookout.' Laurel sighed, making a face.

'They're opening the shutters, got flashlights on their guns…now they're entering the shop…left two guys where we were by the fountain, third guy in the pawnshop window.'

'You see if they've got scopes on their guns too?' I asked. 'Might not look too kindly if they see you looking at them down yours.'

'Can't tell from here, but if one of them looks this way, what do you want me to do, shoot them or wave?' she asked, in her serious voice. She checked the rifle was chambered. She wasn't kidding - and after what we'd been through already tonight, I'd be surprised if her's was the only itchy trigger finger in the group.

It was another one of those weird moments, like a disconnection from reality. Again, people were expecting me to make the call - people better qualified, surely, to make this kind of choice?

I tried to reason it out, lay the facts in front of me. First and foremost; if these were Deserters, another part of the group we'd fought earlier, then getting the first shot off now would be a hell of an advantage for us, with a long-range rifle from the top of a tower block. Many a spree killer had picked the same sort of situation for their mental breakdown.

But if we fired first, that's what we'd be. Killers. We'd be the bad guys in this. That whole situation with the Deserters earlier, they'd been clearly in the wrong, and we'd just defended ourselves. Firing first, that's different. We didn't even know if these were Deserters. They could have been the CDC's people - Sydow Security out gathering supplies and intel, perhaps even in touch with GCR.

On the other hand again - there was no telling who they were, not from here. The safest option then, the only safe option really, was to take the third option.

'If they scope up here, tell us to duck,' I ordered, trying to put some authority in my voice, 'we all get down. Pretend like we're not home. If they come knocking on the tower or start shouting up to us, then we know we're rumbled, but unless that happens, we keep quiet. Too much risk involved in making contact again tonight.'

That sounded a lot better than "let's hide".

'I can get with that.' Lucile nodded.

'Smart play, I bet.' Neville assented.

'Look, down on the road they came in by.' Anita said, her voice dropping lower. 'They're coming.'

'My turn again yet?' I asked everyone. Damian handed me Neville's binoculars.

It took me a moment to spot them, but Anita was right, they were coming. Zeds. Dozens of them, out from the city centre, like we'd seen them doing earlier in the day.

'Everyone, be really really quiet…' Morgan whispered, her voice barely a breath. 'They're not just on the road…'

I didn't need the binoculars to see the ones moving around in our car park - dark figures dotted here and there, some brighter for wearing white before they turned, now stained with red and brown. They must have moved out this way from that fuck-up at Smith Casey's Garage.

'Good job we didn't light a flare,' Laurel muttered, 'we'd be up to our arses in zeds.'

'They're about to be though,' Neville said, and I could tell he was scrunching his face up. 'Still think you're right though, let's not expose ourselves…'

'So to speak.' Laurel added, drawing a tense, quiet titter from Morgan.

I watched the zeds get closer to the plaza, drawn to the area earlier by the gunfire, then drawn more closely to the shopping precinct by the approach of that truck, with its big, rumbling engine. Deserters or not, I wished there were some way I could have warned the men over there what was coming without drawing the zombies onto us instead.

But I didn't need to. The soft moans and shuffling feet of the approaching dead were lost to us up here, but down on the ground, their lookout had already seen the dead coming, and the three gunmen in the plaza were aiming their weapons towards the road. I bit my bottom lip as the first of them came up the embankment.

One shot pierced the quiet of the night, and the zombie dropped. That's when the runners in the mob emerged, enraged by the sound of the gunshot, they screeched aloud and began that staggering lope forwards, arms waving as they jostled their way through the slower moving zeds.

Two more shots, and the first pair of front-runners went down, one of them still thrashing, the shot not a kill, but enough to put it on the ground. The gunfire became more rapid - hard to shoot the head when its tossing from one side to the other.

One of the gunmen rose from his position behind the fountain, and kicked the runner as it closed in, planting a boot into its belly that knocked it to the ground, before putting a round into its head. The second shooter and the lookout kept him covered, the zombies coming up the grassy verge in larger numbers, the bulk of the mob closing in - and still below us, stragglers were moving across the tarmac and through the trees, over the Jamesons' graves.

'Never seen so many of them,' Lucile hissed, 'damn, damn...what do we do if they see us?'

'Hope we can defend the stairwell.' I told her, 'Just keep quiet, and we won't have to.' I didn't need the binoculars now. I gave them to her, let someone else have a turn. Those guys would either make it out, or they wouldn't.

More gunshots, different calibre, different weapons, began to sound out. The rest of their party had arrived to join in the defence against the mob. They were managing to hold their own, from the look of it; keeping to single-fire shots and patiently putting down one at a time. They were trained, like Anita had said. But how long would their ammo hold out?

Maybe they had the same thought. One of them closed the shutters on the co-op, and the lookout disappeared from the window, to join the others. Keeping close to the shop fronts, they fought their way back towards their truck, shooting and shoving anything that got close, keeping their little cordon moving. I wouldn't have liked to have been in their shoes right now, in open ground with dozens of those things, it made my skin crawl to think there were so many of them, just a stone's throw from our safe place.

The soldiers made it to their truck, one guy opening the passenger side of the cab, climbing up and in. Someone shut the door on him, and the rest of the squad moved to the back of the truck as the headlights blinked to life. The driver put it into reverse - hopefully not before all his people were onboard - and then turned in the road, mounting the pavement.

'Looks like they all got out.' Anita confirmed, still scoped in.

'Zeds seem to be following the truck, back towards the city centre.' Neville observed. 'At least they're not sticking around here.'

'How many you say be down there?' Damian asked.

Neville shook his head, and stared down, brow furrowed. 'A lot. A hundred, more? There's a lot less bodies in the plaza than are going after that truck.'

'Show's over, everyone.' I muttered, reminding everyone else to keep it down too, 'Back inside. We don't want to get spotted, end up in that position.'

I was last off the balcony, gently closing the door behind me. Everyone else was taking up their seats again, in the living room, or on the kitchen stools. I had already made enough speeches today, done my part to rally the troops, so I just went to sit back down too.

Silence loomed.

'It's your turn.' I reminded Neville.

He picked up the dice, and rolled.

Eventually, the chatter picked up again, the ladies carried on with their poker and we even managed to finish the game in one night. The coolbox of beer, still keeping so-so on the cool front, seemed to be receiving constant refills, so I was feeling pretty tipsy by the time came to say goodnight.

'Stay safe,' Laurel waved to Lucile as her and Damian walked to the stairwell, 'hear things can get interesting on the thirteenth floor…'

'Scandal.' Lucile smirked in reply.

Laurel would be bunking with me again, Anita taking up the Jamesons' bedroom once more. If she were to move in full time, we'd need to redecorate. Maybe go down to the hardware store, pick out some new wallpaper and flat-pack furnishings.

That sent me spiralling down a whole, semi-drunk line of thought about shopping. Nobody would have to go to discount clothing outlets anymore, we could just walk right into high end tailors', get the menfolk some sharp suits, flashy dresses for the ladies - end the world in style and luxury, cooking over survival fires with our silk ties and cufflinks. It made me chuckle at least.

'What're you laughing at?' Laurel asked, her words coming a little sluggish, not quite a slur, but from a place of comfortable intoxication. I was likely the same.

'Just thinking, about things. Stuff.' I shrugged, heading into the kitchen to…put the kettle on. Hmm.

'That's a convenience I'm gonna miss.' She observed, walking up to pat me on the back. 'I'll be getting changed, don't walk in on me.'

'I'll amuse myself, pretending to make tea.' I called over my shoulder, as she disappeared into my bedroom.

I sat down on the arm of my sofa instead, not wanting to get comfortable. I wondered how those soldiers were sleeping tonight. Did they have a big, communal bunkhouse somewhere, or were they working out of a hotel, everyone with their own private suite? By now you know my mind works like this whether I have or haven't been drinking.

Laurel had stayed with me that first night because she didn't want to be alone. Neither of us did. That feeling was still there, but now I was less sure it was about losing people we loved - Katy, Dani. I think now, we were more worried about keeping the ones we still had.

'That a pistol in your hand or are you just pleased to see me?' Laurel asked, as I set the large revolver down by the bed.

I wasn't self-conscious about changing in front of Laurel - the boxer shorts never came off. She wolf whistled as I changed, settling into bed in her oversized sleep-shirt. It was damn cold, so I had to put actual pyjamas on to sleep in, dark, stripy ones. Stripes are cheerful. They promised that tomorrow would be a good day. The liars.

Thirty Two

I think I dreamt I was Garage Guy, the unfortunate accountant we'd met, looking for the gas pump. Everything was really dark, then there was this bright light, and the screaming started. I ran, but my feet wouldn't carry me. Hands reached out and grasped from all sides. I thrashed and struggled, realising it was all a dream, fighting my way up to the surface, through layers of sleep.

Laurel hadn't woken up. I slipped out of bed and did the usual things with the bathroom. Water still hadn't given up on us, so I was able to flush and brush.

Quietly, I got some things from my wardrobe and drawers and got dressed in the living room, putting on yesterday's jeans with a grey shirt and a dark green zip-up hoodie - the clouds were iron grey, set to rain again, so I'd need every layer to keep the cold off. Bloody weather.

Hair brushed and weapons retrieved, I crossed the hall and let myself into the communal apartment to get started on breakfast. Maybe it was some ingrained sleep-pattern from her job, but Anita was already up, bustling around the kitchen, putting glass bottles into a plastic shopping bag, as if to take to the recycling bins. What would we do with all our waste now?

'Morning, Kelly.' She winced, picking the bag up.

'Good morning. You alright?' I asked.

'Shoulder. Now I know it's seeping it's starting to hurt. Think that's just in my head.' She added, setting the bag down by the door. 'Rubbish bags. No idea what to do with them.'

'I'm sure Morgan will think of some ingenious method of recycling the recycling. There anything I can do?'

'For my arm? No, I don't think so.'

'What if you get worse? I think we'd know by now if you were going to turn, but I mean, standard infection? What do we do?'

'There a pharmacy around here somewhere?' she asked.

I shook my head, 'Not anywhere close. Short drive, I can think of two. One near the garage we got the gas pump from, the in-house pharmacy for a doctors' practice. The other one's further in towards the city - possible detour on the way out to GCR.'

'We'll see if it gets any worse….' She sighed.

'We're good for food, water and weapons,' I gestured over the kitchen side, stacked with supplies and scattered with the guns I'd retrieved from last night, 'medicine would be good about now. Especially if we actually need it.'

'You're…a good friend, Kelly.' Anita smiled, putting her hand over mine on the kitchen island. 'Now empty out one of your guns, I'm going to teach you how to stand when you shoot. Can't believe Nev hasn't already.'

'I gave him some wiseass remark about cowboys so I think he wrote me off as a lost cause. Nev, eh?' I hummed, eyebrow raised.

'It's what my Dad always called him. Thought I'd try it out. Too much?'

'Nev. Nev. I don't know. Not saying you shouldn't, I just can't wrap my brain around it.' I told her, taking rounds out of the Cobra. I spun the cylinder to make sure there wasn't a mysterious seventh shot lurking in there, and snapped it back in with a flick of the wrist because I'm way cool.

'Stand there, middle of the room, and do what you'd normally do if you were aiming at something.' She said, leaning on the kitchen island.

I planted my legs apart in the middle of the living room carpet, and aimed for the bedroom door, cupping my own hand and the butt of the pistol with my left, finger on the trigger with my right.

For a moment, I wondered if maybe this was why Edgar left his gun outside of the room. Perhaps he expected they'd turn after death, and had provided us with a means to quickly…deal with them if so. Likely, I was reading too much into it.

273

'Pause…' Anita said, walking over. 'Finger outside of the trigger guard unless you're about to pull. No accidental discharges - its awkward for everyone,' she added with a wry smile, 'that analogy actually helped drill the lesson in for me. In the same vein, gun safety, don't ever point the barrel towards something you don't want to shoot. Safest place to point it is down at the ground.'

'I've been doing that so far,' I said, 'seen enough action-based entertainment to gather that - I know films aren't real, but seemed the sensible thing to do.'

'Good on you. But there's still a couple things,' she said, flicking the fingers of my cupping left-hand until I moved it away from the gun, 'that's called tea-cupping. Cut it out. They're always doing that in films. Must look better on camera.'

'Okay, show me how to do it right?' I asked, offering her the gun out, in the palm of my hand, barrel pointing away from anything we didn't want to shoot.

'Right, here, see?' she said, settling it into a right-hand grip, finger over the trigger-guard. 'Got your dominant hand on first, then here, where you've got your fingers and the uncovered grip? Support hand on there. Don't cross your thumbs here, in line with the back of the gun, but you can cross them here, so it's like you're tying your right-hand thumb down. See?'

'I'm with you…' I nodded.

'If you pick up a semi-auto like mine or Nev's, same grip applies – keeps all your digits away from the moving parts. You don't want to see what happens to a thumb when it gets hit by the slide. Same for catching escaping gasses from a revolver cylinder for that matter.

'Cobra's double-action, shouldn't have to cock the hammer like you do with that antique, but that support thumb, the one winning the wrestling match with the main thumb? Use that to cock when you're using the older piece. You'll have more control over your recoil than tea-cupping.'

'Simple as that?' I asked, taking the gun back, and holding it correctly.

'Despite being a form of combustion,' she said, slapping me on the back, 'it is not rocket science.'

'You feel better about letting the civilians carry guns now?'

'Ask me after we've been in a firefight together, I reserve judgement.' She said, holding up a finger.

'Last night doesn't count?' I laughed.

'Hah! *You* didn't shoot at anyone! Mr Keep Them Talking So Everyone Else Can Line Up A Shot. Good going, by the way.'

'I don't think that name's going to stick.'

'Don't put yourself down on it,' she said, leading the way back into the kitchen, 'tense situation like that, someone needed to be the voice for the squad. You kept them focused on you, so we had all the time in the world to get ready for that fight, then you even tried giving them an out, offering up that diplomatic solution...'

'I was just winging it.' I said, folding my arms.

'I've seen hostage negotiators have worse first days, is all I'm saying. When you met me as well – crazy lady holed up with a gun. Neville had only seen me a few times until then, but he should still have been the one to disarm and come talk me down, right?'

'Perhaps I have some kind of death wish?' I frowned, quizzical. 'Where's this going?'

'You're a better leader for this group than you give yourself credit for.' She said. With a straight face and everything.

'Oh.' I stumbled. 'Thanks?'

She looked like she was about to say something else, drew in breath, but let it out. 'I occasionally overshare. Sorry. If you start on breakfast, I could inventory the new guns?'

'As leader, I delegate guns to the expert, and take up kitchen duties. So it is written.' I added, making a lordly gesture. She smiled. 'Ah, but little did she know, that because

275

we made sandwiches out of all the short-dated stuff yesterday, I actually don't have to do anything…'

'Now you can come help me count bullets and load magazines then. Come on, it'll be fun.' She lied.

We sat on the sofa with the coffee table dragged close, and set about ejecting the magazines from the sidearms, each of them rather like Neville's, which he'd give to Anita - guessing they were of the same manufacture. All three were in various states of half-empty - or arguably, half full. Likewise for their spare magazines that I'd lifted from their vests.

'They've been in a fight or two, if I were to guess.' Anita said, examining a nearly empty mag.

'You're the detective, inspector.' I reminded her.

'Another group if I were to guess, someone else with guns. If it were just shamblers, they'd have spent their magazines and reloaded. Best reason to switch a half-spent for a full mag that I can think of, is if you're going up against someone else with a gun, and might need to throw down some suppressing fire.'

'That seems to be one of their tactics, judging by the one that got away. Not sure if that helps your investigation.'

'Maybe they got into an altercation with those uniforms from last night - could have been loyalist Territorials, or PMC troops. They hauled ass to clear the pawnshop and setup overwatch after they saw the bodies, but I don't know if that's because they saw dead allies or dead enemies.'

'Or just dead bodies in general.'

She nodded to that. 'We're not going to tell from staring at these. They're nine-mill, and I've got a few spares ratting around my pocket. So empty the bullets out of those ones, I'll clear the chambers and we'll see how many usable mags we can get.'

I wasn't exactly sure on how you did that at first, but managed to figure it out.

'Damian and Laurel both have guns, but no pistols. You and me, packing pairs of pistols-' I started.

'Say that three times fast.' She said.

276

I narrowed my eyes at her for a moment. 'Morgan hasn't got any kind of gun. Never fired one either. Do you think you could give her a live-fire lesson?'

'Not sure how Nev would feel about that,' she hummed, 'not sure how I feel about that. She's still a minor but…think I might be more on your side than his, where his daughter's safety's concerned. She's smart, good to have around. If she could shoot, she'd be even better. Not far off service age either.'

'Up for it then? I know it's not like we're burdened by the amount of bullets we're carrying, but a few shots are better than nothing, right?'

She nodded. 'Not here though. When we're out later, if it's safe I'll set up some targets just before we head back.'

Three usable guns, each one with a full mag, plus three mags left over, with around half a dozen rounds a piece in them. Anita checked and reloaded her own weapons before sharing her spare bullets.

'Now everybody's armed. Great.' She sighed, leaning back in the sofa. 'I'm going to be fired so hard if this ever ends.'

'Either that or you'll get a medal. You should deputise us. Officially. There a ceremony?'

'Nobody does that anymore.' She said, perhaps a little despondently. 'Time to wake the rest up?'

'We're burning daylight.' I agreed.

Anita walked down the hall to knock on the Roberts' door, leaving Laurel for an extra minute, while I went to the stairs for the other two. I gave a musical knock on Damian's door, and heard a vague noise from somewhere within.

'This is your morning wake-up call, D. You up and about?' I asked. There was no reply.

Put yourself in my boots for a moment - if this were a normal day, you'd think it was a plain old case of oversleeping, but a vague mumble, in a zombie apocalypse, then no reply to a shout out? I clenched my teeth, feeling a cold sweat break out on the back of my neck.

'Damian, Lucile, anyone in there?' I called out again, pressing my ear to the door.

Rapid, shuffling footsteps grew closer to the door, followed by a rattling, clinking sound. I took a swift pair of steps backwards, and drew out the Cobra, keeping it pointed at the floor with two hands, finger off the trigger. Now would be a terrible time for a practical lesson.

The door opened, and Lucile stood there in a too-big powder blue robe, loose bottoms and white carpet slippers with a hotel brand on the front. Bleary eyed, she blinked at me, and my gun.

'Well shucks. Good morning to you too.'

'Sorry,' I muttered, stowing it, 'thought I heard shuffling feet. Guess it was your slippers…'

'New safehouse dress code.' She yawned. 'Time to move?'

'Sandwiches will be served upon arrival.'

'Black-tie funeral?' she sniffed.

'Put on your best arse-kicking boots. It's going to rain and I'd rather not be digging graves in a downpour with no central heating to come home to.'

'Point.' She nodded, 'We'll be up, see ya in a minute.'

'Right on.' I waved, turning back to the corridor.

Thirty Three

We ate, most people reloading and checking weapons, being sure to lock safeties and aim at the ground while doing so, under Anita's instruction. It's not like we were terrible for it before, or I'm sure Neville would have said something. I think it just gave her a task to focus on, rather than thinking about what came next.

Morgan, wisely planning for the future, took more meat out to be defrosting for tonight's meal. The coolboxes and ice were doing a decent job of keeping the frozen stuff from thawing, but we knew it was just delaying the inevitable. Another day and it'd all be defrosting, we'd have to cook it and wrap it, or we'd lose it.

'Presents, here.' I said, picking up the Deserters' guns from the table and handing them about.

'But it's not my birthday.' Laurel beamed, giving me a one-armed hug, her rifle held in the other. While the flashlight was taped underneath the barrel, with Morgan's help she'd also secured a long kitchen knife to the side as an improvised bayonet. She wasn't getting caught out again.

'Do you just like taping knives on things?' she asked the girl with the hockey-stick-spear. There was definitely an element of the ridiculous about it, but I didn't want to say anything.

'Even if it holds up for one attack, its worth a little tape.' Morgan said defensively.

'Thought they looked like D&Es,' Neville said, helping me pass the new magazines out. 'Doe-Eastwick, they do the standard issue for the Territorial Army and some of the regional police forces.'

'Same one as you had, right mon?' Damian asked, putting his in one of the pockets of his coat.

Neville nodded. 'Seemed a good buy, if the law were using it, had to be good. I've been happy with the purchase, especially recently. Need to pick up a customer review form.'

I held one of them out to Morgan.

Neville did a double-take.

'No,' Anita chided, before Neville could say anything, coming in from the side and gently guiding him be the shoulder away from his daughter, 'no, we're not putting it to a vote, Morgan gets a weapon, and I'm going to teach her how to use it.'

'Really?' she beamed, quickly taking it from my open hand, but not quite snatching it away.

Anita and Neville gave conflicting responses.

'But really, yes.' I said, giving Morgan the nod.

'She's too young-' he tried.

'We've been through this, with Edgar.' I shouted over him.

'Going out is different-'

'Ain't it better she's armed and ready?' Lucile joined in.

'Girl's responsible, she not going to shoot us in de back.'

It hadn't quite escalated into a full blown argument yet, but it was getting that way. Not like Laurel at all to be the diplomatic one.

'What is it you want?' she asked Morgan, putting a hand on her shoulder.

Morgan looked at the floor a moment. 'It's my choice, Dad...' she muttered, 'but...I'll do whatever you think is best.'

Neville left his mouth to hang a moment. 'Uh, I think,' he paused, scratching the back of his neck, 'I think Anita might be right.'

Morgan looked up, eyes unblinking.

'If you can teach her, sure. Just let someone else hold the gun until class is in session, okay?' he pleaded.

Morgan walked up, and handed him the pistol.

'Until you think I won't go blue on blue.' She said.

'It wasn't that, it was never that...' he muttered, bringing his daughter in for a hug. We all got sheepish and turned away at that point.

The rest of us started to pull on our coats and jackets, securing weapons and making last minute checks. I kept Edgar's old gun in the front of my hoodie and took the first aid kit we'd gotten from the Deserters', squeezing it into a jacket pocket - it was only a small thing, a blister pack of painkillers, gauze, bandages, tiny scissors; same setup as Anita's.

With the binoculars in the other pocket and the hoodie underneath, my jacket was starting to feel pretty bulky, but I'd be glad of the extra protection, and the waterproofing.

I didn't think we'd need compasses, not really much chance of us having to do any orienteering, and I never was great at it to begin with. Still, I grabbed one just in case somebody else might need it, pocketing a couple of the flares and passing the others out to Anita, Laurel and Damian - the best shooters or the biggest guns.

'What you thinking?' Damian asked, quietly.

'Sound, bright lights, we know they're attracted to them. These flares could be a great distraction, just thought it'd be good to keep them around.'

'Aye, save it for de right time.' He lilted.

'If we need to use the flares for communication, green's good, red's bad, right?' I checked, raising my voice so they could all hear me. 'Should have one of each.'

'Nice one, Captain Obvious.' Laurel snorted.

I bit my tongue a moment, and started throwing a bunch of sandwich boxes into a bag for the boot of the 4x4, knowing we'd be gone a good long while.

Anita picked up the bag of empty bottles from by the door as we were leaving. 'Lesson plan,' she said.

We filed out into the foyer after the usual trip down the thousand steps, Lucile and Damian nipping into Stan's apartment to fetch the gas pump and something to drain the diesel into - a red plastic bucket with a spout.

281

While they were busy with that, everyone else kept their eyes on the park, watching for movement, except me and Neville. We made another trip into the landlord's apartment, to grab the shovels we'd need for the Masons.

'How you feeling?' I asked him.

'Is it a single father thing?' he asked, face a mask of concern. 'Do people think I'm not parenting her right, that I don't have her best interests in mind?'

'We know you do, its nothing to do with you being a single parent.' I told him, passing the shovels out of Stan's utility cupboard.

'A gun though? You're all sure about this? Her mother didn't even like guns in the house…'

'These are the crazy, modern, flesh-eating times we live in,' I said, picking up the big green medical kit on our way out. 'You know my thoughts on the subject already. Get her ready for the new world, just in case it lasts.'

'She's growing up, Kelly.' He sighed, 'She shouldn't have to grow up too fast.'

'She was doing that before this started.' I smiled with a shrug. 'Kids, man. What's the saying? It takes a village? We're not trying to step on your toes or anything. We just want to help take care of each other, that includes her.'

'I'll think on that…thanks.'

We re-joined the others, leaning on our shovels. It didn't take them long to siphon off the diesel from the white pickup truck and pour it into Damian's tank.

'Start her up, I'll drop these inside.' Lucile said, reaching for the bucket after it was emptied. The smell of fuel was on the air.

'Keep them with us,' I suggested, 'if we see a safe place to tap another likely looking vehicle, we may as well.'

'It going to stink de inside of me ride.' He said.

'Hmm. Kelly's right.' Lucile mused, 'It's for a good cause. If we've got more gas, we get to ride the elevator again.'

'Alright, deal.' Damian sighed. 'You know how to twist me arm.'

He and Neville took up the front seats, the three women in the middle, with Morgan and myself riding in the back again, holding onto the straps.

'Parental suck-up.' I muttered to her, keeping my voice low. Even the middle seats wouldn't hear us over the engine and radio.

She looked at me with wide eyes and pouted.

'That's just cruel.' I shook my head.

'Is it not a teenage daughter's prerogative to emotionally blackmail their fathers into giving them what they want?' she asked, innocently.

'He's tearing himself up over this stuff, seriously.' I said, giving her leg a gentle nudge with my boot. 'Give him an inch next time, he couldn't say no in front of everyone. Next time he asks you to play it safe, do it. For me.'

'You're the one-' she started, but caught herself talking too loud, 'encouraging me to be all independent, now you're saying I should be wrapped up in the bubble?' she carried on at a whisper.

'Not full time,' I sighed, 'just give him a moment to adjust. Let him protect you again, just one more time, before he loses his little girl.'

'He'll never lose me...' she said, swallowing hard.

I reached over, and put my hand on her knee. My throat was tight, and I didn't know what else to say.

With the radio on, the car was filled with the sounds of saxophone and bass. GCR's Jazz block doesn't stop just because the world does. It did however, go on for a good long while. Five tracks must have played - hard to tell with jazz - before we got to the Masons' cul-de-sac, without interruption from the DJ.

Zeds had been thin on the roads, we hadn't passed nearly as many as we'd done on our previous jaunts. Perhaps all the gunfire last night had drawn them towards one place again. The 4x4 slowed to a halt at the mouth of the street, everyone craning their heads to see if we had company.

'They might have moved on by now,' Neville suggested, 'like the zombies leaving the city. Going to where they can find food.'

'Hope so...' Anita shivered.

Damian parked us in the same place as last time, right outside the Masons' house, at the bottom of their path. I let myself and Morgan out of the boot, bringing the shovels out after me. My ears hadn't popped or fizzed yet, so that was promising.

Everyone stayed close as they got out of the car, weapons readied, scanning the gardens for signs of movement. Damian stood with me and Neville at the boot, covering us with his boomstick.

'How we going to do this?' he asked, eyes fixed at the street entrance.

'You've been here before, right?' I checked with Neville.

'Barbecues, birthday parties, picking Morgan up from sleepovers.' He confirmed.

'So you've seen the garden. Is it closed off?'

'Hedgerows mostly, adjoining the houses either side. Stone wall at the bottom, backs onto a field with a playground.'

'Swing set?'

'And a roundabout, see-saw and those seats on springs that go backwards and forwards.' He solemnly said.

'Nice neighbourhood.' I grinned.

'De hell are you talking about?' Damian said over his shoulder, eyebrow raised.

'Trying to lighten the mood,' I wearily sighed, 'I hate grave digging. Once is enough.'

'I don't mind taking a turn, we'll share de shovel.' Damian assured me.

'Appreciate it. Right...garden sounds like it's pretty well enclosed,' I spoke, starting up the path and turning around, raising my voice enough for everyone to hear, 'so I want Laurel up in that window, master bedroom, second door on the left as you go up the stairs. You're playing our lookout.

284

Morgan, keep her company and run out to us if you see anything.'

'Got it. The sprog'll look after me.' Laurel winked at Morgan.

'Anita, let us do the digging. You're not popping those stitches. So if you've got personal stuff you want to gather up…'

She shook her head. 'Nothing here anymore. I moved out when Becky was still in primary school.'

'Then you…just be wherever you need to be. Okay? Lucile, you good to take a turn with a shovel as well?'

'Ain't in my nature to be unhelpful.'

'Then let's do this.'

I turned to face the house, I saw the bodies of the dogs we'd dealt with by the door. They'd been gnawed on, legs shredded to meat, bellies spilled open onto the lawn, flies buzzing. I put my back to them when I reached the door, and waited for Neville to unlock the place, trying not to think about what might have gotten to them after we left. Maybe just the rest of their pack. Maybe.

The other dog still lay by the door, where we'd shoved it aside to get in. Having not heard that sub-audible bark or seen another one of the glassy-eyed monsters, it felt hard to wrap my thoughts around them again, to remember that was all real, and not so long ago.

'So these are them, huh? The ghost dogs?' Laurel asked, moving around it and up onto the first step of the stairs.

'Hope we don't see any more,' Lucile spoke, everyone filing into the hallway, 'snail paced foot-draggers you can get away from, but I wouldn't like to get chased down by a pack of those things. They buzz the inside of your head, sends your balance out of whack. Trip, fall, and I hate to think what comes next.'

Laurel rolled a shoulder uncomfortably, 'We'll keep the front door closed. Doesn't look like they're good with those.' She added, pointing at the scratches on the door.

285

Anita was the last one in, hesitating as she stepped over the threshold. 'Oh…Sam…' she gasped, looking down at the dog in the hallway, biting her bottom lip. 'You poor thing…'

I gave her an apologetic look. She met my eyes and sighed, shaking her head. 'What happened to make them this way?'

'The virus must cross species, mutate, I don't know. First sign of trouble,' I told Morgan, 'you feel your ears pop and you come running to us, got it?'

'If we have to run, I'm so tripping you to get away.' She stuck her tongue out at me. I ruffled her hair, still grimacing at the expression on Anita's face as she looked again at Sam the old family pooch. It was probably old enough to have been bought for her.

Laurel and Morgan went to take their positions upstairs, while Anita showed Lucile and Damian through to the back.

My footsteps felt heavy, going up the stairs. Last time, I'd flown up them in response to Anita's gunfire, but this time my feet didn't want to carry me. Becky Mason's body would be up there, lying on her bed with a neat little hole in her forehead.

I tried not to see anything when I entered her room again, just left my eyes open so I could walk to the other side of the bed, then left them unfocused as I threw the duvet over her body. It worked. More or less.

'We can't carry her like that.' Neville snapped.

'Don't mean to,' I said. 'That'd look great for the burial, wouldn't it? No, I just…can't look. I couldn't look the first time I came in here, and I'm no stronger now.'

Neville looked at me, like he was searching for something in my expression. 'I know. Too much like Morgan.' He muttered, looking down at the form beneath the duvet.

'Don't suppose you know where they kept their bedsheets?' I asked.

'It never came up. I'll go find them…be back in a minute.' He said, hesitating at the doorway for a moment.

I sat down on the edge of the stained chair Anita had bled into, and cupped my head in my hands. I didn't like this, carrying bodies. Once for Edgar was bad enough, nobody should have to do it twice in the same damn week. Unless they work in a funeral home, I guess.

A brief tap on the doorframe drew my attention back up. I blinked through a tear to see Damian standing in the doorway with white sheets in his arms.

'He...needed a minute. I help you.'

I nodded my appreciation, but didn't say anything.

We bundled her up into the duvet, she was smaller than Morgan, definitely not a child, but her growth spurt was coming in later. A life cut too short. I didn't even know her, aside from when Morgan had talked about her. Boy trouble, girl trouble, school trouble. The general troubles of growing up. Troubles she didn't have anymore.

Carefully, we carried her from the room, one of us at each end of the body. Though the door to the main bedroom was closed, I could hear Morgan sobbing from here.

'I know love, I know...' I heard Neville saying.

Thirty Four

Anita was the last surviving member of her family. Her parents, Marianna and Paul, and Becky, her younger sister by ten years, were all laid out before us, wrapped in clean white bed-linen. I stared at the bodies with an empty gaze, thinking about what I'd like done to me, when it came time.

'Cremation, I think.' I said to Neville, sat next to me on a bench overlooking the garden, where Damian and Lucile were having their turn at digging. 'I want to be burned, nothing left of me to rise up again.'

He nodded agreement, but didn't say anything.

I wiped my hands on my jeans for the dozenth time, trying to get rid of something that wasn't there, scratch off the layers of skin that'd had to touch Becky Mason to wrap her in the makeshift shroud. The walking dead I could handle - the actual dead were worse.

Under a grey sky, we dug until around noon, by Neville's watch, hacking three holes into the earth in the middle of the perfect lawn. When it came time to lower the bodies in, I'm not ashamed to say that I avoided it, going instead to tell those in the house that we were ready.

Anita sat in the middle of the sofa in the living-room, amidst bloodstains and chaos; an overturned coffee table, broken lamps and scattered books. My boot crunched on broken glass, but she was slow to react, turning to face me with her face sickly grey.

'Mr Kelly.' She managed a weak smile, wiping at a trail of tears.

'It's nearly time, Anita.' I told her, 'Unless you want a few more minutes?'

'I'll just…pull myself together, okay?' she said uncertainly.

I crossed the room, and sat beside her. 'You are not alone.'

288

She looked at me, biting her bottom lip.

'You're going to get through this. We'll be here for you, all of us, every day.'

She dragged me into a powerful hug, and sobbed into the crook of my neck. 'Fucking, shit…' she choked.

I guess I wouldn't have the words either. I sat there with my arms around her, smoothing down the back of her hair and trying to be as comforting as I could. I don't know how much I helped, because I started crying too. The whole works. My cheeks burned hot with tears, my nose started to run and my chest heaved with the weight of breath.

Seeing Anita's loss, a woman who had nobody left, it broke me, if only for a moment. It was a glimpse of what might soon happen to myself. Without Katy, that'd be me.

We sat there on the sofa until Morgan found us, her eyes raw as well. She sat down on the other side of Anita and the grieving woman put her other arm around her.

With Morgan here, I felt I had to be strong again, I couldn't just fall to pieces like this. It helped me pull myself together, no more heaving, shaking sobs, just steady, calm breaths. I wiped my eyes and gave Anita's shoulder one last squeeze.

'Come on, it's time.' I said, my voice hoarse.

We supported Anita through the back door in the kitchen, just holding a hand while Morgan held the other. When we reached the rough graves dug out of the garden, Neville moved up to stand behind us, between his daughter and Anita, putting hands on their shoulders. Damian and Lucile waited by the graves. Laurel, presumably, was still on watch.

'Is there anything you'd like to say, Anita?' Neville quietly asked.

'No, I - I can't…' Anita choked, eyes squeezed tightly closed, her face twisted into a mask of pain as tears rolled off her chin. Her knees buckled, the three of us helping her to kneel, Morgan going down with her to wrap her into another

289

full-body embrace. 'They can't be…and…too young…' she coughed between ragged breaths.

I gave the nod to Lucile, who took the first shovel of earth and cast it over Becky Mason's grave. Damian began to fill in Marianna's. I took a couple steps back, composing myself again, sniffing back tears. Neville took my place and knelt beside Anita and Morgan, the pair of them surrounding her with support, comfort. Her family might have been gone, but as long as this group stuck together, she'd never be far from friends. Never be alone.

It was quieter indoors, away from the grief; but leaving the graveside would have been cowardly, and not at all like the "we'll be here for you" message I was trying to send.

So I only went inside for one moment, to grab a box of tissues from the wreckage of the living room. I passed it to Neville, who drew some out for the girls, letting them stem the flow of tears. I stayed a polite distance back, and waited, my face set into a grim expression, a tissue kept aside for myself.

Damian and Lucile filled the graves. It seemed to take a lot longer than when me and Neville filled in the ones in our little park. Takes longer to watch. At least with the shovel in hand you can focus on the labour.

I was glad she hadn't wanted to bury the dog. The sky was looking greyer as time wore on, the rain an ever looming threat, bringing the cold front with it.

Neville helped Anita to her feet, Morgan offering support with her shoulders under an arm. Anita's eyes were still shut tight, I wasn't sure if she'd opened them since we came outside. They helped her into the house while Lucile and Damian patted down the graves.

'She going to be okay?' Damian asked, uncertainly.

'She's hard as nails.' Lucile sniffed, wiping her eyes. 'This was a big fucking hammer, but she'll come through.'

'All we can do is just be around for her,' I said, 'be a shoulder when she needs us, have her back. But don't treat her like she's fragile, she won't like that.'

'Got it.' Lucile nodded, looking at the house uncomfortably. Grief is hard to face.

I led the way back inside. Neville and Morgan were on the sofa with Anita again, just holding her hands. Lucile and Damian went to the living room too, but I went upstairs, and down the hall to the master bedroom.

Laurel was just wiping her eyes.

'Oh, uh, hey.' She sniffed.

'You too?'

'Fuck off.'

I sat down next to her on the bed, and put my arm around her. That's why everyone hugs at funerals, they can't think of anything else to say. I was tempted to remind her we need to keep an eye on the street, but some things were more important right now. So I just brought her in tighter, and she tilted her head onto my shoulder.

'I'm not losing anyone else.' She sighed, chest rising and falling in deliberate, careful breaths. 'Nobody dies. Starting now.'

She rose from the bed and picked up the rifle she'd left by the window, holding it across her chest like a child might a teddy bear. I stood next to her, one hand on her shoulder.

'It's a deal. We're all going to make it through this.'

'I'll keep an eye up here,' She said, voice still rough, another tear rolling down to her chin, 'we should be leaving soon though.'

Downstairs, I stuck my head in the living room, but nobody was there. The front door opened behind me, and I spun around, Cobra raised to hip-height - Anita wouldn't have been happy, but I didn't have time for a proper stance.

Fortunately, it was only Neville, carrying the plastic bag of empty glass bottles. His eyes widened a moment as he saw someone pointing a gun at him, then his expression softened as he realised what'd happened.

'That a gun, or are you just pleased to see me?'

'Both.' I said, stowing it in the holster. 'What've you got there?'

291

'Anita's lesson plan,' he said, holding up the bag by way of explanation, 'figured target practice was a good use for the recycling, so she brought it with us.'

'How's she doing?' I asked, as he closed the door and busied himself with the locks.

'I thought she needed a distraction. I know how hard it is for the mind not to dwell on loss. I was…devastated,' he sighed, 'when my wife died. But if I didn't have Morgan to take care of, it'd have been a whole lot worse. You push through for other people.'

We walked through the kitchen, and out into the garden. A lovely wood-panel fence separated the Mason's from their neighbours on one side, a hedgerow on the other. One section of the fence's panels had been destroyed.

A sledgehammer from the Masons' toolshed stood nearby, Damian removing some of the remaining wood with a smaller hammer. It was far from a neat solution, but the archway left by the missing panels meant we could get from one garden to the next.

Ducking to avoid any errant splinters, we made our way through to next door's garden, everyone gathering around an outdoor table. Anita, with red eyes but a strong, calm voice, began talking Morgan through her pistol.

They had it laid out on the table, magazine detached, and a bullet out. Morgan pressed it into the magazine and slid the clip into the weapon with uncertain motions.

'Like this?' she asked.

'You got it.' Anita sniffed, wiping her eyes, 'Now, you might want to practice that a bit with an empty mag, so you can do it faster.'

'I will.' She said, voice serious, but with a trace of excitement.

Neville went to the bottom of the garden with the bag of bottles. Before the wall at the edge of the property was a chest-deep planter, most of the flowers there no longer in bloom, but some green fronds remained. He spaced the bottles out along the edge of the planter.

Anita began talking Morgan through her stance, correcting her teacup grip and aiming. They were pointing the pistol towards the house however, as Neville was still downrange. Muzzle discipline.

'Any pressure in everyone watching?' I asked.

'Start moaning and shuffling your feet,' Morgan replied, 'give me some motivation.'

'Back in a second, just going to warn Laurel...' I said, ducking though the fence and back into the Masons' to shout up the stairs.

'Stuck on guard duty while the fun happens. Wish her luck from me.' She replied.

Finished with the bottles, Neville came back to stand with the rest of us, behind the gun and off to the sides.

'You've got seven shots in that magazine,' Anita said, taking a step back from Morgan as well, 'take your time with each shot, and when the gun's empty, reload and put the safety back on, just like I showed you, okay?'

'Got it.' Morgan nodded, gun in both hands, pointed at the ground. 'Are we going to be running out of here pretty quick afterwards?'

'Double-quick.' Neville confirmed.

Morgan refocused her attention back on the targets at the bottom of the garden. They weren't too far away, twenty, twenty five feet maybe. She drew in a steady breath, raised the gun, and on the exhale she pulled the trigger.

The flat, low *pop* of the gun was accompanied by the sound of the bullet striking off a chip of concrete planter, an inch or two away from the bottle.

'Take your time, little slower now.' Anita encouraged.

Pop. Smash. Everyone gave a little cheer as the beer bottle shattered into green shards. I could feel Morgan's grin from here, but she just about managed to stop herself from doing an arm-pump. Instead, she settled on another bottle, and fired again.

Another swing, another miss, but it didn't deter her. She tried again, and once more, on the second shot, smashed her target. I looked at Neville, who looked back at me. I saw my own faint smile mirrored in his face. Morgan fired again, snapping our attention back in time to see a third bottle falling to pieces.

Her confidence building, she took aim and fired again, striking another one of her targets, broken glass tinkling down onto the lawn.

'Go on girl!' Damian cheered.

Morgan's last bullet must have landed just beneath the bottle, chipping concrete and knocking it backwards into the planter, un-smashed.

'Shi- I mean, crap.' She self-censored, looking over at her Dad.

'Four out of seven, I'll take that,' Anita said, giving Neville a weak smile, 'how about you?'

'More like three and a half. But good enough,' Neville replied, hugging his daughter, 'for a beginner.'

'Don't forget to reload, and put the safety on,' Anita reminded her. Sheepishly, she did so, swapping magazines within her jacket, reloading and clicking the safety on.

'Guess we should get moving now?' Lucile asked.

'Reckon so.' I gestured towards the fence, letting folks go before me. I picked the shovels up and gripped the hand-holds at the top with one hand. They were heavy, but I wanted a hand free for doors and guns. I considered taking the sledgehammer Damian had used on the fence, but we were suitably armed as it stood.

'Good shooting,' Lucile congratulated Morgan, giving her a pat on the back as they went into the kitchen. 'Better than my first spell at the range. My Pa was about as encouraging as yours too…'

'Here's hoping I don't have to shoot anything more dangerous than the recycling,' Morgan shrugged with a faint smile, 'maybe I'll have exactly half a chance.'

Anita and I brought up the rear. I didn't have any words left to speak, so I just gave her un-injured shoulder a squeeze, and followed her in. She cast one last look over the garden, the

294

disturbed soil where her family was buried, the broken fence, and probably a dozen memories of happier times.

'Should have buried Sam too.' She sniffed, the corner of her mouth twitching up. 'But...no, let's get out of here.'

We piled back into our ride with no disturbance from dogs or zeds. The pack must have moved on, like the mobs of shamblers, roaming around in search of food. Taking up my seat in the boot with Morgan, I offered her a fist to bump. She took it.

'Feeling confident?' I asked.

'No,' she scoffed, 'I didn't expect to be a crack shot at lesson one but I thought it'd be easier than that. Guess that's why Dad puts hours in at the shooting range.'

'Let's just hope you don't have to use it...'

'Comforting, thanks, arse.' She narrowed her eyes at me.

We drove out of the cul-de-sac and back onto the main roads, burned out cars, smashed shop fronts and broken houses rolling by; along with the occasional dark shape shuffling down side streets. The sporadic groups we'd seen over the last couple days seemed to have moved on, probably joining up with bigger hordes, leaving only the odd straggler behind. That thought didn't bode well.

'Hey, up front,' Laurel asked, 'why no radio?'

I peeked my head above the seats, looking between Laurel and Anita's heads. Neville leaned forward in his seat, peering at the dim radio display.

'It's turned on.' He called back, fiddling with the volume control. 'Set to GCR, but all we're getting is silence. It's as if they've stopped broadcasting.'

'Turn it up, full.' Damian told him, 'Think if they were off de air, we wouldn't find de station. Listen, careful...'

He found a quiet stretch of road, and let the car roll to a stop. Neville put the radio up to full volume. The station was still broadcasting; but not music, and no commentary from Carl Sachs. It was broadcasting silence, with a little background fizz from white noise. The sound of an empty studio booth.

'Shit.' Neville muttered. I didn't know if he was thinking the same, he twisted in his seat to look over at us. 'Whatever's going on, it is not good for our chances of making contact with the CDC.'

Laurel leaned forward, 'We need to get antibiotics for Anita's shoulder, but what first?'

Eyes turned towards Anita.

'GCR.' She said, her voice still a little raw from crying, 'We may already be too late, but we have to try. If it's a step towards getting the hell out of this city, the pharmacy's going to have to wait. I'll live.' She added, through gritted teeth.

Thirty Five

Damian pulled back onto the road and began to drive a little faster. Everyone started to check their guns - even Morgan was at it now.

'What could it mean?' Damian asked.

'Could have just gone for a piss.' Laurel suggested.

'Wouldn't have left the broadcast on, he's a professional DJ.' Neville replied.

'Yeah, would have queued songs up.' Anita chimed in. 'Could be an emergency somewhere in the building.'

'Someone might be hurt.' Damian agreed.

'We've got first aid, but if they've got zeds inside the walls...' Lucile frowned, letting the words hang for a moment. 'What do we do? Help them or bug out?'

'Help them if we-' Neville began.

'-but if there's too many-' Lucile interjected.

'Then we handle-' Laurel tried.

People started to talk over each other, words getting caught up in a tangle as everyone tried to get their ideas across. I knelt up in the back and stuck my head between Laurel and Lucile.

'Hey!' I called out, firmly, but not shouting. 'We're on our way. Let's just see what the situation is when we get there. Damian?'

'Yeah?' he acknowledged, tilting his head to show he was listening.

'Don't drive us straight up, slow down as we come out of that wood. Remember that flipped car? Stop there if it's clear. I'll get out and scout ahead, make sure it's safe to bring the 4x4 through.'

'Need any backup?' Neville offered.

'Safest to go in pairs. Everyone else, stay with the vehicle.'

297

'What if you hit more trouble than you can handle?' Morgan asked. 'Not saying I'm coming with you, just asking.'

'We won't be far from you, just searching around corners, making sure we don't drive into a mob like we did last time.' I reassured her.

We hit the stretch of woodland with the expensive properties, and I made another paranoia-check of my weapons and ammo. Between revolvers little and large, I had twelve shots loaded, but it was my bayonet I kept a tight grip on as we drove down the secluded road.

'Big houses out this way,' Lucile said, eyebrows raised as she gazed out the window, 'wouldn't be the worst thing in the world if we had to fall back into one of these...'

We slowed to a stop as we reached the edge of the wood, where the car had flipped to avoid something in the road. The body at the end of the bloody smear that led from the car was conspicuous by its absence. I crawled to the back of the boot and opened it up, Neville getting out of the passenger side door, and closing it so gently that it wasn't fully shut.

'Leave the boot open for me,' I said, grabbing my baseball bat, 'in case this bright idea goes horribly, terrifyingly wrong.'

The road turned a right angle to the left a little ways ahead. I met Neville on the front lawn of the corner house, and passed him my bat before drawing my bayonet. He approached the side of the house to peer around, while I kept close to the wall.

'Got one here,' he muttered, 'back to us, shuffling towards the corner down to GCR. We going to take it out?'

I nodded, and reversed my grip on the bayonet, better to thrust downwards with. 'I'll go first, stay a little ways behind me.'

I crept off the lawn and onto the pavement, stepping softly and carefully, avoiding any broken glass or debris, unlike the first time we came here. I didn't know what was around the corner, so I resisted the temptation to ready my gun as well. Neville was only a few yards behind me, I wouldn't need it.

I could hear its ragged breathing as I drew closer, hissing and wheezing to itself as it took deliberate, shuffling steps towards the GCR broadcast mast, which towered a clear storey or two above the rest of the roofs in the neighbourhood.

It had worn a light blue jacket in life, a waterproof with a university Skiing Society logo stylised on the back in blood stained white. Its figure was slim, probably a girl, but with a buzzed short head of hair. I tried not to think too much about it, as I drew within striking distance.

I raised the heavy bayonet, and plunged it down into the back of the zed's skull, punching through bone with a wet crunch. It collapsed to the pavement, never knowing I was there. I couldn't help but be a little pleased with myself, but that was short lived. I looked down at my bloodied bayonet, and quickly wiped it off on the former student's jeans.

'Shit…' I heard Neville swear just behind me, turning around just as I heard the moan of another zombie, sending the hairs on the back of my arms on end.

It staggered out of the open doorway of the house on the corner, stumbling down the steps and landing face-first on the path. That made me pause, just for a moment. The fall knocked the wind right out of it, stopping it mid-wail.

Neville didn't stop to smirk. He crossed the pavement and brought my bat down on its head, one swing, and the zombie stopped writhing.

'Hope nothing heard that…' he mumbled, looking about.

'Think we're good.' I said, giving him the thumbs up.

We kept our heads down and moved quickly along the street, just in case. The road continued for the length of a few houses, carrying straight on but with a corner to the right at the end, in the direction of GCR.

'At least this road's clear. Still got your bi-nocks?' he asked, crouching down behind someone's garden wall.

I did. I got myself up next to him and we took out our binoculars, looking well ahead down the long stretch of road between us and the gates of GCR. Same collection of parked cars as yesterday, only with no zeds between them this time. Or at least, none that we could see.

The gates to GCR were closed, but zeds were pressed against them - I tried to count, but Neville had me beat.

'Between twenty and thirty, if I had to guess,' he sighed, 'plus there could be more on the other sides of the fence, can't see from here, that house on the left is blocking the line of sight.'

'Be a good place to put our backup though,' I suggested, 'if they've got a window overlooking the car park, or maybe with a line into the building itself, we could get a clearer picture.'

'If it's all gone tits up inside, I'd definitely feel better if Laurel had a position like that.'

'Can't see anything between us and there, but if those zeds catch sight of the truck coming down this stretch of road, say goodbye to that plan.'

'Or…we could use that…' Neville thought aloud. 'Get Damian to drive by, draw the zeds away, we can get right up to the gate.'

'Not a bad idea, but we don't know if they'll open the gate, or if Sachs and his people are still in control over there. Not sure if announcing our presence is going to go down well if there's new management, like those bastards from last night.'

'So how do you want to play it?' Neville asked, nodding. He didn't sound disapproving, but didn't sound like he was fully on board either. I didn't blame him. Getting through the zeds would be a challenge. Getting in without being seen might even be impossible.

'Get Laurel and Morgan up in that house on the end. Morgan for backup, while Laurel might be able to scope in to get us some more info, also works to watch our asses while we crawl through the fence with that set of bolt cutters.'

'Nice,' Neville nodded, checking over his shoulder to make sure we were still safe, 'bring Anita, Damian and Lucile in with us?'

'Yeah. Enough firepower to make strangers think twice about taking us on, enough familiar faces for Sachs to know it's us.'

'Right. Sounds doable to me.' Neville said, taking a deep breath.

'You…okay?' I asked uncertainly.

'Just don't want to end up in another firefight.' He said, 'its one thing shooting at things that can't shoot back. Different, when the bullets are flying your way too.'

'So we do this carefully. We could just be overreacting to someone going for an extended bathroom break…' I shrugged.

'Hope so…' he hummed. 'Where shall we park?'

I looked not down the road to GCR, but to our left, as if we'd go straight on and follow the road around its turn.

'Over there, down to the next right. Let's take a look…' I muttered, leading the way.

Again, we kept low, just in case. There were only three houses before the road turned again, and coming up to the edge of the house on the corner, I crossed my fingers that the road was clear.

'Yes!' I grunted, satisfied. 'We can park down there, road's clear of zeds and the houses on this side probably just have a fence or a hedge between gardens.'

'So we park up, break into the house on the end, and then bust through gardens? Going to be a bad day for the fences of Greenfield.'

'Depends. If Laurel's got a good position in that house, then it'll do for us. All we need is a clear bit of fence to get through, but it'd be good if we had her somewhere useful.'

'And Morgan somewhere safe.' He added. 'Alright, we better get back to them…'

We made it to the 4x4 without any fuss, the boot lid still agape. I climbed in through there while Neville got in the front again.

'Result?' Laurel asked.

'Don't take the next right, go for the one after.' I instructed Damian. 'We're going to go around the back, it's clear. Laurel, Morgan, we're going to get you set up to watch our backs, while the rest of us go in through that big green fence.'

I began to rummage through the toolbag for something to cut the thin but rigid mesh with; fishing the set of bolt cutters from the bottom of the bag, heavier than they looked. They were spotted with something at the business end, but the brownish specks chipped of under my nail, not rust. Gods know what Uncle Rob was using these for.

'How we going to deal with de front door? If it's locked?' Damian asked.

'That's a fair point, I'd still lock up, even with that fence.' Anita said.

'I wanted to go in quietly,' I thought aloud, 'can't risk the door being watched by someone unfriendly. We'll find another way in. Might be able to crowbar a window open.'

'Or two,' Anita suggested, 'go in from two sides on the ground floor, sweep it, meet in the middle. How many ways upstairs?'

'Just the one set of stairs.' Neville supplied.

'Not ideal...' She frowned.

'We'll make it work. Just be careful.' I reminded everyone.

Damian drove us by the first right and down the second, switching off the engine at the top and letting it coast along, negotiating around less parked cars than were down the other side. He eyed up a couple small white vans as we rolled by, weighing them up as potential sources of diesel.

Three houses up from the last, he parked in the middle of the road. Wouldn't be much point pulling into a parking spot if we had to make a speedy getaway.

I let Morgan get out of the boot first, then dragged the tool bag to the edge with me, handing the bolt cutters to Neville, and a crowbar to Anita, keeping one for myself. Neville opted to leave my bat in the car with Damian's, but Lucile and Morgan kept their sporting equipment.

302

The house on the end was stone-clad around the foundations, and white panelling above, trimmed up with hanging baskets. The windows were faux-lead panelled, modern glazing. It wasn't exactly my taste, but it was definitely a family home. Could mean trouble.

In silence, we made our way to the house, Damian locking up behind us, as usual. I crept to the edge of the front garden, another manicured lawn with a path up to the frosted glass door, and took a look down the side of the building.

There was a decent sized gap between the hedgerow that formed the edge of the back gardens, and the wire mesh fence that ran around GCR. After the fence, we'd be squeezed into a gap between it and the building, a few feet wide. Easily enough for the smaller crowbars to jimmy a window.

'Alright, so far so good, no zeds coming our way,' I reported, coming back to the rest of the group, assembled in front of the house. 'Anita, any ideas on how to get in?'

'I'll search the flowerpot, you're taller, get the door lintel.'

'Spare keys outside the house?' I asked, incredulous.

'They've got an alarm box,' Anita pointed, up at one corner of the building, 'power's out so we don't have to worry about it going off. If they've got a coded alarm, the family could leave a hidden spare – if someone found it they'd still need to know the code.'

I reached up and felt around on the lintel above the door, but didn't get anything other than damp, mossy fingers. There was nothing under the large urn of flowers beside the door, but while she was crouched down there, something else caught her eye. She picked a small rock up from the bed of stones the flowerpot was nestled in, and twisted it open, retrieving a key from within. Neat.

'You can get these for about a fiver. Professional second-storey type would probably have found it,' She observed, 'but your average burglar is more likely to smash the window and reach for the lock than look for something like this.'

She tried the key in the door and led the way into the house. A corridor ran down to the kitchen, with stairs on the right. I went in behind her, gun in one hand, bayonet in the other, and nudged open the door on the right with my foot.

'Living room, goes through to dining room.' I called out.

She continued on to the kitchen, while I went through the living room and met her at the other end. Kitchen-diner then. There was a round pine table with five mats in place around a wilting floral arrangement. Five potential zeds, a whole family, somewhere in here.

'Who does that?' Anita asked, pointing at the dying flowers. 'That's where you put the condiments.'

I met her eyes, bright for a moment, but the light soon faded, her expression turning sour as some memory drifted up and took her.

'They must take it off the table for breakfast. I know I couldn't live without brown sauce on my bacon sandwich.' I said, trying to bring her out of it.

She walked over to the kitchen sink, holding her head over it for a moment and taking a shuddering breath. She sniffed back a tear, and then looked out of the window. I turned to do the same, the window in the top of the back door, twitching the net curtain out of the way.

'Prefer ketchup on bacon.' She said. 'Clear in the garden.'

'And clear upstairs,' Neville said, coming into the kitchen. 'But poor line of sight on GCR's second storey.'

'We'll try over the garden then. If we've got no shot there, then we'll have to go ahead without a lookout.'

'Laurel said anything about me, from yesterday?' he asked, keeping his voice low.

'She was pissed, just blowing off steam. She's not going to put a bullet in you, if that's what you're worried about.'

'Was actually just hoping she didn't hold my actions against Morgan. If she's going to be watching Laurel's back, I don't want there to be any tension.'

'Hah, don't worry Neville. They're cool. Now, get the others searching this place,' I said, 'Anita and I will check out the next house over.'

'Good luck.' He nodded to me, but went to Anita before he set about it, giving her another declaration of our support. I think he also said that ketchup has no place on bacon.

Eventually we found a set of keys in the kitchen which unlocked the back door, leading out onto a deck, two steps above the garden. The grass was getting a little on the longer size, a kid-sized football half buried in the growth.

At the bottom of the garden, a wooden panel fence separated the boundary between this one and the next. From here, it looked as though any upper storey window on the left side would have a shot into the upstairs corridor.

'Boost me over the fence.' Anita said, holstering her weapon as we approached. She tossed her crowbar over, but I left the bolt cutters on the garden table.

'We could just smash our way through.' I suggested, giving the fence a little push. It was quite sturdy.

'Make noise, this close to the place we're sneaking in to? You're supposed to be smarter than that.'

'I think I just wanted to see more wanton destruction. You sure you want to go first?' I asked, 'I don't mind.'

'Ladies first. I'll help pull you over, if you're worried you can't make it on your own.'

'Got me.' I confessed.

I crouched slightly to brace myself, and cupped my hands for her boot. It was textured for extra grip, plus moist and muddy from the damp grass, but I managed to help her get high enough to swing a leg over.

Sat atop the fence in what could not have been a comfortable position, she offered out a hand. I wiped mine off on my jeans before taking it, then placed one hand on the top of the fence. I jumped, pulling myself, scrambling for purchase on the panels and after a moment, getting my arm over.

From there, a leg, and from there, an undignified but successful drop to my feet on the other side. Anita swung her other leg over, coming to the ground much more gracefully. She'd had help.

This garden wasn't as well kept as the other, the grass here was in need of a few sheep before it got the lawnmower treatment, and rather than decking or steps up to the back door, there was a pile of loose bricks next to paint tins and some boxes under a tarp. The back door was old, wooden, and Anita's crowbar found purchase after a good shove and a few false starts.

'This going to be loud?' I asked.

'Hopefully not. I'll be gentle.'

'Did you-'

'See if it was locked? Yeah.' She grunted, straining at the crowbar. Wood creaked, and began to splinter.

Rather than applying more pressure, she wriggled it deeper into the door, and rocked pressure back and forth, the wood straining and groaning. It went on for more than two minutes, or a subjective hour in my head. The softly-softly approach would make less noise, and with thirty plus zeds probably within earshot, we were taking caution over speed.

Eventually, she gave one long pull on it, and the sufficiently weakened, rusted, elderly lock gave way, a crunch maybe half as loud as throwing the phonebook on the floor.

Her face twisted, ears straining to hear the moaning of anything inside. All I could hear were the faint moans and rattling of the fence from the zeds we already knew about.

'I think we're good.' I said, taking my bayonet out.

'Then let's do this.' She nodded, pistol drawn.

Thirty Six

Laurel got into position in an upstairs bedroom, one of the few rooms in the house that didn't look like it was newly gutted, though it wasn't exactly finished. The bed, draped over with a dust sheet, was at a good height for her to kneel, resting her gun on the window ledge.

Plastic sheeting was down in most rooms, with wallpaper stripped or first-coats painted most everywhere else. Toolboxes, cordless drills and stacks of construction materials were here and there, but unless we suddenly needed to barricade ourselves inside, or maybe put up a partition wall, they weren't going to be much use to us.

The kitchen floor was down to bare boards, not much there besides an old stove and a tea making setup on top of a small fridge. Looked as if the apocalypse had ruined somebody's renovation plans. Neville moseyed over to the biscuit tin the workmen had left, and inspected the contents.

Out in the garden, Lucile and Damian had set a shiny new aluminium ladder up against the hedge, and were dropping a second one down the other side to make climbing over easier, in case we needed to make a retreat.

The plan was to head back over the ladders, grab the set on this side of the garden, and use it to quickly get over the fence back to the first house – we could just go straight down the gap between the houses and the radio station, but that'd lead zeds right to the 4x4, rather than leave them clawing at a hedge.

'Mwant one?' Neville asked, popping a chocolate biscuit in whole.

I accepted, and gestured with it gratefully, before joining Anita at the living room window. It was a bay, so stuck out a little ways from the side of the house. Without curtains, we were pretty exposed, but it did get us a good look at the zombies pressed up by the gates.

'Neville was about right. Must be at least thirty.' She reported, 'Looks like there's more around the corner of the fence too. Our side's clear, but this could be the beginnings of a horde forming. Wonder what drew them in…'

Morgan tapped me on the shoulder.

'Everything okay upstairs?' I asked.

'No, you need to come see this…' she cringed, swallowing hard.

Anita and me both went with her, to the bedroom where Laurel knelt on the covered bed. She scooted over, and nodded out the window.

'Take a look, in the car park,' she said, 'took me a minute, I wasn't sure, but…'

A familiar looking black SUV was parked up inside the GCR fence, having pulled into a spot nose-first. Both front doors were still open, no sign of anyone nearby. There were a lot of black trucks in a city of Greenfield's size, but it was too much of a coincidence, especially after we'd suspected foul play already. I'd put money on the back window being shot out.

Several zeds also lay dead between the SUV and the doors, as if the gates didn't open and shut fast enough – they had to fight a retreat.

Anita went first. 'Shit.'

'Yeah,' I concurred, 'reckon it's them?'

'Looks like.' She sighed. 'At least now we know what we're dealing with.'

'In my head, this was the worst case scenario…' I groaned.

'Arseholes want a way out of the city too.' Laurel spat, 'After we got the rest of their crew, they're running scared.'

'Could be it…' I frowned, thinking back to our earlier visit to the radio station. 'Or maybe they've been based out of that station the whole time.'

'The sixth man, Carl Sachs' little slip of the tongue?' Laurel asked. 'You said he mentioned there were more in his group, people who went out to get things for the signal relay.

Figures you can't get kit like that at the hardware store – Deserters probably went to their old base to strip it for parts or something.'

'How many shooters could we be looking at?' Anita asked, hand unconsciously sliding towards her gun.

'One woman had a shotgun, but my gut says that was just for show, probably not loaded, and probably not a hostile. Makes two survivors from last night,' Laurel started.

'And maybe one more guy,' I carried on, 'when we were there last, we figured there might have been someone hiding from us. If Sachs and those two women are being held there against their will, the Deserters would need someone to keep them in line while they're out scavenging supplies. But Sachs was asking people to come to GCR the first time we heard his broadcast,' I said, shaking my head.

'Could be they gave him a beat-down for that, somewhere you didn't see the bruises. Or…hostages.' Anita suggested, 'Leverage, bargaining chips, hero points, maybe even a last vestige of civic duty. The Deserters round up survivors, and use them to get in good with the CDC. If they're in contact at all.'

'Yeah,' Laurel scoffed, 'but for all we know they're keeping the women and tossing the men to the zeds. DJ gets a free pass because he's the voice bringing people in.'

'Urgh,' I grunted. 'We could think about this all day, but we're not going to get any answers.' I stood up, and made for the doorway. 'I'll tell the rest. Anita, hope you're ready for some gunplay.'

'You want to give diplomacy a chance first?' she asked, following me down the stairs. I stopped on the last one.

'Maybe. I tried it with them last time and it didn't get us anywhere. On the other hand, when the bullets start flying I don't know if I'll want to crap my pants and run away, or take out some disproportionate revenge for Laurel's ear.'

'Either is a reasonable response, but don't lose your head while you're about it.' She warned, stopping me at the bottom

309

of the stairs, 'Best to keep your wits about you, whether you're fighting or flighting.'

'I didn't get a shot at these guys last time,' I sighed, 'if they're pulling some bad shit here, I don't know if I'd forgive myself for not standing up.'

Anita smiled, but it came across hollow. 'You've got a better attitude than some police I know.'

'This has been a hard day for you, I know.' I reassured her. 'If you want to sit this one out, there's nobody here who'd think less of you. You should be getting bedrest or something.'

'I'd think less of me. I'm not letting you go in there without backup.'

'Then let's do it, before I lose my nerve.' I nodded.

I gathered the rest of the team in the kitchen to relay the news. The Deserters, or what was left of them, were holed up in GCR, likely only two or three men, but we could be wrong. Still, that was their SUV outside the station, and it'd be no coincidence they drove up this way to patch up their wounded man.

'Five against three.' Lucile said. 'I'll take those odds, they're between us and the endzone.'

'Six,' Neville corrected, sounding hopeful, 'Laurel's got a shot into the building from upstairs, if we can fight them near the right windows.'

'I want to try talking to these guys first though,' I told them, 'If we can talk them down without a fight, then nobody has to get shot.' – It felt an easier thing to say than "nobody has to die".

'Doubt they in a listening mood,' Damian said, 'if they know it's us, might be likely to shoot on sight.'

'Still. Costs nothing to try.' Neville said, approvingly. 'We can always shoot them afterwards.'

'We got lucky, first time,' Damian reminded him, 'caught them out at de co-op. This their place. I back you up,' he said to me, 'but are you sure we ready?'

'I can't think of anything else we can do,' I gestured, opening my arms, 'but if you can, I'll take suggestions.'

'I got nothing,' he said, 'let you know if something comes up.'

'We all ready?' I asked.

'Weapons checked?' Anita followed up.

Neville popped out his pistol magazine and eyed it up, Lucile did the same then Damian followed suit with his, one of those we'd taken from the Deserters outside the co-op. He had it stuffed into a pocket in his coat, with the shotgun ready in his hands. Neville and Lucile still had their bats to hand too. Anita, presumably confident her two pistols were loaded and ready, did nothing. I followed her example, trying to mirror her confidence.

At the bottom of the stairs, I called up to Laurel and Morgan. 'We're heading in now. Keep us covered, and if it looks like we're making a speedy getaway, be ready to follow suit. If you hear shots and none of us make it out of the building…' I hesitated, leaving a flat note of tension in the air, 'We're leaving the 4x4 keys on top of the fridge in the kitchen. Get out of here when it's safe.'

'Don't talk shit,' Laurel scoffed, coming to the top of the stairs, Morgan just behind her, 'you're coming back.'

'If you don't, I'll kill you.' Morgan added, patting the pocket with her gun in.

'Stay safe guys.' I said, hoping it wasn't for the last time.

True to my word, Damian left his car keys on top of the fridge. Everyone ready, I led the way out to the garden, bolt cutters in hand, down the makeshift steps and to the base of the ladder. It was unfolded and side-on to the hedge, not propped against it. The one down the other side was still folded up and just leaning, not ideal for climbing in a hurry.

'Lucile, ladies first,' I gestured, 'Stay low, keep us covered.'

Neville held her bat as she climbed the ladder, Damian and I both with a hand on to steady it. She flipped a leg over, reaching a little for the ladders propped on the other side. This was the risky part, if we were going to be spotted by the

311

zombies at the gate, it'd be now. She cast a look over her shoulder to check, but didn't say anything.

Carefully, she climbed down and out of sight. A moment later, the ladders moved, there came a couple clicking and clacking sounds, then the unfolded ladders went into position, side on to the hedge.

'Damn it,' she spat, voice low, whispering through the hedge, 'ground's too uneven here, liable to fall off and bust something if we had to get up in a hurry. Better off leaving them closed.'

'We'll make it work,' Neville reassured her, just as quiet, leaning towards the hedge slightly. 'How are we looking?'

She put the ladders back together, slowly, quietly, and propped the back against the hedgerow. 'All clear, don't think I've been seen.'

'Me next, I'll start on the fence.' I said. Hearing no objections, I started up the ladder, Damian footing it for me again while Neville held the cutters.

The hedge was wide enough to be a reach for Lucile's legs, but I was taller by a clear foot or maybe more. Still, the angle you had to twist to make the step from one direction to another made it uncomfortable. It felt like the ladder was going to go, but Lucile had it held firm on the other side.

Awkwardly, I made my way down, the supports on the reverse-side of the second latter making it tricky for someone with big feet; I could put less than half of my foot on the steps, but I'd rather have that than attempt an escape up an unsteady ladder and break my leg in front of a crowd of zeds.

Neville passed the cutters back before I went out of sight. Once at the bottom, I kept low, and moved for the fence. The green wire mesh wasn't particularly thick, but there were many strands - not like a chain link fence with a two inch gap between the squares, these gaps were so narrow you could barely fit a finger through – probably a good anti-undead design choice.

It made getting the cutters through awkward at first; I had to jam them into the mesh vertically and lever open a wide

312

enough gap to snip with, but after I'd cleared a few snips it got easier, the sharp, heavy blades of the cutters snapping through the fence links without causing much of a ruckus - the sound of a dozen zeds hammering on the gates would hopefully mask my vandalism as background noise.

I snipped maybe two and a half feet across, one and a half feet from the ground. Because of the horizontal wire that ran across the verticals every couple feet, the piece I'd cut out of the fence was still whole - and could have been used as some kind of improvised barbecue grill.

By the time I was done, everyone else was over and waiting. I left the cutters by the fence and got down onto my front, wriggling beneath, from grass onto asphalt, the leather of my jacket saving me from soaking my hoodie on the grass. Once on the other side, Neville and Anita passed me their crowbars, and I got out of the way. We were hidden from the zeds at the gates here, but it still felt too open.

'Just going to check we've got a window around the other side too…' I whispered, moving off around the back side of the building. I didn't poke my head out for very long when I got around the opposite side, just enough to check we had an accessible window. Then I made my way back.

'Alright, we're good, another window on the other side,' I hooked a thumb as Damian was struggling through. Anita, already in, kept poking at the back of his coat where it was snagging. 'You and Damian head around the other side,' I continued, voice still soft, 'we'll get this one. You'll be spotted by zeds, but they're not getting through the fence anytime soon.'

'We'll thumbs-up around the corner when we're through,' Anita muttered, 'then give it a count of five minutes from entry to leaving your room. Listen at the door. After five, open it,' She instructed, 'then we start to clear, quietly. Don't be jumpy, confirm targets before shooting, the extra second could save lives. We'll meet at the reception.'

Once Damian was through, I handed them a crowbar, and we split up. I helped Neville to his feet, then he went to work with the other crowbar, prying up the sash window. It was plastic, PVC, but not a new fit, so finding a gap wasn't too hard. He strained at the crowbar a moment, then started teasing it as Anita had done the door earlier, working it like a pump until finally - *snap*.

It was louder than I would have liked. I put that to the back of my head, and went to the back corner again, waiting for the signal Anita and Damian were in. A minute later, I got it, Damian leaning around to give a thumbs-up. The sash window went up, and we were good to go.

Neville helped Lucile get up to the window and climb through. He looked as if he was going to struggle to get up himself, then he stepped back from the window a moment, while the legs of a chair were offered through.

He took it, simple office furniture, dark metal with blue padding, and set it up to give us a boost. After he'd swung a leg through and bobbed his head to get in, I did the same, finding myself standing on an old sofa, several blankets strewn across it as if someone had been sleeping there.

'Five minutes,' I whispered, 'wait and listen.'

Thirty Seven

I sat by the office door, half slumped, resting the side of my head against it to better hear the corridor beyond. I could dimly make out the wailing and moaning of the zombies outside, hear their fists beating against the rigid wire fence. Every now and then I thought I heard something from upstairs, a cry of pain, the shuffle of movement, a closing door, but I couldn't really be sure.

Neville sat on the chair behind the desk, all but wringing his hands as he looked about the room, glancing over signs of its recent occupancy - the slept-in blankets, a bottle of pop by the sofa, candles beside a pristine copy of a recent bestseller on the desk.

It seemed like a good long while since we'd broken in; the soreness of catching my leg on the windowsill had faded, and was being replaced by pins and needles from my odd seating position. I looked over at Neville, and tapped my wrist. He checked his watch, and counted up fingers - one, two, three, then made an 'ish' gesture.

Lucile was just leaning against the wall with her eyes closed, having picked a spot between two old vinyl records under glass, signatures of the bands and recording dates on white cards beneath. This studio had hosted some big names over the years. Guest appearances, live sessions. Not my sort of thing, less Some Bad Men, more dance-groups and wedding playlist wonders.

I followed the train of thought from my favourite band and arrived in Katy Station on the outskirts of Depression Town. No leads. Nowhere else to look. If she was alive and well, she'd have found me by now - come to the flats, gone back to her old place.

Only explanation that let her still be alive was her being out of the city, got away on one of those ambulances from the hospital, found out it was too dangerous to return. Started

315

making a new life. I liked that thought. If she wasn't here, at least she was safe, somewhere. I held onto that, wished for it. Apparently, it passed the time.

'Time.' Neville muttered, slowly rising from the chair. Lucile shrugged herself from the wall, and returned her gun to hand. She and Neville had left their bats by the bolt cutters outside - no good to them in the close confines of the building, and no sense bringing a club to a possible gunfight.

I got up and opened the door a crack, stomach a-flutter from what we were about to get into. I took out the larger of my two guns. It felt more reassuring in my hand than the antique.

'Anything?' Lucile whispered behind me.

I shook my head, and opened the door wider, moving out into the corridor. Four doors were down the left side, three had name plates for radio executives or DJs, I wasn't really sure. The fourth, I remembered from my deliveries here, was a toilet. And, you'll be delighted to hear, had soft loo roll. My brain went on a ten second tangent about that probably being the first thing to run out of at home once we went on the tinned fruit diet.

Neville took the first door, standing off to one side, reaching for the handle. I knelt down on the other side, and as he let it swing open, pointed my gun in. Though the light was dim, there was enough to see nobody was home. I felt pretty stupid, kneeling there on the threadbare carpet, but we repeated the process for the next door.

Just before we did the third, motion caught my eye at the end of the corridor, but I did as Anita asked, kept my cool, didn't panic, and gave a long hard look down that way. It had been the woman herself giving a quick glace around the corner. A moment later, she and Damian appeared in full view.

We checked the third room, while they made their way up the corridor, towards the reception area, glass doors looking out over the parking lot.

I felt like my voice was trapped now, heartbeat rising in my throat, knowing we were now going to climb the stairs, and come face to face with the Deserters again.

Anita pointed down the corridor she'd just come from, and put her thumb up. I did the same for ours. Then she pointed upwards. I nodded, then pointed to her, then to Neville; the two people with the most tactical training. Damian might have had the bigger gun, but they knew more of what they were doing.

Neville and Anita led the way up the stairs, stepping softly, slowly, quietly, and in line with each other. They stopped just before the little landing at the top, the doors propped inwards by rubber stoppers. Neville went on the left, Anita on the right, just enough room for them to comfortably be side by side, then after a look, she held up her fingers, and made a countdown of three.

It happened fast.

They took the extra step to the landing, knelt down and leaned out of the stairwell, guns first. Maybe that wasn't the best way to go about the diplomatic approach, but none of us had thought that going in guns-out was a bad idea, given that these people had already shot at us.

They say you get further with a kind word and a gun than with a kind word alone. We were about to find out.

'Freeze! We aren't-' Anita barked. I didn't see what happened, but something glass smashed against the floor, there was a muffled swear, then Anita got louder. 'Hands up, don't fucking go for -'

Bang, her gun reported, the sound flat and dull. She hadn't even had time to threaten. Someone cried out in pain as something else clattered to the ground, crockery and cutlery. He'd been bringing food and water to his injured squadmate. We'd caught them at lunchtime.

Anita's gun barked again, but it was quiet compared to the overwhelming volume of shattering glass that followed - a glass door, an office window perhaps. For a few seconds after

317

the deafening clamour, I could hear more glass falling from the frame with soft tinkling whispers, until Anita spoke up again.

'We're not here to fight!' she yelled. 'If you can still hear me, I've got no interest in shooting you again.'

'I'm hit!' someone called out, ignoring her. 'It's those scavs from last night!'

'We don't want anyone to get hurt,' I called, cupping my hands but not taking another step upwards, 'we were here the other day talking to the DJ about getting evacuated. Came back to check in when we heard the radio silence.'

There was a moment's quiet, before the apparently wounded one called back.

'The Deputies? Shit, throw up all your guns and we'll talk.'

'That's not going to happen,' I calmly stated, forcing down the rolling uneasiness in my gut, 'we've got all the cards here. You've two wounded, you're low on ammo, and…' I hesitated a moment, almost telling him about our shooter in the upstairs bedroom, but I thought it better to keep that secret. 'And well, we're not.' I finished. It came as lame as it sounds.

'I'm armed enough,' the injured man shouted back, 'I've got a grenade. Could roll that down the corridor and you wouldn't be making any more threats.'

White hot panic rolled up from my legs to my head, bringing me out in a cold sweat. Would we be able to run fast enough?

'Bullshit.' Anita spat, 'You wouldn't use a grenade in here, even if you had one. Shrapnel would go through this drywall like paper, you'd be lucky to survive.'

'What have I got to lose?'

'You're still alive.' I reminded him, 'That's something, and look, we don't want a fight here. We can all walk away. We've got some medical training,' Lucile the First Aider cleared her throat but I ignored her, 'we can patch you, and your wounded buddy up. My offer from last night stands, we'll even throw in some food, got a picnic with us in our vehicle and everything.'

318

'Where did you park? It's crawling with rotters outside.' The man asked, strangling a cry of pain. I doubt getting shot is a pleasant experience no matter where you take it. 'You assholes let them through the fence?'

'No, we didn't,' Anita reassured him, not rising to the name-calling, 'came in through it with a pair of cutters. Knew you were in here so we didn't want to take any chances, but you're between us and a line on evacuation - so if you don't want to get shot again, I suggest you give yourself up, and crawl into the corridor where I can see you.'

'It usually take this long to talk people off a ledge?' I muttered to Anita, moving to stand closer.

She shook her head. 'He's stalling.'

'Fuck this...' I growled through gritted teeth, 'How's your partner doing, the guy who took a bullet last night?'

'We're doing good, what's it to you?'

He'd already lined sarcasm up as a favoured response for all our previous enquiries, which made me think there was trouble in paradise, and he didn't want to show weakness.

'He's in no condition, his partner's down too. Only one shooter to worry about.' I muttered to my point-men. Despite my gut being in knots, I was still trying to help.

'Rush?' Neville asked.

'On my queue.' I nodded, looking to Anita. 'Mace him.'

She bore teeth in a smile, but there was a manic nervousness to it. We were about to go into danger, against a desperate man with an assault weapon and nothing to lose, you've got to be a little crazy to face that. Especially when you're forgoing your gun for a can of compressed gas.

I took the flare out of my jacket, and stepped into the corridor, keeping low, dimly noticing the dropped sandwich tray and half-shattered drinking glass. Neville covered his side, making sure Anita and I weren't flanked. I didn't have time to explain what I was going to do, but I hoped she catch on quick.

'Flash out!' I yelled, mimicking the voice of a thousand faceless gaming avatars, lobbing the un-lit roadflare through a

319

broken glass door on the right side of the corridor. I had expected that to be it, but Anita made a "bang" to go with my imaginary flash, putting another bullet through the office's corridor window.

The bluff, the shock of breaking glass, I hoped it was enough. Cobra in hand, Anita at my side, we rushed into the room, yelling incoherently. The soldier had rolled onto his side, protecting his eyes and ears, but leaving himself open to a swift boot in the coccyx - hopefully taking the fight out of him, while Anita kicked the assault rifle away.

He looked up in horror, eyes wide, expression pained, realising he'd been played. Seeing the end, he reached for a sidearm on his leg. That's when Anita sprayed him in the face with CS Gas – also known as pepper spray, or mace. Standard police issue. A streamer of the stuff landed home, and immediately his snarl of anger turned into wails of pain. I felt a brief flash of sympathy, I'd been caught by some splash from that stuff before, and it can burn the skin, let alone the eyes.

Sympathy didn't stop me from disarming him, straddling his kicking legs and taking his pistol. He tried resist, but the pain was too much. Swearing and hissing, he made all kinds of promises about what he'd do to us, but the sound of shots from the corridor snapped my attention back. Brief bursts of small, automatic fire were filling the air.

'Watch him, I'll go!' I called out, struggling to my feet and pointing the Cobra towards Neville's side of the building, keeping myself as close to the shattered glass doorframe as I dared.

Yeah. I'd told the firearms-trained police officer to sit and wait, while I, the postman, went into a firefight against a Territorial with a machine gun, wielding a six-shooter. Adrenaline is a bastard, but I must have said it with some conviction because she stayed put.

Neville was, presumably, back down the stairwell, taking cover. I caught a glimpse of a black-clad trooper diving back into the doorway at the end of the corridor, and saw a magazine fall to the ground. He was reloading. He'd shot at

320

my friends and he had the balls to try it again. I stepped out into the corridor to one-up my previous Maddest Thing record, set not thirty seconds earlier.

I raised my gun, and walked forwards, slowly, measured steps that didn't shake my aim. Neville, Lucile and Damian saw me coming their way, and backed me up; Neville leaning around his corner, Damian coming out into the corridor and crouching on one knee, shotgun to his shoulder. Lucile watched the rear – there was no more room, we made a line across the corridor, surely the easiest targets in the world, and waited several long heartbeats, for the shooter to surface again. I'm proud to say we kept our cool. But even then, it still went tits up.

The black-clad soldier spun around the corner, gun to his shoulder, and fired. The Cobra bucked and kicked in my hand, twice, maybe three times, sounding more like Laurel's rifle than any of the other pistols in the group. Neville fired several measured shots, to my - panicked pow-pow-pow. Damian's shotgun went wild, blowing out a ceiling tile and sending dust and a bundle of wires down to hang over the corridor.

In the aftermath of the gunfire, I heard a woman scream somewhere in the building, but my attention was pretty well focused on the job at hand.

The man staggered backwards, I couldn't tell who'd got him, but he must have been hit. He leant against the windowsill at the end of the corridor, back to the glass, which was already punctured by one bullet hole, cracked into a web.

He looked down, a white man in his early twenties, with his eyes wide and mouth open. Weakly, he tried to raise his gun again, but then the window shattered into a jagged cloud, and red mist burst from the front of his head. He hit the floor face down. Which was a blessing.

That might have been overkill on Laurel's part, but you couldn't say she didn't have timing. We had one Deserter blinded, one with a gaping head wound and one still unaccounted for. I turned to Neville to say as much, but then I realised why Damian shot the ceiling.

Thirty Eight

'Says that the other's been bitten – oh my Gods…' Anita gasped, coming into the corridor. I'd already seen it, but the bottom of my world was too busy dropping out to comment.

Damian was sprawled out across the corridor, eyes closed, his shirt staining red around his gut and coat going a much darker brown near the shoulder. A pool of blood began to spread slowly across the lino beneath him. Chills rose up from my feet and froze me on the spot - I couldn't believe what I was seeing.

Lucile saw it too, but she slid down on her knees at his side.

'Oh shit, oh my fuck…' she gasped, making like she was about to press down on his shoulder or his chest, but her hands wavered, uncertain. 'Damian, Damian can you hear me?'

He slowly moved his head to look at her, opening his eyes groggily. 'How bad?' he asked, his voice shaking, 'It hurt like hell, Lu.'

Anita was next by his side, taking out the small FAK that I'd used to patch her up with days before. Would she be able to save him with that little thing? Rather than jumping to help, I just stood there. Useless.

'That's good Damian, if it hurts that's good.' Her voice took on a firm, calm tone, the way that EMTs talk to you when they're loading you into the back of the ambulance.

'Don't…feel so good from here, seen?' he said weakly, tilting his head up to look down the length of his body. When he saw the bloodstains spreading across his clothes, he lowered his head again, bearing his teeth in a defiant snarl. If pain was good, he was going to lean into it.

'What can I do?' Lucile panicked, breathing hard, panic taking over, forgetting whatever training she'd had in her service days.

322

'Your shirt - blood's pooling underneath, so he's got exit wounds. Need to slow the bleeding there while I stitch him up front.' Anita frowned, concentrating as she ripped open Damian's shirt with the aid of the tiny scissors.

I watched the oozing blood until it touched Lucile's knee, but she didn't seem to notice as it soaked into her jeans. She stripped out of her jacket and hauled up the bottom of her t-shirt, a dark parody of undressing for your lover, leaving her kneeling in the blood in her staining jeans and black sports bra.

Damian hissed through his teeth and looked up at the ceiling, his cool exterior crumbling slightly. 'Ah, shit!' he lilted, his voice going higher with fear, what'd happened perhaps sinking in - the reality that there were no emergency rooms to be rushed to, no doctors to come save him…and I still found myself rooted in place.

Neville touched me on the shoulder, just that little touch being enough to bring me out of my daze. He lifted his gun, pointing towards the office where we'd left the temporarily blinded Deserter.

'Go,' he muttered, his voice sounding like it came from the bottom of a well. 'I'll keep an eye out here.'

I didn't say anything, I don't think I had any words in me, I just walked around them, as soft-footed as I could. I'd tell you I trusted Anita and Lucile to see him through, but there was a lot of blood now. I wasn't sure what to think.

'Am I going to die?' I heard Damian ask, sounding as distant and muffled as Neville had, coming over the sound of an increasing buzz in my ears.

'Let me have a look at you and we'll see…' Anita comforted him.

I entered the office, broken shards from the shattered window were everywhere. As it crunched underfoot, the soldier, curled up into a ball, gave an involuntary twitch.

He must have caught himself at it, so he tried to regain his composure, unfurling himself and edging to sit up against the wall by the desk. He'd been spitting curses a moment ago, but the gunfire and the mace must have taken the fight out of him. I thought we'd landed a shot on him too, but he must have taken it on his vest.

I closed the door, the bottom pane was still intact. He began to draw in deep breaths through his nose, letting them out through his mouth.

The soldier probably figured them for his last breaths, and at that moment, I wasn't sure if they wouldn't be. The weight of my guns filtered back through my foggy brain, Edgar's old piece in my jacket and the Cobra, still in my hand, grip slick with sweat.

I found a chair, an uncomfortable thing meant for visitors, and parked my arse in it. Outside, I could still hear voices, but couldn't tell what they were saying, even with most of the glass from the corridor windows spread across the floor. The closed door was just the illusion of privacy, but I still needed something to distance myself from what was happening outside.

Thoughts were racing about my head, jockeying for position, trying to decide which one I'd dwell on first. Would Damian be okay? Were we safe yet? What was I going to do with this guy?

People were handling Damian's injury, as much as we could right now. Neville was looking out for them, making sure the last soldier didn't come into play. That left me to handle one man, unarmed and incapacitated. Problem was, I didn't know how.

'Please,' he begged, as if reading my mind, 'don't kill me. We were just trying to get by...'

I made some kind of grunting noise, my eyes unfocused. All that energy I'd felt, the anger, the pumped-up "let's do this" vibe, had ebbed away.

'At the store last night,' he carried on, 'Sorry it went down like that, that's not how we wanted it - sure as hell not how I wanted it. Captain Ipsom, he was just paranoid, man.'

'What?' I barked, irritated. I'd heard his words but they didn't mean much. I'd just wanted him to repeat them, but instead, he took this as an interrogation.

'After we got this place secure, we let some people in. One of them turned. I had to put him down. Then he didn't want to let anyone else in - if they had supplies, a couple times we took their stuff then kicked them out. But I didn't want to! He was in charge, I just…didn't want to be next.'

'How?' I asked, finding my voice, wrestling it back to normal from angered, 'How did you get set up here?'

'We were already packing our bags before the order came to fall back to Orphen, most of our base really. Couple people higher up than Ipsom tried to make us stay, but there was a fight, some people got shot. Most of the Territorials went to be with their families, some took off to join the CDC. We were the ones with no family nearby. We just wanted to survive.'

'But the radio station, why here?' I pressed.

'Base had fallen to infighting, we weren't staying with the people holed up there. Loyalists. Here, there was the fence, the broadcast equipment, we could wait out the worst of it, then we'd be able to call for help if the all-clear sounded. Ditch our uniforms of course, we weren't going to survive this shitstorm then get tried for dereliction, not to save some southern politicians.'

'So you come here. Sachs has already got something going, but you put yourselves in charge. This Ipsom, he rips people off, you do a bit of scavenging. That's how you survived.'

'Yeah, yeah. Then this group comes, trailing rotters. We end up under siege, day before your first visit. We burned through most of our ammo, end up mostly on sidearms before I figured out a way to draw the horde off. Stop shooting, then make a bigger noise.'

'House alarms.' I nodded.

'You know it.' He said with a tinge of pride, his face still red raw from the mace. 'I climbed the fence and found a house with a working alarm. Had to make sure they were all gonna come so I stuck around long as I could, then got out through an upstairs window.'

Like Dani and Laurel. I nodded, thinking it over. This guy seemed pretty clever. That trick with the alarms was a good idea, and now he was cooperating, answering all my questions. He was brave too, brave enough to lead the horde off when he could have just waited behind the fence. I hoped that bravery wouldn't mean he'd try something stupid if I dropped my guard.

'Sachs, the intern, the older woman. Why'd Ipsom keep them?'

'Couple of us spoke for the farmer, thought we might need her experience should the worst happen, and that pretty young thing, Ipsom had an interest in her, if you know what I mean. Sachs, he brought people in for us to take supplies from, or get our pick of any "experts" he called them, like Mary. Captain knew our meaning about Mary's skills and took it to heart, started making plans. We nearly had a doctor, but his group got cold feet, probably smelled something off. I don't blame them – I wouldn't be here if I had another option.'

I wasn't sure if his penitence was faked for my benefit, or if he really was sorry for everything he'd been a party to here - the old "I was just following orders" excuse. There was no way for me to be sure.

I remembered hearing a scream just before the shooting started. That suddenly seemed very important.

'Your last man, where is he?' I asked him, standing up. His eyes flicked to my gun.

'Isolation. Bathroom. He got bit last night, getting back through the fence. I was bringing his last meal.'

'Anyone with him? Where are the women?' I pressed.

'No, its isolation,' he repeated, 'But the women are in the back rooms probably, where you met with Sachs the other day. Are you going to let me go?'

'No sudden moves, and we'll see,' I grunted, bending to retrieve my un-lit flare. 'Stay put.'

I walked out into the corridor, a little clearer headed, more focused than before. Neville was nowhere to be seen - I

326

assumed he'd gone to find the last soldier, the infected man. Even if he was turned now, Neville could handle it.

'Is he going to make it?' I heard Lucile ask, her voice rough, tears streaking down her face.

'It's possible to survive this sort of injury.' Anita comforted her, sparing time for a reassuring look. She'd probably trained to treat gunshot wounds at some point. 'One in his shoulder, that's not a problem – but down here…He could have been hit in the bowel, bladder or kidney. All can be fixed with surgery…' she muttered, 'but we don't have that luxury.'

Lucile's face paled, and she hugged herself with blood-streaked hands, smearing red at the tops of her arms. She didn't even notice. Even though she'd washed out at the sight of internal organs, she'd must remember all this from her medical training. Poor woman was just too damn worried to do anything about it.

'The main, immediate risks of being shot in the abdomen are blood loss or infection as the bowel contents run out…potentially causes some nasty stuff.' Anita went on, readying items from her little kit, 'Damian is bleeding badly, so that's a good sign, believe it or not. He's not likely been hit there, just a big blood vessel…'

'So we stop the bleeding. Stich him up.' Lucile shivered, taking deep, shaky breaths. 'Let's do it.'

I turned away and went right, away from Damian, towards the back. The glass in the door to the corner office hadn't shattered, but two neat bullet holes had cracked through it. I stopped to look behind me, at where Damian lay, Anita and Lucile attending.

Going by eye, the bullets lined up. The auto-fire from that soldier, probably started low and bucked high, catching Damian's gut, then up to his shoulder. When we shot him, his aim when higher still, over Damian and into the door. I looked up, and saw bullet-holes along the ceiling too. It was a good job Damian had been crouched, or he'd have taken more than a couple.

327

I could hear sobbing now, coming from the other side of the door, and Carl Sach's smooth voice cooing that everything was going to be alright. I'd seen enough death now to know what to expect. I opened the door, and there it was.

Mary, the older woman with the empty shotgun from our earlier meeting, was dead; green and black checked shirt stained around her chest, up near the heart. She'd died quick. Beth, the radio station intern, was knelt crying beside her, Sachs to her side with an arm over her shoulders.

'Alright there dear,' the DJ mumbled, 'you're okay, we're all going to get through this...'

They didn't look up at the opening of the door, but I sensed my presence was noticed after I walked away, back towards my own wounded. My people needed taking care of first.

'Where do you need me?' I asked, taking off my jacket, throwing it towards the stairs, away from the blood and the remains of the dinner tray our surviving soldier had been carrying.

Without anaesthesia, or the painkiller of exhaustion that Anita had used when I patched her up, she set about stitching closed the two holes in Damian's flesh - twice in, twice out, the needle and thread making two puckered little holes in his skin, pulling the little ring of damaged tissue together. One set of stitches for his shoulder and one for his belly, sterilising the needle first with my lighter, then wiping it clean and burning it again between. When she'd finished and cleaned it again, the needle's tip was pretty blackened, but if the heat bothered her fingers, she didn't show it.

Damian groaned and hissed and kicked his legs as the needle passed through his skin, and through her stream of calming, steady words, Anita asked me to sit across his legs. Despite writhing everywhere else, he had enough self-control to keep his chest fairly still while Anita did her brisk needlework, cleaning the worst off with sterile wipes and covering the sewn-holes with an antiseptic cream afterwards.

Judging by the few bullet-holes in the walls around us, one of those guns on full-auto wasn't a recipe for accuracy, but in a narrow corridor you only had to get so lucky. I was snapped out of that thought when Sachs appeared above us, a satchel in his hands with a red cross on the front.

'It was theirs,' he explained, passing it to Anita, 'I'm sorry, I didn't know you had wounded, would have brought it to you sooner. I just…Mary. Take it, take whatever you need, if it'll help.'

Anita opened the satchel, heavy canvas bound in leather, and inspected the contents. 'Thank you, Mr Sachs,' she gratefully said, 'it'll help.'

Sachs sheepishly shuffled back down the corridor, stopping for a moment to look into the room where the mace-eyed soldier lay. He said something to the downed man, but I couldn't quite tell what. Sachs smiled gently, then walked away. I kept my gun close by on the floor, just in case.

We had to roll Damian onto his side, a pained moan escaping from his mouth. Then we threw Laurel's bloodied, ruined shirt away. She'd left her jacket off, and goosebumps had broken out all over her skin, along with a cold sweat.

'Same again big man,' Anita said apologetically, readying a needle and thread from the medical bag this time, something presumably more military-grade. She certainly seemed to have an easier time of it.

I hate needles. I'd watched the first time because I was still in shock, still not thinking clearly. This time, with the dripping blood and the slippery skin, it was enough to make me gip. I fought it back down, and tried to distract myself.

'Where's Neville?' I asked Lucile.

'With the last soldier.' She sniffed, meeting my gaze with watery eyes, 'He's been bitten, feverish, hasn't got long left.'

Dani's memory came to mind again, in the home she shared with Laurel and Katy. I shoved that away too, I had enough things to make me sick right now.

'Laurel and Morgan know what's gone on?'

'Neville went to the window and shouted. They wanted to come over, but he told them to stay put - said the gunshots might draw more people, and they were to signal if they saw anyone.'

I nodded. We waited in silence then for Anita to finish her work. I stared over my shoulder, back down the corridor at the dead soldier with his little machine-gun. It might seem stupid to you, but I decided then and there that we wouldn't be bringing that gun with us, no matter how desperate we were. Not just tactically - because it was loud, ammo-thirsty and looked prone to spray-and-pray…but because it'd shot my friend.

'All done, bar the bandages.' Anita said.

The wounds were now stitched, but there was still work to do, patching him over with bandages and antiseptic gels. Anita must have done this before, not just taken a few days on a course - she was calm and collected all the way through, which must have rubbed off on Lucile. She remembered her training, confidence building as they worked.

They put more bandages and padding on his front once the back was done. From the needles and the blood-loss, Damian was looking like hell, covered in drying blood and the odd smear of antiseptic paste from an errant finger here and there.

'How I doin'?' he asked, giving me a weak smile. I think he was drunk from the pain.

Damian had asked me maybe twenty minutes ago, if I was sure we were ready to take these guys on. I'd brought him in here. I'd stood in that corridor. I didn't ask him to stand and fire next to me – I knew I wasn't solely to blame for his injuries, but my hands felt far from clean.

'Nothing a little hair of the dog won't cure, we'll go for beers when you're out of recovery, yeah?' I gallows-humoured, but the wheels were already turning in my head. I knew what we had to do, to give him the best shot at surviving.

'Those bullets left nasty exits.' Anita sighed, wiping her hands down with more of those little sterile towelettes. 'I think we can manage the blood loss until you have time to heal. Infection is your biggest risk right now, probably not from the bowel, injury didn't smell bad...but we need antibiotics.'

'So, we can just sack a pharmacy, right?' Lucile asked, hopeful. 'We were going to do that anyway, for your bite.'

'No...' Anita said, a little too harshly, staring at the ground. She shook her head, as if dislodging a painful memory. 'We need hospital grade antibiotics to be sure, meds from an IV, not just pills. It wouldn't hurt to re-do his and my own stitching with real medical equipment either, or at least the stuff in the TA's bag...We need to go to a hospital.'

'You're sure, dead sure?' I asked. This was what I'd been thinking a moment ago, just about word for word. I didn't know how I'd go about suggesting it to everyone else without making it sound like I was looking for Katy.

She nodded.

'Zeds are out of the centre, pretty much, but if there are any hot-zones left, they'll be the hospitals,' I warned, 'I'm on board, but it's a risk.'

'Mercy was the real epicentre of the outbreak,' Anita reminded us, 'so we have to go back to County. I told you how bad it was there. But at least it wasn't Mercy.'

'You comfortable going back?' Lucile asked, concern wrinkling her face. 'There must be somewhere else, somewhere safer. A local surgery, a vet, dentist's...'

'I'm not a doctor,' Anita shook her head again, 'maybe if Lucile or I had real, full medical training we could make do with less, but our best bet is a hospital. The sooner the better.'

'Alright, we'll-' I said, taking a step back, scratching my head.

'No,' Damian intoned from the floor, his voice deep, 'nobody going to risk anything for me. I won't let you. I make it, I be fine.'

The three of us looked at each other, Anita, Lucile and I. Anita knew she didn't have to go back to County General, but

331

she also knew it was Damian's best bet, maybe even her best bet. Lucile's face was simply a mask of worry for Damian. I don't know what mine said about me. Guilt over his injury? Another foolish hope to find my fiancée? We each shared a determined little nod.

'You don't get a vote.' I told him.

Thirty Nine

The upstairs toilets of GCR were a little bigger than the one downstairs, a simple closet with a lock. Upstairs were the stalls, four in a line down the left side of the room, sinks on the right. The walls and floor all tiled in the same beige squares, with safety-glass windows breaking up the monotony on the far wall.

Despite the windows, the room was as gloomy as the corridor outside. They must only use the generator to power the transmitter, wasting no power on lighting - though I hadn't noticed a chill in the building, so assumed the heating must still be working, somehow.

The door to the end stall was open, Neville standing a ways back from it, talking to somebody in a low voice.

'He used the house alarms, huh?' he muttered in response to something, before turning his head to me. 'How's Damian?'

The look of concern on his face suggested he wasn't just asking about our Islander friend, but everybody.

'Anita thinks he'll live,' I said, giving a thumbs-up for my own condition, 'but we need hospital antibiotics to be sure.' I walked towards Neville and the last stall, footsteps echoing around the acoustically-endowed radio station toilets.

The soldier in the end stall was sat atop the closed toilet, and had been relieved of his weapons and tactical vest, as well as most of his blood, if his skin colour was anything to go by - white as a sheet, hair soaked with sweat, just like Dani. The infection was burning away the human, and would soon leave him a husk.

'Postman's here,' he groaned, scratching at the edges of an improvised towel bandage that covered his left arm – guess they didn't waste real medical supplies on the dying. 'Do I have to sign for anything?'

If he remembered me from last night, and had the capacity to joke, I guess he had more of his wits left than Dani had by the end.

'He wants to check out early.' Neville explained, 'But the rest of his squad wanted to wait until after.'

'Why?' I asked the soldier.

'Not enough-' he broke off to cough, a deep, smoker's hack, like he was trying to clear something off his chest that just wouldn't budge. 'Can't afford the bullets...' he eventually croaked.

'We won't find much of a resupply here,' Neville went on, 'they came under siege and used most of their ammo. Those SMGs and assault rifles will be more trouble than their worth, without the bullets to feed them.'

'Seems a waste to leave them, after we're all dead.' The dying man said, blearily looking up from his seat on the porcelain throne.

'You might be dying, but we haven't decided if the other one is.' I told him. It came out harsher than I intended.

'Someone survived?' he wheezed, surprised.

'Was bringing you a sandwich,' I paused, suddenly feeling a little apologetic, 'sorry, that kind of went on the floor when we shot at him, but he'll be fine once the mace wears off.'

Neville gave me a look, as if to say "cut the small talk".

'Right,' I acknowledged him. 'Mr Soldier-man. We're here for a line on evacuation, but when we were last here there was a problem with the receiver. You get it fixed?'

He nodded. 'Scrapped a news van we found, rigged something up.'

'Back in touch with the CDC?' Neville asked for me.

'They said backup's not coming for us,' the soldier grumbled, 'we have to get to them. Can't spare the manpower.'

'Makes you think what state they're in?' I wondered aloud. 'Where were you supposed to go?'

'VBC Studios.' He said, trying to clear his throat, but having little success. His voice was becoming raspier by the word, as if he were being strangled. 'Said, soon as we could…they're leaving by tomorrow night…'

The soldier began to slide forwards, off the toilet and onto the tiled floor, supporting himself on all-fours while wracking coughs shook his body. Blood marked the tiles with each heaving convulsion, splattering them like somebody flicking paint at a canvas.

'Please!' he choked between coughs.

Neville already had his gun to hand, but I placed a hand over the top of his barrel before he could raise it. I put up my revolver, and looked Neville in the eye.

'It's my turn.' I told him.

Maybe he was right, it'd be easier to kill someone when you didn't know them, even if it was a mercy to pull that trigger. I guess I was about to find out. Even though this man had fired on us, tried to kill us, nobody deserved to go through such a horrible death, only to come back as something even worse.

I pointed the gun.

I pulled the trigger.

Crack.

My ears rang with the gunshot, echoing around the tiled toilets as if we'd been standing in a cave. Neville said something, but I couldn't hear it. He was right. It was easier. Even the rolling unease in my stomach was beginning to subside now. Is that fucked up? Killing somebody calmed me down?

I tried not to dwell on it - told myself I did him a favour, perhaps more than he would have done for me, had the tables been turned. Neville followed just a little behind me as we walked together out into the corridor, where Damian was standing on his own two feet - though supported by Lucile and Anita.

'We're going to have a nightmare getting back to the truck,' Anita shook her head, 'Obviously we can't get him under the fence, so even going the direct route isn't an option.'

'Hurt enough already…' Damian grimaced agreement.

335

'I'll lead the zeds off, and somebody can get the 4x4 through the gate.' I volunteered. Neville was about to protest, but I got out in front of him, 'Yeah, I'd be glad of backup, but you won't talk me out of it, we need to get going, fast.'

'Actually, was going to ask why we don't just take their SUV?' he suggested.

'He's not critical,' Anita reminded us, 'but the sooner we can get an IV running and re-do his stitching, the better.'

'Me scars are gonna have scars, butcher.' Damian snarked.

'Whiner.' Lucile chided, 'Take a few bullets and you go all soft on me.'

'Be ready to leave in five,' I told everyone, 'got to finish up here. Meet you downstairs.'

Neville went ahead of them on the stairs, should Damian fall, though between Anita and Lucile he had plenty of support - even if Lucile's height meant he was more leaning on her than being carried. While they went their way, I went the other, to fetch Carl Sachs.

He and Beth were still in that back office with Mary's body, some kind of supply room now. Boxes of tinned food and dry pasta adorned every surface, with a camping stove and various utensils set up on the desk like a rudimentary kitchen.

'I'm sorry for your loss. Truly. But we've got to leave soon, see to our wounded.' I sighed, 'I have to know first…are the CDC really at the VBC Studio?'

'That's what their Lieutenant said,' Sachs reported, standing up to meet me, leaving Beth behind the desk with her tissues and tears. 'They're expecting to be gone before sundown tomorrow. But I'm not going anymore.'

'What? Why?' I floundered, 'I was going to ask if you two wanted to come with us, once we'd seen to Damian.'

'Somebody's got to keep the signal going,' he said, a glint in his eye, 'tell everyone else where to go, what to do, how to fight the rotters. I can't do that anywhere but here.'

'Your intern?' I asked.

336

'Terrified,' he said, dropping his voice though it was unlikely she wouldn't hear him from ten feet away, 'hasn't been out of the building or looked from a window since she got here. She went out there, she'd be paralyzed.'

'Then what do you want me to do with the last soldier?'

'Conrad. Let him be.' Sachs nodded, 'He was the best of them, or at least, far from the worst. We need someone who can shoot, protect us. Without Ipsom, he might remember his job was to protect people.'

'What if he wants to go to the CDC too?'

Sachs chewed it over for a moment. 'Then there's nothing I can do to stop him disappearing in the middle of the night. But I don't think he will.'

'I'll go talk to him,' I said, offering my hand out to shake. Sachs grasped it. 'We'll keep the radio tuned. Update us, for as long as your generator holds.'

He smiled and nodded. 'Good luck out there. Keep the doctor's bag, call it a parting gift. But you ever need a place to run back to, we'll be here...hopefully.'

'We're leaving in a couple minutes, borrowing the SUV but we'll bring it back. Could you come down and get the gates for us?'

'If you're taking their truck, no need, senior staff had remotes for the gate - juniors had to make do with a code,' he added, going to write some digits on a piece of paper. 'The truck has my remote, had to ditch my car a while back, but keep the code as well, should the batteries die.'

'Thanks, Mr Sachs,' I smiled, glancing back down to Mary, 'I hope everything works out here. I'll see you later, with any luck.'

I turned and left, walking down the bullet-pecked corridor and over the broken glass, into the office where the soldier sat, back against the wall, knees drawn up to his chest. From his expression, I could tell his eyes must still burn, but he opened them enough to gaze up at me.

'Is it time then?' Conrad the soldier asked.

'Time for what?'

'Finish me off…' he shrugged.

'I thought about it,' I told him, 'you shot at us, and one of your squaddies has put one of mine in the hospital. You get how dangerous a trip that's going to be?'

'Shit,' he spat, 'he might have been better off dying, for your sake.'

I ignored the twinge of anger that brought on, tilting my head and trying to smile it off. 'But despite all that, I'm going to let you live.'

He frowned, like he didn't believe me.

'I wasn't lying when I said we didn't want to kill anybody. We're just trying to survive too, leave the city, and get somewhere safer. So I'll do you a deal.' I added, echoing last night.

'I'm listening…' he said, leaning forwards slightly, letting his legs drop so he was spread out, rather than hunched up.

'Stay here. Protect Sachs, Beth, and anyone else who comes up to those gates. Help him keep the generator running, the signal up, and help him keep food on the table.'

'I do all that, and what?'

I knelt down beside him, and dropped my voice. 'You get to fulfil those oaths you swore, to protect the people of the Republic in times of dire need, to stand above the rest and say that you are a warden - a protector. Voison's first and last line of defence, the shield that sheltered our people during the air raids, the high wall that blocked landing after landing on the coasts. You get to live. Maybe even make up for everything you were a part of here. Be a hero, if you're lucky.'

Holy shit, his eyes were actually welling up.

'Okay, yeah,' Conrad sniffed, 'I'm game.'

I rose up, and rolled a twinge out of my shoulder. 'The SUV. Where are the keys?'

'Sun-visor, we wanted them to hand should we need to escape in a hurry.' Conrad replied, wiping his eye with a pained expression. Ah, maybe he wasn't crying at my little speech, he had just been pepper-sprayed after all. Damn, I'd thought I was getting better at talking a good game.

'I'm going to borrow it, to take Damian to the hospital, but I'll bring it back.'

'Whatever you say, man.' Conrad grunted, standing.

'I'll leave your gun at reception. I doubt you'll shoot me in the back, but can't be sure. Sorry.'

'That's fair. I wouldn't, but it's fair.'

'We can't spare any more ammo, but neither can you.'

'Hmm.' Conrad thought for a moment. 'Knife. Combat knife. We all have them in our boots, six inches or so. Be enough to go through that fence and maybe into a rotter's face. If you come back, the fence might be cleared, could roll straight in.'

'Way better than crawling under the fence. We'd appreciate that. But don't put yourself in too much risk, they could still scratch you if they get a finger through. Not sure if that's infectious, but…'

'I'll wear gloves. Maybe even put the knife on the end of a broom.' He shrugged again, 'I suggested all this crap to them, but did they listen? Unwilling to adapt from the shoot and loot strategy…' he trailed off, and sniffed again. 'Been a hell of a day. Guess I'll see you if you come back with the vehicle.'

'I will. See you later.' I nodded, bidding my farewell.

Sachs seemed to trust this guy, at least a little. Knowing he had a knife in his boot made me reluctant to turn my back on him, but I tried to keep my cool as I crunched my way out of the room, closing the door behind me - just in case. I also grabbed the submachine gun from the pool of blood around the near-decapitated soldier at the end of the corridor, should Conrad get any ideas about spraying any remaining rounds at us. I'd leave it at reception.

The rest of our little group had assembled at the front doors, and were looking out at the zeds gathered around the fence. Their numbers had grown by perhaps a dozen, brought here by the gunshots. That left quite a mass of bodies to plough through, but for something as big as the SUV, it shouldn't have been a problem.

'The last soldier?' Neville quizzed, 'I didn't hear any gunshots.'

'DJ Sachs vouched for him, and despite my ever-increasing paranoia, I think he's sorry for shooting at us. Hey,' I pointed a finger at Lucile before she could jump in, 'we didn't come here to kill, and we're all alive, for now. Conrad, the soldier, might keep Sachs and Beth alive a while longer. That's good, right?'

'They not coming?' Lucile asked, sucking on her teeth, 'Neville told us about the CDC's big move-out.'

'Sachs is going to keep the radio up as long as he can, public service announcements, make sure everyone whose still out there knows where to go, and how to fight.'

'Can we be making tracks, yeah?' Damian grumbled from where he lent on the reception desk, 'I don't want to rush anyone, but…'

'He's right, we'd better be moving.' Anita said, gesturing outside, where it was beginning to rain, 'You got the keys?'

'They're in the front,' I told her, 'Leave his gun here, he'll need it when we're gone.'

'Trusting you,' she raised an eyebrow at me, pulling the piece out the back of her jeans, and setting it on the desk.

We made for the door.

Forty

'Gate remote is in the SUV, but I've got the codes too,' I added, patting my jacket pocket, 'Neville, you able to give a shout to our ladies across the way while we get into position?'

'They coming with, or staying put?' he asked, opening the door and holding it for us.

It was a good question. Mercy Hospital was the centre of Greenfield's outbreak, but County General had been the scene of some pretty gruesome shit too, from everything Anita had said, and as evidenced by Katy not being here.

'Not sure,' I muttered, as we gathered under the shelter just beyond the doorway. I let out a long sigh, scuffing my feet. 'Neville. I don't want to bring Morgan to the hospital - it's going to be crazy dangerous. But the longer we wait, the more trouble Damian might be in. We can't afford the time dropping her off back at the Towers and she can't drive herself.'

'I ain't leaving him,' Lucile said, tapping her recovered bat on the ground, 'Anita neither – Can you drive?' she directed at me. 'Could Laurel take her back?'

'Laurel would never go for it, if there's a fight, she'll be there. I brought you all into that fight D,' I told him, 'so I'm not bailing now.'

'I'd have to take her back,' Neville nodded, 'but you'd be down a shooter.'

'If you want to keep your girl safe - go mon.' Damian groaned, 'If it too bad in there for four fighters, five won't be much better.'

'But what about six?' Neville scowled, eyes fixed on the zeds gathering by the gate.

'You don't mean…?' I asked.

'I don't think she'll shoot any of us in the back,' Neville said, like he was talking himself into it, 'and damn, we can't afford the time.'

341

I looked at Damian, bloodstained and battered. 'Looks like we're doing this - okay. Neville, go fetch the girls, you should be alright to get out the way we came in, then take Damian's ride.'

'Not a scratch, yeah?' Damian said, managing a pained smile, 'Keys are on top of the fridge, remember?'

'Meeting you on the road to Mercy?' Neville asked.

'We'll be out quicker, I'll slow down to let you catch up.' Anita nodded, 'I'll drive our side.'

With that, I offered Damian my shoulder, and helped Anita support him to the SUV. The back window may have been shattered, but the soldiers had cleared out the glass already, save a couple sparkling pieces on the foot-mats.

It wasn't quite such a steep step as into Damian's tank, but getting the large man up was a challenge, narrated by his grunts and hisses of pain. We had him sat up in the left side back seat, Lucile in the middle, holding his hand, while I called shotgun for Anita - literally, I had Damian's shotgun, safety on, barrel down, between my legs. The rain had speckled the headrests in the back with the odd drop, but neither of them mentioned it.

I told her about the keys, so Anita flipped down the sun visor on the driver's side and caught them as they slid out. There were a load of different keys on the ring, but only one of them was clearly for the vehicle. Where'd they get this thing from? It definitely wasn't military, or it'd be more like Damian's.

I opened the glovebox to get the gate remote, a blue plastic thing about half the size of a phone, but I waited for Anita to drive us into gate-position first, reversing out of the parking spot and coming head-on about fifteen feet back from the gate.

'They're going to flood in after us, as soon as that gates start to open,' she said, 'hope nobody's at the windows behind us, we need all eyes on us.'

'Ready?' I asked her, gesturing with the remote.

'Give Nev and the ladies another thirty seconds,' she replied, running her hands over the steering wheel and down to the gear-stick, familiarising herself with the feel of the truck, 'Get myself ready and set too...' she added, adjusting the position of her mirrors, though I doubt that's what she meant.

County General. Anita had made it sound like hell, and that was the least screwed of the two hospitals. She'd made it out of there, fought her way to a motorway checkpoint, losing people all the time, only to find out it was worse on the other side. Going back to County, she would have been reliving the whole thing. Throw that on top of burying her family and patching up some serious post-firefight injuries, I was surprised she was keeping it together at all. I put my hand over hers, on the steering wheel.

'Everything's turned out pretty shitty,' I said, waving at the zombies, 'but we've made it this far - and we're gonna go the distance. We'll be with the CDC by tomorrow night. We're getting out of here. We're going to be fine. Okay?'

Anita half-turned her head, and sniffed back a tear. 'Yeah, I'm alright. Going to need another breakdown later, but I'll hold for now.'

I squeezed her hand before letting go. 'Ready to do this?'

'As I'll ever be.' She cringed.

I clicked the little "open doors" symbol on the remote, and after a moment's hesitation, the bisected gate began to slide open. The first of the zombies, a woman in a once-fluffy, once-white bathrobe, was already reaching a hand through the widening gap, and stumbled forwards as the gate opened further, the rest of them piling in behind, coming straight for us.

As soon as the gates looked wide enough, Anita revved the engine, setting off hard, slamming into the front rank of the miniature mob and not stopping there. She ploughed through, tyres mounting over fallen zeds, crunching up and down as they encountered resistance and pushed on through it.

It was like being on a really bumpy country lane.

343

The SUV pressed on, through the gates and through more zeds, coming to clear road after only a few seconds. I looked behind us, craning my head over the seats. Lucile's height made it easier to see out of the smashed back window, even with her sat in the middle.

There were a fair few broken figures staying on the ground in the car park, but most were crawling or running after us as we slowly made our way back to the woodland road, barely faster than their runners. We wanted to bait as many of them as possible, but I wasn't sure of the range on the remote. I said as much to Anita.

'Damn. I'll turn us around, we'll make a second pass.'

Once we'd reached the top of the little hill, Anita did a quick turn in the road, mounting the curb, not bothering with three-points. Then she went right back towards the radio station. The faster of the zombies had pulled away from the mob, it felt too small to call it a horde just yet, but they were easily dodged as the SUV drove on towards the gates again.

'Why're you swerving?' I asked her, not sounding critical or anything.

'No sense damaging the car if you can avoid it.' She explained.

We drove by the gates again, avoiding the main body of the zeds as they came towards us, though this put us uncomfortably close to some parked cars. I clicked the remote to close the gates, and looked over my shoulder once more as we drove by. It looked like they were struggling to close, some of the crippled zeds were blocking it.

'Fuck,' I cursed, 'last thing we needed. Those gates won't close unless those bodies are cleared.'

'Too many of them still coming after us for you to get out,' Anita warned me, 'guess I'll have to thin them out a little more.'

She found a break in the parked cars, and used it to execute a much more careful turning manoeuvre, backing into the open spot, coming out a little, then having to back in again. The road was too narrow for much else.

344

Then she set the SUV on the warpath. This time, she didn't swerve away from the massed zeds. She rammed the SUV into the bulk of the mob, sending bodies sprawling, knocking air from dead lungs - if I'd not known these things were emotionless, I'd say they just got a nasty surprise.

Anita then reversed, and came in again. Twice. Three times, smashing the standing ones, trying to catch them on the left or right side of the bonnet rather than head on – I guess she figured we'd be less likely to damage the engine. When most of them were knocked down, broken and writhing, she drove over them, clear through to the other side, then put the truck in reverse and did it again.

'Cathartic?' I asked her.

'Very much so.' She said, struggling to change gear as one of her tyres spun in something slippery that I tried not to think about.

She pulled us forwards again, and opened her door slightly to look out, as if she were checking her parking at the supermarket. 'You're clear to shift those bodies, but be careful. I'll cover you from here.' She added, undoing her seatbelt and taking out her gun.

We got out, and I noticed the gore caking the underside of the SUV. Some of it squelched to the tarmac as I watched. I turned away, and went for the gate, drawing my bayonet from my belt – not everything was truly dead yet. I had to set my boot to the back of a few necks, quickly coming down with the steel blade, three or four times.

Once nothing was moving around me, once the carpet of bodies lay still, I dragged them out of the line of the gate, leaving the ones that'd fallen too far in - Conrad or Sachs could handle those, I wasn't sticking around here longer than I had to.

Bloody smears and unpleasant memories were all that marked where the zeds had fallen in the gateway. I'd managed not to get any real gore on my hands, grabbing unbloodied sections of clothing to drag from, and wiping my bayonet carefully and thoroughly before I slid it back into the sheath.

We mounted up again as I clicked the gates closed, and drove for the woodland road to meet back up with Neville, Morgan and Laurel. Despite never getting blood on me, I felt unclean, and unclipped Anita's first aid kit from her belt while she was driving; fortunately it was on my side. I used one of the disinfectant wipes on my hands, but it was awkward to unclip, so just held onto the FAK rather than re-clipping it.

'How's it going back there?' I inquired.

'Ya know,' Damian piped up, 'It's not that bad.'

I'd have believed him if we didn't hit a pothole, drawing a groan of extreme discomfort.

'I'll make it, don't worry mon.' He tried again.

'I've heard of people coming through worse,' Anita said, keeping her eyes on the road as we negotiated the suburbs, 'not seen it first hand, but there was a senior officer in our precinct, shot up twice as bad. He pulled through.'

'Yeah?' Lucile asked, hopefully.

'He rode a desk ever since. Shot went through his spine, made it hard to walk.' She told us in an offhand fashion, 'But you shouldn't need PT when you pull through. You'll be okay.'

'Make me believe it next time…' Lucile muttered.

Neville was actually waiting for us when we reached the wooded road, having pulled the 4x4 slightly to the side. He must have seen us driving over the zeds at the gate, and knew what we were doing. Anita pulled us up alongside and rolled the passenger side window down, leaning over to speak.

'Any complications?'

'All good here,' Neville gave the thumbs up, 'straight to County General?'

'If it all de same to you?' Damian shouted up.

'You heard the man - let's move.' Neville nodded.

We led the way, Neville following a few car lengths behind, just in case we ran into trouble and had to stop suddenly. I didn't pay much attention to the road - or the occasional bit of foot-traffic Anita dodged, bumped or straight-up crunched through. At first, it was because I'd volunteered

346

to load everyone's guns, Lucile passing forwards the box of shotgun shells. But once the fresh shell was pumped, my cylinders filled and Anita's magazine swapped, I found myself wrapped up in my own thoughts again, thinking on what our next move should be.

If this were a game of chess, I'd be a rank amateur, thinking only a couple turns ahead. Damian and Anita were in trouble, one more than the other, but trouble all the same. Ironic that during an infectious undead plague we were having to worry about regular old bacteria.

Once we had the meds we needed, once we'd got our pieces back out of danger, it'd be late – fully into the night. Even with the zeds clearing out of the centre, I still figured the hospital to be teeming with them - trapped in private rooms, rattling drawers in the morgue, or just shambling down corridors, unable to find their way out – hospitals are mazes at the best of times.

We certainly couldn't spend the night in there. We could head straight for the VBC Studio, make ourselves known to the CDC - they were our line on evacuation, after all. With the zeds moving out of the centre, it might even have been fairly safe, though I wasn't willing to bet anyone's lives on it, while we knew our own place was secure.

In the end, it'd have to come down to a vote. De-facto leader or not, this was too big of a decision for one man to make. Besides, there were supplies at home we'd do well to bring with us, no telling how short food and water would be behind the CDC's walls.

When I surfaced from my list of pros and cons, we were rumbling through the outskirts of the city centre, down a road lined on both sides with exotic restaurants of various price ranges and food hygiene standards. The closer to the centre we got, the fancier eateries became kebab shops - one of them seemed to have caught fire in the last day or so, and burned through to the takeaways and pub on either side.

The zeds were still here, thinner on the ground, but ever-present. A handful down a side street, some trapped in the

347

flats above the diners, banging on the windows. I saw one chewing on a bare leg, the rest of the body hidden by the van the poor bastard had tried to crawl under.

It wasn't far now. The buildings were reaching the odd storey higher, the pavement becoming more worn. We crossed a once-busy junction, leading onto part of the city's ring road, where we saw a newly built hotel reaching just a little higher than our apartment block. It was called the Gatehouse, and marked the entrance to the city centre.

We drove in, making our way to the hospital, heedless of the one-way system that'd formerly made centre-driving a maddening experience. Some of the buildings towered overhead, a mixture between dated offices and new-build steel and glass. Other, nicer aspects of Greenfield town centre stood as yet more reminders that this wasn't just a day on the high street - where quaint little independent stores stood with their doors and windows smashed, looted, burned, or the sight of somebody's tragic end.

County General Hospital was a little further, in the more student-oriented quarter, nestled between a couple university buildings and a swanky business park. It formed a blocky C-shape around a parking area - there were never enough spaces, so most visitors had to use a nearby multi-storey parking garage. Today was an exception. Not much call for visiting hours anymore, the place looked desolate. Evidence of the infection however, was hard to miss.

In the nearly empty parking lot, several of the cars that remained were in a similar state to those we'd been passing on the roads - some the victim of collisions, rushing to the road and crashing into bollards or railings meant to protect pedestrians. Others had bloodstained interior windows, blocking from sight whatever horror had taken place within.

I looked up at the hospital itself before we drove around the side; taking in the sight of what we were about to head into. The gore-smeared glass, dark figures moving unseen behind, did not fill me with confidence. One window on the second floor had been smashed open, and an improvised rope

348

of bedsheets thrown out, which would have landed the daring escapist on top of a shelter over the front entrance.

But we pulled passed all that, around the side of the building, to the Accident & Emergency entrance. It was down a broad alley, formed by the side of the hospital and a wall beside the Uni's Engineering Department building. You could easily get two ambulances down it without sucking your chest in, but we wouldn't have to worry about other traffic.

Once Anita had reached the end of the bay, she carefully turned the SUV to face back the way we'd came, positioned to drive away easier, should we need it. She pulled forward enough for Neville to do the same, and once both vehicles were lined up and backed close to the doors, she let out a deep breath.

'Okay,' she reassured herself, 'we can do this.'

Forty One

Wide sliding doors led into the A&E Department, a large shelter overhead so folk weren't being unloaded from the ambulance in the rain. Cigarette bins stood at either side of the doors, but according to Katy, most of the EMTs here were total fitness nuts so they were mainly for people who'd driven their loved ones in, then needed to take the edge off once they were being seen to.

Under the shelter, the lights were off, but inside the hospital, everything was lit up. They must have had a pretty robust emergency power system - I suppose you'd have to, with patients on life support you can't risk a poorly timed power-cut.

As we dismounted our truck, that thought lodged home. If the lights were on all night, any zeds coming by this part of the city would see them. The hospital would definitely not be empty - but I couldn't see any shamblers from here. Maybe they'd heard our car doors slamming, and would be here any minute.

'You see it?' Morgan asked me, hugging herself with one arm. 'There was a bike in staff parking, up front. Katy's, I think.' She added, hooking a thumb over her shoulder.

I shook my head. 'Didn't see it. Anita told us staff got out with the patients, cops and soldiers though. No reason to think she wasn't with them. Can't have taken her bike if she was in an ambulance.'

'I hope so,' Morgan sniffed, twitching her frown into a brief smile, 'maybe she'll be at VBC, waiting for us.'

'I hope so too.' I told her, before we went to join the rest of the group.

They had formed a rough line before the hospital's doors, stopping just where the yellow lines marked the drop-off area. Damian was leaning on Anita's left, but she had her gun out and ready in her right. Lucile stood on Damian's other side, her own pistol gripped in both hands, with Neville and Laurel either side of them.

'No guns,' I ordered, coming up beside Neville.

'The hell not?' Laurel asked, tilting her head to the doors, 'This place is going to be crawling…oh, bastard.' She clicked the safety on her rifle. Everyone else lowered their weapons slightly, but didn't holster them.

'Don't blame you for being scared. I'm going to need a change of trousers after this is done,' I told them, 'but we've got to hold our shit long enough.'

Laurel huffed her amusement.

'We go quiet, for as long as we can.' Neville finished for me, 'Bats and blades, everyone.'

It took them a moment, gathering up their courage and readying their too-close-for-comfort weaponry. I had my bayonet already, and Laurel's improvised version would have to do - that hammer on her belt might have saved my life, but against more than one zed at a time, it'd be better to run.

'Any of your training cover this?' I asked Neville and Anita, raising a hopeful eyebrow.

'Not specifically,' she hummed thoughtfully, 'but get your bats up front, I say. Anything they don't smash outright will get knocked down - leave that for Laurel and Morgan to deal with.'

'You and Lucile on point then.' I told Neville, 'I'll cover the rear - Anita, keep our man Damian upright, at least until we find a chair or something to wheel him along in.'

'We have an escape plan, if this goes south?' Neville asked, simply going along with the command to stand at the front as we faced an entire hospital full of walking corpses.

'Run back to the vehicles. Nobody gets left behind. Go home and try a pharmacy?' I suggested.

'VBC Studios are closer,' Neville said, 'and they might have the stuff we need for Damian. Could even check there first.'

Anita shook her head. 'My gut says hooking up with the mercenaries is a one-way trip, once we're behind their

351

barricades they might not let you civilians out again, or me. They'll mean well, it'll be for our own protection, but if they don't have the meds, Damian could die. If it's bad in the hospital, they wouldn't try to save him - puts more people at risk, and they're trying to save as many people as they can.'

'Well-meaning, but not helpful?' I summed up.

'Not saying for sure, but that's my guess.' She nodded.

Neville tutted. 'Alright. Let's be careful.'

I called out the marching order again - Neville and Lucile with their baseball bats at the front, Morgan and Laurel behind with their taped-on-knife spears, Anita and Damian behind them, with me at the rear. A tiny, evil part of my brain whispered that it'd be easiest for me to run away, but a braver and equally chilling part pointed out the one at the back usually gets picked off without anyone noticing. I'd have to be doubly on my guard.

The halls and hubs of the A&E Department were at least partly familiar to me. Often, when I'd finished at the Post Office, I'd walk to the hospital to meet up with Katy for a ride, her place or mine.

While the other nurses weren't keen on letting people wander during the busy intake periods, they knew me enough to let me walk to the waiting area of whatever sub-department Katy was working in that day - Trauma Centre, Respiratory, Fracture, Paediatrics - the Emergency Department had to be like a little hospital all to itself just to handle the varied nature of its patients.

'Trauma's where we need to be,' I called out from the back, as we entered Triage, 'they have a small surgical room, think there's a medicine store for it nearby.'

'Ya don't sound too sure, Kelly.' Lucile accused.

'It was my fiancée who worked here.' I said, defensively. 'But it's a locked "staff" door in full view of the nurse's station, only seen white coats and scrubs using it, so it's not a broom closet.'

'Alright, but what if -' Lucile was about to say.

'Quiet - you hear that?' Anita shushed us, holding up a hand for silence.

It was just a quiet noise at first, a bumping sound, something you hear when you're at home alone, and the quiet's getting to you. Then it came again, louder, closer - the sound of footsteps down a corridor - heading towards us.

The nurses' station overlooking the waiting area always reminded me of a little fortress, blocking the passageways that sprawled out to its sides and rear from the never-ending tide of sickness and injury. Its chest-high walls suddenly looked even more defensible.

'Desks, go, keep your heads down.' I muttered, giving Anita a little nudge, who spurred the rest of the team forwards, quickly and quietly passing through the easily-cleaned plastic chairs of the triage waiting area, and into the nurses' station. I stayed out and crouched behind, six computer desks, six chairs, they filled the space to capacity, but did as I said - crouching or kneeling out of sight.

Thump. Thump-Thump. The sound grew closer, accompanied now by the definite squeak of boots on the linoleum flooring. From the footsteps, there had to be at least two, maybe three, walking out of step with a slow, easy purpose - not a shuffle.

More people. I hadn't counted on this. Zeds, yeah, but living people - we'd been burned by that already. With Damian now kneeling behind the desks, out of the fight, I didn't like our chances if these people were heavily armed. I left his shotgun propped against the side of the desk, but hoped the rest of the group had switched to their guns so they could back me up when this went wrong.

'Don't shoot!' I called out, remaining hidden just in case.

The footfalls stopped, I figured just at the end of the central corridor, towards the Respiratory Department.

'I'm alone, and unarmed.' I lied, 'Just looking for some medicine.'

I waited for a response, but didn't hear one, though straining my ears, I did hear something - a ragged, shortened breathing, like an asthmatic after a long run. They were as tense as I was.

'You hear me? Don't shoot, okay?' I called out again.

They *hissed*.

It brought the hairs on my arms and the back of my neck to stand on end, a cold flush washing down my back, an utterly primal, base reaction. Whatever made that noise, it wasn't human - but it sure as hell wasn't a zombie either.

I stood up, bringing the shotgun with me - the safety was on, I wouldn't use it unless I needed to, but facing some new threat, I might. As I rose, I saw Neville and Anita had done the same, guns in hand, they must have figured we were dealing with people too, and gotten their firearms ready. We were all wrong.

They had been soldiers, these two, wearing grey fatigues stained dark with blood around their throats, but sporting no other injuries. I thought there was something familiar about these two, but I couldn't place my finger on it until I heard it.

Upon seeing us, they threw back their heads, exposing gore-slick throats and bloodstained chins, and unleashed an unearthly, animal screech, carrying down corridors and hallways in the silent hospital.

We had met these before. In the forecourt outside Smith Casey's auto-shop, a zombie that walked like the living. It too had a single injury to the throat, no other wounds like the rest of the zeds we'd encountered - put that with the scream that draws in the horde, and we were in trouble.

'Some shuffle, some run,' I spat, propping up the shotgun again, drawing my bayonet with the satisfying whisper of steel on steel, 'these bastards walk like people.'

'And then ring the dinner bell for their buddies.' Neville added, readying his bat. 'How do we play -'

We weren't prepared for what came next.

The one in the forecourt had caught me off guard like that too, a burst of speed unlike anything your Average Joe human could do - maybe an athlete, a sprinter, but not me. They rushed forwards before we had a chance to spread out into a fighting position, but rather than reaching over the desk or going around for the entrances like regular zeds would, these fuckers jumped. *Jumped.*

With a blood-curdling screech, they launched themselves over the chest-high wall, a leap more feline than human, crashing in amongst my friends, one sending Neville sprawling, dazed, the other landing on Morgan's back, knees first, as it struggled to reach Anita. My friends cried out in shock or pain, letting out curses and fearful, panicked cries.

All except Lucile - she answered their cry with her own, roaring as she brought her bat down in an overhead swing on the one that'd landed on Morgan, the one closest to her and Damian. The aluminium of her bat dented at the impact, but a sickening crack left us in no doubt that she'd hit the skull.

She let out a brief grunt of satisfaction at what she'd thought was a killing blow - but she was premature. The force of that impact - enough to dent a metal bat - would have dropped a zed for good. We knew that. But whatever this... thing was, it didn't seem to care about the fatal blow.

It was forced back off of Morgan, staying low but stumbling as it tripped over Neville's legs, the enclosed space working against it. Despite the blow to the head, it was still snarling, now guttural and rough, as opposed to the dry screech of the dinner bell.

The other soldier took a glance over its shoulder, from where it was pressed down on Neville's chest, its pale, bloodless hands struggling with Neville's as they fought. Upon seeing the other one fall, rather than continuing the fight it dropped its attack, and scrambled for Lucile, boots digging into Damian's gut and Neville's crotch as it used them as stepping stones to claw out at her, managing to grab the front of her shirt.

I was too far away to help her, but the downed creature was near the entrance, and getting quite ably to its feet, no sluggish shambler even with the cracked skull.

From behind, I plunged my bayonet down into the back of its head, where the neck meets the brain stem - or so I

355

guessed, biology was never my strong subject, but the spine connects all brain function to the rest of the body - if that was gone, I figured it wouldn't matter how tough its skull was.

Like a puppet with its strings cut, the ghoulish horror succumbed to gravity, falling on the spot. My bayonet had become lodged in the spine, and rather than fight to free it, I fought to free Lucile.

After it got her shirt, it must have yanked her closer, but she'd lost balance and came falling into the same heap everyone else was in - her hand flew out for support, but landed on Laurel's rifle, sending the weapon skittering away and offering no help in her fall, hitting the floor cheek-first.

Laurel grabbed the back of the soldier's fatigues and pulled, but she was as ill-prepared as anyone else, having fallen onto her arse as everyone tumbled from the creature's first pounce. Without a good grip, her fingers slid free, letting the soldier snake its neck down for a final bite to the side of Lucile's neck.

Sadly for the soldier, it wasn't to be.

A growl of challenge erupted from Morgan's throat, something I'd never heard even in her most fierce hockey matches. She plunged her spear into the soldier's side, catching it under the armpit, a soft spot. She too was laid half on her back, propped up on one elbow, her other arm fully extended. It was an awkward position to strike from, but it seemed to work. From what we'd seen of the other zeds, they wouldn't have been put off their lunch like that, but this thing was.

It snapped its head to her, its newest enemy, and let out another rough, dry screech - this close, I could see its bared teeth, and was hit by a wave of unclean, stinking air, its breath carrying the smell of rancid meat.

Rather than press the attack however…it twisted the other way, letting the spear pull free of its flesh with an irritated tug of its body, crawling fast on hands and feet like some ungainly spider. It loped off down the right-side corridor, towards what had been the miniature Paediatrics area.

356

Then it stopped where the corridor turned off, and spun around to face us again, letting a burbling hiss through its teeth once more. I watched as it straightened itself out, its movements jerking and tense – I was sure I could hear bones cracking back into position as it rose again to full height. I felt its eyes on me, and met its gaze right back, suddenly feeling very vulnerable, my people on the ground before me, my weapon buried in the other one's neck.

I broke eye contact first, looking down to see Morgan getting to her feet, her short spear held across her body, tip pointing towards the soldier-zed. She snarled, a wordless defiant sound, taking a step closer, over Lucile, jabbing her spear forwards like some tribal warrior.

The thing took one last look at her, cocked its head, and walked off down the corridor, smooth as you like.

Forty Two

'What the fuck was that?' Neville groaned, getting back to his feet. There were clear, bloody bootprints on the front of his winter coat, where the soldier had straddled his chest, doubtless the bruises beneath would match.

'Son of a bitch…' Lucile breathed, an involuntary tear in one eye as she picked herself up off the floor, rubbing at her jaw. 'What the shit? That just happened right?'

'Everyone okay? Nobody bitten?' I asked, looking over my shoulder, keeping my eyes open for the horde that'd surely come to investigate that screaming.

'We need to move,' the new Morgan said, looking over her shoulder as she read my mind, her long braid whipping about, 'sooner rather than later.'

Damian, leaning on a desk this time, got back on his feet under his own steam. His head hung forwards slightly, his brow soaked with sweat and his eyes looking increasingly sunken.

'It put a fuckin foot in my stitches,' he grimaced, 'think it ripped. I go with de girl, we need to move.'

'Further in, or bail?' I asked.

Anita answered for the rest of the team. 'We press on, go loud if we see another one of those…'

'Ghouls.' Morgan called it, with a certainty that was hard to argue with, even if she was probably pinching it from a video game or trashy fantasy novel. You teach a girl to shoot and suddenly she goes full commando.

'Fuck it, it's as good as anything.' I nodded, pointing a finger down the left-side corridor. 'But that's the way to the Trauma Centre. Closest to the rest of the hospital. We've got to move quick if we want a chance of dodging the horde.'

Damian sat down in a wheeled office chair, and cast a quick, slightly embarrassed look at Anita. 'It be quicker than walking,' he shrugged, the motion making him twinge. We

358

formed our marching order again, and made quick progress down the corridor towards the Trauma Centre, rolling Damian along.

The first thing we passed were the diagnostic rooms, half a dozen individual little spaces lining a broad corridor scattered with flipped gurneys and pools of blood. They were equipped with various bits of medical apparatus, from a simple office setup with handheld instruments and computers, to treadmills and modern x-ray machines, little more than a table with an arm-mounted scanner.

Footprints milled here and there; the shuffling, scuffed prints of zeds, and the clearer bootprints of the police or mercenaries - or perhaps the ghouls. They seemed capable enough of imitating the way people walked, but these prints looked older, the blood all dried up. Had to be days ago.

Handprints were also spread across the white walls, particularly around the doorways and windows of each room, as if people had taken shelter within and the zeds had tried to gain entry. In one doorway, they must have found success, as the door hung off its hinges. I didn't look within, but my imagination treated me to images of a frantic struggle, followed by a swarm of hungry mouths.

We moved down the corridor in silence, save for the gentle rolling of Damian's wheels, Anita negotiating her way through the fallen gurneys – we couldn't put Damian on one, too filthy to risk near an open wound.

'How much further do you think? Might be worth finding a clean set of wheels.' Anita asked.

Bang.

I spun around, the noise coming from behind me. I saw a flash of movement at the end of the corridor, forty or so yards away. I couldn't be sure, but I had a hunch that ghoul was following us…or maybe *stalking* was the right word. I swallowed down a tense lump in my throat.

I heard the banging noise again and stepped forward, awaiting another move from the ghoul, but it wasn't from our entourage. It was coming from one of the diagnostic rooms.

359

The curtains had been drawn, but I could see the outline of a fist beating down on the glass, and heard a muffled moan from within.

'Let's keep moving,' Anita urged us, forgetting about the gurney.

'Keep your eyes open everyone,' I warned them, 'at the risk of sounding overly dramatic, I think we're being followed.'

'That thing is hunting us?' Morgan asked, tightening her grip on her spear.

'I don't know what it's doing. Sure as hell not behaving like I've come to expect these things to. We've seen ones that can run – my guess is they were the marathon runners back when the world was sane. Those two ghouls, they were both in uniform. Maybe there's something to that.'

We left that corridor with an eye over our shoulder, just as more fists started to beat on the glass in the rooms around us, a rising moan coming from each room. I swallowed my fear once more, and kept the rear guard as we headed for the trauma centre.

We followed the signs down a couple corridors and twisting turns, navigating what surely made sense on the building plan, but to us rats in the maze, it seemed hopelessly complicated. We caught no more sight of the ghoul, but that could have been due to its caution rather than our vigilance. I did not like the sound of a thinking zed.

Eventually we arrived in Trauma's little reception area, much like the last, only smaller. A handful of seats over by the windows overlooked grounds at the rear of the hospital. My eyes glanced over a coffee table scattered with old magazines, but fixed on the machine nearby, a sudden urge for a strong, hot coffee making my mouth water. We'd passed no place untouched by the infection, but it seemed quieter here than elsewhere.

'Trauma closed pretty early,' Anita muttered, 'there was an outbreak here, one or two infected, nobody got hurt but the ward was quarantined after that. Well. Would have been. CDC didn't have a chance to put up any curtains before they were run out.'

'So, not expecting company?' Neville asked.

'Shit, I didn't expect zeds to walk like folk and stalk like cats,' Lucile grunted, 'I'm expecting all hell to break loose any minute.'

'She's right,' I piped in, from the back, 'keep your guard up. Surgery's just up ahead, I think.'

'We can read signs too…' Morgan pointed, up on the wall.

Stare down one undead horror and you start to take liberties. She was growing more confident, no doubt about that. Without a word, she took a nurse's badge from the desk, the kind with a magnetic strip for opening restricted areas. Good thinking.

I eyed up the coffee machine once again, and considered suggesting a break to everyone. Nerves were surely fraying, if my own were anything to go by - but I shook that idea off. Firstly, we didn't need the caffeine jitters right now, and secondly, I didn't bring any money.

Down a hallway from the Trauma waiting area, around a corner, and we were there, a set of lime green double-doors in a staff-only corridor, pleasantly devoid of any blood or gore. Morgan used the nurse's laminate to buzz the doors unlocked, then our spear-carriers nudged the doors wide, Neville and Lucile heading in after them, bats raised.

'Clear,' Neville announced.

We piled in behind him, and it was as if a weight had been lifted from my shoulders. Even though we were still in the hospital, still in the midst of this horror show, this place had an air of calm about it; completely removed from any of the stains of the building's recent history, it was just a normal day in here. Well, aside from us trespassers.

The theatre was split into two rooms; the operating table and medical equipment being divided off by a windowed wall and glass doors with a disabled-access style button at an easy height for opening with one's rear. To our left sat a huge sink, deep enough to wash your whole arm in, with half a dozen taps.

Every surface was pristine clean, kept from the wandering zombies and those weird ghouls by the electronic lock. Rather than the glaring, bright lights of the corridors, the operating theatre was dimly lit, with an adjustable spotlight over the operating table in the centre of the room, currently turned off. It took me a moment to realise it, but soft, classical strings were playing gently through speakers in the ceiling. That might be why this place seemed so relaxing.

I closed my mouth before anybody could see me standing agape. Suddenly, a sliding sound spun be back to face the doors. Morgan had stuck her hockey-spear through the handles, making an improvised bar – though surely the lock would still be engaged.

Anita let out a deep breath. 'You know I'm not a doctor right?'

'You got to do your best to pretend,' Damian smiled at her, 'and I do my best not to die, yeah?'

'You're not going to die,' Lucile said quietly, moving to hug him, albeit gingerly, 'you hear me?'

He nodded, flashing her a toothy smile.

'Lucile, you should have more experience with this type of injury. Shake off your nerves and help me.' Anita said, 'Laurel, you don't mind the sight of blood? You can swab.'

'Aye aye,' Laurel nodded, face set grim despite her casual response.

'Anything I can do?' I asked. Neville stood next to me, volunteering as well.

'Doesn't seem to be any antibiotics in here,' she said, opening stainless steel drawers and cupboards, 'just surgical equipment, monitors, antiseptics...got everything I need. Apart from what we came here for...' she added with a sigh.

'How are you holding up?' Neville asked her, moving closer and lowering his voice.

'Not good, but there's worse off. I'll make it.' She replied, 'Find me antibiotics. Anything with a name ending in cycline or cillin - I'm stretching my training as far as I can here. Half a dozen IV bags and a dozen boxes of pills should be more than enough for both of us. Just have to hope we get lucky and respond to them, no bad reactions.'

'Bad reaction?' Damian asked, listening in. He sat on the surgical table with Lucile's help, who then eased him onto his back.

'Vomiting, diarrhoea, fever. Don't worry about it, most people respond just fine.' Anita assured him, but I detected a note of strain in her voice. She wasn't doing too well herself.

'Anything else we can do? Does he need blood?' Neville asked her.

'If you know how to administer a blood pack, be my guest, Nev.' She frowned, coming over too harsh, 'He could do with it, sure, but I'm out of my depth here as it is...'

'Real comforting there...' muttered Laurel, as she wheeled over a trolley loaded with suture equipment. 'I know you need a compatible type - Type O being the best cross-match donor, and blood packs have to be refrigerated, but warmed up before transfusing. Beyond that, I can't say if there's a danger of giving him too much or too quickly, and if he's got a rare blood disorder then all this barber-surgery will be useless.'

'Cyclines and cillins it is then,' Neville nodded, 'I can think of a few.'

He returned to Morgan and myself, by the scrub area doors. Laurel, Lucile and Anita began scrubbing their arms, jackets off, sleeves rolled up. Morgan would help them into one of the nearby surgical aprons afterwards. "All the gear and no idea", as the saying goes.

'Know where this supposed storage room is then? Reckon it'll have all we need?' Neville asked me.

'Pharmacy in the main building will have the pill-form antibiotics. I've collected prescriptions from there before, not on a main thoroughfare so should be less zombies, in theory. As for the IV stuff, makes sense it'd be near surgery, have it close to hand. The room I was thinking of isn't far.'

363

'Too much to hope the pills would be in there too?' Morgan asked.

I shook my head. 'Pill form's generally prescribed for home use, which means going through the pharmacy. I know some patients can get IVs at home, but I'm not sure if that'd be kept in the pharmacy or in another storage area. We might get lucky, but I wouldn't count on our luck too much.' I shrugged.

'I dunno,' she cocked an eyebrow, 'we're here in belly of the beast and still alive.'

'Let's try to keep it that way. You mind staying here, guarding the door?' Neville asked his daughter. Perhaps he was taking my advice on making her feel useful.

She offered out the nurse's lanyard to us, Neville taking it, then removing her spear from the door handles. 'Knock out shave-and-a-haircut, and I'll remove the bar.'

'Why bother with it? If it's an electronic lock you don't really need it, do you?' he asked.

'We're on emergency power Dad, no knowing when or what's going to lose juice. Makes me feel better.'

'Alright. Stay safe.' He added, kissing the top of her head.

'Besides, what if the ghouls know how to use the keycard? Spooky.' She gestured, complete with an 'Ooooh.'

Her first shooting lesson, her first real crisis, and her first battle with the undead - and she'd kept a level head through it all. I gave Neville a look as we stepped out into the corridor, which he returned with an uncertain, vague smile.

'She could be worse.' He muttered.

The doors closed shut behind us, and we heard Morgan slide her spear into place. It wasn't ominous at all.

Forty Three

We stood there for a moment, in the middle of a long corridor, lit from above by halogen lights, the usual hospital smell of disinfectant replaced with the distant, faint odour of the dead. To either side of us were options, doors we could check, signs we could read, but for the first time since we started risking our lives, neither one of us made to move.

'Feel better when we've killed it.' Neville said, his voice muted.

'Same.' I agreed, keeping my voice down too. 'It probably knows we've split the group.'

'Smart enough to walk like it's still alive, and if it's been following us, it's probably smart enough to try taking us unaware.'

'No silent treatment then,' I told him, 'if it comes for us, we take it out, even if it means going loud.'

He grunted the affirmative, eyes locked on one end of the corridor, as if waiting for the ghoul to stick its head around. 'What about the others?'

'They've got the door, and a whole heap of guns. Unless it can crawl around in the ceiling panels, they'll be alright. Now come on,' I added, 'that med storage room should be down this way.'

Neville and I walked left. I'd read somewhere that if you ever got lost in a maze, like that was an everyday thing, that you should put a hand on the wall and walk. Takes you down all the false corridors, but eventually you have to reach the exit. We could have split up, just to check the doors along this corridor, but being more than five feet apart felt like a bad idea with Morgan's aptly named ghoul lurking about.

The first door we came to from the surgical room was another of the same, which Neville buzzed open with the lanyard just to check it out, carefully opening the door a crack

365

rather than swinging it wide. For once, caution wasn't required - the room beyond was as empty and quiet as our own.

'What did the doctors do? Pitch in to clean up before they evacuated?' he though aloud.

'You complaining at the lack of a bloodbath?' I smirked, checking over my shoulder again. It was only the second time since we'd walked the dozen paces from our door.

'At this point, finding an empty room is too much of an anti-climax...'

'Here we go,' I said, as we reached the door at the end of the corridor, a set of double doors propped open by a pair of rubber stoppers. Beyond was yet another thoroughfare, but with some seating built into the walls near a snack machine. It was at that very machine where I'd glimpsed this door, the one I suspected to contain our much needed medical supplies.

Neville was flicking his head back and forth along the new corridor, making sure we were alone, while I tried the handle. Damn thing was locked, and it wasn't an electronic job either, we'd need keys.

'Coast is clear,' Neville reported, 'how're we looking?'

'Bad news. We're either going to need to bust this door down, or find a set of keys.' I told him.

He didn't say anything, but took a step or two backwards, pulling the rubber stoppers from the doors as he went. They were the sort of easy-swinging doors the doctors would have to push gurneys through, so they wouldn't offer any actual protection from zeds, but the sound of them bursting open would at least give us a warning.

'Nurse's station back there could have keys.' I said, staring back down the way we'd came. If the ghoul was following behind us, it'd make sense we'd cross paths with it again going that way. 'We'd make a fair bit of noise breaking into this without them.'

'Hmm,' Neville nodded, 'its safety glass, and I'm betting a decent lock. Door doesn't look heavy duty though – if we'd brought a crowbar I'd try it.'

'Wonder if the horde's arrived at reception yet. If we don't get what we need at the nurse's station, are you willing to go all the way back to the truck?'

'Crowbar means meds, meds mean our people stay alive,' he said, 'not thrilled at the sound of trekking back and forth all night, but if that's what it takes, I'm not backing down. Let's move.'

We set off back, passing by our surgical room and returning to the Trauma waiting area. I had my Cobra in one hand, bayonet in the other, while Neville followed a couple feet behind me with the wooden bat held ready.

Both of us strained our ears a moment, hearing a banging noise coming from…somewhere. Sounded like the floor above. Probably just a zed trapped in another room, nothing that could get us from here, but it was the last thing we needed, something else to think about.

I was starting to sweat as I searched the drawers behind the nurse's station, throwing folders and papers here and there, looking for a key ring, or even just a single spare.

'Must have kept one around somewhere,' I muttered as I searched, moving on to the next desk, flicking through their in-tray just in case it was hiding between forms.

'Maybe they needed the spare already, in the panic,' Neville suggested, taking his eyes from the corridors to check the window, where the rain was beating down hard now.

'Anita said she escaped with a lot of the medical staff. That key could be halfway to Danecaster. But…what about one of the staff who didn't make it?'

'I see where you're going with this. Find a medical zed, put it down and see if it had a key.'

'But where to start. We can't just go looking for one. We'll hit more than we can handle.'

'Anita,' Neville said with certainty, 'if they had to isolate patients, they'd have had to isolate staff too. If they were in a hurry they might have forgotten to hand their keys over.'

Suddenly, light flashed beyond the window, brief but bright. For a split second, I'd thought it could have been a searchlight, maybe somebody trying to signal us. But then the rumble of thunder followed up, the rain picking up intensity once more.

I made a wordless sound of irritation. 'Like I wasn't on edge enough.'

'After what we've been through, you're afraid of thunder?' Neville asked, raising an eyebrow.

'I'm one of those weird people who like storms. This is going to ruin them for me.'

We went back to the surgical room, where Neville knocked his secret knock to Morgan. I heard the stick being slid back, then Neville buzzed us in with the keycard lanyard.

'Back so soon?'

'Pit stop,' he told her, 'got a question for Anita.'

We got back in and closed the doors, shutting off the creeping tension once again. Inside, the three women had donned full surgical gowns and masks, and were reapplying Damian's sutures. He was lying on his back, sterile surgical paper towels forming a square around his wounds. Morgan must have found the CD player, as the seasonal strings had been replaced by some classic soft rock.

'They found some local anaesthetic, so he's at least numbed up a little this time. Our friend still out there?' Morgan asked.

I shrugged. 'Biding its time.'

'Anita,' Neville asked, pressing down an intercom button near the surgical doors, 'we need keys for the meds room, and can't find any at the nurse's station. There a doctor or nurse in an isolation room who might still have theirs?'

She didn't respond for a moment, and I wondered if she had to press something to talk, though that'd seem like a design fault.

'Remember where we noticed we were being followed?' her voice crackled, sounding further away than just the other side of the glass. 'I'm pretty sure some staff put themselves in there, one or two. Not sure what room though Nev. Can't you bust the door down?'

368

'Prefer not to, too much noise. We'll check those rooms, save that as a last resort.'

'Once more, into the breach.' Morgan said.

Back out there, we retraced our steps, through the waiting room and into the warren of corridors, following the signs for the reception this time, knowing we'd hit those diagnostic rooms first. At every corner we came to, one of us would lean around before we went ahead, and it's a good job too. I snapped my head back, before I'd been spotted.

'It just walked by the end of the corridor again.' I muttered to Neville. 'Think it's staying between us and the exit.'

'Aren't we giving it too much credit?' he asked in the same low tone.

I shrugged one shoulder. 'We've seen what it can do. It's faster and smarter than anything else out there. Why not?'

'It'll take one of us to keep an eye out for it while the other searches for the keys. Or we can attack it straight off.'

'I'd feel more comfortable with it gone. I'll play bait, you wait for your moment. Shoot if you need to, but if we can do this without...' I added, stowing my piece.

Neville didn't look too happy about that, but kept his hands firmly on his borrowed bat as I walked into the diagnostics area, following a safe distance behind me. I dragged a gurney across my front with one hand, pushing it down the corridor so I had something between me and the inevitable surprise attack.

Up ahead, we heard a noise, like somebody knocking something over, but I had no idea what. Could have been the rumble of distant thunder for all we knew.

'Don't like this.' Neville said, my thoughts exactly.

We walked by the rooms, their occupants beating fists down on doors or windows, nearing the end of the corridor. It was like that part in a horror movie where you know the jump-scare is coming, but you just don't know when.

So I took the initiative, decided I'd surprise the monster, not the other way around. As I came into range, I shoved the

369

gurney left at the end of the corridor, and moved for the right, ready to grapple – but nothing was waiting for me.

Figuring the attack would then come from behind, I turned to see the gurney knock into the wall with a soft bump. If it had come for my back, it'd have at least banged into it, but I needn't have worried. The ghoul had other ideas.

Above the gurney, one of the ceiling tiles was missing, tiny motes of dust still drifting down. It'd shoved the tile up and climbed into the crawlspace. No small task with a ceiling height of maybe eight feet.

'Shit,' I spat, 'it's in the ceiling.'

The words had barely left my mouth before there was an almighty crash, as it kicked its way down through the suspended ceiling in a shower of dust and gypsum – landing right on top of Neville.

My backup wasn't going to be taken for a fool though. Rather than being knocked to the ground with the ghoul on top, he managed to stumble to the side, bouncing off a blood-streaked window with the ghoul taking much of the impact, but it'd wrapped an arm around his neck, holding on tight.

I moved to assist, but the ghoul pulled Neville this way and that, as if it knew staying still would let me line up a strike with my bayonet. Neville certainly did. Rather than prolong the struggle, his face already turning red, he threw himself to the ground, where the ghoul would have made an easy target, lying atop him.

The damn thing was too smart though. Before I had a chance to strike, it was backing off him, crawling backwards with more speed than the human body should have been able to manage. I hauled Neville to his feet with one hand, and pointed my blade towards it with the other, threatening.

It just sat on its haunches, slit-neck twisting about as it craned to look at us from different angles, sizing us up. A low, burbling growl filled the corridor, sounding not unlike a lion, or possibly even an outboard motor.

Neville recovered the bat and we spaced ourselves out across the corridor, giving us both room to manoeuvre if it pounced at us again. Damn thing didn't – just tilted its head back to scream, turning that rumbling purr into an ear-splitting shriek. Neville rushed forward with the bat, trying to cut it off, but it scampered away from his swing, twisting and bounding away, back into the corridors between us and the rest of our people.

'Scared, huh?' he called after it, his voice shaking slightly.

'I know I am.' I told him, checking behind us. 'If it called any zeds to reception, they'll be on us in a minute. We need to move fast, no point doing this quietly now. I'll watch, you shoot.'

Neville nodded agreement, taking out his pistol and wasting no time. He turned to the closest diagnostic room, and kicked the door, using what I can only assume is some kind of approved technique, since it only took two boots to burst open.

He moved in, and I heard the moan of the occupant followed by the sound of it being knocked over, taking a vase or something with it. Neville didn't waste a shot though, emerging a moment later after the now all too familiar sound of a crunching skull.

No luck in that room, he moved on to the next, barely breaking stride as he got to vent his frustrations out on another flimsy door. I let him to it, trusting him to get the job done, while I went to check for zeds coming up from reception.

A runner was just rounding the corner as I did. It spotted me from the other end of the corridor, and made straight for me. I dragged that gurney back with me as I withdrew back into the diagnostics area, giving the runner something to tangle with before it got to me.

The runners don't have the agility of the ghouls. It came around the corner, arms flailing, and crashed into the gurney. The ghoul would probably have done some kind of kung-fu flip, but the runner went face-first onto the floor, where my bayonet found an easy target in the back of its head.

A gunshot brought my attention back towards Neville, who was emerging from one of the rooms with a ring of keys in his hand.

'Let's go!' he called out.

We ran for the exit, and now we were familiar with the route back, we made it to the nurse's station near our surgical room without issue. The ghoul must have thought better of tangling with us again so soon, but every rumble of thunder, I felt sure would be that damn thing bursting through the ceiling.

Forty Four

There wasn't much we could do to block it from above, but the ghoul, if only with that scream, seemed able to direct the attention of the zombies. If it knew where we were, it seemed likely that it'd drag the horde towards us. So we set about rearranging the furniture from the waiting area into a makeshift barricade at the mouth of the surgical corridor.

With a sofa dragged lengthways, we wedged it in with chairs pointed back-down, resting on the arms, then piled the rest of the chairs on and finally stuck the coffee table on top for good measure. It was hardly the Aelium Wall, but it didn't have to hold for a hundred years. Just long enough.

'Want me to stay out here and keep watch?' Neville asked.

'Hells no. Let's get that cupboard open and get back inside.'

It took him a moment to find the right key. I checked the other end of the corridor, where we'd closed the doors, for approaching zeds. Fortunately, we were alone. For now.

Lights in the room flickered to life automatically as we entered, leaving the door open just a crack behind us. Along one wall were wire baskets and plastic tubs of varying colours, everything from medical dressings to epi-pens were individually wrapped in clear vacuum packing, some of the baskets near to overflowing, but others almost empty, with scattered stock littering the floor beneath.

'Looks like they managed to get some supplies out with them,' Neville observed, making straight for the tubs, scanning quickly over them. 'Hopefully not everything we need.'

Along the back wall were refrigerators, and since everything was clearly labelled I had no problem finding IV bags, but hadn't brought anything to carry them in. I looked around, and saw a little kit bag with a big red cross on it. I knew these things usually had a defibrillator in them, but guessed that wouldn't do us a whole lot of good – whereas the bag, we could use.

I piled the contents out on the floor, then Neville began loading in the meds while I held the bag open. He'd also thrown in a few IV-starting kits, and by some miracle had even found tetracycline pills by the box full. The taxpayer value of what we were looting from this room was probably immense.

'Think we've got enough?' I asked, taking a wheelchair from a rail by the door, an improvement on Damian's current mode of transport.

'Kelly, I think we've got enough for everyone to get shot.' He said, looking about the room. 'This place is a treasure horde – the stuff in here's going to be in pretty high demand soon, if it isn't already.'

'We can't exactly take it all with us, and these IVs must have been in the fridge for a reason, we can't store it all. But keep the keys. Maybe just knowing this is here will be worth something, in case the CDC's people want to come for a resupply.'

He locked up on the way out, while I got Morgan's attention with the musical knock. Back once more in the safety of our operating theatre, Neville told Anita we had the goods. She was sat up on the table with her top off, getting her wounds re-dressed.

'That's great news.' She said, showing no sign that Lucile's needlework was bothering her. They'd finished with Damian, who seemed more comfortable in his new wheelchair.

'We should be done here in two shakes,' Lucile chimed in, 'what's our exit plan?'

'As we thought, that ghoul-thing brought zeds to reception,' Neville answered, 'not sure how many. We fought it again to get the keys, but it got away. Not before calling for backup again.'

'Took out a lone runner, so I think it's just shamblers we've got to worry about. Not sure how many are between us and the exit though. Could be a handful, could be a hundred.' I said.

374

'Worth finding out?' Neville suggested.

I shook my head. 'Ghoul might have done us a favour with that second scream. Dragged them away from reception, but there's more than one way to get there. We could loop around through the Fracture Clinic, come at our exit from a different angle.'

'That'll work.' Laurel said. She was watching Lucile stitch Anita's shoulder back up. Unlike the improvised kit we'd been using, the surgical room had tongs, grips and all kinds of sinister little hooky things. Guess there was room for that in the bag too, once it'd been wiped down.

'Bring that kit with us when you're done, Doc.' I said to Lucile through the intercom, 'Got room for it in the antibiotics bag.'

True to her word, it didn't take long for her to finish Anita's stitches. Her service training, forgotten upon seeing Damian shot, must have been coming back to her. She set about cleaning down the instruments and wrapping them in clean paper towels.

'We know the dosages for those?' Morgan asked, pointing to the bag over my shoulder.

'It's printed on the boxes for the pills. The bags…' I shrugged. 'Hoping Lucile does.'

Suddenly, all the lights went out.

'Shit.' Neville cursed.

'Language.' His daughter checked him.

The large free-standing surgical light came back on, but it was the only light in the room. Somebody angled it towards the door, though I couldn't tell who. Damn thing was blinding after a few seconds in the pitch black.

'Seems like their power's going out. Lights must have run off solar panels or something.' Lucile said, 'Could be switching over to a gas generator, or…maybe that's it for power now.'

'Either way, we need to be making tracks.' Neville nodded, moving for the door. 'If that ghoul's half as smart as it seems to be, it'll make the most of this.'

'Wonder if it can see in the dark?' I asked.

'I know I can't.' Laurel said, leading the way back through the glass partition. She recovered her rifle, and flicked the flashlight on. The rest of us soon followed suit.

'More duct tape when we get home.' Laurel muttered to Morgan, as she struggled to find a comfortable way to hold both her spear-stick and flashlight.

Neville opened the doors, checking right as I went left. Between the storm outside and the lost power, the hallways of the hospital were black, lit only by the white beams of our torchlight. My side was clear, but I heard Neville swear again. We weren't alone.

Our barricade was doing its job, holding back a group of pale faced, bloody-mouthed shamblers. They reached over the pastel blue furniture with arms red with death up to their elbows. The mixture of hopeless wailing and wordless snarls took on a disturbingly eager note upon seeing us.

'It's leading them after us.' Neville said.

That gave me a chill – but the last thing we needed right now was a panic. I needed Neville's best to see us through.

'Nothing we can't handle. We've beat it twice now – it knows it won't survive a third.' I told him, putting conviction in my voice though I wasn't sure I bought it myself. 'Back it up, this way, we're further into the hospital but the ghoul should already have cleared the way for us.'

Unless it was leading a flanking wave up our other side. I didn't voice that thought. It was bad enough I'd had it, without putting it in other heads too.

I led from the front, Neville right behind me as I cleared the next set of doors, going left again as he went right. This time we were clear, but had to wait a moment for the rest of them to catch up with us.

Anita was pushing Damian's chair, the big man holding his shotgun with a firm grip. The local anaesthetic they'd given him had numbed his wounds, but obviously hadn't sent him out of it. Morgan was standing by them, with Laurel and Lucile bringing up the rear this time.

'Hear any noises from above, move, quickly.' I advised the group, 'Rotting bastard tried getting us from above.'

'He get a face full of buckshot if he tries anything.' Damian said, 'I not going through all this just to get done like that.'

'Too bloody right.' Laurel said.

Every now and then the lights would flicker, exposing the things we couldn't see in the beams of our lights like the flash from a camera. These halls were just as bad as the rest we'd seen, toppled gurneys and pools of blood, smears of ichor and bullet-holes peppering the walls.

We were moving beyond what I was certain of with the hospital layout and had to stop at the next junction to check the signs on the walls. While I plotted a route, racking my nervous brain, everybody else kept their eyes on a corridor, or in Neville's case, the ceiling. Meanwhile, the rumble of thunder was constant, and seemed to be getting closer, with the flashes of lightning through distant windows generally not helping ease the mood.

On top of all that, the ghoul was out there. A corpse that could walk like the living, and seemingly, think like a predator. It was even more dangerous than the runners, but was it smart enough to know where we'd go next? It'd found us in the surgery, and I can only assume it'd led that mob straight for us.

That meant is was tracking us, even now. It knew we wouldn't go through the zeds to get back to the entrance, leaving us with only the one way out of that corridor. It couldn't have predicted our moves from there, surely. However…it did seem to know where we ultimately wanted to be.

'This way.' I decided after a moment's hesitation, trying not to let my sweating palms get the better of me.

'You sure?' Anita asked, 'We could go straight ahead, be at reception inside of ten minutes.'

377

'It knows that.' I said, forcing my voice down to keep it calm. 'It herded us out of surgery, expects us to make the next quickest run for the exit.'

'Bullshit, how do ya know that?' Lucile asked.

'Strike and retreat.' Neville said, his eyebrows climbing higher as realisation took him, 'It's been whipping us up, trying to make us panic so we break and run.'

I hadn't thought of that, but it was close enough. I nodded.

'It expects us to go straight for the exit. But we can outfox this corpse. There main exit puts us out overlooking the car park. Head left around the building, down the run to A&E and we can be in our vehicles before it even knows we're gone.'

'Slip right between its fingers.' Anita said. 'Alright, lead on.'

I did as I was told, taking us further into the hospital, and wondering how long our shy friend would wait in ambush before he realised we weren't coming. Maybe he had another trick up his sleeve for just such an emergency. I tried not to dwell on it, as I listened at every corner and checked the signs at every intersection.

The scream had done a good job of clearing out the main corridors, but zeds trapped in rooms or locked into larger wards harassed us constantly, trying to break down the doors of their prisons as we walked – and rolled – on by.

Up ahead, a large window had been smashed out, someone probably making their escape through it. Now the broken window let the storm in, curtains soaked, rain dripping into a puddle on the floor, diluting the blood into pale red swirls.

I checked the window out as a viable escape option, wouldn't save us a whole lot of time, but could have been useful if it wasn't directly overlooking the body of the last person who tried. He'd got tangled in the bushes and a zed must have lent through and munched on him. Though his legs were skeletal from the knees down, he was still trying to pull himself free.

We weren't far away now though, heading along the final corridor, making quick progress. Here and there were the remains of broken barricades and discarded weapons, smashed furniture and a fire extinguisher left by the ruins of a patient's skull.

The main hospital reception was a huge, sweeping thing, with staircases on either side of a circular double-height space. Large, ceiling-height glass offered some weak light on the front of the building, with shielded reception desks on the ground floor and offices above. The disabled access lift was the scene of a poor wheelchair-user's last stand. Looks like they'd taken a few with them before taking their own life with a pistol. I considered heading over to loot it, but I wasn't putting my hand into that bloody mess for an empty gun of an unknown calibre.

We weren't there to stand around gawping. The doors were mostly automatic, but with the power out we just used the normal ones, holding them open for Anita to push Damian out. We used the stairs while they had to snake down a short access ramp, all the while keeping an eye on the building, looking for something watching us from within. Seemed we'd gotten out alright.

'There it is.' Morgan said, breaking formation to come up beside me at the bottom of the stairs. She was pointing to a parking space just up ahead, but I'd already seen it. Katy's bike. Her helmet was still on one of the handlebars.

Part of me was in denial. It wasn't her bike. People can have the same bike. The same helmet even. But in my heart, I felt it, knew it was her ride.

I wiped an errant drop of rain from between my eyes, blinking hard so it wasn't joined by anything. 'Help me with something.'

I called the group to stop for a moment, and vaulted over the low railing between the path and the car park, not bothering to find a gap. In one of her saddlebags she'd kept a cover. I unfurled it, thick tarpaulin, and with Morgan's help, I secured it over the bike, fastening it beneath.

It was purely symbolic, but entirely necessary. I may not have had a clue if she was alive, or where she was, but I knew her pride and joy was safe. It was like a promise for me. That I'd never give up hope. If we could survive the shit the last week had thrown at us, then I was sure as hell she could too.

'Sorry to hold us up.' I apologised, stepping back over the railing with Morgan, re-joining the group.

'That was worth a minute's pause.' Anita said, though she didn't look happy to be in the rain, 'We need to keep the memories of those we've lost…or just those we can't find.' She added.

I looked back over my shoulder at the covered bike, and nodded. I think…just finding one last trace of her…it gave me some closure. A knot in my stomach unwound, but there was a burden that hadn't yet lifted from my shoulders. I'd done all I could to find Katy – now I just had six other people to make sure survived, and I was determined to succeed.

We turned the corner at the end of the building, descending down another set of stairs and a wheelchair ramp at the mouth of the A&E bay. That's when things went wrong again.

Forty Five

Though they were far from us as we turned the corner, it was hard to miss the wall of zeds pressed up against the A&E doors. They'd opened automatically when we came in, but with the power out they were just glass walls now. There were other doors of course, but they pushed inwards rather than out, meant for shoving gurneys into the building.

The stained remains of hospital gowns were in fashion with the zeds pressed up against the doors, most of them must have been patients of one department or another – there were zeds wearing casts or trailing IVs from their arms. Standing between the taller figures though, were zombies we'd been lucky enough not to see yet. Colourful pyjamas torn and bloodied.

I glanced at Neville, the only father in the group. His jaw was set, eyes blankly staring ahead. Anita must have abandoned Damian for a moment, as she came up beside him, putting an arm around his shoulder.

'They're not children, Nev.' she quietly said. 'I had to do for my sister what needed to be done. If their parents were around, they'd want the same. If they come for us, we cannot hesitate. Not even for a second.'

'This disease, this infection, it's evil.' I said, turning around to face the rest of the group, 'It takes away, destroys, all of what a person is, all of what they'd ever be. It takes control of them, makes them walk around, spreading the virus, hiding behind the faces of the victims it claims. It uses our humanity against us. It wants us to be afraid. It wants us to hesitate. We just have to remember – that they aren't people anymore. They had that taken from them.'

'Most humane thing we can do for them would be to put them down.' Lucile agreed, 'But that'd put us at too much risk. If we had the bullets I'd say we should shoot them, send every one of those poor bastards to a peaceful rest. But we can't spare the rounds – or them.'

'So we run to the vehicles, and get the hell out of there. Works for me.' Morgan said, taking her dad's hand, reminding him that he hasn't lost her. I set off moving towards our two trucks, leading by example I think you call it.

We couldn't really hear the zeds on the other side of that glass, save for the occasional pounding of fists, but in my head I was playing their usual soundtrack. The moan. That rasping breathing. I tried to ignore it, and listen to the rain pounding down on the shelter instead.

That's when the ghoul threw the fire extinguisher.

They shouldn't have been allowed to do that.

It pitched the damn thing over the heads of the waiting mob like it was nothing - the glass shattered outwards as the press of zombies took the rest of the pane with it, stepping over the shards of broken glass in bare feet. They'd reach the trucks long before we would, even if we didn't have to be pretty careful with Damian. There was only one thing for it then. We had to fight.

'Go loud!' I shouted over the rising moan of the dead, all too real now, 'Keep calm, pick your targets!'

'Firing line, we shoot from left to right!' Anita ordered, 'Nobody shoots the same target. Form up, now!'

A good manager, so they say, knows how to delegate. As the group's sort-of leader I like to think I understood the strengths of those around me. Anita was a good shot, well trained and disciplined. She'd suffered devastating personal tragedy on a scale that I couldn't even comprehend, and was still up and fighting.

'You heard her, line up!' I yelled.

We formed a firing squad to either side of Damian, lining up like riflemen in a colonial era battle. If only we had another rank in front and behind, to back us up while we reloaded our muskets.

'Shirt and tie, on the left.' Laurel called out, punctuated by the almighty *crack* of her rifle, louder than the thunder overhead.

'Soldier, far right.' Lucile said next, needing two shots to drop the mercenary – I guess all soldiers don't become ghouls.

She didn't panic after the first miss, taking her time and aiming again. Laurel's rifle was at a comfortable range with its scope, but our handguns would struggle until the conflict came in closer. If we hadn't thinned the herd by then, we'd be in trouble.

'Nurse.' Damian said, raising his shotgun to his shoulder, fortunately the one furthest from his injuries. He still grunted in discomfort as the buck of recoil punched back – one shot had been enough though.

'Mostly naked patient, right side.' I called out, bringing the heavy Cobra to bear, gripped just how Anita had shown me.

I slowly squeezed the trigger, concentrating so much about just keeping the sights lined up with the zed's head that the kick of the weapon took me by surprise. The side of its head disappeared, but it slumped sideways before dropping down, taking another with it.

Following the pattern, sticking to the plan, Morgan had already dropped her spear and lined up a shot, calling it and firing only once, taking out the leading zed that'd broken from the herd. She knew she lacked the skill for a long range shot, so took the easiest she could, leaving those further away for her father and Anita.

I learned from that, and as the next few shots rang out, Neville and Anita firing off one or two rounds a piece, we started from the end of the line again – call a target, shoot it.

Laurel never missed a shot, but the rest of us weren't so skilled. Damian fudged a blast from his shotgun, but the pellets were enough to rip through sternum and spine, putting a zed on it back, even though it wasn't truly dead.

Morgan let her nerves get the better of her, firing four shots to bring down one particularly elusive target, but I was

383

little better, taking two rounds to hit a zed wearing a damn neck-brace. Its head was practically a stationary target.

We'd been down the line maybe three or four times, it was hard to remember, but the zeds were gaining ground slowly but surely. After his last shot, Neville called he was empty, Anita passing him her spare pistol as the line fired again, already having been using the one Neville had given her.

'Cease fire, move back!' I called out, grabbing Damian's chair and dragging him backwards. You should always ask permission before assisting a wheelchair user – unless there are zombies involved. Just take it as an open invitation.

We gave ground, then repeated the process. Zeds have no instinct for self-preservation, save for the ghoul, I guess. No head for strategy, the average shambler will keep coming until one of you is dead. That's what I was playing on. Keep them in good pistol range until we either ran out of bullets or they ran out of bodies.

I hadn't forgotten about the ghoul though. It was throwing this wall of zeds at us to keep us occupied, I was sure of it. Bastard was probably running through the building, heading for our rear, or positioning to jump from an upper storey window at us. That was the other reason I called to move back – so we could see the front of the building, and weren't anywhere near a window.

Look at me. I can outsmart the deceased.

Laurel ran dry first, her magazine the smallest. Without a spare one to reload, she slung her rifle over one shoulder and pulled out her pistol for the next go around. After that it was me and Damian, loading bullets and shells into our weapons one by one. It took longer than I expected, with the other gunslingers having to pick up our slack at the cost of their own surely-dwindling ammo.

Fortunately, there weren't a whole lot of zeds left by the time we'd reloaded. The mob, maybe forty strong, was now reduced to half a dozen of the slowest, most crippled zeds, plus a few writhing, injured forms on the concrete.

384

'Hold fire!' I shouted out over the ringing in my ears. Be a wonder if we didn't get tinnitus from all this. 'We can finish these ourselves. Morgan, cover Damian in case our friend shows up.'

'Got it!' she said back, her voice a mix of nerves and excitement. I recognised the tone. Her blood was up.

Bats were recovered from the ground and I put my bayonet in hand. The clubs led the way in, Neville and Lucile picking left and right, splitting the little knot of zeds into two groups, holding their attention on the closest meal, distracting them from my bayonet and Laurel's hammer.

Anita's telescopic baton was never going to smash a head without some serious work, but it did just fine for its intended purpose. She knocked a zed to the ground by whacking the back of its knees, subduing the perp.

That made them easy pickings for the rest of us, and with these being the slowest of the zeds, it didn't take us long to finish off the rest of them. We were well practiced by now. That's probably why the ghoul ignored us, and went for Morgan.

That, or maybe it was personal.

The first we knew of its attack, Laurel was still pulling her hammer free of the back of a zed's skull. I heard Morgan call out the danger, but it was on her before we had a chance to move, appearing from the front of the building with startling speed. We'd moved too far forwards to engage the zeds, lost sight of its approach right at the last moment. Guess it was smarter than me.

Morgan had already put herself between the building and Damian, the injured fighter abandoning his chair to dash towards us, getting out of the way of the fight. He might have been able to shoot in his condition, but tangling with the ghoul up close might have been more of a liability than a help for Morgan.

She'd thrust her spear out to meet the ghoul as it rushed her, jabbing her knife through the remains of its Kevlar, just under the ribcage. Bullet-proof vests don't do much against knives. It'd been enough to hold it from taking her down immediately, but the ghoul's arms were longer – he'd either been lanky in life, or changed in death.

It tried to claw for her face and neck, but she'd turtled up, putting her head down and hunching her shoulders. With her hair braided up, it couldn't find much purchase there either, though she'd probably want to wash her hair tonight.

The whole exchange had taken perhaps four or five seconds, but it didn't take many more for Neville to charge forwards. He swung his bat underarm, going for the ghoul's knee like he was whacking the hockey ball across the pitch. I swear the damn thing was lifted off the ground with the force of the blow.

The shattered knee buckled, pitching the ghoul over onto its back as it fell. Neville didn't let up though, bringing the bat down again, aiming for the head – but it threw up an arm to deflect the blow, knocking it aside rather than blocking it outright.

You're giving me that look again, like I'm giving these things too much credit, but wait until you see one yourself. They know how to move, they know how to fight. If it didn't have its windpipe on show I might have believed it was just some psycho too.

Neville recovered from the deflection and swung again, lower, meaning to break the other leg. Again, the ghoul wasn't going to let this happen, kicking and screaming in wounded rage, but it was for nothing. He brought down my old bat, swung once more in revenge, to shatter the other knee.

It was still swinging its arms, trying to claw out at Neville, when his daughter shot it dead.

Their skulls might have been thick enough to take a solid blow, but a bullet to the brain will still take them out of the fight.

'Thanks.' Neville gasped, breathing hard, bringing her in for a tight, one-armed hug.

'You too. Wasn't worried, not even a little.' She added with a long exhalation of breath, trying to calm a rapidly

386

beating heart. I knew the feeling, though it was getting less with every fight.

'Sons of bitches might have hard heads,' Lucile said, clapping Morgan on the back, 'but cooler heads prevail, my Pa always said.'

'Is there something in my hair?' Morgan asked her with a worried sort of smile.

Lucile had to stand on tiptoe to see, but she picked out what appeared to be a whole nail, somehow snagged off the ghoul in her hair.

'What was it?' she asked.

'Best you don't know.'

'Urgh.' Morgan cringed. 'Let's get out of here before we soak.'

'You heard the lady, let's move.' I said, wheeling Damian's chair over to him.

'I'll walk, but be worth putting it in de back.' He said, taking pained steps towards his big blue monster.

I folded it up, and stowed it in the boot.

'What's next?' Neville asked. 'We giving Conrad his truck back?'

'I mean to keep my word – we'd have struggled to get Damian out of GCR without it,' I said, 'but let's get our wounded home and seen to first.'

'Not sure we can make two trips out and still have enough diesel left to drive to VBC tomorrow, if that is still the plan?'

'Sachs said they'd be out of there by sunset, yeah. We'll have to make some fuel stops on the way home. You take the lead, stop whenever you see a vehicle we can tap.'

Neville nodded, and we saddled up. I kept Anita company in the commandeered SUV, Damian having returned to his 4x4 with Lucile.

'That could have gone better.' I said, belting myself in.

'Could have gone worse.' She reminded me.

'Yeah. Guess it could.' I muttered, looking out over the parking lot as we drove by, Katy's bike covered under that tarp.

Forty Six

'Looks like he's stopping.' Anita said, breaking gently.

We were coming through a residential area, not-quite outdated terraces on one side, with wide, open fields on the other – maybe ten minutes out from the hospital, since there was no traffic. I hadn't been paying much attention, lost in my own thoughts, but at the sudden stop I perked up.

The storm must have been blowing over, as the rain was easing up and I couldn't remember hearing thunder in a while. The day was wearing on though, the dinginess of cloud cover would soon be giving way to the dinginess of night, but for now, there was still enough miserable grey light to see by.

'Must have seen a likely candidate for fuel.' I thought aloud, undoing my seatbelt as we pulled up just behind the 4x4.

Neville and Lucile were getting the pump and bucket from the back, Laurel moving off to inspect a nearby sedan. Morgan was keeping Damian occupied, presumably.

'Working class neighbourhood,' Neville said, before we could ask, 'I've seen a few vans and pickups here before, betting they've got the fuel we need.'

'If it ain't written on the filler cap then we shouldn't chance it. Good way to kill a car, putting the wrong gas in.' Lucile said.

'Owner's manual will probably be in the glovebox though.' Anita offered.

Lucile nodded at that. 'But if not…'

'Then no, don't take the risk. I'll go double check what this thing uses,' she added, hooking a thumb at the SUV, 'be nice of us to return it with something in the tank.'

'Filling up the truck for the assholes who shot Damian,' Lucile shook her head, 'not sure I can forgive him. That Conrad. For being a part of that.'

'He seemed sincere, that he didn't want anything to do with how the rest of his squad were acting.' I said, trying to be diplomatic. 'But I get it. I haven't forgiven him really either. In time, maybe, he'll be able to forgive himself.'

'Guess we'll see.' Lucile sighed. 'But if he shoots you when you take it back, don't come bleeding to me.'

It came out harsher than she intended, I think. An awkward silence hung for a moment, before Neville cleared his throat.

'If this thing with the CDC goes south, maybe we should start scavenging as much gas as possible.' He suggested. 'Who knows when we'll get more? Might have to last us years.'

'A year, at best.' Lucile corrected him, thankful for the distraction, 'Fuels have expiry dates. Diesel's better than petrol, but all gas goes bad eventually.'

'Well, I just learned something new.' I hummed, scratching my chin. 'The number of post-apocalyptic films I've seen that now have gaping plot holes is staggering.'

'So if we can't get with the CDC, long term we need to be somewhere with solar panels, or a wind turbine.' Neville said.

'Then our biggest worry will be calm, cloudy days. Geothermal would be dandy, but now we're pipe dreaming.' Lucile grunted, 'We'll get to searching anyway. We definitely need this for the short term. See if we all survive through to the long game.'

I looked over my shoulder, where Anita was flicking through the SUV's manual, checking the fuel type. 'No, Lucile, why don't you stay? Neville can go with Anita.'

I suggested it not because I suspected Anita and Neville were growing closer, but because I knew it'd stress Lucile too much to not be with Damian right now. She'd saved his life. I think that earned a few minutes respite.

'Appreciated.' Lucile said, flashing me a tense smile, 'Don't want to leave him while we're out here like this.'

'Think he took down at least as many zeds as you, and that was while sitting down.' I smirked.

Anita and Neville went off with the bucket and pump, gun and bat in hand. We'd burned through a lot of ammo in the fight outside the hospital, but as far as I could tell, there was no reason for the zeds to have stuck around here once they left the city centre.

This route would lead to castle tower in a near enough straight line, so the horde that'd passed by last night might have even come through here. Between that and the sight lines we had over the open fields, it felt as safe as anywhere.

Laurel was keeping an eye out for us from atop the sedan she'd been peeking at, standing up on the roof with her rifle up, scanning windows and the like. With her out there, I felt confident that nothing was going to sneak up on us, so climbed into the front passenger seat in the 4x4 – Morgan, Lucile and Damian in the back.

'How's it feeling?' I asked him.

'Think I be a lot worse if not for de local,' he managed a strong smile, 'but not that good besides. Could sleep for a week.'

'Straight to bed with you when we get back.' Lucile said.

'That a promise?' he grinned back.

She snorted, while Morgan looked down to hide her expression.

'Yeah, he's fine.' I chuckled. 'What about you?'

'Me?' Morgan asked. 'Peachy.'

'Yeah,' Lucile joined in, 'you handled yourself like a fighter in there. Where'd you pull all that from?'

She shrugged, not meeting anyone's gaze. 'Everyone else has been fighting, all week. All I did was make tea and stuff. So…I guess you could say it's been *brewing* for quite a while.'

Damian started the opening notes of a belly laugh, but cut them short with a drawn out 'Oooh…' – I couldn't help but laugh myself.

'One liner puns?' Lucile asked, incredulous. 'Girl takes out a couple zeds and thinks she's action hero material.'

'Glad to see it hasn't affected you. Big man there was throwing chunks after our first close encounter.'

391

'You get used to it.' Damian nodded, settling down into the seat, getting comfy enough to nap.

'Hope so.' Morgan quietly spoke. 'Don't mean to be a burden on anyone. When it comes to the fighting, I'll be there with everyone else.'

'Proud of you. Your Dad is too, I bet. He hasn't nagged me about you in a while.'

'He do that a lot?' she asked.

'Maybe not anymore.' I smiled. 'Right, I'm going to keep an eye out. Shout if you see zeds.' I told them, pointing at Morgan. 'No taking them on by yourself, Morgan the Barbarian.'

I left them to it, and approached Lucile's vantage point atop the car. It was parked on the other side from us, away from the houses, overlooking the playing field. It looked like a decent enough area, worn but well maintained – the paintwork on the swings and slides in a nearby playground was all chipped, but there was no broken glass or damaged equipment.

Neville said this neighbourhood was working class, and it did remind me of where I grew up, a little. People might not have polished the silverware every day, but they took care of their space in the ways that mattered.

'Something in the trees.' Lucile said, not taking her eye from her rifle scope.

Across the open field, at most two hundred yards away, was one edge of Cemetery Park – I suppose the field was technically a part of it as well. The park hugged a huge swath of suburban Greenfield, and went a long way towards winning the it the "Greenest City In Voison" award on a semi regular basis. The trees there were old, towering things, the park a mixture between maintained recreational centres and wild greenspace, fit only for hikers and foxes.

'What is it?' I asked, hand reaching for my gun.

'Movement,' she muttered, 'could be people, or ghouls walking like people. I'm at the edge of my scope range and they're moving through tree cover.'

392

'Come down from there, just in case.' I urged her, offering a hand down. She stepped onto the bonnet, then took it, jumping back down to the road.

'Who do you reckon? Best guess?' I asked.

'People hiding out in the woods. That'd sound right to me. Getting away from any looters, and hopefully the wandering dead. It's not a bad idea – especially if you knew your way around Cemetery Park and could fix up a decent rabbit snare.'

'Can you?'

'Hah. I got this rifle from a hunter, but I ain't one,' she shook her head, 'could shoot you a buck at that range – on a good day. But don't count on me to skin and butcher it.'

'I think they only have deer at the animal farm corner, in captivity. It's not quite *that* big of a park.'

'Wasn't suggesting it, just…illustrating the point.' She shrugged. 'Wonder what happened to the petting zoo. If dogs go all weird, maybe other animals can catch the virus too.'

'The people who work there don't do it for the money. They'd have come to get the animals out.'

'Maybe that was them,' she said, tilting her head back to the woods, 'outdoors types, working in the park so they'd be familiar with it. Wouldn't rate any buildings in the park for defensibility though.'

'Don't suppose you need a fortress if the enemy will never reach the gates. Hmm…' I thought, trying to put myself into the position of someone making their home in the park.

'What're you thinking?' she asked. 'You want to make contact with them?'

'No…I'd rather play it safe. We've got wounded and if they're not friendly, or not human, then we're running a risk. I was just thinking what I'd do if I were them.'

I looked over the houses on the street, walking close enough to see the front doors and living room windows. Scratch marks stood out against painted doors and windowsills.

'Reckon we've seen enough crowbars in action to hazard a guess at what left those marks.' I said to her.

'People then. Living people.' She said, taking in a deep breath.

'Always a relief to know they're out there.' I said, stepping back closer. 'Especially…with what you've been through?'

'Wasn't quite so emotionally invested in that first group,' she said, meeting my gaze with a pained look, remembering the one she did love. 'But yeah. Would suck hard to lose any more people…' she trailed off, looking over to the treeline. 'And…knowing there's more people out there…that's nice too. You know?'

'I know.' I said, standing by her, looking to the trees myself. 'She might not be dead. Still got hope.'

'Me too.' Laurel quietly said, finding my hand with hers.

I didn't say anything, but when she squeezed, I squeezed back.

We stood like that for a moment, looking out over the trees and fields, a breeze passing over to rustle the grasses that were already starting to look a little overdue for the council's mowers. Eventually, we drew our hands apart, both folding our arms.

'Ghost dogs. Maybe ghost cats too.' Laurel muttered, 'Ain't seen any cats around. Birds neither. And you'd think with all the rot and dead about that carrion feeders would be having a ball.'

'Maybe they can tell the meat's tainted, flew away from the cities to be clear of it.' I suggested.

'Either that or we're going to get a murder of zombie crows swooping down on us one of these days.' She shivered. 'Now that was a bloody horror film.'

'Ugh, don't remind me. Katy made me watch that when we first started dating, I hated it. Sound of cawing made me twitch for days.'

'Wonder if we'll get to see another movie again…' Laurel said, looking thoughtful.

394

'If we have enough fuel for the generator, which will apparently expire in a year or so, then we could watch one tonight. Sit down as a group. Popcorn and everything.'

'I mean a new release. There were a few films coming out I was looking forward to. Bet the cans are in some distribution centre somewhere, never gonna make it to the pictures.'

'If the world gets back on its feet, I imagine there'll be more than a few zombies movies getting made.'

'They'd be documentaries, I guess. I'll miss the comic book movies. Doubt those sequels will get picked up again after this.'

'We'll have to find the original comics.' I sighed. 'Never did get into them. Prefer a book. Apparently that means I don't appreciate the artwork enough.'

'It does.' She grinned. 'We got sent old comics in our care packages while I was on border guard. Had to learn to read slower, take in the pictures, or you'd burn through an evening's entertainment too quick.'

'They didn't have TV in the mess, or whatever?'

'There are only so many times you can watch the same library of donated tapes. Not even discs. Tapes - which you had to rewind the old fashioned way, no menus. Republic's "standing army" is a joke. No wonder we outsource it all to professionals. They could probably afford satellite TV, we barely even had satellite phones.'

'No wonder Conrad's squad deserted. Why bother taking care of the country, if it never took care of you?' I shrugged.

'On the bases, you get bombarded with all these nationalistic posters, music, news, whatever.' She waved her hand. 'Even the tapes, I bet they sift through them before sending them to us. No movies about government corruption, or the horrors of war – not that I saw much horror on the border. That's a recent addition. But I guess some of that sticks with some people.' She frowned.

'They decide to go career, buy into the whole "Voison the Beautiful" shtick. They forget about the lousy funding, the poor treatment – the fact we're still conscripting for mandatory service despite being in the age of mobile phones and the Wireless.' She continued, barely pausing for breath. 'Territorial. More like Vestigial. Should have either disbanded or folded into the PMCs decades ago. At least they're actually trying to help people, using all that money to save lives, not just pulling back to Orphen, protecting their own asses.'

She finally seemed to run out of steam. That must have been a long time coming.

'Think it's nearly time to head back?' I asked.

'I could use a drink. And a smoke. And some food.' She added with gusto, 'I'm sure I'll get sick of barbecue eventually – but today is not that day.'

Forty Seven

Neville and Anita returned with diesel a few minutes later, Neville carrying a sloshing green gas can, Anita with the bucket and pump.

'Found this in the back of one of the pickups.' Neville said, indicating the big green can. 'Truck was diesel, so I'm betting this will be. If you're alright with that.' He added, to Damian.

'Gamble on it when we get home.' He nodded, still half asleep.

'What's the plan then?' Neville asked me, most of us gathered around the boot as Anita returned her kit.

'Go home, drop everyone off, then you, me and Laurel will take Conrad his SUV back. Fingers crossed, it'll be the most uneventful thing we ever do.'

'Can't seem to leave the front door these days without needing to shoot something.' Anita seconded.

'What do you want us to do?' Morgan asked.

'Gas up the generator so we can use the lift, and make sure Damian settles in. Might as well get started on those IVs.' I said to Lucile.

'I'll do what I can.' She nodded.

'Bet that bag of meds will be worth its weight in gold when we get to the CDC,' Neville said, 'but it's worth a lot more to us right now.' He said, with a glance at Anita. 'How're you holding up?'

'Sore. Itchy. Paranoid.' She said, rolling her shoulder uncomfortably. 'Looking forward to some industrial strength blood-cleaners and reading the info sheet on the antibiotics. You don't have to be teetotal on all of them – some of them just make you a lightweight.'

'Looks like I'm playing nurse and bartender.' Lucile raised an eyebrow. 'Let's get the patients home then.'

I nodded, and without further ado, we got back into our vehicles and drove on, taking the near-enough straight line to castle tower. I was sure that Anita would be able to hear my grumbling gut over the engine – there was still radio silence from GCR, but I suppose Sachs would have his hands full dealing with the bodies.

'Think I'm starting to get a fever too.' Anita said after a few minutes driving. 'Don't feel too warm, but I'm sweating.'

'You want me to take over?' I asked.

'I'm good. Don't feel dizzy or anything.' She added quickly, 'Just getting…the, uhm…' she paused. I think it was the first time I'd heard her afraid to speak.

'Cold sweats.' I finished for her.

'Yeah.' She muttered.

'Aren't they a later stage symptom of…?' I asked, thinking of Dani lying there in her bed. I didn't check her temperature, but she was soaked with sweat.

'Yeah.' She repeated. 'Most of the time.'

'What do you mean?'

'I saw patients at the hospital present with slightly different symptoms. Some had muscle cramps, or limb spasms. Migraines. All the infected ended up with a fever at some point. Most of them burned up, then went cold. Some skipped the burning, went straight for clammy and soaking.'

'How can one virus present with so many different symptoms, in so many different people?' I frowned. 'I was never great at biology, but I thought they were pretty predictable?'

'You heard the term "superbug" before?' she asked.

'Hospital illness, resistant to treatment.'

'Yeah.' Anita nodded. 'They adapt. Mutate beyond the standard format. That's what makes them harder to treat.'

'Mutate.' I dwelled on that word for a moment. 'Like the dogs, and the runners. And the ghouls.'

'And fuck knows what else, yeah.' She said again.

We drove on in silence until castle tower was visible between the rest of the buildings, then Anita began to slow

398

down, dropping further back from Neville than our usual distance.

'Quarantine me.' She said, her words coming out strained. I turned to look at her, and saw her eyes were shining with tears. 'If I go, I won't take anyone with me.'

'We don't know you're infected,' I said, turning in my seat, 'and until you drop dead in front of me, I will stand by the fact that you are not. How quick do they turn?'

'I've heard it anything from an hour to two days, both from bites. Both from people. We don't know how different it is from anything else. It could be carried weaker, or worse, another mutation or…'

'Stop.' I said, forcefully. So forcefully she actually stopped the SUV, but that's not what I meant. 'If you are going to turn, then you have my promise that I will do what has to be done. But I don't think I'll have to. Take your medicine, get some rest.'

'But what if I turn, tonight?' she asked, hands leaving the wheel to cover her face as her shoulders shook.

'You ever see someone go from upright and talking, straight into one of those things?'

'No…' she answered.

'Then you aren't going to turn over dinner. If it makes you feel better, there's a lock on the bathroom door in the Jamesons' place. Sleep in the bathtub tonight if you have to – but I don't think you'll need to. Antibiotics. Bedrest. You will be fine.' I said, stressing every word of the last part.

She wiped her eyes, and gave a great big sniff, her chest heaving.

'Rough day?' I asked.

'You could say that.' She nodded, putting us back into gear.

We pulled up outside to find nobody had missed us. Morgan and Lucile had taken the probably-diesel can down to the basement to gas up the generator, rather than testing it out in Damian's truck, which was more useful than the elevator.

When they came back up, Lucile gave us a smile.

'Sounds healthy. Think we're good, people.'

'Right, we'll get going while we've still got some light.' Neville said, 'You take care of them, you hear?' he said, looking to Anita and Damian, not worried about his daughter for once.

'Straight to the IVs when they're upstairs.' She said, taking the medical bag from me. 'When they're all set, we'll get to cooking.'

That reminded me of the food we had in Damian's ride, packed lunches we'd never eaten. Our food supply was healthy, but they could probably do with it at GCR, and might go a ways towards building some trust between us again, like them giving us their medical kit.

Morgan gave her dad a peck on the cheek before saying goodbye. She was about to head back inside, when Neville grabbed her, pulling her in for a hug.

'Proud of you, sweetie.' I heard him mutter into her ear.

'Love you, Dad.' She said back, hugging tighter. 'Stay safe.'

She gave me and Laurel a wave too, before slipping into the elevator with the rest of them.

'You've got a great kid, Neville.' Laurel said.

'She takes after her mother.' He said back.

'Hah!' she barked a laugh. 'Come on, let's get going. I'm dying to eat.'

Neville and I took Damian's, leaving Laurel to bring up the rear in the borrowed SUV. I got into the passenger seat while he topped up the tank, but I could smell gasoline even before that – took me a moment to realise the bucket in the back was giving off fumes. Damian wouldn't be too pleased but if it kept his ride moving, he couldn't complain. Still, we drove with our windows halfway down, letting the last of the drizzling rain in as we let the fumes out.

'She'll be okay, I think.' Neville said. 'If things don't get back to normal. If they stay this way. She's strong, stronger than I ever knew. She'll be okay.'

400

I didn't need to add anything to that. The quiet between us on the drive wasn't strained or awkward – for a nice change, it was amicable. There wasn't anything that needed to be said. Or so I thought.

'How are you coping?' he asked after a few minutes. 'Her bike, left behind there.'

'Anita said some staff got away in the ambulances, and they got separated. She could be anywhere, alive or dead. I think…' I struggled, swallowing a lump in my throat, 'I think I've done all I can for now. There's nowhere left to look. She's either alive, or she isn't, but I…can't find her now. Gone, either way.'

Neville reached across to squeeze my shoulder as I very intently studied the scenery out the window. He had to change gear, so it didn't last very long, but the support was still there.

'Got to concentrate now on getting everyone else out alive.' I said. 'We'll set off for the VBC Studio at midday tomorrow. Sachs said they were moving out before sundown. Hard to tell when that'll be based on today,' I said, waving a hand at the passing storm, 'but around five, I guess?'

'Should give us plenty of time to make our introductions.' Neville chipped in. 'Could take them to the hospital store room if they wanted, or bring them by here if they're short on food.'

'Not sure about the latter, but definitely the hospital, if we need something to, I don't know, earn their trust. But if it turns out the food situation is crappy wherever they want to take us, might be good to have a stash hidden. Selfish I know, just taking care of our own, but if that's how we've got to survive, I'm sure the CDC will manage just fine without us.'

'I'm with you. If it comes to it. My daughter might be able to hold her own in a fight now, but what's a father to do if he can't put food on the table?'

'We'll assess the situation, then make our call. Who knows? Maybe their safe zone is all roses and we'll never have to fight another rotting corpse ever again.'

'Unlikely…' he said, drawing the word out. 'But wouldn't it be nice?'

The little neighbourhood around GCR was clear of all undead movement, until we came to the fence around the radio station itself, where a couple of strays had pitched up against the green mesh and were trying to chew their way through. They weren't near the gate though, so we managed to open it up and just drive straight in – over the bodies of those we'd dealt with earlier. It was getting quite messy on the road, but I tried not to look at the gore. Or listen to the crunching.

Conrad was looking down on us from an upstairs window, but didn't have a weapon in sight. He disappeared into the building as we parked up and got out. I knew Neville would be holding his gun behind his back, but Laurel wasn't so subtle, standing half-behind the rear end of the SUV with her rifle out. At least it wasn't pointed at the doors as Conrad came out to meet us.

'Didn't think you'd bother.' He said, 'Guess my estimation of people is a little off these days.'

'How's the face?' Laurel asked, ever a beacon of diplomacy.

'I'll live.' He said, just taking it on the chin. 'How about your man? He pull through?' he asked, seeming genuinely concerned. Probably didn't want another body on his conscience.

'Should do. Hospital was dangerous, but I think we cleared a lot of it out.' I said. 'Things alright here?'

'Lot of blood on the lino.' Conrad shook his head. 'Sachs hasn't broadcast anything yet. But we did get a message from the CDC. I'd have put it on the radio myself, but I wanted to see if you'd come back first.'

'What's the message?' Neville asked.

'Timetable's moved up. They're evacuating the VBC building and setting off in-convoy at three in the afternoon. Plan is to link up with another group of refugees and head to Sydow. Apparently the city's a fortress now, totally under

Sydow Security's control. Government has written off everything save the capital.'

I wonder if Conrad would have really declined to broadcast that, if we hadn't brought the SUV back. Pays to keep your promises, I guess. It was good to know, even if it didn't accelerate our timetable much.

'Thanks.' I said. 'Offer's still open if you, Carl and Beth want to come with us.'

'I'll see what happens.' Conrad shrugged, 'Sachs might come around, but Beth, she…hasn't said a word since the shooting started. Think she's broke from it. We take her out beyond the fence, think we're asking for trouble.'

'Good luck then,' I said, taking a step forward, and offering out my hand. Hesitantly, eyes flicking to my bayonet as if expecting some sort of trick, he took it, and we shook.

'You too. Good luck, Mr Kelly.' He said.

'That food I mentioned before the fighting started. It's yours. Goodwill gesture.'

Laurel raised an eyebrow at that, but I'd already decided. We couldn't take it all with us anyway, and it was only sandwiches, soon to expire. She helped me pile them up on the reception desk, but didn't say a word to him.

We got back into the 4x4, Laurel keeping a wary eye on Conrad, but our paranoia was misplaced this time. We drove out of there, over the bodies and into the neighbourhood without any trouble. I felt myself relax as we headed through the woodland, on our way back home to a well-deserved meal.

Anita had worked out we'd last four months at castle tower on three meals a day, but with all the running around we'd been doing, we'd forgotten about the lunches we'd now given to GCR. Rationing might be easier if we kept ourselves busy.

The skies darkened into night as we headed on back for the evening, the visible area around our vehicle drawing in, until it was just us and our headlights. We still had the windows cracked, just to let the gasoline smell out, otherwise we'd probably never have heard the gunshots.

'Hear that?' Neville asked, eyes flicking from the road a moment, glancing out of the driver's side window.

'Someone's in trouble.' Laurel said, as if someone was just off to the headmaster's office. She unbelted and shuffled over to the other side of the passenger seats, peering out into the deserted streets as we rolled on by. 'Sounded far away, but hard to tell with all these houses around.'

The first shot was soon accompanied by several more, a brief exchange of short pops and loud cracks, followed by the chattering of an automatic weapon. They did indeed sound far away, but I wasn't hoping to get a closer look.

'Get us out of here, Nev.' I said, 'Trouble follows us enough, don't think we need to go looking for it.'

He nodded. 'City's been pretty quiet these last few days. Early on I heard a lot more of this.'

'First off it was all the confusion,' Laurel piped up from the back, 'people weren't sure what was happening and who was trying to kill them. My guess…people settled down for a bit, but now they're running out of food or water. Probably the have-nots trying to steal from the hoarders like us.'

'All the more reason not to get involved.' Neville agreed.

Forty Eight

Mist was rising up as we pulled into the car park at home. Neville let us into the foyer and locked up behind, while we called the elevator down. Man, it was good to skip the stairs. After a day like today, I'd have crashed in Stan's place if the food wasn't up on the fourteenth. My stomach and Laurel's were practically harmonising gurgles at this point.

The warm scents of tonight's meal drifted down the corridor as the elevator doors opened up. Smelled more like a roast dinner than a barbecue, but that's sort of because it was trying to be. Candlelight flickered through the open doorway.

We took our shoes off and went into the Jamesons' place, where Morgan was supervising boiling vegetables in the pot on the camping stove, which was set next to the real one in the kitchen. It looked as if she'd already boiled and strained off some of the veg, and had them sitting in their own pans on the real stove. She'd even kept the water for gravy.

'Sorry if you were looking forward to more barbecue.' She said over her shoulder as we came in, 'We had all this fresh veg to use up, and if you eat too much meat and no veg, well, not being able to flush properly anymore will be the least of our worries.'

'Speaking of that, is the water still working?' I asked.

'For now, thankfully.'

'I'm going to go clean up. We all probably should, don't know when we'll get a chance again.'

'That's what we figured. Lucile's taken Damian down to her place for a sponge bath, but I was waiting for you guys to get back. Need someone to mind the veg, and there's a joint of beef and a load of chicken in the oven.'

'The oven still works?' Neville asked, reaching for the oven door.

'No!' Morgan said, getting in front of him. 'But it's still a good thermal insulator. There's a joint of beef in there, chicken

405

breasts and sausages wrapped in foil – it's not all for now, or might not be. This is experimental cooking here.'

'How're you cooking then?' Laurel asked, craning to see through the tiny glass panel, from which came an orange glow.

'Disposable barbecues. I'm hoping the temperature will get high enough for long enough, since they cook well enough in an open space, why wouldn't it work in a closed space?'

'We're still getting something though, right Morgan?' Laurel asked, folding her arms. 'There a backup plan in case?'

'Something in there will definitely be cooked.' She hurriedly said, standing between us and the oven. 'Sausages and chicken ran the risk of being overdone, hence the foil, but it was a thick joint of beef, might be bloody in the middle.'

'Ugh,' Laurel moaned, obviously a fan of rare meat, 'I can only take so much food talk right now. How long?'

'Could be a while…' Morgan teased.

Laurel's face fell, and I'll admit, mine did too.

'But there's chips and dip in the living room.' She shrugged, making for the door.

She'd even put the tortilla chips into bowls rather than leave them in the bags. We didn't talk for a good couple of minutes, just set about the snacks until the rumbling in our bellies had died down. Neville and Laurel hadn't snapped at each other in a while, so I felt comfortable leaving them in the lounge while I checked on the boiling carrots.

I heard the door to the Jamesons bedroom open, and turned around to see Neville going in.

'Hey.' I heard him say to Anita, before mostly-shutting the door behind himself.

Laurel was still sucking her fingers clean when she came into the kitchen and bumped me with her hip.

'You first, or me? For the shower. I'm assuming I can borrow yours again?' she asked.

'You go first. It's not like there's any hot water I'll be missing out on anyway.' I shrugged, poking the carrots about with a spoon.

'Cold showers all around. Guess nobody's going to be feeling the love tonight.' She added in a mutter, tilting her head back to the bedroom door, where you could just about hear Neville and Anita quietly talking.

I grunted an affirmative, but didn't comment. 'Go on, may as well go now.'

'Can't see myself being long, cold enough up here as it is, without staying alone too long in the shower.'

Once she'd left, I could hear more conversation between Neville and Anita, but didn't feel like eavesdropping, so went out onto the balcony. She was right. It'd not exactly been warm all day, but even with the hoodie on under my jacket, it was freaking cold up here. No wonder Morgan was playing around with the oven rather than standing out on the balcony.

The mist that'd begun to creep up as we were parking was starting to take hold now, casting everything in a shroud of grey. I wiped my cheek as a speck of rain fell, but it wasn't heavy rain like this afternoon, just that slow, damp air that comes with fog. I could still make out the shapes of the cars in the parking lot, but they were fuzzy silhouettes now.

'So this is it.' I said to the misty Greenfield night. We were leaving tomorrow. Evacuated in a CDC convoy to Sydow, capital of the midlands – Conrad had said it was a fortress now. A fortress with a lot of hungry human mouths to feed, no doubt. But at least they were human mouths.

I didn't want to leave. I wanted to wait. To stay here, like Katy had told me, just a few days ago. It seemed like months since I'd seen her, since I'd put that ring on her finger, a promise that we'd always be together. A promise neither of us seemed able to keep. I stood there shaking, mostly from the cold, but partly…just because. I leaned my elbows on the balcony and hung my head, letting the dark thoughts creep in.

It'd beaten me. The city. The new world. It'd taken from me the one thing I felt mattered in my life. What did I have, if not her? A so-so job with no future prospects. A decent apartment that was only getting dearer. Not even any friends I cared enough about to risk my life for.

But that wasn't true anymore. I sniffed back a wave of tears and drew myself back up to full height. I did have people I'd risk my life for, and they'd do the same – they had *done* the same – for me. This virus might have split me up from Katy, but I'd go on. Even if I never found her, she'd want me to go on living.

I looked over my shoulder, at the curtains and the soft glow of candlelight around the edges. Warmth. People. Life would go on whether or not I stayed out here in the cold, feeling sorry for myself. I turned from the mist-shrouded view of the dying city, and walked back into the apartment, wiping my eyes.

Lucile was just taking her boots off.

'He settled down for the night?' I asked.

'Yeah, out like a light.' She said, heading over to the stove. 'Got his and Anita's meds pushed through straight away. Good job you didn't pick up the slow-drip stuff. They'll still need another treatment or three, but they won't be hooked up to the bag for hours 'n hours. You see anything of Anita?'

'Neville's talking to her.' I hooked a thumb over to the door, 'Guessing no news is good news.'

'Today has been an…eventful day.' She sighed, straining the cooked carrots from one pot into another, and dumping the cooking water into the larger pan.

'Here's hoping every day is boring from now on,' I said, 'I've had quite enough excitement for one lifetime.'

'I'll drink to that.'

I left her with the cooking, padding in my socks across the hallway to my apartment. Laurel had lit candles enough to just about see by, placing the little covered tea lights on the floor, lighting a path from the front door to the bathroom and bedroom. I went to the kitchen first though, as I could still hear the shower running.

There were more candles around here somewhere, or so I'd thought. They must already have been in use – Morgan probably took them in her search of the building – but I spent a couple of minutes searching drawers and cupboards, looking behind pots and pans, places I knew they'd never be.

Laurel left the bathroom with her towel wrapped beneath her armpits, and on the tall blonde it did not reach far down her thighs at all. She'd had her shortened hair held up while she showered, but unclipped it as she turned towards my bedroom, shaking it down and flicking it with a hand. The roll of her shoulders threatened to drop the towel, but she closed the bedroom door before I got the whole eye-full. That was about the moment I remembered to avert my gaze anyway – not just out of respect for Katy, but Laurel herself.

I must not have made a whole lot of noise searching those cupboards, and standing in the darkened kitchen she never saw me. That was probably lucky. Awkwardness avoided. I crept over to the front door, and pretended to be coming in for the first time. I didn't think she'd appreciate me perving on her from the shadows.

'You out yet?' I asked the bedroom door.

'Just. You can borrow my hair clip if you want. I hate washing my hair cold, it always goes weird.'

'Thanks. Are you decent?' I asked.

'Sure, come in.' she said.

I opened the bedroom door, expecting to find her wearing my dressing gown or having already gotten changed – but she'd just been laying clothes out, and was still wrapped in her towel, walking around to her side of the bed. I tried not to stare at her legs as she bent to retrieve the clip from the nightstand.

'So uh,' I faltered, 'cold shower as bad as I'm expecting?'

'Did me good, I think. Bracing.' She quickly added, throwing me the clip. 'Now go, let me get dressed. And pick your tongue up off the floor.'

'Tell it to my good ear.' I said, waving a dismissive hand.

'Oh-ho, you did not just ear crack me. You'll pay for that one.' She said, pointing a threatening finger, though the twitching of her lips didn't seem all that intimidating.

409

I shut the door behind me, smirking, and went straight into the bathroom. Maybe a cold shower would do me good.

It's impossible for a man's eyes not to wander. No matter how long you've been in a relationship, even been married, biology wants guys – and girls – to check each other out. You might be perfectly happy with your sex life, your partner might mean the world to you. But if a well put together member of your preferred gender flashes a lot of skin, its only natural to find your eyes wandering. So I told myself.

Wandering thoughts on the other hand, are what cold showers are for. Ten minutes since I decided I was going to go on living for Katy's sake, and already shit like *this* was happening. I let the water freeze me back down before I started with the shower gel. The memory of her touch wasn't even a week old yet.

It was probably the most unpleasant shower I've ever had – the cold water sapped every breath of warmth from me, so I was quick as could be, but still had to scrub myself from top to bottom – just not the hair. Like Laurel, my hair did not like being washed in the cold. It'd itch something fierce the next day, so I left it tied up, under the ridiculous looking ducky-themed shower cap Katy had bought me for a joke. Thankfully, it lived under the sink so Laurel hadn't seen it.

I shivered and towelled my way to dryness and put my jeans on before leaving the bathroom. I wasn't letting her get a look at my legs. But she'd already left the bedroom by the time I got there.

Once changed into my winter pyjamas, heaviest dressing gown and slippers, I was beginning to feel the ghost of warmth coming back to me. I retrieved my pistols; the antique and the giant, putting them into the roomy pockets of my robe along with their bullets. I wasn't expecting trouble next door, but I'd never cleaned them and it was probably about time I learned how.

As I'd guessed, the gunslingers were playing with their toys again. Neville and Anita sat on the sofa with Morgan, their pistols and tiny tools in carefully separated tea-towels

410

before them, slides off, magazines out and all kinds of intricate, tiny pieces arranged before them. They were cleaning the weapons down with cloths and little brushes, oiling parts I'd never hope to identify.

Damian's shotgun and Lucile's pistol were placed next to the coffee table, forming an orderly queue, so I added my guns to it. It was family bonding time, I didn't want to get in the way of that.

Lucile must have been getting her shower, so that did mean I found myself alone with Laurel at the kitchen island. She must have had a gun cleaning kit too, either that or Neville had way too many. Her rifle was broken down into several pieces – but it was a simpler affair than the semi-automatic pistols, I guess, as there weren't half as many.

'Really blows the cobwebs out, right?' she asked.

Unlike everyone else, in PJs and robes, she'd just changed into clean jeans and a t-shirt, with a long sleeved cardigan over the top. It wasn't her usual style, but if it kept her warm, she needed it. I suppose packing up nightwear isn't essential when you're fleeing your home. Anita must have borrowed hers from another tenant.

'It blows alright. Wonder when the next time we'll get a hot shower will be?' I thought aloud.

'Any time we want, if we can be bothered.' She shrugged. 'Head to a camping supply store. They do fancy ones, but at the basic end they're just a massive bag with a shower head you can put water into. Warm the water up first and we've got hot showers. The black ones will warm themselves up in high summer.'

'You know, all these post-apocalypse movies are starting to seem a little far-fetched to me.' I said, not meaning the plots. 'Good showers are easy to come by, you can loot new clothes from anywhere and gasoline goes out of date. So why is everybody always dirty faced, wearing the same ripped up outfits and still hunting for gas like it matters?'

'That shit wouldn't look as cool on bicycles.' She shrugged, poking down her rifle barrel with a little rod.

411

'Horses?' I suggested.

'Then you'd be complaining about that. Wondering where they get the feed from, how they stable them, shoe them, who mucks them out…'

'Probably. I'll give you that one. My willing suspension of disbelief can only ignore so many unanswered questions. Anything I can do to help with…this?' I asked, gesturing at the rifle.

'I got it, thanks. But you can stay. I mean, not like you've got anything else to do?' she added with a smile.

I returned it. 'Sure, I'll stay.'

Forty Nine

Tonight was open bar night. When the meat was about ready, Lucile went to see if Damian was up to moving, but he declined in favour of bedrest. He'd been shot, so we didn't hold it against him, but it didn't stop us celebrating ourselves.

Lucile took Damian some food down first, then Morgan plated up vegetables, various meats and covered it in gravy, I poured drinks. Everything was on the menu. Beer, wine, spirit and mixer – though Neville took his whisky neat. Lucile was a while coming back, so we'd started eating without her, gathered around the kitchen island like we had done that night with the Jamesons.

It was a tight squeeze, but with Damian and the old couple no longer with us, the six of us got around the island without too much elbow bumping.

'Ate, then went right back to sleep.' Lucile said, tucking into her roast with gusto. I poured more red into her glass, it'd almost been emptied on the first attack.

'I can't tell if I'll sleep or not. Don't know if I'm exhausted or wired.' Anita said between forkfuls. The oven experiment was a partial success, sausages and chicken were safely cooked after a good long wait, but the beef was too bloody for my taste, cooked bleu.

'More wine, better than any sleeping tablet.' Laurel saluted, raising her glass in a manner that suggested I fill it with sauvignon.

'Eat, drink and be merry for tomorrow we get the fuck out of here.' I said, topping her up. 'As much as I have loved my time in this wonderful city, I think it's time we were moving on.'

'Here's to Sydow, and the CDC,' Neville said, raising his tumbler in toast, 'may their walls be strong and their larders stocked.'

'And their guns never run dry.' Laurel added, clinking glasses with him. We all joined in, Morgan with her uncouth beer bottle, myself with a tall glass of rum and cola, but after that it was all quiet until we'd finished eating – it was a meal hard fought for, and everyone wanted to enjoy it.

However, once it was over, we had business to take care of, even if that business was conducted while drinking around firearms – something I'm pretty sure they tell you not to do in the owner's manual.

Our little group had quite a lot of nine-mill pistols floating about thanks to those Territorials, but the ammo situation was sliding towards its inevitable conclusion. Where once Neville and Anita had enjoyed a healthy supply, those same bullets were spread across five guns, and with Neville's pawnshop M1943 no longer sporting a full clip, he took his piece back from Anita, leaving Lucile and I the only ones without a nine-mill.

Given we had our own guns, it wasn't a problem, but it left everyone with only one full magazine for them, with Anita carrying the leftovers in a near-full mag for herself. I reckoned we'd get by though – Damian's shotgun and Laurel's rifle were still stocked up, for now at least. Laurel's pockets didn't clink with brass the way they used to.

Once the pistols were sorted and reloaded, freshly oiled and cleaned, I topped up everyone's drinks and told them all to get comfy in the lounge. That ran us out of available seating, but before I dragged over a stool from the island to perch on, I found Morgan a notepad and pen from the kitchen.

'Team meeting, you're in charge of the minutes.' I told her.

'From day saving hero to secretary in just a few short hours. My career is in the toilet.' She sighed.

I climbed up onto the stool and faltered for a place to put my drink down, sat up in the middle of nowhere. I think that's why it went down faster. Sure.

'So…' I started, my usual oratory self, 'bit of a busy day. But we made it through. Good job everyone.' I paused, for

414

refreshment. 'Tomorrow might be worse though. We've no idea what we'll find when we get to the VBC Station. Neville, throw me a worst case scenario.'

'Overrun, by Deserters, or looters, some kind of arseholes at any rate. They shoot first and don't stop shooting until we're driven off or dead.'

'Okay. That's actually worse than what I was thinking, but yeah. That's a very real possibility. But what's our best case, Laurel?' I asked, passing the ball. It was a game Gladys had tried at the post office, trying to get new ideas from people but you could only talk if you had the basketball.

'If everything comes up roses, we get evacuated to the promised land. Fortress city protected by the mercenary company who specialise in security services.'

'Like what?' Morgan asked. She didn't have the ball, but I let it slide. The ball was imaginary.

'Small scale? Bodyguards for diplomats, politicians, suits in big business.' Laurel started, 'But up from that I know they've done event security for international talks, and been hired in to patch holes in base defence for military and government installations.'

'So they're the ideal defenders then?' I asked.

'Pretty much.' She nodded.

'What about weaknesses?' I probed. 'I'm not saying we're going to fight them, but what do we need to be prepared for?'

'Been wondering about that.' Laurel said, 'They don't have a lot of vehicle power, at least on a military grade. No tanks and very little light armour, they don't need it. So mostly they've got trucks and busses.'

'Like the guy on TV,' Neville chimed in, 'guarding a bus full of infected, outside of Mercy Hospital.'

'I saw that too, yeah. That was Sydow Sec. Guess they dropped the ball on that one, but who was expecting the living dead?'

'Hopefully they've got their shit together now.' I shrugged, going over to the kitchen to refill my drink. 'So they're good defenders, but weak on the transport.' I shouted back. 'Convoy could be vulnerable then, or over-capacity, if they've got loads of refugees.'

'Maybe we should load the truck up with supplies, join the convoy in our own transport?' Anita asked.

'It is the next best thing to a military ATV,' Lucile said, 'hells, some of the trucks I rode in during my time were a sight worse.'

'I'm reluctant to load her up if we've got to abandon it though,' I weighed in, 'If they don't want to take it or they end up commandeering everything we have anyway, I'd rather our supplies be…' I struggled for the words.

'You want a contingency plan,' Neville nodded, 'in case things don't work out. We should be able to leave the CDC and get back here, with supplies waiting for us.'

'Pretty much.' I sighed. 'Somewhere between the best and worst case, there's the reality. Sydow is probably going to be overcrowded and hungry, no matter how defensible their security forces and CDC doctors can make it. If they can't feed us, I'd rather know we can run to someplace where we've still got a chance.'

'I hear you, I guess.' Lucile rolled a shoulder, 'But it doesn't quite sit right. If we've got food, maybe we should try bartering it with them?'

'It's an option,' I told her, 'but even then. Better we have our supply here, hidden away.'

'There's still more we can take from the co-op.' Laurel reminded us. 'We were in a bit of a rush to leave, but those soldiers who went in after us didn't leave with anything.'

'Yeah, they were a little busy.' I raised an eyebrow, remembering the horde roaming around outside our front door. 'We do that tomorrow then, if we're in agreement. Clear out the last of the co-op supplies and squirrel them away in castle tower, anything we're not taking with us.'

'You made us clear out all the apartments,' Morgan complained, looking to Anita, 'and you want us to fill them again?'

416

'Nah, not restocking cupboards,' I said, 'but hiding things. Reckon the top of the elevator cab would be a good place, and the bottom of the shaft.'

'Rats.' Morgan threw in.

It drew a few confused looks.

'We have rats, if you remember.' She said, jogging my memory. 'The other day, up in this very apartment.'

'You didn't think to mention this sooner?' Anita cringed, checking down by her feet.

'Wasn't very big…' she apologised. 'But if we have rats then anything we leave behind has to be pretty well boxed in. They'll gnaw through anything in time.'

'We haven't seen any in days though,' I thought aloud. 'Maybe they were just fleeing ahead of the zeds.'

'Could be.' She said, 'But still. Anywhere we can get traps from? Or anything else we can do? Minimise our losses.'

'I'm not an expert.' I admitted, putting my hands up.

'Seal everything up tight,' Lucile supplied, 'plastic tubs, metal containers, the harder it is for them to get into something the more likely they'll sod off to find something easier to eat.'

'Then we leave behind everything tinned,' I suggested, 'reduces weight in our packs and leaves behind the stuff most likely to survive. Suggestions on hiding spots?'

'Top of the elevator cab was a good shout,' Laurel said, 'but if we're thinking of spreading the stash out, then what about kitchen bins? Take out the old garbage bag then put a new one in, and bag up our tins inside that one. Don't know about the rats, but if I were looting a place I'd probably overlook someone's bin.'

Woman had a point, I threw her a thumbs up, but Lucile was already in with another suggestion.

'The dumpsters around back, glass and metal recycling,' she said, 'who's going to look in there?'

'If we're talking general hiding places, I've seen killers and drug dealers hide weapons in all kinds of places,' Anita came in, leaning forwards, 'Rip the upholstery beneath these cushions and it's just empty space. Then you've got your loose

417

floorboards, ceiling tiles, false backs on cupboards, stuffing the mattress…'

Morgan was scribbling down the suggestions on the notepad, so we were covered if we couldn't remember this in the morning. I for one did not intend to stop drinking until bed time. Whenever that happened to be.

'So we've got our hiding places,' I said, after she'd finished writing, and no more suggestions were forthcoming. 'We know where we're going to squirrel away our nuts for the winter. But what nuts are we taking with us?'

'How do you reckon they'll be fixed for water?' Neville asked Laurel.

'Probably okay? If they've been filling water bottles non-stop since this started then they'll be fine. We've still got water, so I imagine a city with military engineers is keeping the pump stations going.'

'Either way, we probably won't have to worry about it. That's good.' I nodded. 'So we take rice, pasta, noodles – lasts ages, and its light for how much food you get once it's taken on water.'

'Going to be a bit bored if we're stuck eating rice forever.' Morgan said. 'Taking any jars of sauce?'

'I think we'll have the bag space between us. But we'll leave, say, a third of the dried stuff here? In case shit.'

'In case shit…' Morgan hummed, writing on her pad, possibly word for word. 'The meat's going to be done for, come tomorrow morning. We'll have to cook it up if we're going to squeeze a couple more days out of it. We can bust up some furniture for the oven, my experiment wasn't a total failure, can definitely be improved upon.'

'Another job for morning.' I said. 'Everyone got a nice big backpack tucked away somewhere?'

There was a nod from everyone, Morgan and Anita had apparently seen some in their search they could get to.

'Probably looking at half food, half clothing and whatever else you need. I don't mind if you want to bring hand luggage too but at least leave one hand free for a gun.'

418

'Small wardrobe allowance,' Laurel hummed. 'Better leave behind your formals, everyone.'

'Damian's not going to be up for carrying much,' Lucile said, 'I can carry his pack if someone covers me.'

'No, I'll get it.' Neville offered, 'I'll wear it on my front, another pack would weight you down too much.'

'You saying you're stronger than me, Neville?' Lucile grinned, 'You looking to arm wrestle?'

Neville laughed. 'You'd probably win that. I just mean…I'm taller. I'll carry the weight and keep moving better.'

'Probably right there.' She snorted. 'But I aim to pull my weight. I'll take the shotgun then. Stop you getting eaten.'

'So we know what we're looting, and we know what we're packing, and we know what we're hiding. We've got our weapons sorted, and our shit is generally together. Any other business?' I asked, taking a long sip from my drink.

'Think that about covers it.' Neville nodded, looking around, to a room of bobbing heads.

'Right. Let's drink. I think we've all earned it.'

Fifty

I drank to remember. I drank to forget. I drank because the bottle was nearly finished. What I didn't do was drink too much. After that bottle of rum ran dry, I stopped. As safe as castle tower was, none of us could really bear the thought of being too drunk to defend ourselves if the need arose, and besides, we'd need to be sharp for tomorrow.

Despite stopping myself short of overindulgence, I woke up with a sore head, dry throat and a weight on my chest. I'd shared the bed with Laurel again - her arm was draped over me.

Carefully, I extracted myself from the warm covers, regretting it almost instantly. Winter was coming on fast this year, and without the benefit of central heating the only things keeping me warm had been the duvet and Laurel's increasingly confusing company.

I looked over her sleeping form, deep in the dreams that white wine apparently brings her, and felt the churn of mixed emotions in my gut. Was Morgan right? We were getting close? Or were we just sharing a bed because we didn't want to be alone? How far would loneliness and loss take us? She was my fiancé's best friend.

I dressed warmly again, putting a black long-sleeved undershirt on, with another blue t-shirt over the top, finishing it off with the hoodie again. If I got too warm I could always stuff it in my bag or something, but if I was this cold inside…

Jeans, boots, hair and teeth brushed, and I was about ready to face the world. Laurel was stirring in the bedroom as I used the bathroom tap to wash down some paracetamol for my headache. I didn't mean to wake her, she could have slept in – her bag was already packed anyway. But we'd need to move eventually, and there was work to do before then.

Only after I swallowed the pills did I consider I'd just used up medical supplies for a hangover headache. A habit a

420

decade in the making, it'd be tough to break, but we'd all need to be sharp today. It was worth taking a couple pills of the most common medicine in the world for.

This morning I seemed to be the first person up and about, so set to doing the list of jobs we'd set out from last night. Firstly, I broke all the eggs into a giant mixing bowl and whipped up a campsite's worth of scrambled eggs, adding an equally large dose of salt and pepper as I went. By the time the chopping board came out for the salad peppers, Anita had left her borrowed bedroom.

'Feeling any better today?' I asked her.

'Don't feel any worse,' she said, with a faint smile, 'and I'd expect to be, if I were going to turn.'

'Did you end up uh…sleeping in the bathroom?' I asked, tentatively.

'I couldn't get comfy, even with the drink. In the end, I just cuffed an arm to the headboard. But hey,' she added, gesturing at herself, 'I'm alive. So I guess…I owe you an apology for yesterday.'

'You freaked out,' I said, meeting her eyes, 'that could happen to any of us.'

'Still. I'm sorry I went off like that. Embarrassing.' She cringed. 'Looks like I'm on the mend now anyway. Thanks.'

'Even if Damian hadn't have been shot, we'd have gone to find medicine for you.' I told her, meaning every word. 'We don't have many people left. Got to take care of those we do have.'

'I know.' She smiled, looking about the kitchen, avoiding meeting my eyes again.

'Help me with breakfast?' I asked.

'Sure.' She sniffed, 'Yeah.'

We set to making an industrial sized serving of scrambled eggs and peppers, with more of the sausages from last night warmed up on the side. Since we'd learned that some people can't stand tomatoes or mushrooms, we cooked those in separate pans, for people to add as they please. Fortunately, we were all good with the peppers.

Morgan had talked us into saving the seeds, and found plastic food baggies to put them in once we'd separated them from the gooey bits. I didn't know anything about growing food from supermarket veg, but she seemed to think it was worth a shot, and we had time to spare.

As Neville, Morgan and Laurel filtered in, we were just adding grated cheese by the fistful to the still-gooey eggs. They were coming along nicely as Lucile and Damian came through the door, met by a chorus of greetings.

'Good to see you up and about.' Neville said with a handshake.

'You keeping your spare hanky in there yet?' Laurel teased.

Anita gave him a careful hug. 'She's not a bad nurse, right?'

'You missed out on a good party last night.' Morgan told him.

Finally, it was my turn.

He looked at me, and the slow smile that'd been playing on his face as he met the rest of them turned into something a lot more serious. A look I won't forget in a hurry.

Anita had come from a position of power, she was used to being the one saving the day, so she struggled to look me in the eye and express it, but Damian could. I was just his neighbour, a casual acquaintance – and I'd risked my life to save his. Not just against one zed, or a couple of gunman, but against a whole damn hospital full of nightmare zombies and freakish ghouls. He looked at me with such gratitude that I felt I could touch the sky.

Even if I still felt largely responsible for his injury.

'Thank you mon…' he beamed, taking confident steps forward, though I could tell his injuries pained him. He put a hand on my shoulder, and gave me a slow nod, his eyes closed. When he opened them again, they were watery. Lot of tears going around recently.

'Thank you everyone, you saved my life last night. I will never – never,' he stressed, voice rough, 'forget that. I owe each an every one of you.'

'I'll take mine in cash, big man.' Laurel joked. We laughed, and he did too, letting the tears run down in the growing stubble covering his chin. Me and Neville were looking overdue a session with the razor too, but we had more important things to do.

'No speeches.' I said, before anyone could start. 'It's breakfast time. Good to have you back with us.' I told him, giving his good shoulder a squeeze.

We ate our eggs with random perishables and sliced bread. The antibiotics pumping through Anita and Damian were effecting their appetite, but with Lucile's encouragement they managed to get down a reasonable portion. Laurel and Morgan did their best to make up for it, while Neville and I watched from the balcony windows, eating stood up. It was too cold to go out, but the mist was clearing, so we had the view, and were far enough from the kitchen that we could talk in private.

'Time do you make it?' I asked him.

'Ten, ish.' He said, checking his watch.

'I want to be setting off at two. Little early, but I want to get a look at the place before we commit to it.'

'Should the worst-case scenario be the real one.' he guessed.

I nodded. 'You ever been into the VBC building?'

'Once. I had an interview there, before I started working for the firm. Don't remember much though, this is going back years.'

'Probably not that important to have an interior map anyway,' I shrugged. 'If they're legit then we won't need one. If we can tell they're not on the level then we don't go anywhere near them.'

'There's a warehouse building across the street. Could get us a vantage point, but if they're as defensively minded as

Laurel says then they might have somebody watching it, and take offence at us getting into firefight positions.'

'Suggestions?'

'VBC's on an intersection. That warehouse is directly across on one side, car park on the other. But across on the diagonal is a row of fancy apartments. If we can break into there through the back, and get to a window or a balcony a little ways away, we can use our binoculars to get a look at the studios. Less chance of us being spotted.'

'That's what we'll do then.' I said, returning my attention to the eggs for a moment. 'If everything looks good we'll show ourselves, drive up to the front gate. If something's off...'

'Then we get back here.' He nodded, having a forkful himself. 'But what then? Long term, I mean. It seems like this thing isn't just going to blow over.'

'I don't know...' I faltered. The subject matter, the implications, they were a little heavy for breakfast. 'Keep in touch with GCR I guess. Use their radio to reach out to people, expand the group, safety in numbers.'

'That could attract unsavoury sorts, like the Deserters, or just be an advertisement for people looking to rob us.' Neville warned. 'Not saying it's a bad idea. But there's always a risk.'

'Safest thing would be to stay here and starve to death, but I mean to go on living.' I said. It must have come out with more anger than confidence, as Neville gave me a worried look. I flashed an apologetic smile. 'I know. But any troublemakers who cross our path...they'll get what's coming to them.'

Neville and I both looked over to Damian. 'We'll be better, next time.' He said. 'Surviving these days, we'll have to get ruthless.'

'We've already done our share of mercy killings. And regular ones.' I added. 'But so far nothing we've done has left a bad taste in my mouth.'

'Except...Dani, maybe?'

I hadn't forgotten. But I had forgiven. I shook my head.

'Had to be done. I knew it then, but I was having a hard time coming around to it. If the same happened again…if it had to be you, or Morgan, or anyone else…'

'You'd do it?' he asked, his gaze intent.

'And I'd want you all to do it for me.' I answered.

After breakfast, it was time to pack up our bags. Laurel helped Lucile and Damian, since her stuff was basically all ready to go. She'd had to dump a couple of her shirts and pairs of jeans to make room for rice and pasta, but at least she'd been joking earlier about bringing her date-night heels.

I'd suggested we get packed up before we made our final raid on the co-op, and stashed all the supplies. That way we'd have a bit of thinking time about things we'd forgotten or needed to add, rather than rushing about at the last minute and leaving our toothbrush behind or something.

By eleven, we had our bags stowed in the Jamesons' flat, and split up into two groups to tackle the co-op and stashing jobs. I'd be taking Neville and Laurel to the shop, while everyone else stayed behind. All we had to do was load up the 4x4 and dump the groceries by the elevator. They had to find places to hide it.

With boxes from the storeroom, bags from the counter and help from a few trollies, we emptied out the co-op, taking everything that'd last – trollies full of more dried foods, tinned fruit and produce that'd no longer be called fresh, but might still be worth something for Morgan's seed collection. The potatoes especially. Some of them were starting to sprout already.

While Neville drove the first load back home, Laurel and I kept at it, bagging packets of jelly sweets, hard candy and liquorice on top of spices and cooking sauces, cordials and soda pop, going from the essential food that'd keep us alive to the non-essentials that'd keep morale up. I wouldn't be able to stand boiled rice for more than two meals without some jalfrezi or hoi sin sauces.

Basically…we emptied the shelves. The only things we didn't load into a trolley or bag up were the newspapers and

425

magazines, the contents of the fridges and freezers, and the booze. We had plenty of that back in castle tower already, and as Neville's watch went ever further past twelve o'clock, we were running out of time, so had to join up and assist the others.

Anita's team had been stashing supplies all over the tower, starting with nestling a trash bag of tins and several three-litre water bottles amongst the recycling, and moving into Stan's apartment to get creative with his kitchen bin, sofa upholstery and the linen drawers already concealed beneath his bed.

It was a pattern that continued right the way up the building, save for our own apartments – stashing supplies here and there, leaving only one or two tins of our least favoured foods visible in the cupboards every apartment or so, hoping that'd create the illusion this place had already been searched, if anyone were to come through. To help that image along, we left a few apartment doors open, smashed the odd plate, and left odds and ends scattered about from upturned drawers. The hard part came to when it was time to do that to our own places.

'I'm not hacking into my sofa to hide tinned tuna.' Neville said to Anita, folding his arms.

'We've got a winning formula here Nev, let's stick with it.' Anita pleaded, holding the bag of tins in one hand, a kitchen knife in the other.

'I ain't keen on ruining my couch neither,' Lucile said, giving her a stern look. 'If looters ain't been put off by the first twelve floors of jack shit then I'd say they deserve a break.'

'We have managed to hide almost everything…' Morgan pointed out to her. 'Should be enough?'

'Fine, fine,' Anita conceded, 'but don't come crying to me when we've no tinned tuna.'

'Oh, I won't…' I muttered.

With our sofas safe, we stashed the remaining food and drink in the more conventional hiding places – under beds, on top of cabinets, under the sink, behind the towels in the bathroom, while still leaving the odd tin or jar of sauce scattered about the remains of a ransacked kitchen. It was oddly cathartic, tipping my drawers out across the side, making my place look a dump, but I wasn't looking forward to having to clean it up.

If we ever came back.

Fifty One

For what we hoped would be the final time, we pulled on our
jackets, strapped on our bags and checked our weapons.
Loaded up with the oversized camping bags, we were a little
too big to all fit in the elevator at once, so I tapped Morgan and
Laurel on the shoulder, got them to wait back up with me.

As soon as the doors closed shut, I let my mouth run.

'I love her. I always will. But with all this going on, I can't
keep hoping that she's okay, or that I'll ever see her again if
she is. I'm not just *moving on*, not like that, I'm not going to
forget her, but I have to *move on*, argh, move past, keep going.'

The words tumbled out, no thought given. They were
heavy words to carry, and I needed to share that burden.

Morgan looked down at the carpet, eyes flashing brief
anger before her lip twitched down. Laurel reached out,
touching my arm.

'I know what you mean.' She said, taking a long blink. 'I
know this plague has taken one sister from me, and I can't bear
thinking it's taken the other.' Her eyes turned then to Morgan.
'But I'll take family anywhere I can get it. She loved you,'
Laurel croaked, eyes flicking between us, 'both of you. If she'd
have been able to come here, she would have. If she had a way
of getting you a message, she would have.'

Morgan reached out to touch Laurel's arm, but Laurel
brought us in for a group hug, squeezing the life out of us.

'Making me cry, you shit.' She grunted at me. 'We're not
just going to get over this, I know…but we…'

'Need to get past it.' I finished off the thought for her, my
voice coming out as rough.

I heard Morgan sniff and felt the tears roll down my
cheeks too. I buried my head in Laurel's shoulder for a
moment, trying to regain my composure.

'We stick together, okay?' Morgan asked, breaking the
hug first. But keeping a hand on our shoulders. 'No matter

428

what happens. Nobody else gets left behind. We don't lose anyone else.'

I nodded, my throat too tight to speak.

We summoned the elevator and boarded in quiet, riding the lift down to some small amount of sniffles and the drying of our eyes. The tears had been brief, so the mirrored panels beside the doors were kind to us, showing we didn't look like we'd been crying. Not that anyone would have looked at us sideways.

Whatever the next few hours would bring, be that safety, disappointment or another firefight, there was finally a sense of closure. Not for Katy. That'd be a long while coming. But for Greenfield. For the world. We didn't think things would ever be the same again. There would be no 'going back to normal'. We had to take care of each other, not just for a few days, but maybe forever. With such good people around me, I could live with that.

On the ground floor, chairs had been tossed about and potted plants knocked over. The doors were open, everyone waiting outside, with Anita writing on the lobby windows in red spray paint, probably from Stan's apartment.

'*Dead inside.*' I read, joining them in the car park. 'Think it'll be enough?'

'Short of politely asking people not to come in, I think we've done all we can to keep our refuge secret.' Neville said, picking up Damian's bag from where it lent against his leg. 'Suppose we could drag a few corpses over for authenticity, but I doubt anyone looking to loot is going to be put off by that.'

'Yeah, I mean, we aren't.' I shrugged. 'Come a ways since day one.'

We weren't planning on bailing from the truck in a hurry, and with me and Morgan holding onto the straps in the boot, there'd be help on hand if we needed to grab the bags and run. I've been joking about how big Damian's cargo space is, but seven full sized camping backpacks made an admirable start at filling it up.

We'd at least doubled, if not tripled Anita's four-month food estimate with our scavenging – it's scavenging when we do it, and looting when it's someone else. It felt a shame to leave it all behind, but it wasn't like we couldn't get to it again, if we needed to.

As Neville started the engine, the radio tuned into GCR, and finally, Sachs was broadcasting again, even if it was just music, and no announcements. If we didn't make it out of Greenfield then we'd need to keep building our bridges with those guys. A radio relay would be a valuable tool in a world without mobile phones.

I did the food maths in my head as we drove. It didn't take long. An optimistic twelve month supply at full rations would stretch to two years if we rationed. That'd be long enough to figure out how to farm, right? Get some seeds from a garden centre, head to the library for some kind of How To Guide. Morgan could figure it out.

For a minute or so, I wanted to turn us around – say it wasn't worth the risk, meeting the CDC, or whoever else might be out there. Tell people we didn't need anyone else's help, that we could make a go of it on our own. Neville and I had talked this morning about setting up our own community.

But there was a safety in numbers that couldn't be denied, and plenty more risk involved in either isolating ourselves, or advertising our small, well stocked little haven. No, the best course would be to try the CDC, to see what it's like behind the walls of Sydow.

As comfortable as I'd become with the idea of killing man or zed, I wasn't crazy, or, heh, *dead inside*. The idea of safety and protection outweighed all other arguments – and had I not sworn to myself I'd do what was best for these people? Keep them safe? Yeah. Sydow was the place to be. If not, we had our backup plan.

VBC Studios was on the outskirts of the city centre, where the high streets and commercial districts petered out into hotels, flats and warehouse space – but you were still only a ten minute walk from the nightlife.

The zeds had been getting thicker on the ground again, drawn back towards the city centre by something. It was a little disconcerting. I'd figured they'd have spread out into the suburbs by now…but what was our theory? They were going where the food was. Wherever people made their presence known. If they were coming back towards the centre, they were following something. The assembling convoy, I hoped.

We were driving through a residential area a little further out, the last row of old terraces before the dual carriageway that brought traffic into the heart of the city. That's when we heard the gunfire. Neville pulled us over immediately, off the main road and down a side street, into the terraces.

'Was that aimed at us?' Lucile leaned forward, between the front seats.

The gunfire continued, small arms and chattering automatics – like we'd heard last night. Maybe the same people were fighting again.

'No, we're out of sight, must be someone else.' Laurel said.

'They're really going at it.' Neville commentated, like we couldn't hear it already. He turned in the road, creeping back to the corner we'd come down, but pulled up onto the curb instead, like we were parking.

'Where do you think it's coming from?' I asked from the boot.

'Knowing our luck, right were we need to be?' Laurel grimaced. 'Why can't things just got smoothly?'

'It's quarter past two.' Neville said, turning over his shoulder. 'If they're shipping out in convoy, it'll be moving soon. Can we afford to wait?'

We didn't have to.

The gunfire suddenly grew closer, and we fell quiet, listening intently. After a moment, the sound of roaring engines grew louder.

'Heads down!' I called out, everyone bar myself ducking out of sight.

In the boot, I figured I was far back enough to remain unseen, as vehicles began to speed down the main road we'd just been on. The first of them was a military Humvee, charcoal grey. The firing position in the roof, the one I'd seen them mount machine guns and rocket launchers to in the movies, just had one soldier with an assault rifle, firing back the way they'd come.

The next vehicle was a civilian sedan, pecked with bullet holes, though the solider hadn't been shooting at them before they sped out of sight. A pickup truck came next, figures holding onto a bar above the cab, firing pistols at the soldier, or the sedan. It looked as if the convoy was under attack before it'd even finished gathering.

'Come up, they're not looking our way.' I said.

We watched as another Sydow Sec Humvee chased out of sight, probably hoping to catch up with the pickup. A classic green Panther, an old van and a pair of motorcycles went next, with a large truck thundering along behind them – I recognised its fire engine-like profile as the truck we'd seen pouring soldiers to investigate our co-op.

Gunfire chattered from the rear of the truck, and I just caught sight of the soldiers firing there, as the main body of their pursuers caught up to the chase. Gods, what had driven them to this?

A blue people carrier – a real soccer mom's car – was sporting two gunmen from the sides and another from the bloody sunroof, firing more pistols and a long rifle. I didn't see if anyone's shots hit home, but the chase was only in our sight for a moment before it passed along.

The carrier was followed by another couple of motorcyclists on dirtbikes, but these weren't dressed in full, proper leathers as the others had been. After them were more ordinary looking cars with battle damage, hard to tell then who was in the convoy and who the aggressors were. After a couple of minutes, the gunfire faded and the engine noise died away.

'Should we follow them?' Neville asked.

'Might get shot by either side.' I warned, 'Take us to the VBC, quickly! There might be some soldiers there who know what's going on.'

'Yeah, can't hear gunfire anymore,' Laurel said, 'maybe the convoy led the shooters off, could still be people there.'

Neville had us back on the road and turning the corner while still gathering speed – guess he didn't want to be in sight for any longer than necessary. We crossed over the carriageway and into narrower, winding streets, seeing evidence of the battle all around. Some of the parked cars had lost their wing mirrors, or had their windows shot out. Even the walls were scarred with chipped brickwork from stray bullets.

We didn't bother with the original plan – sneaking up for a vantage point. We slowly drove up into the centre of the intersection, Neville flicking the 4x4's hazard lights on, and rapidly flashing the headlights.

The building was a square affair over half a dozen stories, with a walled off parking lot, the gates currently opened. Though there was an entrance on the street, it was much like the foyer of castle tower – all glass – so had been covered over with what looked like a mixture of bedsheets, tarps and bin bags, so the zeds couldn't see in.

When nobody called out to us, we pulled around the side, and up the little incline into the parking lot. It was mostly empty, but had the capacity for twenty or thirty vehicles. Judging by the tents and marquees that'd sprung up in the parking lot, I'd say it might have been at capacity just a few minutes ago.

They'd probably split up, drawing the attackers off in different directions across the city, hoping to meet back up somewhere on the road. That's what I'd have planned for…but that didn't do us much good. We were supposed to join up with that convoy. Now it was gone, split up and under attack. Even if we found them, there was a chance they'd shoot us on sight.

'Think they all scrambled.' Lucile said, looking out of the window over the shanty camp. 'Both sides.'

'Wonder what they was fighting about?' Damian asked.

'Could be anything,' I said, gritting my teeth. 'But it's fucked up our plans something fierce, whatever it was.'

Quiet fell, broken only by the soft sounds of the radio, turned down since we heard the gunfire. I hung my head and tried to think of a way we could hook up with the convoy – predict where they'd be on the road maybe? Or maybe…

'Lucile, Anita, get that gate closed,' I ordered, crawling to the boot door, 'Morgan, wait with Damian in the car. Neville, Laurel, we're going inside.'

'I reckon they packed all the good stuff with them when they left,' Laurel said, 'there'll be nothing left to take.'

'Not trying to take anything. Trying to find something. Maps, plans, a post-it note, anything that'll tell us where they're going to try joining the convoy back up.'

I got out of the boot and pulled the cobra into hand, eyeing up the overlooking windows for any surprise shooters. People were getting out, but not with the usual speed and enthusiasm I was used to by now.

'Could be they just scattered Kelly,' Lucile said, approaching me with an apologetic look. 'Gone off to secret safehouses Gods know where.'

'Or they're all making their own way to Sydow.' Neville added, arms folded, 'might be no catching up to them, but at least we know where they're going.'

'Main roads are a rush hour from hell,' Anita reminded them, coming to stand beside me, 'if they had a plan to drive out of this city then they knew a road that was open. Finding that information out for ourselves could cost us more than time and fuel.'

'So we go inside and see if they left instructions.' I said, firmly, breathing a little too hard perhaps. 'So come on, let's move, before somebody comes back and gets the wrong idea.'

'He's right, we've come too far to turn back when the answer could be in there.' Morgan said, 'Even if we can't find the convoy, just knowing what roads to take would help.'

'Hey!' Damian called, from still inside the 4x4. 'Got to come hear this! Talking about de convoy!'

We ran to the front of the truck, gathering around the doors as Damian turned up the radio. It was Carl Sach's buttery announcing voice, but with an edge of concern, not its usual jovial tone.

'…spoke with the acting Commander, who said they spoke with their Director General. Do not go to VBC Studios, the convoy has been forced to scatter – they're all making their own way to Sydow, but I told them you were on the way. They said they can't come back for you, but there is something…a long shot. Sydow Sec had a supply train coming down from Kilmister, they're diverting it to pass through Greenfield but you've got to be quick – it was already getting close.'

'Damn it!' I cursed at the radio.

'When? What station?' Neville gestured wildly.

It was as if Sachs could hear us.

'You need to get to city station and be at platform eight in less than thirty minutes. They can't wait for you. If you can't be there, just get somewhere safe. Either way…hope I'll be hearing from you guys real soon. Good luck, Deputies.'

Fifty Two

I'd never seen us move so fast.

We were back in Damian's big blue monster and reversing before I'd quite had a chance to grab onto something in the boot. Neville spun us around in the car park, throwing me against Morgan with an apologetic gasp as the wind was knocked out of me.

I managed to right myself as we stormed onto the streets of Greenfield city centre. VBC Studios was not far from the train station. Not far at all. Neville turned us left, speeding down the side street and onto the main road – a week ago, traffic would have been pretty heavy around here, but now it was smooth sailing, onto a different part of the dual-carriageway, and we were practically there.

Neville crossed four lanes, not heading for the train station's small parking area, but meaning to drive us straight up to the front doors.

Greenfield Station wasn't a particularly grand affair – a little old, a little dated, but the area outside had been freshened up for the Greenest City awards. Set down from the main road, the station was separated from the sidewalk by a sloping, curved fountain wall of stainless steel, bringing you down into a plaza of planters and benches. When the weather was nice they even had table tennis outside.

The station's edifice was all old stone arches, but around that skeleton they'd bolted steel and glass, for the more modern look. Between that and the fountain, it was actually a fairly pretty place to look at. On a good day.

Today the view was spoiled by the drab CDC tents erected between the greenery, with gurneys and scattered supply tables tossed around by the ravages of a struggle some days ago. More than one of the marquee tents had been burned to its skeleton, nothing but ashes and the blackened remains of cot beds standing beneath.

436

The glass walls of the station had also been covered over with opaque white tarps – emblazoned with yellow and black stripes. Quarantine, if I had to guess. Did they even realise they'd quarantined the station we were supposed to escape through?

My mind raced for another way in – but I knew there wasn't one. You couldn't see them from here, but there were high walls with barbed wire around the parking lot, and if we spent the time driving to the other side of the tracks we'd be met with the giant retaining wall of the hillside opposite. My train of thought, so to speak, was derailed by the chatter of gunfire.

'Fuck, no!' Neville shouted, breaking hard before we reached the bottom of the ramp, and reversing up, looking over his shoulder. He'd seen the men emerging from the tents, and they did not look friendly.

GCR wasn't a private broadcast, and there must have still been some of those arseholes from the convoy close enough to intercept us. As of now, I had no clue what their problem was with us, or the Mercs, but since they were firing at us it was definitely an issue.

'Get ready to fight!' I yelled, as Neville backed us to the top of the ramp. 'We're going through them.'

'There's got to be like, ten, twelve guys down there!' Lucile panicked, 'We can't take on that many!'

The gunfire petered out as we were out of sight, but that meant that the sound of another engine could cut through the new silence. Something big, with a lot of grunt – a charcoal grey cousin of our own 4x4.

The Sydow Sec Humvee charged into the plaza at the bottom of the ramp, just after the curtain wall. They'd done what we'd done, come up the curb using a pedestrian crossing. But unlike us, they didn't have to curve down into the plaza. They were straight into it, barrelling down the corridors formed between tents, scattering and distracting the gunmen.

'We go through them!' I yelled again, opening the boot and turning back to bellow orders. 'Laurel, sniper, up here! Damian, cover her! Everyone else, with me!'

I had no fucking idea if they were going to do what I said, but I should have known by now that these people would listen to me. The idea of being in charge was still pretty fresh, and as much as I'd tried my damnedest, I'm sure I'd always have doubts.

I didn't see Laurel and Damian setting up, but I heard the crack of her rifle before I felt the presence of the others at my back as I strapped on my bag. I helped them into theirs, left Laurel with her's, and picked up Damian's heavy pack, straining my left arm but trying to put that out of my head. Neville had agreed to take it, but I needed him shooting.

I moved for another one of the plaza's entrances – the stairs. While the ramp provided access near the doors for wheelchairs, sightseers and the occasional ATV, the stairs led down into the planters and tents.

It was a more exposed route down, but the low wall that shielded the ramp wouldn't have been much better – best thing would be to close as quickly as possible, make use of the confusion that Sydow Humvee had bought us.

Neville and Anita capitalised on it straight away – as we crossed the open ground between the stairs and the nearest planter, one of the gunmen was stumbling around the corner of a tent, checking his shoulder. They were sparing with their shots, but more than enough hit home, spraying the side of the tent with red mist as he dropped.

The shots brought a renewed hail of gunfire, but none of it seemed directed at us. From within the rows of tents I heard a woman scream – 'Get down!' – followed by the loudest gun I'd ever heard. It was like Laurel's rifle firing on automatic. The thundering, chugging sound of the weapon deafened us to everything else.

I led my team around the side of the tents, sticking to the planters, going for the right side of the building. The fighting sounded like it was coming from the front doors, so we'd go in

438

through the side. I checked to make sure everyone was following, and was pleased to see them staying low, moving one at a time while the others covered.

At the top of the stairs, crouched behind the chest-high wall, I saw Laurel in position, but over the booming noise of the machine gun, I couldn't tell if she was firing – until the gun suddenly stopped. Maybe the operator had been shot? But whose side were they on anyway?

Another series of shots rang out, punctuated by two thunderclaps from behind me, Laurel taking out unsuspecting shooters. When the hail of bullets from the machine gun didn't resume, I figured it was as safer time as any to move.

'Shooter, on the stairs!' I heard someone shout.

'Hostile?' another voice answered. No telling if they were Sydow's people or the convoy raiders.

'He's our sniper!' a third voice called back, 'Put your guns down and walk, this doesn't have to go worse for you than it already has.'

The third voice was the voice of reason. Made sense if that'd be Sydow, but I wasn't in a mood for taking any more chances. If they had the guns and the skills, they'd be right behind us after they'd finished dealing with these arseholes.

I waved until I got Laurel's attention, then made a beckoning motion, followed by holding up one finger, hopefully she'd get that meant "one minute". I knew she'd be exposed coming down those stairs – Damian keeping her from just making a dead sprint for it, so we needed a distraction, and I knew one that'd worked before.

'Anta, flares.' I whispered, taking the green and red fireworks out of my pocket.

She understood, taking out her own. 'Green?'

'On the count of three…' I began, letting her finish the countdown in her head. On the third beat, we ripped the end of a flare each, and tossed them into the tents without a sound, coloured smoke billowing skywards. We'd picked green – hopefully Sydow would recognise them as military flares, and green for the friendly colour.

439

There came the sounds of swearing, followed by something being knocked over. Someone else started barking orders and within moments the gunfire resumed, though perhaps more frantic and panicked than before.

Laurel and Damian didn't stop when they got to us, they kept on running, the tall woman supporting the large man in a mad dash for the side of the building. It'd be worth a few fresh stitches if we managed to catch this train.

Past the planters and the plaza, the confusion and the gunfire, we made it to the taxi rank, a sheltered turning circle for pickups and drop-offs near the car park. The quarantine tarp still blocked the doors I knew were there, but Lucile grabbed hold of a seam and found the zip, pulling upwards as I did the head count. 'Nobody left behind,' I thought with pride.

I took the lead, going for the glass doors beyond the tarp, but they were locked. I couldn't see the mechanism, so I figured it had to be electronic, stuck into lockdown as the power went out. I doubted the doors were bulletproof glass though.

Standing back, I fired once, shattering the left door, and leading the way into the building, Lucile holding the tarp so everyone could get through. On one hand, we were out of the gunfire, on the other hand, I think we'd have been safer in it.

'Mother of fuck.' Morgan gasped, bringing her gun into a ready position, but holding fire.

The main body of the station stretched away before us, a few concession stores on the right, a coffee shop on the left, all the shutters down. Daylight came in patchy through the skylights, and muted through the tarp that covered the front of the building. But it was enough light to see the blood by.

People must have come here for evacuation before us. A lot of people. The tiled floors were a mess of luggage, bloody smears and footprints – the milling footprints of wandering zeds, all of whom had gathered at the front of the building, pressing their mass against the windows and doors in a shuffling, moaning horde. There must have been a hundred of them.

The gun battle outside had shattered several panes of the glass walls, letting a handful of zeds here and there press right up against the tarp – a matter of time before it broke or came away from whatever had fixed it to the walls.

Luckily, they hadn't heard my shot amongst the din outside, nor heard Morgan's swearing. As everyone else came in behind us, I knew it'd be just a matter of time until we were spotted. I handed Damian's bag back to Neville.

'I'll be bringing up the rear,' I muttered, turning away from the horde and back to my people, 'Neville, make sure everyone gets on that train. Head for the platform bridge, the stairs will slow the shamblers down, but I'm going to draw their attention.'

'What?' was the general response from the group.

'They're going to burst through the walls and attack those soldiers in the back, a whole horde of them.' I gestured behind me, 'If Sydow survive that firefight then they'll still be in deep shit from the zeds. I might be cutting them off from getting the train with us, but at least they might live to see tomorrow.'

'No time to argue,' Laurel said, 'let's go, now or never.'

Neville adjusted his grip on Damian's bag, and set off across the station, sticking to the right side, where the concession stores and public toilets were. I brought up the rear, just behind Morgan.

Archways led towards fast food joints and the first platform, with stairs to the platform bridge in the middle. We got through the archways unseen, and began climbing the stairs. When we were at the top, I waved everyone to keep going, then took out my red flare.

'Over here!' I yelled, igniting the flare, 'Right here you braindead bastards!'

I stood on the top of the steps, waving the red flare and firing my gun twice into the ceiling, to the sound of breaking glass. It must have been enough to convince them the firefight wasn't all that interesting, as no sooner had the shattered panes rained on the tiles, than runners were shouldering their way through the pack. They'd been at the front of the horde, but they were making better ground that I was, standing still.

I swore some more, tossing the flare their way and getting myself onto the platform bridge. It spanned all eight platforms, with glass walls overlooking the lines and platform coffee shops, stairs heading down at every number. The group were already at five, but I was catching up fast.

Suddenly, at six, Morgan was knocked off her feet.

It came out of one of the stairwells, tackling her like a football player. Her head would have smashed against the hard tile floor if she hadn't turned in the fall, taking the impact on her backpack. Like the ghouls at the hospital, this one was in military camo.

Further ahead, it was Lucile and the supported Damian next in the line, but they hadn't even seen her go down, let alone were in a condition to help.

Willing myself faster, I pumped my legs and surged forwards, screaming wordlessly at the ghoul – unlike the zeds, these things had a sense of self preservation. By being the loudest, meanest looking thing in sight, I hoped I'd scare it off.

It sort of worked.

The ghoul leapt back off of Morgan, the young woman dragging herself out of my path before I tripped over her. I'd thought about using my gun, but I'm an average shot at the best of times. Running forward, firing my revolver single-handed, I stood more chance of shooting Damian in the back.

Instead, I hit the ghoul with all the force and momentum I could muster, not trying to bear it to the ground as it had done Morgan, but simply trying to knock it flying. It'd changed its stance to meet me, planting its feet apart, half crouched and waiting – but the end was in sight for me and my people. I was the irresistible force, and he was just another movable object.

With what I assume to be the force of a battering ram, I shouldered the ghoul off its feet, knocking it backwards, where it slid a couple of feet across the tiles. That's when I opened fire.

Bang. The first shot missed as it tried to regain its feet.

Bang. My second took it just under the neck.

Bang. I pressed my gun up to its head before pulling the trigger.

But that wasn't the end of the gunfire.

Morgan was backing up, firing down the bridge at the way we'd just come, where an uncomfortable number of runners were pouring up the stairs, every bit as fast as we were. I holstered my gun, back at my hip.

'Go!' I ordered, unbuckling the bag strap on my chest.

'Not leaving you!' she shouted, still firing, 'Nobody gets left behind!'

'Don't plan on staying – take this!' I said, thrusting my bag at her. She took it in one hand, and kept firing with the other. She'd actually managed to get a couple, but there were more where they came from. 'Go!'

She growled, but listened to me, tossing me her gun. I didn't know how many shots were left, but they'd be enough. They had to be. I adopted the grip Anita had taught me and fired at the oncoming runners, emptying the magazine in four or five shots. I only managed to get one before the distance became dangerous, but with that last shot the downed zed managed to trip the two behind it.

I ran on, shoving the gun into my pocket, steaming for platform eight, the end of the bridge, while drawing out Edgar's old pistol, my only loaded weapon. I risked a glance over my shoulder and saw that the runners were closer than I expected – three of them, the others still lagging far behind.

These would get me if I didn't do something.

An abrupt turn and I was face to face with them, raising my gunhand and pulling the trigger without trying to think about it. I let the damn thing practically run onto the barrel of the gun before I blew the back of its head off.

I thrust out a stiff-arm tackle to block the other one while I cocked the pistol with my thumb, just about managing to wrestle the gun into position and fire before the third runner was on me, ragging at my clothes, trying to throw me off balance. It worked.

I fell into the wall and bounced off, landing face down on the ground. Before it could come down on my back, I rolled, smacking it in the face with the butt of the pistol as it knelt beside me – the force of the blow, fuelled by sheer terror, knocked it backwards long enough for me to get back on my feet. I cocked the pistol, kicked it in the face, and fired as it hit the ground. It would have been cool if I didn't miss and fire again.

The fastest of the remaining runners was closing the gap again, two platforms away, but this time I could steady myself, hold the gun properly, and take it out with my remaining two shots. Now all my guns were dry, but at least I had no pursuers. I was clear.

I reached the top of the stairs to platform eight, and saw the train at the platform already, a mixture of flatbed cargo carriers and steel boxcar containers. They hadn't stopped the train though, it was still moving, slowly but surely. They couldn't afford to stop – that platform had a fair number of zeds scattered about – in amongst luggage and scenes of violence. I had to move fast.

Damian and Lucile were already out of sight, presumably they'd managed to climb into a container, but everyone else had waited, confident they could just leap onto the flatbeds that came next. Laurel shot a zed near the bottom of the stairs, while Anita plugged away at a small knot of them moving towards us from the far side of the platform.

'Go on, go!' I shouted as I took the stairs, seeing the train begin to noticeably pick up speed, 'I'm right behind you!'

Anita and the overburdened Neville jumped onto the flatbed, Morgan not bothering to run further up the platform to get them, just taking a half jump-half stride onto the next flatbed back, still holding onto my bag.

'What took you so long?' Laurel asked, before jumping onto the one with Neville and Anita.

I didn't have enough breath to answer. I just ran as the train began to pick up speed in earnest, reaching the bottom of the stairs and launching straight into a sprint – blind panic setting in at the thought of the train leaving without me, but I was easily within distance to catch it up and jump aboard Morgan's flatbed.

I put on a final burst of speed to make the jump – and came crashing down to the cold, rough concrete, the wind knocked out of me, something wrapped around my ankle.

'No!' I heard Morgan cry out, over the sound of the rolling train, and the ringing in my ears.

'Look out!' Laurel echoed in my head, the crack of her rifle cutting through the ringing.

I turned in time to see one zed drop to the platform, half its head missing, but a fast, low shape was moving down the stairs, in military fatigues. Another ghoul.

Laurel's rifle cracked again as I tried to stumble to my feet, kicking the bag strap that'd gotten twisted around my foot, but she must have missed it. The ghoul jumped on my back, but I'd barely gotten my balance. I came crashing down again, but not before smacking my head against a steel bench.

Breathless, dizzy, and I think possibly bleeding, I became dimly aware of someone's shouts for me to get down.

I tucked my head down as multiple shooters opened up with pistol fire – I guess at this point it was shoot straight to save my life, or shoot badly to save me from a horrible death.

The weight on my back suddenly went slack, and I rolled a shoulder to knock the thing off of me, my head pounding with the strain.

I got to standing, groggy, and managed to start putting one foot in front of the other, building speed to try and match the train – there was still one more flatbed to jump into.

But as I turned to make the final push, to jump onto the back of the rolling train, the world lurched sideways, my vision turning grey. A dim little thought told me that I'd hit my head a lot harder than I thought, and that for some reason, my shirt was wet.

445

As the train left the station, I tried once more to get back on my feet, but putting weight on my left arm was agony. I fell onto my back and craned my neck to look down myself.

There was a bullet hole in my jacket, up past the elbow on my sleeve. The jacket I'd bought to ride on Katy's motorcycle. I could feel my hoodie and my shirt were really wet, but I couldn't feel the wound yet. Was that a bad sign? Or was I in shock? And was *that* a bad sign?

I looked around the platform, my world spinning as a wave of dizziness hit. It looked like zeds were climbing on the ceiling, but when the world settled down again I could see they were just coming at me from everywhere else. Down the stairs. Along the platform. Over the other tracks. Man. There were quite lot of them.

I reached into my pocket for the loose bullets for the Cobra, dropping a few of them as I tried to load them into the gun with my shaking hands. I tried to sit up, but the world didn't like that, doing its best impression of a washing machine as the bile rose up in my throat.

I took aim towards the stairs, and fired. I don't think I hit anything, but that wasn't really the point anymore, was it? I was fucked from the moment that strap got caught around my foot. It was over.

'At least I got everyone else out.' I said, letting the Cobra fall from my grip, clattering to the concrete. I'm not sure if I was saying it out loud or if it was in my head.

I'd told Neville I'd wanted Morgan to be prepared. I guess she was now, even if I had to look out for her, one last time. Maybe if I'd have thrown her gun back she'd have been able to reload and get that one off me. Then again, Morgan might have shot me in the head, rather than the arm. Would that have been so bad?

'Just too damn slow.' I muttered, fishing in my pockets for Edgar's Tetley, the single, lone, loose, last bullet.

Poor kid. She'd be devastated to leave me behind. But at least she still had her dad. Still had each other. Still had Anita. She'd need people too, her sister, her parents, all gone.

446

'Think I did okay.' I replied, pushing it into place, fingers in my left hand going numb. Dizzy, I flicked the chambers closed.

Like Lucile and Damian. His folks were gone. But weren't Lucile's from Sydow? Nice. Maybe they'd find each other. They'd do alright there then. Providing he took his meds, and got some new stitches. Maybe Lucile would go back to her medical training, have a change of career.

'Just…better luck next time.' I said.

I didn't have anyone left. They'd gone without me – I told them to, but I'd be lying if I didn't say there was a sting to it. Someone could have jumped off the train. But no. Probably for the best.

I closed my eyes, feeling the tears welling up behind them. I saw Katy's smiling face, her cute nose and that little stud. So many memories. So many things left to say.

Then I saw Laurel standing beside her, tall and strong, a pain sometimes but worth it. I couldn't help but wonder…maybe there was something there, after all. I mean, I was thinking of her. With the last bullet loaded, it was her I now saw, here as I got ready to end it all. Right before…

I pressed the gun under my chin.

Edgar Jameson left me this gun while he took pills with his wife. That's how they checked out of this world. Their end was peaceful and quiet. With his gun, I'd have the same – I wouldn't kick and scream as the zeds tore my flesh. I wouldn't give them the satisfaction.

One shot, and it'd be lights out.

My hands shook as my finger tightened on the trigger.

Go on. Just one pull, and it's over.

My grip was so tight it was painful.

It's not giving up. It's not losing.

I felt myself begin to sweat as the zeds closed in nearer.

You got everyone out. You won.

I closed my eyes and took a deep breath.

That's when I pulled the trigger.

Afterword

Before you move on to your next literary adventure, please take a moment to rate this story on the Kindle Store, and leave any thoughts or comments on the page (no spoilers please).

Reviews are **vitally** important for indie-writers like myself, as more reviews mean more readership. It doesn't have to be a long review, just throw however many stars at me as you feel the book deserves, and tell me why you did, or did not, give those stars. Two sentences, and you'll not only make my day, but support me in writing future stories.

Your feedback and critiques are all welcome - the good, the bad and especially the constructive. If you enjoyed the book, share it with your friends. If you didn't enjoy the book, you could share it with someone you don't like – that'll get 'em.

You can follow me on Facebook or Twitter for updates, future stories and other bits and pieces.
https://tasorsby.wordpress.com/
https://www.facebook.com/TASorsby/
https://twitter.com/T_A_Sorsby

Thanks for reading,
T.A. Sorsby

Printed in Great Britain
by Amazon